92
Sci fic

ROBOT BLUES

ROBOT
BLUES

MARGARET WEIS
AND DON PERRIN

A ROC BOOK

ROC
Published by the Penguin Group
Penguin Books USA Inc., 375 Hudson Street,
New York, New York 10014, U.S.A.
Penguin Books Ltd, 27 Wrights Lane,
London W8 5TZ, England
Penguin Books Australia Ltd, Ringwood,
Victoria, Australia
Penguin Books Canada Ltd, 10 Alcorn Avenue,
Toronto, Ontario, Canada M4V 3B2
Penguin Books (N.Z.) Ltd, 182–190 Wairau Road,
Auckland 10, New Zealand

Penguin Books Ltd, Registered Offices:
Harmondsworth, Middlesex, England

First published by Roc, an imprint of Dutton Signet,
a division of Penguin Books USA Inc.

Printed in the United States of America

ISBN 0-451-45581-9

I'm so sad, got the robot blues.
I'm so sad, got the robot blues.
I'm so sad, got the robot blues,
my robot done drank up all of my booze.
I'm so sad, got the robot blues.

My robot took my girl for a walk.
Said all they'd do was sit and talk.
When my girl got home, she gave me the news.
She and my robot was takin' a cruise.
   (And they was leavin' me behind!)

I'm so sad, got the robot blues.

Anonymous, circa 2064

CHAPTER 1

The means by which enlightened rulers and
sagacious generals moved and conquered
others, that their achievements surpassed the
masses, was advance knowledge.

Sun-tzu, *The Art of War*

The man followed the woman into the motel lobby. She never glanced at him, never noticed him. No reason she should. He was an unprepossessing type of man, the type whom witnesses are likely to vaguely describe as being of "ordinary build," "average height," with "no distinguishing features." He kept his eyes on her.

The woman was attractive, or rather she might have been if she had taken more care with her hair, her makeup, and her clothes. Her hair was shoulder-length, brown, lacked shape and body. Her clothes—a medium-length skirt and mannish coat—suited her trim, perhaps too thin figure, and that was about all that could be said for them. She had a preoccupied, studious air about her that was disconcerting, as if part of her were really somewhere else. She carried a shabby overnight bag that appeared to have been hastily packed, for the tail end of a blouse fluttered out from the side.

Slung over her shoulder were a small, worn purse and the strap of a computer case. The case was made of high-quality leather, appeared to have been packed neatly and with care, with no odd bulges, no loose straps or unbuckled buckles. She kept her hand possessively on the computer case; the purse was forced to trail along behind. Obvious where she placed her priorities.

The man entered the lobby almost on the woman's heels. No need to keep his distance. The hotel was attached to the busy Megapolis spaceport and the lobby was crowded with people, either wanting rooms or checking out.

The lobby was circular, with a gigantic vidscreen almost two stories high that loomed over guests, while a smiling personage with excellent teeth welcomed them to the Megapolis Spaceport Hotel, inviting guests to register at one of the automatic registration machines to be found conveniently in the lobby.

A long line of restless people had gathered at the automatic motel registration, which machines may have been convenient but were, unfortunately, not working properly. There were three registration machines. One was out of order. An alien with credit problems was tying up number two, arguing loudly with the machine. The third machine was functioning, but at sublight speed. When a real live motel employee made the mistake of showing up, he was immediately mobbed and disappeared precipitously.

The woman took her place at the end of the line for the sublight registration.

The man took his place in the line behind the alien arguing with the machine, ensuring that he would probably be able to remain in the same place for as long as necessary. The woman would move along more rapidly, but that was all right. The man didn't need much time. He just needed proximity and a clear shot.

The woman shifted the computer case to a more comfortable position, yawned, blinked her eyes, rubbed them, and yawned again. She looked groggy, exhausted. Those jump-flights were killers. When you finally get to sleep, a steward wakes you up to tell you the ship is going into hyperspace and would you please make certain your webbing is fastened, don't eat or drink anything for the next hour, and try to relax and ignore the fact that your insides feel like they're now on the outside.

The man knew what flight the woman had taken. He counted on the fact that she wouldn't be operating at one hundred percent efficiency. Odds were that she would not have noticed him anyway, but he didn't rely on odds, never took chances.

She arrived at the front of the line and did precisely what the man had been expecting her to do. She placed the overnight bag on the floor at her feet, shoved the computer case to the back, brought her purse to the front. She reached inside her purse to retrieve her plastic. Sliding the card into the machine, she leaned forward to let the machine scan her eyeball, and said "Darlene Mohini" in a sleepy voice. She repeated her name when the machine announced tersely that it hadn't understood her.

"Darlene Mohini," she said again, irritably.

The machine asked Ms. Mohini if she had reservations.

"Yes." She yawned again. "One night."

The machine found this agreeable, indicated that it would have a room key for her momentarily.

Dull-eyed and drowsy, she waited.

The man reached into his suit coat pocket, drew out a small derringer that fit neatly into the palm of his hand. He held his suit coat folded over his right arm. Under cover of the coat, he raised the gun, aimed, and fired.

A tiny projectile whispered through the air, embedded itself in the flat base of the woman's leather computer case. The projectile was small, about the size of a needle. The man's aim had been true. The projectile slid neatly into a seam in the leather, disappeared.

The registration machine handed over a plastic chit. The woman took the key, started to leave. A person standing behind her stopped her, indicated that she'd forgotten her overnight bag. Smiling in a weary, preoccupied manner, the woman reached down, picked it up, and trudged off in the direction of the airlifts.

The man, task complete, stepped out of line with the muttered comment that this was going to take all day and he didn't have the time. He walked through the motel lobby, beneath the blaring vid sign that was now regaling the guests with the wonders to be found on Megapolis. The man paused at the news counter to buy a news/entertainment chip for the flight back. Seating himself, he slipped the chip into his pocket viewer, settled down to watch.

Another man, walking past, stopped, asked him if that was today's news chip.

"Yes, this is today's."

"How'd the Megapolis Bombers do? I think they're overrated this year."

"See for yourself." The man held up the screen, then said in a low voice, "Clean hit. The transmitter is in her computer case. You should be receiving the signal now."

The other man nodded. Sitting down beside the first, he leaned over to look at his neighbor's viewer. This second man was middle-aged, graying, developing a paunch. He was dressed in a rumpled, ill-fitting, and inexpensive suit.

"What's the assignment?"

"Simple. Eavesdrop on her conversations. Record them. That will let HQ know for certain she's the one we want. Keep an eye out especially for this person." The first man inserted another chip into his viewer. The picture of a cyborg appeared on-screen.

The cyborg was of indeterminate age, bald, with acid burns on his head. His eyes were deep, penetrating. His left side was mechanical: cybernetic arm and leg, with—according to the description which was scrolling beneath the picture—a detachable hand that could be replaced by anything from a small missile launcher to delicate instruments. The leg was reported to have a special hidden compartment where weapons were stored, but that information could not be confirmed. The cyborg was also said to have augmented hearing and a specially designed left eyeball with infrared vision.

"Jeez!" said the second man, impressed. "He looks scary. Is he? Or is that all for show?"

"It's for real. So's he. Former field operative for the Feds. He's independent now, pulling down big bucks. His name is Xris. He's the leader of a mercenary team called Mag Force 7. HQ has information that Mohini's now a member of the team. If she's the mark, she'll hook up with the cyborg. If not, we drop it, start over."

"He won't look like that, will he? I mean, don't most cyborgs hide beneath fleshfoam and plastiskin and all that?"

"Sometimes he does, sometimes he doesn't. Depends on the job. But you shouldn't have any trouble recognizing him. Watch." The static vid shot on-screen changed to an action shot of the cyborg walking down a street.

"Notice the peculiar gait," said the first man, hitting the replay button. "He walks lopsided, as if the physical half of him is at war with the mechanical."

"Weird, huh?"

"There are other people on the team," the first man continued. "Mohini might make contact with any of them. You'll find them all on here." The first man removed the chip, handed it to the second.

"Uh-huh. A lot of bother, if you ask me, but then who is asking me, huh?" the second said glumly. "Why didn't you just kill her when you had the chance? You could have, I suppose?"

"Oh, yes," the man said flatly, without emotion. "But my orders are specific. We need to make certain she's who we think she is."

"And since when are the bosses squeamish about taking out the wrong person?"

The first man shrugged. "It's not that they worry about taking out the wrong person so much as they want to make damn sure we take out the right person. Get it?"

"Not really, but then I'm not being paid to get it, am I, huh? You're leaving town, I hear."

"Yes, it's my son's birthday party tomorrow and I promised him I'd be home in time."

"Really? How old is little James, Jr., now? Must be about four, huh?"

"Seven," the first man said proudly. "Already in third form. *And* captain of his school soccer team."

"Seven! Already? Time flies, huh? Last time I saw

him he was a rug rat. Well, say hi to the wife and eat a piece of birthday cake for me."

"Sure thing. Oh, and remember, transmit all info to HQ and then sit tight. Shadow only. Wait for orders."

"Right. I know. They were very specific about that." The man shook his head again. "All a lot of trouble for nothing, if you ask me. Be seein' you. Have a good one."

"You, too."

The two parted. The first man hurried off to catch his spaceplane, the second bought a news/entertainment chip. He plunked himself down in a chair in the motel lobby, took out a small vid machine, slid the chip inside, put the earphones on, and appeared to prepare himself resignedly to be informed and/or entertained.

In reality, he was listening to the clear, distinct sounds of Darlene Mohini, inside her hotel room, kicking off her shoes.

CHAPTER 2

There are five types of spies to be employed: local spy, internal spy, turned spy, dead spy, and the living spy.

Sun-tzu, *The Art of War*

It was automatic for Xris to check for a tail every time he went anywhere, automatic to glance at the rearview cam display when he pulled away from the curb, automatic to glance at it a second and third time as he propelled the rental vehic through the congested city streets. Automatic, he didn't even think about it, he wasn't particularly expecting it, and so it took his brain a few extra seconds to latch on to the fact that—by God—he had company.

The gray two-door. Thinking back, he recalled having seen it ease out into the street about a half kilometer behind him when he'd left the hotel. It was now accompanying him along the boulevard, keeping the same distance, both of them heading into the city.

"Maybe you and I just happen to be going the same direction," Xris said to the gray two-door, eyeing it on the display screen. "Let's find out."

The boulevard was a spacious four-lane principal road, divided by a wide expanse of green lawn, dignified trees, and a well-disciplined creek. Bisecting a residential district, with attractive but not ostentatious homes for Megapolis's burgeoning upper middle class, the boulevard was only lightly to moderately traveled.

Xris took his time, signaled, and made a right-hand turn.

The gray two-door turned right.

Driving at a medium pace past rows of houses, Xris signaled, turned right again.

The gray two-door cruised along after him.

"Should have a sign marked 'In Tow,' " Xris muttered. "Well, this should clinch it."

He turned right a third time.

So did the gray two-door.

Xris was stumped. He had no doubt that he was being followed. Making three right turns in succession is an old trick used to spot a tail. But the gray two-door was so damn obvious about it. Plus, why tag along? Why not just use any of the innumerable electronic tracking devices available on the market? Attach it to the car, bring up the blip on your screen, and follow your subject from the comfort and privacy of your own living room.

Xris pulled his vehic over to the curb, shut down the air cushions. The vehic dropped to street level. The gray two-door stopped as well. It had moved up on him, due to the fact that the streets in the residential neighborhood were only a block to two blocks long.

Xris sat in the driver's seat, glared at the car through the rearview cam.

"I might have known," he said to the car. "Didn't take you long, did it? Who? And how much?"

He wasn't going to get answers sitting here. He had parked in front of a nice little brick house with a two-vehic garage, a dog slumbering in the Argasian sun, and a toddler on a tricycle. Xris climbed out of the vehic. The dog woke up, began barking at him.

Xris made it clear to the dog that he had no designs upon either the house or the toddler and strolled down the sidewalk. He allowed himself the thought, in passing, that this was the sort of neighborhood, the sort of life, he and Marjorie had always talked about buying into—complete with dog, kid, and trike. He allowed himself the thought, allowed himself the pain. It had been going to come anyhow. This way, he could control it.

That done, he could focus on this little problem.

The gray two-door remained where it was, parked in front of a house similar in design to the brick, except that it was built with stone and had a cat in the driveway.

Xris walked up to the gray two-door, leaned down to peer through the tinted steelglass. Recognizing the man inside, Xris stood up straight, drew in a breath, then tapped on the window. The man inside touched a button.

"I'm going to the Space and Aeronautics Museum," Xris informed the man politely. "It's about ten kilometers north on the boulevard, to your right. I'll wait for you at the lights."

"Good to see you haven't lost your sense of humor, Xris," said the man inside, his voice coming through the speaker hidden in the blastproof door. "I wouldn't want to spoil an educational outing. Why don't you step inside? We need to have a little talk."

The door clicked, swung open.

Xris entered, sat down in the passenger's seat, shut the door, which was soundproof as well as blastproof. Relaxed, making certain he kept both hands in plain sight—and also making certain the driver kept both his hands in plain sight—Xris pulled out a twist, put it in his mouth.

"You know I can't tolerate cigarette smoke, Xris," said the man.

"I'll chew it," Xris said. "So, Amadi. It's been a lot of years. I heard you had retired."

"I did. I was. They brought me back."

"Once a Fed, always a Fed, huh, Amadi?"

"Something like that." Amadi smiled.

He must be pushing seventy now. His black hair was gray, his swarthy complexion seamed with wrinkles. He'd kept himself in shape and he was doing fine financially—if Xris could judge by the well-cut suit and the designer silk tie. The bureau must be keeping him on retainer. Not surprising. Jafar el Amadi was the foremost authority on the Hung—one of the richest, most powerful criminal organizations operating in the central part of the galaxy.

Amadi had also been Xris's super on his last job with the Feds. The job that had gone very, very bad.

Xris settled back into the cushy seat. A series of small
beeps came from his left arm. Shoving back the sleeve
of his own well-cut and expensive suit coat, Xris rolled
up his shirt cuff, revealing a mass of gleaming steel, LED
lights, complex wiring. He made a few necessary
adjustments.

He noted Amadi watching, saw that the man's smile
was a bit strained.

Xris wiggled the fingers of his left hand. "It's the temperature of the skin that's the problem. Hard to main-
tain. You don't want the plastiskin too cold—you touch
someone and they think they're being grabbed by a hand
from the grave. You don't want it too hot, either, although turning up the heat sometimes comes in handy.
I can soft-boil an egg—"

"Cut the crap, Xris," Amadi said, the smile gone. "I
was at the hospital when they brought you in. You're
damn lucky you're alive."

Xris shrugged. The matter was open to debate. "I'm
going to be late for my meeting at the museum. Let's
make this short. How's the wife and kids, Amadi? Oh,
and don't bother asking me about mine."

Amadi's dark eyes flickered. "I guess I can't blame
you for being bitter—"

"No! Really?" Xris was shocked. "How long had the
bureau known Armstrong was a traitor? Before or after
Ito and I walked into that goddamn munitions plant and
got ourselves blown to hell and back?"

"It wasn't until after, Xris, I swear—"

"Then why didn't you tell me the truth? Why didn't
you tell me it was Armstrong who set us up, not Dalin
Rowan? You let me go for years thinking that my best
friend had betrayed me. You let me go for years carrying
that hatred inside me. God knows what I would have
done if—" Xris stopped, clamped down hard on the
twist, so hard his jaw started to ache. He hadn't meant
to say that much. Looking at Amadi brought back a lot,
a helluva lot.

The arm beeped again. Xris ignored it. He could have
hard-boiled an egg about now.

Amadi was watching him carefully. "So—you found Dalin Rowan."

Xris chewed. The tobacco juice slid down his throat, erasing, for the moment, the faint metallic taste that never seemed to leave his mouth, always reminded him that he was more metal than man. He had to be careful here, very careful.

Xris grimaced, stared at the windshield. "How'd you find out?"

Amadi shrugged. "Someone hacked his way into our computer system a couple of months ago. Neat, sweet, clean. The job had Dalin Rowan's footprints all over it. He was searching for files on the Knights of the Black Earth. Imagine my surprise when, a few days later, you and your team manage to stop the knights from turning His Majesty the King into the universe's largest carbonated soft drink."

Xris looked blank. "Gosh, I'm sorry, Amadi. You got the wrong information. I heard about that incident on the GNN news. Their anchorman was the would-be assassin, wasn't he? Warden, that was his name. I'd love to take credit for saving the king's life, but we were light-years away at the time."

"You were a lot closer than that." Amadi tapped a finger on the steering wheel. "You were the one who shot up that hotel, destroyed one of the regicide devices. That poisoner of yours—what's his name, the Adonian Loti—he and the character in the raincoat took out Warden, who was the knights' backup assassin.

"Oh, I can't prove any of this—Olefsky's Wolf Brigade whisked you and your team away before anyone could spot you. The Lord Admiral concealed the Loti—or should I say the Honorable Ambassador from Andonia? All handled very neatly. His Majesty is safe, the Knights of the Black Earth are destroyed. We've been told from the highest level that the case is closed. Fine." Amadi shrugged. "Case closed. But there's another case that's wide open."

"Which is?" Xris swallowed the remainder of the twist.

"The break-in of a top-secret naval installation."

"The Navy called in the bureau on that one, did they?"

"You know damn well the Navy didn't call us in. They've shut the lid so tight you couldn't pry it loose with a concussion grenade. They won't even admit the damn base exists, much less that someone actually managed to crash their security and waltz right in."

"Well, that's the military for you," Xris said. "Always got to have their little secrets."

"That's where you found Dalin Rowan, wasn't it, Xris?" Amadi said. "That's where he was hiding. You found him and you were going to kill him, weren't you? But he talked his way out of it. He was the one told you about Armstrong."

Xris had to phrase this next question carefully. Deep inside, he was doing a little exulting, but he needed to make sure he was right. He took out another twist, took it out of a golden cigarette case that had the Royal Seal embossed on it. A gift, from His Majesty, from the first time Xris had done the king a favor.

"You got it all wrong, Amadi. I heard about Armstrong from a gypsy fortune-teller. She saw it in my cards. As to Dalin Rowan, you guys gave him his new identity. I would have thought you would have kept tabs on him."

"We gave him a new identity to protect him from the Hung. After he testified at the trial, he was supposed to take his new ID and disappear."

Xris leaned back in the seat, folded his arms. "Let me guess what happened after that—Dalin Rowan took a new ID, all right, only it wasn't the one you had fixed up for him. His disappearing act was for real. Hell, you can't blame him, Amadi. You know the Hung. Dalin Rowan all but destroyed them. He put their top men in prison. He bankrupted their operations. If there's one person in the universe the Hung—or what's left of them—would like to see hanging in a Corasian meat locker, it's Dalin Rowan. And yes, the Hung leaders are stashed away on some penal planet, and yes, they don't have any cash, but that won't stop them—"

"It isn't stopping them, Xris," Amadi said quietly.

"They have cash, apparently. Reserve funds we didn't know about. Their people are still on those penal colonies, but you and I both know that guards and supply ship captains can be bribed, that orders and money and drugs and God knows what all flow in and out of those places. And you know something else, Xris." Amadi eyed him. "If we know you have access to Dalin Rowan, the Hung know it, too."

"How?" Xris's lip curled around the twist. "Got a few more traitors left in the department?"

"Damn it, Xris!" Amadi slammed his hand on the steering mechanism with enough force to rock the vehic. "We need to talk to Dalin Rowan! He's got information we can use. He's bound to know where the Hung kept those reserve accounts. Either that or he can go through the old files, track the information down. It's there. It *has* to be there. We just missed it the first time around."

"Sorry, Amadi," Xris said coolly. "It's been years since I've seen Dalin Rowan. I guess you'll have to crack the Hung on your own."

Amadi was grim. "You think you can protect him, Xris? Think again. You're good. But you're not as good as the Hung. They have the money, the manpower, the resources. Bear Olefsky's Wolf Brigade won't be there to rescue you the next time. Rowan'll never know what hit him. *We're* his only hope."

Xris glanced at his watch. "Been nice seeing you again, Amadi, but I've got to go. I'm going to be late for my appointment as it is. Are you going to keep following me? If so, I can make it easy for you. I'll mail you my itinerary for the next few weeks."

He put his hand on the latch, found it was locked. "Open the door, Amadi. Unless you want me to kick it open." Reaching down, Xris pulled up his pants leg, revealed gleaming steel. "If I use this leg to kick open that door, you won't have much of a door."

Amadi pushed a button. The latch clicked.

"I could make things tough for you, Xris."

"You could," Xris conceded, "but you won't. I just might happen to bump into Dalin Rowan on the sidewalk one day." He opened the door, climbed out. "If I were you, I'd go back to collecting my pension."

He slammed the door shut, waited on the sidewalk for Amadi to drive away.

Amadi didn't move. He had his hand on the speaker controls. He was going to say something, make another appeal, a final offer.

The cat in the driveway yawned, stood up, stretched, came over to Xris and rubbed around his legs. Xris knelt down, petted the cat, all the while watching Amadi, who decided he wasn't saying anything, after all.

The gray two-door rose on its air cushions, floated off down the street.

The cat rolled over on its stomach and purred. Xris knew how the animal felt. He could have very easily done the same.

CHAPTER 3

Men! The only animal in the world to fear!

D. H. Lawrence, "The Mountain Lion"

Xris's euphoria had evaporated by the time he reached his own vehicle. The bureau was barking up the wrong tree, but that was small comfort. The fact that they were giving chase was disheartening. And Amadi had been right about one thing . . . well, okay, he'd been right about a lot of things, but one was most critical. If the bureau dogs were on to the scent, Xris could be damn sure that the Hung would be panting along behind.

That crack about traitors had been a cheap shot. The bureau was a good organization, but it *was* an organization, employing millions of people spread out all across the galaxy. Not surprising to find those whose credit had gone critical, who would be willing to sell a name, a number. The Hung were very good at finding desperate people, very good at using them.

"The one advantage we have," Xris said to himself, as he climbed into the car under the watchful eyes of the dog and the interested eyes of the toddler, "is that everyone is looking for *Dalin* Rowan. Nobody's looking for Darlene."

That had been the whole point in talking to Amadi— to ascertain if the bureau knew that the female Xris had abducted at gunpoint from the top-secret naval base had once been his former partner and best friend. He had also once been a male.

"The ultimate disguise," was how the detective who had tracked Darlene down had put it.

Years ago Federal Agent Dalin Rowan had infiltrated the crime syndicate known as the Hung. A genius with computers, Rowan had managed to worm his way into their systems, had not only gained evidence against them, but had also sent their financial empire into a nosedive. The leaders were jailed, the small fish fled to calmer waters.

The Fed protected Rowan; he testified at the trial behind an opaque bulletproof screen, using a voice scrambler. (The defense had successfully challenged holographic testimony). When the trial was over, the bureau had a new identity all prepared for Dalin Rowan. But Rowan had already taken steps on his own.

Michael Armstrong had been a Fed agent. He'd sold out to the Hung. It was Armstrong who set up Xris and Mashahiro Ito to die in that munitions factory. A short time later, Armstrong was found dead, murdered. The Hung, of course. Armstrong's usefulness to them had ended, and they'd rid themselves of a potential threat. That was what the bureau claimed.

Dalin Rowan knew different. Armstrong's credit with the Hung hadn't run out. He wasn't a threat to the Hung. He was a threat to someone else, someone in the bureau itself.

Rowan hadn't been able to find out much; just enough to make him nervous about accepting the bureau's phony ID. Dalin had to disappear completely, utterly, leaving no trace. A few months of hormone treatments, the operation, and Dalin Rowan was dead.

Darlene Mohini was born.

Darlene Mohini's phony identity was so good that he—she—managed to gain security clearance at the very top levels of the Royal Navy. She became a code-breaker, a code-maker. Her abduction—by Xris—had forced the Royal Navy to all but shut down for seventy-two hours while they changed their codes. Xris had ruined all that for Darlene; he'd blown her cover and now he felt responsible for her safety. She was a valued part

of the Mag Force 7 mercenary team now, as well as—
once again—a trusted friend.

He and Darlene both knew that the Hung would be
after her; they should have figured the bureau in on the
hunt, too.

"Thank you, John Dixter, for keeping her secret,"
Xris said quietly, maneuvering the vehic down the
boulevard.

John Dixter, Lord Admiral of the Royal Navy, knew
the truth. He knew about Dalin Rowan, about Major
Darlene Mohini, about Darlene Rowan. The bureau was
searching for Dalin. But what about the Hung? Who
were they searching for?

Xris had no answers. He fretted and fumed and
thought of this possibility and that possibility and only
when he realized he had no idea where he was or how
he got there did he force himself to snap out of it. He
and Darlene had discussed all this; he'd made the best
possible arrangements to protect her, short of locking
her in a lead-lined container and sealing her up in cold
storage.

"If the Hung are going to end my life, Xris," Darlene
had said to him, "they're going to end my *life*."

And so she was working with the Mag Force 7 team,
a group of mercenaries who were for hire to anyone
who had plastic enough to be able to afford the best in
the business. Someone could, apparently. Xris was on his
way to the Megapolis Space and Aeronautics Museum to
meet with Dr. Michael Sakuta, curator, who'd expressed
an interest in hiring the team for a job.

Xris checked the map in the rental vehic, discovered
that, although part of his mind had wandered, the other
part was right on track. The residential section gave way
to an elite shopping district, and where that ended, the
manicured lawns of the museum began.

Xris parked the vehic and mounted the broad marble
stairs to the staid, columned portico. He entered a side
door, showed the pass that had been sent to him by the
curator. He was told how to find the museum's offices,
and walked into the gigantic, echoing foyer into a throng
of schoolchildren, who had stopped to gape at a side-

by-side comparison of an ancient Atlas rocket booster and a compact, powerful Naval spaceplane.

Xris paused to listen to the guide, who was describing Earth's first moon landing to the group of now giggling children. The kids had probably been to Megapolis's moon on school outings. Glancing around the enormous room, Xris found Raoul and the Little One. He did *not* see Amadi. Xris hadn't really been expecting to. That tailing business had been mostly for show—to shake Xris up, jolt him. Xris gave Amadi credit. He'd succeeded.

As for keeping Xris under surveillance, Amadi wasn't the least bit interested in Xris's business, except to hope maybe Xris might lead them to Dalin Rowan, and Amadi surely knew better than to figure Xris would make a blunder like that. As for the Hung, if they didn't know it, they soon would. Xris nominated several likely candidates as Hung spies, fixed an image of each of them in his mind for later reference, and strolled over to meet with Raoul and his diminutive cohort.

Raoul was staring at something—Xris couldn't see what—with fixed intensity. Xris wondered what had captured the Adonian's attention. It could be anything from a holographic rendering of the solar system to a trash receptacle. Dr. Quong had once described Raoul's thought processes as comparable to butterflies in a sunny meadow: flitting happily this way and that, alighting on a bright-colored flower, staying for a time, then fluttering off again. In this instance, Raoul was transfixed by an illuminated and animated soft drink dispenser.

The Little One, muffled in raincoat and fedora, stood patiently at his friend's side, watching Xris. The cyborg attempted to arrange his mind to meet the telepath's searching scrutiny. A hopeless task.

Walking up, Xris tapped Raoul on the shoulder. "Most people come to look at the exhibits."

Raoul—not the least surprised—turned his unfocused gaze languidly on Xris, then sent it wandering vaguely about the museum. "Whatever for?"

Xris was relieved to see that Raoul was dressed quite conservatively in a dark suit, white shirt, and hat. This outfit was such a radical change from the last Xris had seen Raoul in—lime-green silk lounging pajamas—that Xris forgave the nipped-in waist on the suit jacket, the mauve spats, which matched the mauve cravat, and the six glittering earrings. Raoul had sleeked back his long black hair into a ponytail. A homburg perched at a fashionable angle on his head and he carried a walking stick with a pearl handle. He had only a hint of mauve on his eyelids, a touch of mascara, and a soft pink lipstick. This was apparently Raoul's version of the well-dressed academic.

The Little One tugged on Raoul's coattail. The two spoke silently in whatever manner they communicated. Raoul's gaze shifted back to Xris. His eyes focused, his gaze sharpened, the mauve eyelids narrowed.

Xris scowled at the Little One, but by that time it was too late.

"He says you are upset, Xris Cyborg," Raoul murmured.

"I'm upset," Xris snapped. "Let's leave it at that for the time being. We're late as it is. Sakuta's offices are upstairs. We'll walk. You have your passes?"

"Of course."

Raoul cast one last lingering glance at the soft drink machine, then followed Xris toward the stairway, located some distance away from the main crowd. Since the staircase led only to the museum offices and was marked EMPLOYEES ONLY BEYOND THIS POINT, the staircase was little used.

"Ask him"—Xris jerked his thumb at the Little One—"if anyone's taking an unusual interest in us."

"He says that one gentleman is extremely taken with my hat," Raoul replied.

"Not quite what I had in mind," Xris said.

"No, I didn't suppose it was."

Raoul looked to the Little One, who was standing on the stairs, scanning the crowd. At length, the fedora shook back and forth.

"No, Xris Cyborg. No one is focusing his or her thoughts on us at the moment."

"Good," Xris said.

"No one is focusing his or her thoughts on Darlene Rowan, either," Raoul continued imperturbably.

Xris glared at the Little One. "Just once, I'd like to have a private thought in my head. Just once. Would that be too much to ask?"

The small telepath cringed and sidled closer to Raoul, who rested a protective hand on the Little One's shoulder.

"He has no way of knowing, my friend. The concept of privacy is unknown among his people—"

"Save it for Doc's thesis." Xris snorted and climbed the stairs in glum and ill-tempered silence.

Raoul and the Little One accompanied him, the Little One occasionally tripping over the long raincoat he wore. The two were holding one of their incomprehensible conversations.

"I was only going to inquire . . ." Raoul was saying in a loud whisper that echoed up the stone staircase.

The Little One waved one hand, made a tugging motion.

Raoul hushed, listening to the Little One's silent reply. Xris found the discussion highly irritating. He could have ignored an ordinary conversation between two people, but he couldn't help listening to these two, couldn't help trying to fill in the blanks, so to speak, trying to guess what the Little One was silently transmitting. And Xris always had the feeling that they were talking about him.

Which, in this case, they were.

"I know he's in a bad mood," Raoul responded, "but I don't see any harm in asking . . ."

The Little One was holding forth again, apparently, because there was another burst of silence from Raoul. Xris gritted his teeth, bit back an order for them both to shut up.

"It's only once a year," Raoul said, aggrieved.

Xris came to a halt on the first landing. "What is it?" he demanded.

"It is nothing, Xris Cyborg," Raoul demurred, lowering his purple-hued eyelids. "I was going to request a leave of absence, but the Little One maintains that you

are not in a good mood and that therefore this would
be an inappropriate time to approach you—"

"Leave of absence? What for?" Xris demanded, then
remembered. "Oh, hell, is it that time of year again?
No, I may need you for this job."

He began climbing the stairs again.

"But if you don't need us?" Raoul pursued, assisting
his small friend, who was having difficulty traversing the
broad stairs. Xris slowed his pace, though he did his best
to make it look unintentional.

"It's a very important holiday on my planet," Raoul
continued solemnly. "One that is fraught with religious
significance—"

Xris glanced sideways at the Adonian. "It's a carnival!
A week of brawling, carousing, and drunken orgies."

"As I said"—Raoul was grave—"it is fraught with religious significance. I was unable to attend last year and
my spiritual outlook on life was considerably diminished
as a result. I would very much like to attend this year
and renew myself. The Little One will, of course, accompany me."

The cyborg knew better than to pursue the subject of
Adonian spiritual outlook. People made adult vids out
of those. Xris eyed the Little One, who was nodding the
fedora. "What does he do during the riots?"

"We do *not* riot," Raoul said, dignity affronted. "The
Little One finds the experience cerebrally stimulating."

Xris grunted. "I'll bet he does."

"May we therefore request a leave of absence?"
Raoul asked.

"You can request it," Xris said in the tone which
meant *No way in hell.*

He marched on in silence. Raoul sighed. The Little
One fell over his raincoat.

Xris could almost hear the words *I told you so* ripple
through the air.

At the top of the third flight of stairs, they entered an
outer office. An efficient and attractive female receptionist, whose choice of eye shadow and nail polish received
Raoul's mark of approval, told them that they were ex-

pected and the professor would be with them shortly. She had barely finished speaking when a door in the back of the office opened.

"Ah, here's the professor now," said the receptionist.

"Dr. Sakuta." Xris extended his hand—his right hand, flesh and blood and needing no adjustments as to temperature. "These are my colleagues, Raoul de Beausoleil—"

Raoul offered the fingertips of his hand. "Charmed," he said, and meant it. Dr. Sakuta was a very good-looking man.

"And this is the Little One," Xris added. "I spoke to you about him."

"Your telepath." Sakuta nodded.

"I trust that's still all right with you," Xris said. "Nothing personal, just a routine precaution."

Sakuta gazed at the Little One with an abstracted air. The professor blinked, looked up. "Oh, yes, certainly. Fine with me. I quite understand. In your line of work, you must be careful. If you'll just step into my office? Forgive the mess. They're renovating this part of the building."

Entering his office, Sakuta offered the one visible chair in the room to Xris. The professor whisked a drop cloth off another chair, which he gave to Raoul. Sakuta glanced uncertainly at the Little One; obviously no chair was suitable for the small empath, who came only to Xris's waist. The Little One took his accustomed place beside Raoul, plopped down on the floor, and made himself comfortable.

"Is he all right like that?" Sakuta asked in a low voice.

"He's fine," said Raoul, melting. "Just perfectly fine. Thank you so much for caring."

Sakuta shrugged and walked around another piece of cloth-protected furniture to reach the chair behind his desk. The room smelled strongly of paint. Half the walls were a different color from the other half. A jet-powered ladder stood on the floor, airbrushes gathered around it. The painters were nowhere to be seen. Perhaps the professor had told them to take the day off.

Sakuta sat down at the desk, then—blinking again—

he stared at the open door. "Oh, dear," he said, and started to stand up. "This is very confidential."

"I'll get it, Doctor," Xris offered. Rising, he shut the door, returned to his seat.

"Thank you." Sakuta gave them an apologetic smile. "All this turmoil"—he made a vague gesture to the walls—"it's been a considerable strain. So difficult pursuing one's work. The constant distractions . . ." He blinked at them again, gave a deprecating laugh. "It's silly of me to complain, I know. Having one's office remodeled isn't exactly a catastrophic event. But my life revolves around my work."

In his forties, good-looking, with his dark eyes, Van Dyke beard, trimmed mustache, and luxuriant black hair, Sakuta looked as if he would be more at home among the rich and famous in the gambling casinos of Laskar. Instead, he was just another goofy, absent-minded prof.

"I can imagine how much it must upset you," Xris lied sympathetically.

"So can I," Raoul said, and sighed deeply. "Your work must be fascinating. And your rockets," he added in a breathless tone, "they must be so big!"

"Cut it out," Xris muttered, and gave the Adonian a surreptitious kick in the shin. Aloud he said, "We don't want to take up your valuable time, Professor. If you could just explain the nature of the work you want to hire us to do—"

"Oh, yes, certainly." Sakuta sat forward in his chair, regarded Xris with bright enthusiasm. "What do you know about space-age archaeology?"

"Enough to pass the final."

Sakuta appeared shocked at this response.

Xris grinned. "It's a joke, Professor. Archaeology wasn't my field. Sorry."

Sakuta's expression cleared. "Ah, yes. I understand. My nemesis was economics. At any rate, on the planet of Pandor, which you will find located in the Zeta Three quadrant, some construction workers have made a historic archaeological find. They have uncovered the wreckage of a prehyperdrive spaceplane."

"I don't remember much from my archaeology class," Xris said, "but I do seem to recall that prehyperdrive craft aren't that rare."

"You're quite right." Sakuta seemed genuinely pleased with Xris's answer. Xris had the feeling he'd earned an A for the day. "The spaceplane itself is not of interest. We have several on display already. It is what's inside the spaceplane that is of inestimable value."

He had dropped his voice; his eyes were moist. His hands actually shook with excitement.

"What is it?" Xris asked, envisioning nothing less than a chest of jewels or maybe—considering Sakuta's interests—a case of antique microchips.

"A robot," Sakuta said, his voice soft with reverent awe. "Not just any robot," he added hastily, seeing that Xris was underwhelmed. "This is one of the first robots designed by scientists to undertake space flight. On its own." Sakuta looked from Xris to Raoul, apparently expecting them to leap out of their chairs and go bounding about the room. "Surely you understand the significance?"

"Oh, I do!" Raoul breathed, half rising. "I truly do." He licked his lips.

"Look, whether we understand it or not doesn't really matter, does it, Professor?" Xris said, shoving Raoul back into his chair. "I don't suppose you want to hire us to write a research paper on it."

"No, sir." Sakuta looked slightly abashed. "You're absolutely right. You have your areas of specialization and I have my own. It's just that this discovery . . . well, never mind. No, the reason I am hiring you is to recover this robot."

Xris leaned back, automatically reached for a twist, saw Raoul raise a disapproving eyebrow, and desisted. Clasping his hands together, elbows resting on the arm of the chair, he regarded the professor speculatively. "What's wrong with it?"

Sakuta was taken aback by the question. "Why, nothing's wrong with it . . . that I know of. It's very, very old, of course, and I think we can safely assume that most of its circuitry is corroded. And it probably sustained a certain amount of damage when the plane in which it was traveling crashed into the planet, though my colleague who first reported the find stated that, in her estimation, the robot was in excellent condition, all things considered. I'm not sure I understand your question—"

Xris was shaking his head. "Look, Professor, from all indications, it sounds like you need to hire a salvage team, not Mag Force 7. We're a crack commando outfit. I have the best men and women in the business on my team and you'll pay the highest rates in the business for us. And if all you want us to do is dig out some moldy old hunk of scrap metal—"

"Ah, I see. I wish it were that easy." Sakuta smiled briefly; his smile faded. He ran his fingertips back and forth on the desk pad, back and forth, staring down at the pad all the while.

Xris recognized the signs. He waited patiently.

Sakuta looked up. His face was tinged with a faint crimson. "I ... I am deeply ashamed of myself. I could never have imagined ... Ethical considerations aside, I ..." He lapsed into silence.

Suddenly he clenched his fist. "But, damn it, this is too important!"

Sakuta shut his eyes when he spoke, as if he feared to see the condemnation of his visitors' faces. "I'm committing a terrible act. I know that, but I can't help myself. Gentlemen, I am hiring you to steal this robot."

CHAPTER
4

Thieves respect property. They merely wish the property to become their property that they may more perfectly respect it.

G. K. Chesterton, *The Man Who Was Thursday*

Sakuta sat, sweating, shaken.

He might have been asking us to assassinate the prime minister, Xris thought, amused. Raoul had leaped to his feet and was solicitously pouring the professor a glass of water from a carafe on the desk.

"Thank you," said Sakuta faintly.

"My pleasure." Raoul was about to rest a comforting hand on the professor's broad shoulder, except that Xris growled. With a jerk of his head, he ordered the Adonian back to his chair.

Sighing deeply, Raoul obeyed, patting Sakuta's hand tenderly as he left.

The professor never noticed. He gulped the water, wiped his lips fastidiously on a white handkerchief, which he then returned to his breast pocket.

"Who is in possession of the robot?" Xris asked.

"No one, at the moment. It is still inside the wreckage of the plane, where it was discovered. The Pandoran government officials have taken into their empty heads to fear that the ship is contaminated—some sort of ancient virus or bacteria that may infect and kill everyone on the planet. They are, of course, completely wrong. Any expert would tell them so. Several have. The plane crashed in a desert environment. My colleague has inspected the spaceplane thoroughly and reported finding only trace amounts of radiation and no bacteria or germs of any kind, ancient or otherwise. The Pandoran government refuses to listen. And, I must admit, we haven't gone out of our way to convince them. Their irrational fear is buying us time."

Xris shifted in his chair. "Professor, I don't mind bending the law on occasion—"

He was forced to wait to continue until Raoul recovered from a fit of coughing.

"—but galactic salvage law clearly states that any debris which falls from space becomes the property of the planet on which it falls. If the Pandorans want this robot for their own Space and Areonautics Museum, then—"

"That's just it!" Sakuta cried in a hollow voice. "If they wanted it for a museum, that would be fine with us! We could arrange to have it exhibited here on loan. But they don't. They are terribly afraid of it. They intend to destroy it."

Xris frowned. "Legal action, then."

Sakuta was shaking his head. "We are in a quandary, gentlemen. We could go to the galactic court and ask for an injunction to stop the Pandorans from destroying the robot, but that would take weeks of legal maneuvering and we don't have weeks!

"The robot and its spaceplane were discovered during the excavation of a construction site. The Pandorans are far more interested in proceeding with their construction than they are in saving the robot. They simply want to be rid of it. They have threatened to bring in bulldozers and"—he shuddered at the thought—"cranes to remove it to a safe area where it can be destroyed."

"Money ..."

Sakuta was now impatient. "We've offered them ten times the value of the robot. They've refused. They keep yammering about flesh-eating viruses. I tell you, gentlemen, I have had nightmares about rough, hulking Pandoran construction workers—"

"You, too?" Raoul was sympathetic.

Sakuta regarded them with pleading eyes. "It wouldn't

be precisely stealing, would it? We would still honor our commitment to pay them for the robot. We are simply ensuring that we save it for posterity."

Xris considered. "You want to hire us to travel to Pandor, retrieve this robot—"

"I will give you a crate that we have specially designed for it."

Xris resumed. "And then you want us to smuggle the robot off-planet—"

Sakuta looked stricken. "I know that this means breaking the law. Perhaps it's not feasible—"

Xris waved that small consideration away. "In the interests of science." He looked over at the Little One. "Well? Is he telling the truth? Is this on the level?"

The telepath gazed steadily from beneath the fedora at Sakuta, then nodded.

Raoul gave the professor a charming smile—to apologize for ever dreaming to doubt him—and turned to Xris.

"The Little One says that Professor Sakuta is telling us the truth, Xris Cyborg. But not all the truth."

Sakuta frowned slightly.

Raoul hastened to continue, anxious that Xris should understand. "Professor Sakuta greatly desires this robot, my friend, far more than he is admitting to us. The reason: His colleague considers the robot to be in working condition with its memory intact. If so, it would be the first prehyperdrive robot ever recovered capable of offering us an eyewitness account of conditions in the galaxy hundreds of years ago. Scholars galaxy-wide will be willing to pay enormous amounts for the opportunity to study the robot and its files. The museum will reap tremendous financial benefit, as well as widespread publicity. Professor Sakuta himself stands to benefit greatly and has already signed on with a publicity agent to handle his lecture tour."

Sakuta's face was extremely red. The professor attempted several times to speak, gave it up, drank a glass of water, straightened his tie, and then regarded them with an air that was half ashamed, half defiant.

"Very well. I admit it. Yes, we will stand to profit by this discovery—"

"To a considerable extent," Xris inserted dryly.

"But I assure you, gentlemen, that money is not a motivating factor. The significance of this discovery, from a scientific and historical perspective, is beyond measure—"

"Except to your accountant." Xris cut off the professor's earnest protests. "Relax. We'll take the job. We'll meet and plan the operation tonight. Tomorrow I'll let you know the estimated cost. I take it you want this handled ASAP."

Sakuta had regained his composure, though he still looked faintly embarrassed. "I would have you on Pandor this moment, if that were possible. Yes, as soon as you can make your arrangements. The . . . um . . . money will not be a problem. The museum is prepared to pay whatever you require."

Xris grunted. "I'll bet. Still, I'll send you an estimate, along with the contract."

Sakuta was alarmed. "Do we . . . do we have to . . . put this in writing?"

Xris grinned. "Don't worry. The contract's worded quite carefully. It's for your own protection as well as ours."

"Of course." Sakuta managed a strained smile. "You are professionals. That is why I turned to you for help. I have made up a dossier which contains information on the planet, its people, the location of the robot—everything I thought might assist you."

He handed over a disposable electronic notebook. Xris accepted the information, stood up.

"One more thing. Where do we deliver it?"

"What?" Sakuta appeared genuinely confused.

"The robot," Xris said patiently.

"Oh, yes! My goodness. Of course. Delivery. Um . . . I don't suppose that bringing it here would . . . No, I can see that wouldn't do."

Xris had been shaking his head.

Sakuta was baffled. "I'm afraid I have no idea . . . I'm

so unused to this sort of thing. Have you any suggestions?"

"Pandor . . ." Xris recollected. "It's near the Void, isn't it?"

Sakuta nodded.

"There's a place known as Hell's Outpost. I see you've heard of it." Xris grinned at Sakuta's shocked expression. "It's not bad. A quiet place. Everyone minds his or her own business. Perfect for our transaction. Meet us there. We'll let you know when."

"I'll be there," Sakuta promised, though he didn't look happy.

The professor rose, moved around from his desk. He extended his hand, shook hands with each of them, had only slight difficulty in retrieving his hand from Raoul's affectionate grasp. He walked with them to the door of the office.

"I'd give you a tour of the museum," he said, "but this has left me with an upset stomach. If you wouldn't mind . . ."

Xris assured him that, much as they would love to view the exhibits, they were on a tight schedule. They walked down the hall. The receptionist was not at her desk—rather to Xris's disappointment. She had seemed to regard him with a certain amount of interest. Of course, he was wearing a suit that hid his cybernetic leg, his fleshfoam and plastiskin hand, and a wig that covered the scars on his bald head.

Xris considered waiting. The Little One put an end to his hopes.

"The Little One says she is not for you, my friend. She is interested in the professor and the feeling is mutual." Raoul heaved a despairing sigh. "Ah, well. It never fails. The good-looking ones are always straight."

Xris smiled, took out a twist, thrust it into his mouth. They descended the stairs, stepped out into the exhibit area, which was now packed with groups of school-children. Their shrill voices echoed, bounced off the high ceiling. Xris turned down his augmented hearing. They dodged shrieking children, harassed-looking teachers, stoic-faced museum guides, and were near the exit when the Little One suddenly grabbed hold of Xris's right hand, pointed.

A woman stood with her back half to them, apparently deeply involved in studying the brochure she held in her hand.

"She interested in us?" Xris asked quietly.

The Little One nodded.

"I don't suppose she thinks I'm incredibly sexy and hopes I'll ask her to go dancing."

The Little One shook his head.

"Who's she working for?"

The Little One shrugged.

"She is very single-minded, is thinking only of us. Perhaps she is aware that we have a telepath. Do you want me to deal with her, Xris Cyborg?" Raoul asked, his hand reaching for his purse, where he kept a tube of very special lipstick.

"No," Xris said, and continued walking out the door. He watched, out of the corner of his eye, the woman follow after them. "It's nice to know someone cares."

CHAPTER
5

Advance knowledge cannot be gained from ghosts
and spirits, inferred from phenomena, or
projected from the measures of Heaven, but must
be gained from men for it is the knowledge of
the enemy's true situation.

Sun-tzu, *The Art of War*

The Mag Force 7 team was scheduled to meet later that
evening in a small conference room in the Megapolis
Spaceport Hotel, in a room that had been reserved by
Xris under the auspices of a corporate leader gathering
together his regional managers for a sales conference.
When Xris had first been contacted by Sakuta for the
job, he'd put the word out to the Mag Force 7 team—
disbanded since the Knights of the Black Earth affair—
to meet him on Megapolis, gave them the name and
location of the standard business-class hotel adjacent to
the spaceport.

A job for the Megapolis Space and Aeronautics Museum wasn't likely to call for top-level security conditions; no need to travel to the edge of the galaxy, to
Hell's Outpost to discuss their plans at the Exile Café,
for example. Xris guessed beforehand that this would be
a simple job and he'd been right—in that, at least.

What he hadn't counted on was Amadi and friends
dropping by to join the party—*if* that woman at the museum had been one of Amadi's. Logic told Xris she was
a bureau agent. Paranoia whispered that she was one of
the Hung.

Whoever she was, he hoped to throw her off the trail. Xris and Raoul and the Little One drove to the spaceport. No sign of Amadi or any of his agents following. Small comfort. Amadi was good and when he didn't want to be seen tailing a suspect, he wouldn't be seen.

Dropping off the rental vehic, the three merged with the crowds in the terminal, purchased three tickets for an outbound flight, and then lounged around in the bar until it was time for their flight to leave. Xris sipped a beer and studied the professor's notes. He formed a preliminary plan to steal the robot, then spent the rest of the time worrying about Darlene.

Raoul bought the latest edition of the *Galactic Inquisitor* and caught up on the gossip about the Royal Family, began ooohing and aahing over the first official family photos of the newly arrived baby prince, attempted to show Xris, who wasn't interested. The Little One crept into the minds of everyone in the immediate vicinity and, though he expanded his store of knowledge on humans considerably, the telepath caught no one tailing them.

When the flight was called, they weren't around to catch it. By the time Amadi—or whoever was keeping an eye on them, if anyone *was* keeping an eye on them— realized they'd been given the slip, the three were long gone. Xris, Raoul, and the Little One left the spaceport, caught a tram to the nearby spaceport hotel.

Xris had plenty of opportunity for thought, with the result that paranoia fought logic and emerged the victor. By the time he reached the hotel, Xris had worked himself into such a fevered state of anxiety that he posted Raoul and the Little One to keep watch, then used the house phone. Asking for Darlene under the name of Mohini, he buzzed her room.

Having already convinced himself that something terrible had happened to his friend, Xris was startled and relieved and even slightly angry at her voice—calm and sleepy-sounding—at the other end.

" 'Lo?" she mumbled.

All that worry, and she'd been taking a nap!

"Darlene, is that you? Are you all right?" Xris demanded.

She heard the tension in his voice, woke up fast. "Yes, it's me. I'm all right. What's wrong?"

"Has anyone been inside your room? For any reason?"

"No."

"Did anyone make you switch rooms? Offer you cash to move?"

"No, Xris." Darlene sounded exasperated. "And I remember the routine, okay? No maintenance man has been in to 'fix' the phone, if that's what you're worried about."

"Good. What's your room number? I'm coming up."

She told him. He switched off the phone, turned to Raoul. "The Little One latch on to anything? Anybody interested in us?"

Raoul shook his head—carefully, so as not to disturb his homburg. "No, there is no one watching us, no one following us, no one paying the slightest bit of attention to us, probably because I am wearing this drab gray suit, which—while it is in the latest style—simply does not suit my personality. May I add, my friend, that the Little One and I"—he patted the fedora that stood somewhere about waist-level—"believe that you are behaving most irrationally. It would indeed be remarkable if anyone were to have kept up with us after all those twistings and turnings and dodgings and feintings we made at the spaceport. My head is still swimming."

"You're a Loti. Your head is always swimming. As for it being remarkable, the Hung's pretty damn remarkable, and don't you ever forget it. I'm going up to talk to Darlene. You and the leech here find Jamil—"

"I was going to change my clothes!" Raoul protested.

"You're beautiful," Xris assured the Adonian. "The gray brings out the red in your eyes. Go find Jamil, tell him what's up, have him search the conference room. When he's covered it, call Darlene's room, let us know. We'll be down."

"What is he looking for?" Raoul's lashes fluttered.

"Anything. Everything—from bugs to plastic explosives."

"Plastic bugs to explosives," Raoul murmured, attempting to commit the instructions to what memory he had. "Now, about my request for a leave of absence—"

"Go!" Xris said through clenched teeth.

Raoul, offended, went. The Little One trailed along behind.

Xris hoped his orders would survive in translation and that Jamil wouldn't spend the next thirty minutes hunting for rubber cockroaches. The cyborg headed for Darlene's room.

Darlene Rowan listened to Xris in silence and even when he had finished, she remained silent.

Xris stood in the small hotel room, peering moodily out a gap in the curtains covering the sliding glass door. He had a twist in his mouth, was chewing it to a bitter pulp.

Hearing nothing from Darlene, Xris turned.

"Well?" he demanded.

She looked at him, shrugged, gave him a faint, lop-sided smile. "We've known all along this was coming, Xris."

"Is that all you can say?"

"What do you want me to say, Xris?" Darlene's voice sharpened. "That I'm scared? I lived for years being scared. Then one day, it just doesn't seem to be worth the effort. I got tired of my heart clogging my throat every time some stranger knocked at my door. Now I just swallow and go on."

"Yeah, well, swallow this. The bureau's pulled Amadi out of retirement to handle this case. They wouldn't have done that unless something big was going down. And Amadi was making sure that no one saw or heard us talking. He's made the connection, all right. He may not know who you are or where you are, but he knows that I know."

Darlene shook her head, shoved a strand of brown hair out of her eyes. She was composed, slightly pale, but then she never had much color in her face. Her hair was tousled from her nap. She'd thrown on a hotel robe. Her overnight bag was where she'd dropped it on the floor, hadn't even been opened. The only item she'd un-packed was her computer case. She'd placed the portable computer on the table near the bed; she'd probably pro-grammed it to wake her. Darlene turned to it now, per-haps instinctively. Her fingers ran idly over the keys. Her comfort, her solace—the machine.

Xris remembered clearly the first time he'd seen her—her, Darlene, not him, Dalin Rowan. He'd been sur-prised to discover that his friend was a damn attractive woman. He'd been more surprised to hear from his friend that deep inside, that's what Dalin Rowan had always been—a woman. Now that Xris had been around Darlene for a couple of months, he understood.

There had always been something jarring about Dalin Rowan, a dissatisfaction with life, with himself. He'd drifted through life in a kind of dull, gray haze of unhap-piness that only lifted when he was inside his—or some-one else's—computer. Dalin's halfhearted attempts at relationships with women had inevitably ended in disas-ter. They complained that he kept himself shut off from them, that they never truly came to know him.

Even his best friends, Xris and Ito, had never truly known Dalin Rowan. Xris had proved that by being ready to believe Dalin had actually sold them out to the Hung, that he'd been the one to send them into that death factory.

Xris was starting to know Darlene Mohini. He was starting to like her, too, as were all the other members of the Mag Force 7 team. She was more relaxed, more at ease, able to open up, to talk about herself. When she spoke of Dalin Rowan, it was as if she were speaking of some unfortunate friend who had now passed out of her life. She remembered Dalin fondly, a little sadly, but with no regrets.

"I'm not so sure Amadi has made the connection, Xris," she said, tapping the computer keys. "He knows that Dalin is around. All right, yes, it was foolish of me going back into the bureau's files to ferret out that information on the Knights of the Black Earth, but God only knows what would have happened if we hadn't cracked that case. And that's the only link Amadi's got: me snooping around the knights and you putting a halt to their operation."

"If Amadi saw you alone, he'd walk past you in the street and never recognize you," Xris conceded. "But if he gets a close look at the two of us together, that's all the link he'll need." Xris chomped savagely on the twist. "That old man's sharp. His mind'll ring up a 'Xris-Dalin, Dalin-Darlene' match faster than Harry Luck can shove coins into a slot machine. And as far as we know, no one but you ever made the connection between the Hung and the bureau. Odds are, whoever the traitor is, he or she is still there."

"Amadi knows about the traitor," Darlene said. She switched the computer on. "That's why he's being careful."

"Amadi was born careful. When he came out of the birth canal he had his head turned, looking over one shoulder. That's why he's still alive. Did you ever say anything to him about Armstrong's death? About the evidence that someone in the bureau was involved?"

Darlene shook her head. "How could I? I didn't know who to trust."

"And we still don't," Xris said emphatically. "So, here's the deal. You and I split up. Let Amadi and the Hung traipse after me for a while, if they can keep up. Once they see that I'm not leading them to you, they'll lay off, lose interest, follow some other line."

Darlene protested, "But the job—"

"This robot snatch is easy. I've got most of it planned out. Jamil and I can handle it. I was going to dismiss the rest of the team anyway. Give everyone a vacation. I want you to go along with someone—anyone but me. You can have your choice."

Xris ran down the list. "Harry Luck. He's trying to decide whether to go to some high-rolling town to lose what money he made on that last job or to attend some seminars being held on the 'Capabilities of the Dirk Fighter in Close Proximity to Atmosphere' or something like that. He can't decide. Harry's taken one too many stun blasts to the head, but he's a damn good pilot, Darlene. You know—you saw him in action on that last job. And he's devoted to you—"

Darlene shook her head, half smiled. "Not Harry, Xris. He's sweet, but, as you say, he's devoted . . ."

She left the rest unfinished. Xris, grinning, moved on. "There's Dr. Quong. He's anxious to finish that study on the Little One, on Tongan physiology. He could probably use your help. The Doc's a bit touchy, but you seem to be able to get along with him better than any of us. Plus he'd have you eating right and exercising. You could gain weight into the bargain. The Doc's a good surgeon and—" Xris stopped, not quite certain where that was going.

"And if anything happened, I'd have a doctor on call." Darlene grinned wryly. "Sorry, Xris, but if the Hung catch me, all the Doc would be able to do is certify the time of my death. Plus I don't really see myself spending my vacation immersed in the psychological oddities of the Tongans—outré as they are."

"Tycho, then. He's planning to go back to his home planet for a visit. The planet of the chameleons, only don't call them that. They find it offensive. I've been there, met his family. They're a fun group. They all look alike. I mean exactly alike. You can't tell his mother from his father, his brothers from his sisters, his relatives from the neighbors. They can tell each other apart, of course. I think it has something to do with skin pigmentation but I've never figured it out. They're all tall and skinny, like he is, and they blend nicely into the surroundings. Of course, you'd stand out like a red flag on an ice floe, but then so would a member of the Hung or the bureau. Tycho's a crack shot and a good person to have on your side."

Darlene was shaking her head. "You know as well as I do, Xris, that the Hung could recruit someone from the 'chameleons' and then I'd be in worse danger simply because I would be so highly visible."

"Well, Jamil would probably be the best. He's steady, reliable, quick-thinking, ex-military. His only flaw is that he's a bit of a womanizer, but with two wives on different planets I think he's got about as much as he can handle. He'd be ideal, but I need him for this museum job. All that leaves is Raoul. He's been pleading for years to go back to Adonia to attend some weird hedonistic religious festival—"

"Really?" Darlene looked interested.

Now it was Xris who protested. "You can't be serious!"

"But I am. Think about it, Xris. Carnival time on Adonia! What could be better? Crowds of people of all types. Everyone who isn't Adonian wears masks. I'd have Raoul with me—"

"He'd be a big help." Xris grunted. "Especially if your mascara's smeared."

Darlene made a face at him. "Come off it, Xris. You think quite highly of Raoul. You wouldn't have him on the team otherwise."

"Yeah, but I don't know why," Xris returned. "And that's what bothers me. He's a Loti—a habitual drug user. I know it; he claims it himself, I've seen him higher than a jumpjet in hyperspace, yet I've never personally seen him swallow so much as an aspirin. When I assign him to a job, he spends more time worrying about what to wear than he does on how to accomplish his mission—"

"But he gets the job done," Darlene stated.

"True," Xris admitted. "I have to give him credit, in all the years he's worked for me, he's only failed us once, during that Olicien bug thing—"

"And that was under extenuating circumstances." Darlene argued her case. "The Little One would be with him. He could pick up on the thoughts of anyone trying to find me."

Xris considered the matter. "There would be a drawback to the crowds, you know that. An assassin can lose himself among them as easily as you can."

"But he's got to find me first," Darlene returned. "Honestly, Xris, I—"

The phone buzzed. It was switched to nonvid, as per instructions for all the team. Xris answered, not saying a word, his usual technique. Team members were prepared for silence on his end, knew how to respond to it. Anyone who shouted "Hello! Hello?" was definitely a wrong number.

"Jamil here. The room's clean."

"I'll be down in a sec." Xris switched the phone off. He regarded Darlene thoughtfully. "Raoul, huh?"

She nodded, smiled. "I haven't had a vacation in years. This might be fun."

"All right. If that's what you want. I have to admit, it does make a certain kind of sense in a nonsense kind of way. It's sure as hell the last place anyone would figure you going. Once Raoul and the Little One have made their report on Sakuta, I'll send them to you. You can leave tonight."

Xris walked to the door, tripped over the computer case on his way. He shoved it with his foot, kicked it under the desk.

"Lock the door after me," he instructed. "Don't answer the phone unless it buzzes three times, then quits, then buzzes again. Don't—"

"For God's sake, Xris, I was in the bureau as long as you," Darlene cut in, annoyed. "I repeat—I know the routine."

"I know you do," he said quietly. She stood beside him, near the door. He reached up, smoothed back the errant lock of hair that was falling in her eyes. "It makes me feel better, all right? Like I'm doing something constructive when I know all along there's not a goddamn thing I can do. If the Hung are looking for you . . ." He shook his head.

She put her hand on his arm, his good arm, his flesh-and-blood arm. Her touch was cold, her fingers chill. He'd been worried that she was taking this too lightly. She wasn't. She knew the Hung better than he did. She'd been inside their organization for months.

"I'll be careful. I promise."

"All right. And I promise to quit the mother-hen routine."

"I'll lock the door. You'll tell Raoul the signal?"

Xris sighed. "I'll tell him, but God only knows if he'll

remember it. If he doesn't, you can smell his perfume through the woodwork. I think it's lilac today."

Darlene smiled at him—her lopsided smile. "I'll be fine. Don't worry."

He nodded, started to leave.

She stopped him, detained him, her hand still on his arm. "You know this is only a stopgap measure, Xris. I can't keep running away. I can't keep you from doing your job. Yes, I know you don't need me this time around—or at least you claim you don't—but how about next time? And look how I've disrupted your life. And the team. They don't resent me now, but they soon will. Next thing you know, you'll be turning down jobs because of me. This can't go on."

Xris smiled at her reassuringly. "It won't. The best defense is a good night's sleep, as our friend Tycho and his maladjusted translator would say. Or then there's my personal favorite of his, the one about carrying the whores into the enemy camp."

Darlene stared at him, wide-eyed, astonished. "You're not thinking of taking on the Hung yourself?"

"About time someone did. It's not a job we're going to do tomorrow or the next day. It'll take time, planning, money. But I've got it in the back of my mind."

Darlene gave him a playful slap on his metal arm, shoved him toward the door. "I think you've got a gear loose. Go have Doc check you out."

Xris listened at the door before opening it. His augmented hearing would pick up the sound of anyone lurking about outside. He couldn't hear anything, but he popped the door open swiftly, peered out into the hall.

Empty.

Xris thrust a twist in his mouth. "Have a good time on Adonia. I hear the orgies are first-rate. Be sure and take vids."

"It's a religious holiday," she said solemnly. "Raoul told me so."

Xris removed the twist. "Take care of yourself," he said gruffly.

Darlene managed a smile, but she was a bit impatient. "I will, Xris. I'm good at it, remember?"

She shut the door behind him.

He walked away, down the empty, silent hall, and suddenly had the feeling that he would never see her again.

The feeling was strong and almost impelled him to turn around and go back, just to prove himself wrong. But that would be stupid, illogical. Darlene would be insulted and she would have every right to be insulted.

Xris didn't believe in premonitions, gut feelings, or anything of the sort. No kindly premonition had come along to warn him to stay out of that munitions factory where Ito had died and part of Xris had died, too. Dr. Quong would say that this feeling of impending doom was Xris's response to his lack of control over the situation. Amadi had taken Xris by surprise, caught him off guard, blindsided him. There wasn't a damn thing he could do to help Darlene, other than make a few plans that were, in his mind, highly inadequate. He was frustrated, and this was the result.

Xris lectured himself all the way downstairs to the meeting room, and by the time he arrived, he felt somewhat better. Darlene would be fine. Just fine.

As he walked through the lobby, he noticed a man with a pocket viewer, earphones on his head, seated in a chair, staring intently at the screen. Xris noticed five other men and one woman, all with pocket viewers, earphones on their heads, all of them staring with various degrees of attention at the various screens. None of them glanced at him. None of them paid him any attention whatsoever.

"Paranoid," Xris muttered, and continued on his way.

He didn't hear the first man speak two words into a cell phone.

"It's her."

CHAPTER
6

One who is in difficulty and doesn't make plans is
impoverished; one who is impoverished and doesn't
fight is lost.

Sun-tzu, *The Art of War*

"That covers my meeting with Sakuta." Xris was
speaking to the assembled Mag Force 7 team—the
assembled team minus one. "I've accepted the job. Now,
here's the setup.

"Where's Darlene?" Harry asked.

"We'll cover that later," Xris said. "Now back to this
job—"

"I don't think we should start the meeting without
Darlene here," Harry protested.

Xris counseled patience. "She's not coming, Harry.
There's a reason. I'll go into it later. Can we get back
to the job?"

"There's something wrong, isn't there?" Harry said.
"That's why that thing's here for a nothing job like this."

He pointed.

"That's a water pitcher, Harry," Xris said.

"I mean that thing next to it."

The "thing" was a bug-scrambling device brought
along by Quong. The device warbled electromagnetic
frequencies, disrupted sensitive micro devices. Nothing
with a microchip inside it would work while the scrambler was operational. Fortunately for Xris, his inner

workings were specially shielded. Otherwise he'd be flopping around the room about now.

"Yes, Harry, and what's wrong is that you're annoying the hell out of me. Can we get on with this?"

"Sure, Xris," Harry said. Leaning over, he muttered, "There's something wrong, isn't there?" under his breath to Dr. Quong. "Do you know? No one ever tells me."

Xris ignored him, continued on.

"Here's the plan. On most other worlds, it would be easy for us to walk off with this antique 'bot. Just show up, hijack it, leave. Pandor presents a problem—several problems. The first: The Pandorans are extremely intolerant and prejudiced against off-worlders. A spate of serial killings—really nasty stuff—took place in one of their major cities years ago. An off-worlder was responsible. The Pandoran people were outraged. In addition, the native Pandorans blamed off-worlders for stealing jobs and controlling the wealth. Result: They forced all off-worlders to leave the planet and won't let any off-worlders back on. With one exception."

Xris looked to the former military man Jamil, who nodded and took over.

"As you can see by the astral map, Pandor is located on one of the major Lanes leading to the Void. If the Corasians ever decided to attack the galaxy from this direction, they'd cruise down this hyperspace Lane. Because of Pandor's vulnerable location, the Royal Military has maintained an Army base on Pandor for as long as the Corasian threat has been known. The Pandorans don't like it, but they don't like being attacked by the Corasians a whole lot more. Army personnel are the only off-worlders permitted to enter Pandor and they are shuttled directly from the spaceport to the base to avoid contact with the local population."

Xris picked it up from there. "According to Sakuta, a construction site is located near this military base—"

"Is it on base property?" Tycho asked, through his computer-programmed translation device.

"Unfortunately not." Xris shook his head. "That would make this easy. The property is owned by a group

of Pandor developers. They're building a shopping mall
and adding a high concrete wall to keep the sight of the
Army base from offending the shoppers. The site is near
the base, though, which gives us an edge. Jamil and I
will dress up in our best Army officer suits and—"

Quong interrupted. "Imitating an officer of the Armed
Services is illegal. If you are caught, you could be ac-
cused of spying and sentenced to death."

Xris shrugged. "They have to catch us first. And we'll
be on and off that base so fast they won't hardly know
we were there. Where was I?" He consulted his electronic notepad. "Oh, yeah. Jamil and I get onto the base.
We do a little song and dance to pay for our supper.
While he's entertaining the troops, I inspect the security,
make any adjustments necessary. That night, we slip off
base, find the robot, grab it, bring it back, stash in with
out luggage, and depart."

Quong was sceptical. "How big is this robot?"

Xris smiled, pulled out a twist, put it in his mouth. "Oh,
about two and a half meters tall, half a meter in diameter, and probably weighs around two thousand kilos."

Quong sniffed. "And you are going to put that in your
suitcase? You had better take Raoul's luggage instead."

"It wouldn't fit," Raoul said complacently. After a
thoughtful pause, he amended. "Well, yes, it would, but
I'd have to leave half my wardrobe behind." He was excited. "Xris Cyborg, it sounds as if you do not need me
on this mission. If so, don't forget the religious holiday—"

"I haven't," Xris said grimly. He raised his hand, fore-
stalled the Adonian's arguments. "We'll discuss this
later. To answer your concerns, Doc, Sakuta provided us
with a crate for the robot—specially built with moisture
control systems and pillows to keep it comfy and God
knows what else. Jamil and I just have to figure how to
bring the crate onto the base without arousing
suspicion."

"I've got an idea on that," Jamil said. "*And* an idea
for why we're on the base in the first place."

"Good. Well, gentlemen, that's it for that job. Jamil
and I can handle it. There's another matter that I have
to cover." Xris was silent a moment, chewing on a twist.

Finally he said quietly, "I had a visit today. From the bureau. One of their agents—my old boss—bumped into me."

"They know about Darlene!" Harry was out of his chair, ready to run to her rescue.

"Yes and no." Xris motioned for the big man to sit down. "The bureau is aware that the person they know as Dalin Rowan is alive and well. They found his footprints in their computer files. But they don't know anything more than that. And we have to keep them from knowing. Because if they find out, odds are that the Hung will find out, too."

"Damn! What are we going to do? We have to do something Xris," Harry said, his face creased with worry.

"I am," Xris said, rubbing his temples. His head ached. "I'm sending Darlene to Adonia with Raoul—"

"In time for the festival?" Raoul was breathless from the suspense.

"Yes, in time for the festival. You see—"

He would have explained further, but Raoul had leaped from his chair, hurled himself at Xris, and flung his arms around Xris's neck.

"Thank you! Thank you, my friend!" Raoul cried fervently. "You have no idea how much this means to me. I unfortunately have been forced to miss the last three festivals and my friends on Adonia are most annoyed with me since I owe them all parties and now I will have a chance to fulfill my social obligations—"

Choking in a cloud of lilac perfume, Xris endeavored to disentangle himself from the Adonian's fond embrace. "Your main obligation is to take care of Darlene. And don't forget it." He rubbed his cheek where Raoul had planted a kiss, looked suspiciously at the smear of red lipstick on his hand. "What is this? Do I need an antidote or something?"

"No, no," Raoul said reassuringly, patting his hair—which had become mussed in the flurry of the moment—and picking up the hat that had been knocked to the floor. "It is ordinary lipstick. Berry Berry Delicious, if you want the name. It's really quite a becoming shade on you."

"I don't like this, Xris," said Harry Luck grimly. "I don't like it one damn bit."

"I don't much like it myself, Harry, but this is Darlene's plan and it's her decision and, all things considered, I think it's the best we can do—aside from you sitting outside her door day and night with a beam rifle across your knees, of course."

"And maybe that's what we should do," Harry argued stubbornly. "Not let her go traipsing around the universe with Mr. Berry Berry Delicious here—"

Raoul was affronted. He smoothed his hair and regarded Harry with an icy, if somewhat unfocused, stare.

"The Little One and I pledge ourselves by all that Adonians hold sacred—"

"Condoms, lip gloss, and styling mousse," Quong whispered in a loud aside to Jamil.

Raoul's lashes fluttered, but he carried on. "—to keep Darlene Rowan safe and sound, and I will hold myself bound by that pledge and the Little One will hold himself bound—"

"All that binding, sounds like an Adonian party to me," Jamil said, nudging Quong.

"This is not funny!" Harry shouted angrily.

"Harry, listen—" Xris began.

"Indeed it is not," Raoul said, his lip quivering, his cheeks flushed crimson. "If you are impugning our abilities, Harry Luck—"

"I'm not . . . whatever that word is . . . anything." Harry slammed his hand on the table, rattling the water pitchers. "I'm just saying that I don't think it's a good idea to send Darlene off with a poisoner and a telepath when the odds are that some top-notch death squad is after her."

"You *are* impugning our abilities!" Raoul returned, highly indignant. "I promise that we will look after Darlene most assiduously!" He caught hold of the Little One, who, at the torrent of conflicting emotions surging about the room, was endeavoring to hide from them by crawling under the table. "And," Raoul added magnanimously, "I will do something about her hair at the same time."

This pronouncement broke up the meeting. Harry clenched his fists and kicked over his chair. Jamil lay sprawled on the table, helpless with laughter. Tycho fumbled with his translator, trying to find out what Darlene was doing with rabbits. Quong offered to check Harry's testosterone level. Raoul sniffed and held himself aloof while the Little One tangled himself up in the tablecloth.

"Shut up," Xris said. "All of you."

The words snapped. Xris had the feeling he might snap next.

"Harry, sit down. Raoul, get the Little One out from under there. Tycho, recalibrate that damn translator. No one said anything about rabbits."

Jamil raised an eyebrow, exchanged glances with Quong. Harry, his choleric face splotched with patches of white, mumbled something, returned to his seat. Raoul dragged the Little One out from under the table, adding the loudly whispered admonishment that he had better behave because Xris Cyborg was in a bad mood.

"Damn right I'm in a bad mood," Xris said. Taking out the golden case which held the twists, he tapped the case on the table. "This is all my fault. I screwed up. I was stupid. Careless. I had no idea the bureau was tailing me. They've probably been at it for weeks now. Amadi showed himself because he needed to talk to me. If Amadi had been the Hung, I'd have led them right to Darlene. Maybe I already have. I don't know."

He tapped the case on the table, frowned down at it.

Jamil shifted uneasily in his chair, an expression of disapproval on his face. He was ex-military, an officer. Superiors weren't supposed to admit to making mistakes, weren't supposed to show weakness.

Harry Luck, big, brawny, with as much muscles in his head as his arms, kept quiet. Xris would have to explain this plan several times to Harry and even then the big man might not catch on. Thoughts dropped down into his mind like the little steel balls in a pachinko game, bounced around, sometimes hit, most of the time missed. But he was a damn good pilot, one of the very best.

Bill Quong. Doctor of medicine, degree in engineering. He kept them all in good working order, Xris especially. Terse, pedantic, Quong reduced all of life to its chemical and mechanical components. He preferred machines to people and his bedside manner tended to reflect this. He was regarding Xris with professional concern, probably wondering if his electrolyte count was out of whack.

Tycho. Tall, humanoid in appearance, thin to the point of emaciation, he belonged to a race known in slang terms as "chameleons" for their ability to alter skin color to blend in with their surroundings—a handy skill for a sniper and a trained assassin. His people had no facility for any human language, neither comprehending it nor speaking it. He wore a translator for that purpose. Unfortunately, the translator tended to miss a lot. The "chameleon" language was immensely logical, highly structured and consequently had difficulty handling the idiosyncrasies of human speech. Tycho's use of clichés and idiomatic expressions tended to be extremely colorful and possess meanings never intended. He was clearly perplexed by what was going on. Between "impugned" and "assiduously" his translator had probably overloaded.

The Little One, empath, telepath, was staring at Xris from beneath the brim of the fedora. His was a mysterious race, unknown to the rest of the universe, given the fact that they were extraordinarily hideous-looking people (one reason he was muffled to the eyes in raincoat and to the nose in fedora). To leave their planet was punishable by death.

Somehow, somewhere, the Little One had hooked up with Raoul, Adonian, Loti—slang for habitual drug user—and one of the most expert chemists and poisoners in the field. The two were an interesting pair, completely devoted to each other. The empath was comfortable around the Loti, who functioned—generally—in a drug-induced haze of pleasant thoughts and emotions. The Little One, as far as Xris could determine, acted as Raoul's guide dog, leading the Loti around the obstacles and pitfalls of life.

The Little One was now quivering beneath the raincoat, shivering in the emotional windstorm of Xris's anger, guilt, anxiety, and frustration.

Xris looked up. "There's not a damn thing *I* can do to help Darlene except keep away from her; draw them off her, maybe draw them out. So that's the plan. Harry, I gave Darlene all the options. She chose to go with Raoul. If you want to argue with her, go ahead. I don't advise it. She was barely speaking to me when I left."

Harry muttered something unintelligible, shook his head. The others kept silent, so silent that they could all hear the faint whir and hum of Xris's machinery.

"Right," Xris said. "I think that's it. Jamil, how long will it take you to gather everything we need?"

Jamil cleared his throat, sat up straight. "A couple of Army uniforms, standard-issue side arms, insignia, medals, patches—I've got most of those at my place on Esquimalt. Leaving tonight, I can be there by twelve hundred tomorrow."

"Good. Meet me at seventeen hundred hours the day after. I assume we can take a standard spaceplane flight to Pandor?"

"Right. No need to steal a fighter or anything." Jamil was on his feet. "I'm a colonel and you're my aide, rank of captain, arriving to give the Army personnel on Pandor an edifying and informative lecture which they've had scheduled for months, only they just haven't noticed it yet. I'll need Darlene's help to slip it into their computer files. Is that all right?"

"She'll be glad to have something to do. Go on up to her room, tell her what you need. Take Raoul and the Little One with you. The sooner you three leave"—Xris gave the nod to Raoul—"the better."

"Indeed," Raoul said, equanimity completely restored. "I have a great deal to do to arrange for the party. There are the caterers to contact, the menu to consider. I am certain that the house needs cleaning—"

"Just get Darlene off this planet quickly and safely, will you, Loti?" Xris said grimly.

"Of course." Raoul's lashes half closed. He glided over, wrapped a hand around Xris's arm, his flesh-and-blood arm, squeezed it gently. "Have no fear for Dar-

lene, my friend. We will take excellent care of her. And
perhaps she may learn some things about herself at the
same time. She has been shut up inside a prison for the
last several years—"

"She's been shut up inside a secret military space-
base—"

"I don't mean that, Xris Cyborg." Raoul's voice was
soft, low. "I mean a prison of her own design. It is not
her death you should be most concerned about, but
her life."

"What do you mean? What about her life?"

"She doesn't have one," Raoul said calmly. "Good-
bye. Kiss, kiss." He started to glide away, turned back.
The purple-drenched eyes were misty, shimmering,
glazed. "Oh, and you *will not* permit Harry Luck to accompany Darlene to Adonia, will you? To think of him
sprawled on my white velvet couch, in those dreadful T-
shirts he wears, drinking beer, belching, and munching
potato chips."

" 'The horror, the horror,' " Xris said sympathetically.

Raoul swayed slightly on his feet, put his hand to his
head. "Yes, it is, isn't it? Pardon, Xris Cyborg. That last
image has been too much. I feel faint. I believe I shall
go sit down a moment."

"Xris, I—" Harry was looming on the horizon.

"Wait a sec."

The Little One, instead of attending to his distraught
friend, as would have been usual, was standing in front
of Xris.

"What is it?" Xris asked gently. He had a real fondness for the small empath. "Is something wrong?"

The fedora nodded.

"What? Tell me."

The Little One raised his small hands, palms out.

"Something's wrong, but you don't know what," Xris
guessed—correctly, it seemed. "Is it me?"

The Little One nodded his head once, then shook it
again and waved his hands, indicating that yes, he knew
Xris had problems, but that this wasn't what was bothering him.

"Is it about Darlene?" Xris tried again.

The Little One thought a moment, then shook his head emphatically.

"What, then? The job? The museum? Sakuta?"

The Little One considered this. He nodded, but only tentatively.

"Something's wrong with this job? *What's* wrong? Can you tell me? Can Raoul tell me?"

The Little One shook his head, pulled the fedora down around his ears in a gesture of frustration. Stamping his feet, he lifted his hands into the air, turned, and stomped off, tripping over the hem of the raincoat as he went.

Xris, too, was frustrated, considered going after the empath and trying to pin him down, then decided against it. The Little One was obviously as upset with himself as Xris was with him. Nagging at him wouldn't help, might further upset him.

"As if we didn't have enough trouble," Xris muttered. He thought over what might go wrong with the job and, other than the obvious, like being arrested for impersonating an officer, couldn't think of a thing.

Paranoia must be catching.

Xris turned to the next problem, to tell Harry that he couldn't go to Adonia because he'd never make it through customs.

He just wasn't pretty enough.

CHAPTER 7

I always say that beauty is only sin deep.

Saki (Hector Hugh Munro), *Reginald*

The only part of the passport which Adonian customs officers inspect is the photo. On Adonia, they don't particularly care where you are from, where you are going, or how you intend to get there. They're not overly interested in what you are bringing on-world, what you are intending to take off-world, or why you're on their world at all. They only want to know what you look like.

Eons ago, when genetic altering was popular, scientists set out to breed a race of superior people. Wise, intelligent, gifted with all manner of attributes, these people were destined to be rulers and were known as the Blood Royal. The current king, Dion Starfire, and now his newborn son, are the last of that bloodline. At that time, the Adonians also began experimenting with genetics with hopes of producing a superior being—one designed to meet their own standards. The Adonians did not seek intelligence and wisdom. They sought aquiline noses, flat ears, thin thighs, cleft chins, melting eyes, and firm buttocks. If you are beautiful, reasoned the early Adonians, you don't need to think. Thinking will be done for you.

The Adonians succeeded. They created a species of human noted galaxy-wide for extraordinary beauty. Males and females were so wonderfully attractive that the term "gorgeous as an Adonian" passed into popular usage. But it seems that the Creator demands a price for tampering with His creation. The more beautiful the Adonians became on the outside, the less beautiful they grew within, until at this time in their history, they were noted as being a society completely devoid of morals.

The Adonians are not immoral. Immorality implies that one has a sense of the difference between right and wrong. The Adonians lack this. For example, Adonians have passed laws stating that it is legal to "refuse to sustain" a child if it is born ugly. To them, this is mercy killing. The Adonians care about nothing except beauty and pleasure—in any and every form.

Following this line of thinking, one might assume that the home world of Adonia would be a cesspool of iniquity, a den of vice. This is not true.

The Adonians believe that their planet must be beautiful, in order to suitably showcase the beautiful populace. If planet and inhabitants are beautiful, people in the rest of the galaxy will come visit and enjoy, admire and emulate, and—of paramount importance—spend money. Since most methods of earning money (factories, offices, and such) tend to either smell bad or look disgusting or cause wrinkles, the Adonians banned these from their world, which left them with only one major source of income. What they live for—pleasure.

Adonia became a hedonistic paradise. The Adonians have only one entry requirement: You must either be at least passable in appearance or agree to wear—at all times—a mask so that your looks will not offend any of the more sensitive in nature.

As Darlene rode on the Adonian shuttlecraft—one of the most luxurious she had ever encountered—she found herself growing increasingly nervous. The thought of having to pass through customs, of being deemed "unacceptable" in appearance, the possibility of having to wear a mask, was unnerving. Bothered her far more, she was startled to realize, than the thought of an assassin stalking her.

"I'm being silly," she argued with herself. "What do I care what a bunch of vapid, ignorant, egotistic, prejudiced people think of my looks?"

Nevertheless, she did care. Perhaps it was being in such close proximity to so many Adonians on the shuttle, staring at them in awe, listening to them talk about shampoo and cosmetics, the latest fashions, the most exotic perfumes. Darlene caught herself pulling her hair to the back of her head in a vain effort to hide the split ends, and wishing that she'd taken Raoul's advice as to her makeup. Several Adonians glanced at her and hastily averted their eyes.

Raoul himself was in a state of bliss not to be approximated by artificial stimulants. It had been three years, he told Darlene, since he'd returned to his home world for Hedonist Days and he had missed it dreadfully.

"Mummy and Daddy made so much of it," he said during the shuttle trip. The tears of childhood memories glistened in his eyes. "Baking the phallic cookies, setting up the condom tree, mixing the hallucinogens for the punch. That was *my* special job. Then planning the party games!"

"Your parents are dead, are they?" Darlene asked, watching Raoul make a delicate swipe at his nose with a lace handkerchief.

Raoul was forced to pause to think about this. "No, I don't believe so. I'm sure I would have heard. . . . Yes." He confirmed this in his mind. "I would have undoubtedly been informed."

"Did you have an argument?"

"Oh, no. We are on quite good terms. At least we would be, I'm sure, if we ever met." Raoul smiled at her confusion. "You see, my dear, my parents' job of caring for me ended when I reached the age of majority, which—on Adonia—is sixteen. At that age, state payments for the upkeep of children ends. I was expected to go out and make my way in the world. Mummy and Daddy gave me their blessing and a ten-setting adjustable curling iron and we haven't seen each other since."

"You refer to child-raising as a job?"

"What else would it be?" Raoul returned complacently. "Most children are products of test tubes anyway. I refer to my parents as 'mummy' and 'daddy' but they're probably not, biologically. The state pays parents to rear children and they receive a bonus if their children turn out well. Which I did," he added, smoothing his hair and contentedly contemplating his own reflection in the mirror, of which there were many on the Adonian shuttlecraft. "My parents made quite a tidy sum off me."

"There's no affection," said Darlene, hesitantly. "No parent-child bond. That sort of thing?"

"Not necessary," Raoul assured her. "Quite detrimental, in fact. People like you—no offense, dear—have complexes brought on by hating your father and loving your mother or vice versa. Those complexes lead to all manner of sexual problems, which lead to more complexes. We have none of that here. You were a woman trapped in a man's body. Recall how you suffered in your society! On Adonia, such a mistake would have been discovered and corrected by the time you were twelve!"

Darlene's cheeks flushed. She didn't mind talking about herself or her past with her friends, but she wished Raoul would keep his voice down. Several Adonians— who had before turned away from her—were now regarding her with marked interest.

"What about affection?" she asked, hurriedly changing the subject. "Love?"

"Messy emotions!" Raoul sniffed, banished them with a flutter of his handkerchief. "I am happy to say that, for the most part, we have eradicated them."

"I wouldn't say that eradication has been entirely successful in your case," Darlene said with a smile.

The Little One, enveloped in the raincoat, his face covered by the hat, was sound asleep, his head pillowed on Raoul's lap.

Raoul glanced down at his slumbering friend. "I do have some flaws," he admitted, mortified. Sighing, he comforted himself with another glimpse at his reflection. "Fortunately they are only internal. They are not apparent on the surface. Which reminds me. I must change prior to landing."

Raoul gently shifted the Little One to a more comfortable position, cradling his friend on a nest of soft cushions, then left. Raoul had already changed clothes twice, once before leaving the space cruiser to go to the shuttle, once after having arrived on the shuttle, and now once again, in order to disembark.

Darlene was accustomed to shuttle rides in which everyone sat glumly, silently in their seats, anxious to land, anxious to end the wearisome traveling and get on with their lives. Not the Adonians. The shuttle ride developed into a party, a blur of motion, color, and activity, all awash in heady perfume.

Adonians were constantly leaving to change their clothes or arrange their hair or change their hair and arrange their clothes. A sumptuous banquet was served aft. Live entertainment was for'ard. Stewards poured champagne into crystal glasses. The shuttle had a heated pool on board, a masseuse, a sauna. Also a recreational area. Watching the couples (with the occasional threesome or foursome) enter the rec room and later emerge flushed and invigorated, Darlene guessed that the Adonians weren't playing shuffleboard.

"People became so restless on shuttle flights," Raoul explained when he returned. He had changed from a mauve jumpsuit with golden epaulets on the shoulders and matching gold boots to a long flowing pink caftan with billowing sleeves, encrusted with embroidery and glittering with sequins.

"Restless! The flight's only two hours!" Darlene protested. "Why couldn't you just ... read a book?"

Raoul laughed so much he had to leave again to repair the damage done to his eyeliner.

When he returned, he regarded Darlene with a contemplative frown. "Now, do let me *try* to do *something* with your hair!"

While Raoul fussed over her—murmuring despairingly beneath his breath—Darlene studied the other passengers onboard the shuttle, trying to ascertain if any of them might be shadowing her—although, she admitted to herself ruefully, spotting a tail would be a difficult task on an Adonian shuttle. What with all the comings and goings and clothes changing and appearance altering, she probably wouldn't have spotted her own mother.

Was the drop-dead gorgeous Adonian blond woman

seated across the aisle from her the same drop-dead gorgeous Adonian redhead who had occupied that seat on departure? Darlene wasn't sure. She had the dim notion that the woman wasn't a woman at all. Darlene was beginning to think Xris had been right. This trip was a mistake.

But there was always the Little One. The telepath, having awakened, reported through Raoul that no one was thinking about Darlene at all.

"Not surprising, with this hairdo," Raoul muttered. He gazed sadly at Darlene. His voice had the tragic note of a surgeon telling the nurses to pull the plug. "I've done all I can conceivably be expected to do, given the circumstances."

The shuttle landing took forever, the craft settled down very slowly and very gently. "It would never do to jostle the wine," Raoul explained.

When the doors were at last opened, the Adonians rose gracefully, bade good-bye to newfound shipboard romances, and glided toward the exits on waves of rose and musk and violet. The smoke of hookahs lingered in the air. The few off-world passengers, feeling—as did Darlene—frumpy, dowdy, repressed, inhibited, and, most of all, ugly, slumped down in the seats and wished they'd never come.

Raoul was eager to leave, however, and insisted that Darlene come with him. Walking off the shuttle in company with the glittering, beautiful Adonian, she understood now why the Little One chose to envelop himself in the raincoat; she envied him his fedora.

Shrinking into herself, conscious of all eyes on her (disparagingly, it seemed), Darlene Mohini picked up her computer case and her shabby overnight bag and prepared to be thoroughly and deeply humiliated in customs.

She would have almost rather been shot.

CHAPTER
8

So clomb this first grand thief into God's fold . . .

John Milton, *Paradise Lost*

The shuttle landing on Pandor was considerably more jarring to its passengers than the shuttle landing on Adonia. No champagne had been served on the flight; the fragrances in the air were a mixture of disinfectant, boot polish, and machine oil. No swimming pools; the passengers considered themselves lucky to have toilets. The seats were benches, with worn and cracked vinyl cushions. The passengers made no complaint about the discomfort, however. They were all Army personnel, they'd all been in worse places, and there was a full-bull colonel onboard, who was heard to remark to his aide that this landing was soft as a baby's bottom compared to the drop-ship landings he'd made during his days with special forces.

After that, of course, the other passengers—two privates and two lieutenants—dared make no complaint, could only nurse their bruised tailbones and suffer in silence.

As a matter of fact, Jamil's own tailbone hurt like hell, but he knew how a colonel was expected to act. He'd seen more than his share during his years in the Army.

When the shuttle landed, the door opened to blinding, glaring sunshine. The flight attendant—an especially attractive woman who'd been solicitous to Jamil's wants and needs all during the flight (to the glum envy of the two lieutenants and the sardonic amusement of the two privates)—turned to announce that passengers could now disembark.

The privates and the lieutenants all looked at Jamil. It would be the colonel's privilege to leave first, keep them waiting—if he chose. He smiled, waved magnanimously.

"You gentlemen go ahead," he said. "The captain and I will wait."

Standing, he straightened his uniform, adjusted his cuffs, smiled and glanced at the flight attendant. She smiled back. He'd forgotten the effect of a uniform on some women.

The others left hurriedly, the two privates endeavoring to avoid catching the eyes of the two lieutenants. All four grabbed their onboard luggage, which had been stowed in the back, sidled past the colonel and his aide, and hastened toward the door. Jamil could almost see them exhale with relief when they made it out safely. He felt a twinge of regret for the old days.

Xris, in his guise as captain and aide-de-camp, left his seat, next to Jamil and stood aside to allow the "colonel" to pass.

Jamil strode out into the aisle.

"Check to see if the staff car is waiting, Captain."

"Yes, sir," Xris replied, and started off.

"Captain!" Jamil barked.

Xris turned.

Jamil held out his carry-on bag. "And see to the rest of the luggage, will you, Captain?"

Xris blinked, recovered. Returning, he took the bag. "Yes, sir, Colonel, you bastard," he added under his breath. "Don't get used to this."

Jamil grinned, tugged on his cuffs, and walked forward to pass a few pleasant moments flirting with the flight attendant.

Through the plane's window, he watched Xris retrieve the luggage, carry it down the stairs to the tarmac, broiling in the Pandoran sun. Jamil chatted as Xris supervised the unloading of the large crate which contained the visual aid materials the colonel would be using in his lecture, saw it deposited safely on the tarmac.

It must be hot out there, Jamil thought, observing Xris sweating in his heavy uniform as he stood at the bottom of the ramp, waiting to make his report.

Jamil relaxed a moment more in the cool comfort of the cabin, joking with the shuttle pilots and enjoying a chilled glass of orange juice. The flight attendant was writing down her phone number.

She handed it to him. He thanked her, thanked the pilots, and proceeded down the stairs. He couldn't recall enjoying anything in his life half so much as watching Xris salute him.

Jamil returned the salute, glanced around in feigned astonishment.

"The staff car is not here, sir," Xris reported.

Jamil wasn't surprised. The big surprise would have been if the staff car *had* been there to meet them.

"Find out what the devil's happened to it, Captain!" Jamil ordered, but Xris was already crossing over to the small terminal building, his eye on some poor unfortunate corporal.

Jamil strode over to the terminal building, taking his time. He could hear Xris's furious bellow.

"Why the hell isn't Colonel Jatanski's staff car on the tarmac, ready to pick us up?"

The corporal stammered his reply. "I'm s-sorry, sir, but we have no record of any senior officers arriving on base today."

"We'll see about that, Corporal!" Xris stated grimly.

Jamil took a moment to enjoy the view.

Pandor was a desert planet—at least the part on which they had landed was desert. A white-hot sun blazed in a cobalt-blue sky. No need for paved landing strips. The tarmac was red dirt, baked hard by the relentless sun. The buildings of the landing site, and those of the Army base itself, which he could see off in the distance, were low, stone structures, cut from rock that was the same reddish color as the dirt. Singularly unattractive.

Off to his left, at the far end of the tarmac, were two huge hangars. Both had their doors open, to try to obtain some relief from the sweltering heat for the crews working inside. Various signs in Standard Military identified the Army Aviation squadrons based on Pandor. Bombers and fighters and fighter-bombers, these spaceplanes could be used for both land and space combat. Jamil made a mental note of them; you never knew when such information might come in handy.

A sign adorned with an orange skull on a black background hung over the first hangar, announced the fact that the 2311th Bombardment "Thundering Death" Squadron was stationed there. In front of the doors, a massive Claymore Heavy Bomber was winding up its engines for some type of maintenance check, to judge by the grounds crew swarming around it. Next hangar over was the home of the 1073rd Tactical Fighter "Ruby" Squadron. Maintenance crews could be seen working on the Dirk Fighters inside.

By the time Jamil arrived at the terminal, Xris had hauled the unfortunate corporal inside, had him sweating over a computer terminal.

"Punch up the daily routine for this god-forsaken base, Corporal," Xris ordered.

The corporal obeyed. Jamil bent over, glanced at it. The screen lit with the daily administrivia: *Order unit photographs from the base photographic unit, Mess C will be closed at lunch today, The construction area is off-limits to all personnel,* and so forth. Jamil was just starting to get worried when he saw the name Jatanski flash by. There it was: *Reminder to all personnel to attend tomorrow's briefing on "Foreign Object Damage to Spaceplane Engines" to be given by noted aerospace expert Colonel R. A. Jatanski.*

Xris jabbed his finger at the entry, glared at the red-faced corporal, who no doubt saw private's stripes in the cyborg's eyes.

"Uh, s-s-sir, I-I—"

"Get me my goddamn staff car!" Xris yelled.

"Yes, sir!"

The sweating and shaken corporal grabbed the phone; Jamil and Xris could both hear him talking in urgent tones to someone on the other end, probably the Base Commander's aide.

"I was getting nervous," Jamil said in a low voice to Xris. The two had strolled over to the window, in order to give the corporal room to maneuver.

"*You* pull up the daily list then!" he was overheard to say.

"I thought maybe Rowan might have blown it," Jamil continued.

Xris smiled, shook his head. His hands kept reaching for his pocket, kept reaching for the gold case of twists that would have normally been there, was not there now. Due to health concerns, military personnel were prohibited from smoking. Not even a colonel's aide could have broken that rule. Xris put his hands behind his back, clasped one hand over the other's wrist, held them firmly.

"How'd she manage to break into a military computer?" Jamil wondered.

Xris shook his head. "How the hell should I know? That's Darlene's department. She was on their payroll for years, must have found more than a few back doors."

"Your car is on the way, sir," the corporal informed them. "Colonel Strebbins extends his apologies."

Jamil curtly nodded, continued to stand in magnificent and indignant aplomb at the window. Their backs to the corporal, he and Xris exchanged glances. So far. So good.

Half an hour later, a black hovercar, adorned with a small flag indicating colonel rank fluttering from the front bumper, landed in front of the terminal. A private in a very neat, very crisp dress uniform stepped out and entered the terminal. Xris waved him down. The private halted, gave a very neat, very crisp salute.

"Begging your pardon, Sir. The Base Commander, Colonel Strebbins, sends his deepest apologies for the delay. He says that he is very much looking forward to the briefing tomorrow, Sir. Your Room in the VIP quarters has been arranged. Captain, Sir, you will be staying in the transient officer's quarters, next door. Colonel Strebbins requests the pleasure of your company tonight at his table at the Officer's Mess, 1900 hours for 1930 hours, if you wish."

Jamil nodded. "Yes, tell the colonel that Captain Kergonan and I will indeed attend."

The private loaded their luggage into the hovercar. The colonel entered the staff car, relaxed in cool luxury, while Xris gave instructions to the corporal regarding the delivery of the large and clumsy crate containing the "exhibit" materials that was resting on the tarmac.

The corporal gazed at the shining specially designed metal crate, with its myriad dials and gauges, all prepared to provide the antique robot with a constant humidity level, constant temperature, protection from the contamination of unfamiliar environments, and other comforts.

"That must be some exhibit, sir!" the corporal stated in awe.

Xris pointed to the "biohazard contamination" symbol he himself had added to the outside of the crate. "As you can see, Corporal, this should be handled with extreme care. The colonel and myself are the only ones who have been trained in the procedures to allow us to handle this material safely. Anyone else risks doing serious damage to the environment, perhaps to himself. Understood?"

The corporal must have been wondering what all this had to do with the topic of the colonel's lecture, "Foreign Object Damage to Spaceplane Engines," but he said nothing about that, assured Xris that the crate would receive the very best treatment, and asked where it should be delivered.

Xris walked over to the staff car, knocked on the window. Jamil pushed the button; the window slid down.

"Excuse me, Colonel, but the corporal wants to know where you want the crate delivered."

"How the devil should I know?" Jamil said in an undertone, glaring at Xris.

"What was that, Colonel?" Xris said, leaning his head in the window. "Begging the colonel's pardon, but I don't believe that location would be suitable," he added, having heard Jamil mutter, "Up your ass!"

They had known in advance that the crate was going to present a problem. It was equipped with air jets, which eased it gently over the ground. Xris wouldn't have any difficulty getting it to the construction site, but he couldn't very well be seen taking the damn thing for a stroll through the base after dark. Ideally, they needed to stash it someplace near the site. And, at the moment, they had no idea where the best place would be.

Sakuta's map of the base, provided by his colleague, had obviously been drawn up by some ivory-tower intellectual playing at being a commando. It was rife with X's marking the ammunition dump, arrows pointing out the guard posts, and was careful to note in red all the back entrances to every building. Unfortunately, the map maker had not thought it important to include information on such mundane locations as warehouses and storage sheds.

Xris and Jamil had agreed to play this one by ear, ask the right questions, make their plans accordingly. Generally Xris handled this sort of thing; he was good at thinking on his feet. But Xris had now just dumped the whole matter into Jamil's lap. Xris could always retrieve it, if he had to. He was all set to offer a suggestion if Jamil bobbled the ball. This was payback for the luggage toting.

Xris's head was in the window, where no one could see him. He grinned, winked.

Jamil leaned forward. "Have the crate delivered to your room, Captain."

The grin vanished from Xris's face. He said something beneath his breath that no captain would ever say to a colonel and expect to live through, drew back, stood up, and gave the instructions to have the crate delivered to his quarters. Actually, that was a damn good idea. It was just too bad Jamil had to be the one to think of it. He'd be certain to remind Xris of this when the time for paychecks rolled around. The corporal looked dubious, but it wasn't his place to argue with either a captain or a colonel.

Xris took his place in the front seat with the driver.

Jamil sat back in the cushy seat in the rear, folded his arms, relaxed, and prepared to enjoy the ride.

*   *   *

Jamil's quarters were palatial. The army base on Pandor didn't get many high-level visitors—it didn't get many visitors of any level, apparently. Those who came were treated royally. The aide pointed out the "honor" bar down the hall. Each of the rooms had a fireplace (the desert nights on Pandor were chill), marble-topped desk, and bath facilities, and a vid entertainment system.

Xris was not so fortunate, as Jamil well knew, being highly familiar with transient officers' quarters. The cyborg's room was clean and spacious. ("You have ample room for the crate, Captain," Jamil had pointed out.) The furniture was functional—about the only compliment that could be paid it—consisted of a metal bed, a metal desk, and a metal sink. The crate sat on the floor.

Jamil was putting the finishing touches on his dress uniform when Xris knocked on the door. Jamil invited the captain inside, shut the door, and reflexively ducked the swing Xris took at him.

"That's for sticking me with that blasted crate," Xris said in an undertone. He had already taken a twist out of its case, which he had stashed in his steel bag. Thrusting the twist in his mouth, he started to chew. He glanced around. A lift of his eyebrow asked, *You check this place out?*

Jamil nodded, went back to the mirror to make final adjustments. Both officers were in dress uniforms, well tailored with all the proper insignia, patches, epaulets, and suitable metals. Raoul was in charge of the team's wardrobe, and the uniforms were in immaculate state, fit perfectly. Xris and Jamil removed the few extra unmilitary adornments which Raoul thought added "that certain touch."

"All right, we go over the plan again. After dinner—"

"After the port and the toasts," Jamil corrected. "And they'll probably ask me to make a speech."

"Fine." Xris ground the word up with the twist. "After all that, we traipse off to the bar—"

"The head table rises," Jamil said. "That's where I'll be sitting. When we've left, then everyone is free to go to the bar. I'll meet you there and—"

"And you'll send me on some sort of errand—"

"I'll order you to go check out the hall where I'll be giving the lecture."

Xris pondered. "What if some bright-eyed lieutenant wants to show it to me in person?"

"Not necessary. We wouldn't want to take him away from the fun. I have a map. A good one," Jamil added, casting a disparaging glance at Sakuta's map. "I'll stay in the bar and keep the base commander busy."

"If possible, I'd like to find someplace to stash the crate near the construction site. Once that's accomplished, I'll experiment, see how easy it is to get off-base. If I make it, we go with Plan A. If not, we'll move on to Plan B."

Jamil grinned. "My taste for Pandoran stout."

"Yeah. If either plan works, I'll have the 'bot safely stowed in the crate by the time you give your lecture tomorrow. You say—"

"I say that I've run tests and the environment here isn't suitable and so on and so forth and it would be too dangerous to open the crate, so we'll have to forgo the exhibits."

"Plan C, you don't even bring the crate. You explain the same thing. I'll recover the robot during your lecture. We pack up and leave."

"What about workmen at the construction site?"

"I talked to the private when he showed me the room. The window overlooks the site, so it was a perfect opportunity to ask what's going on. He said that construction had halted because of a crashed spaceship they found. Guards are posted, but only on the road leading in. The crash site's about five kilometers away from the main entrance. They've placed portable electronic fencing around the downed ship." Xris patted the compartment in his cybernetic leg where he kept his tool and weapons hands. "Nothing that can't be solved."

Jamil nodded. "It all seems dead easy."

"Yeah, doesn't it?" Xris shifted the wad of soggy twist from one side of his mouth to the other. "I almost wish some little something would go wrong, just to ease our minds."

"Bite your tongue!" Jamil admonished. "Nothing's

going to go wrong. We have every contingency covered and, if all else fails, there's Plan D."

"Biological warfare." Xris shook his head. "I trust it won't come to that. For one thing, I don't want to hang around for twenty-four hours, waiting for everyone to start racing for the latrines. But, just in case, I've located the base water supply and I've got the germ mixture Raoul concocted in a vial, locked up in the crate."

"You're sure this stuff is harmless?" Jamil asked. "We're in enough trouble with the Lord Admiralty over the Major Mohini episode as it is. I wouldn't want to have to explain why we accidentally poisoned a couple thousand military personnel."

"Raoul assured me that the most that will happen is diarrhea and stomach cramps. A mild case of food poisoning, that's what it will look like. I had the Doc check out Raoul's germs and Quong gave it the okay."

"Then I think we've got everything covered." Jamil looked at his watch. "Nineteen hundred. You ready?"

Xris chewed rapidly, swallowed—regretfully—the last of the twist. "You'll keep the speech short, won't you?" he said, his hand on the door handle.

"Are you kidding?" Jamil was put out. "Do you know how many of these ass-numbing speeches I had to sit through in my day? Listening to some blowhard colonel tell all about his experiences during the Faraqu Split, how he held off six thousand crazed Faraqi with his side arm alone?" Jamil rubbed his hands. "Now's my chance for revenge!"

Xris eyed him. "If you think I'm going to sit there and listen to you bullshit for thirty minutes . . ."

"Oh, all right," Jamil grumbled. "But what's it worth to you? Something extra in my paycheck?"

"How about a paycheck at all, *Colonel*? There's that little matter of the luggage, not to mention a robot coffin sitting on the floor in my bedroom."

Jamil bargained. "Five minutes?"

"Three," Xris amended. "And I'll dock you one hundred golden eagles for every minute over."

"Done." Jamil growled. "But you've shattered a dream."

Xris snorted, and the two walked out.

CHAPTER
9

The most peaceable way for you, if you do take a thief, is, to let him show himself what he is and steal out of your company.

William Shakespeare, *Much Ado About Nothing*,
Act 3, Scene 3

"And it was while I was standing in the desert at Far-aqu, with six thousand wild-eyed Faraqi glaring down at me from the heights, with only my needle-gun left to defend myself and the women and children entrusted to my care, that I came to realize that the life of the Royal Army officer is the best life in the universe! God bless us all!"

Jamil sat down amid thunderous applause. He looked out to Xris, seated with the other low-ranking officers. The cyborg was pointing at his watch. Jamil had run two minutes over. That would cost him plenty, but it had been worth it. One crusty old major was actually wiping a tear from his eye. A lovely blond captain was regarding Jamil with admiration.

The base commander made a suitable reply. The officers at the head table rose and departed in state, all looking very solemn and well fed. The meal had been actually quite decent. Colonel Strebbins spent a goodly portion of the meal relating the story of how he had swiped the cook from the 1083rd, stationed on Vangelis II. The port after dinner had been excellent.

Now the officers were free to retire to the more informal and relaxed atmosphere of the bar, a separate room attached to the dining area. The major was pumping Jamil's hand and wanting to discuss the inept strategy and tactics at Faraqu. Jamil made polite excuses and walked over to the bar, where the blond captain was talking to Xris.

"Your speech was so inspiring, Colonel," she said, after Xris had made introductions.

"One might call it 'golden,' " Xris said under his breath, but loud enough for Jamil to hear.

Jamil cut neatly in between Xris and the blond captain. "Captain Kergonan," he said over his shoulder, "I think you should go check on the arrangements for my talk tomorrow."

"Yes, sir, Colonel," Xris said, putting his untasted drink back down on the bar.

It occurred to Jamil that Xris left far too quickly and far too obediently, particularly when he must have noticed the blond captain frowning in disappointment at the cyborg's leaving. Jamil figured something was up, was convinced of it when he saw Xris pause on the way out the door to speak to Colonel Strebbins. Xris might just be making polite remarks about the dinner, but Jamil was on his guard. He asked the captain what she thought of the inept strategy that led to the defeat at Faraqu.

The two were settling down to a comfortable conversation when Colonel Strebbins loomed up. "Wonderful speech, Colonel," he said. "I see you've met Captain Strauss. Best shot on the base with a lasrifle. Had our qualifiers last week."

"Thank you, Colonel." The captain flushed with pleasure at the compliment.

Strebbins turned to Jamil. "Your aide tells me that you have a particular interest in how we run things here on Pandor. He suggested I come over here now and give you the complete lowdown." He glanced at the blonde. "I don't want to bore you, Captain . . ."

"If you'll excuse me, sir?" Captain Strauss gave Jamil a smile, picked up her drink, and left.

Colonel Strebbins leaned his elbow on the bar and

began. "When I took command six years ago, this base had one of the lowest efficiency ratings in this quadrant. Since that time, I . . ."

Jamil listened, nodded, sipped his drink, silently cursed Xris, and swore to get even.

An hour later, the colonel was launching into an account of the base's new morale-boosting program, complete with a description of the enlisted personnel's sock hop and talent show, when conversations paused, heads in the bar started turning, people began looking toward the front foyer.

"By God," Strebbins said, interrupting himself. He set down his empty glass on the counter. "What's all this?"

Jamil, thankful for any interruption, looked to see what all the fuss was about.

Two officers stood in the entryway. One—a pilot—was still wearing her flight suit, carried her helmet under her arm. Jamil raised his eyebrows. The pilot had committed a serious breach of etiquette. You didn't walk into the officer's mess in a flight suit unless you had a damn good reason. The patches on her shoulder indicated that she flew a Stiletto precision bomber, Zircon Squadron. Not stationed here. The fact that she still carried her helmet meant she intended to leave again swiftly.

The other officer wore the standard dress uniform, with the rank of major, though the gold-braided aguillet around one shoulder identified him as an aide-de-camp for a lieutenant general or higher. The major removed his beret and entered the bar area. He walked straight up to Colonel Strebbins.

"This man appears to have urgent business for you, Colonel," Jamil said, lifting his drink and preparing to leave, feeling relieved that he'd been spared an account of the talent show. "I'll leave you—"

"Excuse me, sirs," the major said, including them both in his glance. "I am Major VanDerGard of General Hanson's staff. I have been sent to immediately retrieve Colonel Jatanski."

Jamil gulped, stared. He decided to set down his drink

before he dropped it. His first thought was: Xris. Xris
has set this up, damn him.

Figuring that, Jamil was just about to make some
smart-ass remark when he took a good close look at
the serious-eyed major, at the major's gold braid, at the
uniform that was rumpled with travel. Then there was
the obviously flight-weary pilot waiting in the foyer.

Jamil's gut tightened. Not even Xris could pull off a
stunt like this. Plus he would never do anything to jeop-
ardize the job. Whatever this was, it was for real.

"Yes, Major," Jamil said, hoping astonishment would
cover apprehension. "I'm Colonel Jantanski. What is
it?"

"Sir, you are requested to be the assisting officer for
Lieutenant Colonel K. A. Katchan. As the lieutenant
colonel's commanding officer, you are the first choice for
assisting officer, and the lieutenant colonel has chosen
you. His Special General Court-Martial is to sit for opening statements in thirty hours, and you will need to begin
work immediately."

Colonel Strebbins was grave. "Well, Jatanski, it looks
as if one of your people has gone off the deep end. I
don't envy you this one. Sorry I won't get to see your
presentation tomorrow. This sounds serious, though."

Jamil had read many times the standard author's cli-
ché about a character who feels suddenly as if he has
entered a dream. Jamil didn't dream; he prided himself
on the fact that he slept soundly throughout the night,
was not one to wake suddenly screaming from the throes
of a nightmare.

Not until now.

Now he was in one of those frightful dreamlike situa-
tions in which everything is going wrong, you know it's
going wrong, you want to try to fix it, but you are power-
less to act. Jamil knew he should say something, but
he could only stand staring at the major in speechless
amazement while his brain scrambled to make some
sense of the senseless.

Jamil thought back. Katchan! I remember a Katchan.
He served under me ... but that was *six years ago!* And
Katchan had been a supply sergeant! They don't nor-

mally promote supply sergeants to lieutenant colonel! To say nothing of the fact that I'm not in the Army anymore. I haven't been in the Army for years. I can't serve on a court-martial. I'm not a colonel!

Most of all—I'm *not* Colonel Jatanski!

The game's up, Jamil realized. Someone's found out. Xris and I are going to be doing a long stretch in the brig.

Okay, but if that's true, where are the MPs? The beam rifles? The manacles? The Army doesn't usually play games, especially with people impersonating their officers.

The major was regarding Jamil with respect, Colonel Strebbins with sympathy.

"You look a bit rocky on your feet, Jatanski. Comes as a shock to you, I expect." Strebbins motioned to the sergeant behind the bar. "Another drink for the colonel. Make it a double."

"Thank you," Jamil said faintly. "Katchan is an excellent officer. Never gave me cause for complaint. What"—he put the glass to his lips, tried to look casual—"what is the charge?"

"Theft of government property," the major replied.

Jamil gagged, choked.

"Steady, there, Jatanski," Strebbins said solicitously, pounding Jamil on the back.

Are the MPs arresting Xris right now? Jamil wondered. Is this a ruse to get us both off base without trouble, without publicity?

He set down his empty glass. "I'll have to find Captain Kergonan—"

"That won't be necessary, sir. The captain is to carry on as planned," the major said.

Jamil stared, stunned. "I beg your pardon, Major?"

"General Hanson feels that Captain Kergonan is eminently qualified to carry on in your absence," the major elaborated. "The captain is quite familiar with the subject material and is capable of handling the assignment on his own. Wouldn't you agree, Colonel Jatanski?"

"Yes, eminently," Jamil murmured. He shoved himself away from the bar. Perhaps I can find Xris, warn him. This smells like a trap. "I'll just go back to my quarters, get my gear."

"I'm sorry, sir, but we need you to come straight to the spaceplane. The trial is being held on the command cruiser *King James II,* General Hanson's flagship. It is just now entering this system. Captain Ng will fly us back." The major turned to Strebbins. "If you could send someone for the colonel's luggage, sir . . ."

"Certainly," Strebbins said heartily.

"That won't be necessary," Jamil intervened. He had a few things in his luggage he'd just as soon not be discovered, things like a nonregulation .23-decawatt pistol, the vial containing the water-contaminating virus, the hand-drawn map of the base. "Captain Kergonan will take care of it for me."

"Are you sure?" Strebbins asked. "You don't want to go before old Iron Guts Hanson without a clean pair of socks."

"Yes, no question." Jamil was firm. "Captain Kergonan will take care of everything. If you would give him that message—that he is to carry on in my absence." He glanced uncertainly at the major.

The major nodded. "General Hanson's orders, sir." He reached into the pocket of his flight jacket, pulled out an envelope containing a disk. "I have that in writing. If you could see that Captain Kergonan receives this, sir?"

"I'll see to it," Strebbins said, took the computer disk, stood tapping it on the bar.

Jamil stared at the disk, wished he could get a look at the orders, but it would have been coded to Xris's military I.D. number and personal password.

Of course, Xris didn't have a *real* military I.D. number, nor did he have a *real* password. He'd made that all up, had instructed Darlene to enter it into the military's computer files before they left. Someone had gone to one hell of a lot of trouble to ferret them out!

And for what? Jamil had no idea.

"If you please, sir. The spaceplane is being refueled. The car is waiting." The major was obviously impatient to leave.

Strebbins offered his hand. "Good luck, Jatanski. Glad it's you and not me. Hate these damn courts-martial. Always put me to sleep. And I was really looking forward to your lecture, too. But I've no doubt that Captain Kergonan will manage fine."

"I'm sure he will, sir," Jamil said.

"We have every confidence in the captain, sir," the major added, saluting. He accompanied Jamil out of the bar, into the foyer. Here he introduced Jamil to the pilot, who nodded curtly and intimated that they were running behind schedule.

A vehic was waiting for them outside the mess; not the staff car, with its fluttering flags, but a hoverjeep. The major kept close behind him. Jamil ignored the man, paused a moment, glanced around, hoping against hope to catch a glimpse of Xris.

No such luck.

Jamil climbed in the back of the hoverjeep alongside the major. The pilot sat in front. Major VanDerGard apologized for not taking the staff car to the airfield.

"This is quicker, sir, if less comfortable."

They had all just barely settled themselves when the driver launched the jeep into the air, sped toward the airfield.

The ride was fast and uneventful. No one said much of anything, mainly because no one else would have been able to hear what was said over the roar and rattle of the hoverjeep, which had seen better days. VanDer-Gard must have commandeered the first vehic he found. The pilot sat up front beside the driver, keeping fast hold of her helmet on her lap. She paid no attention to them, never once glanced back. VanDerGard braced himself in his corner, one arm on the doorframe. Jamil kept a firm grip on the back of the seat.

The hoverjeep was covered with a fine coat of the red Pandoran sand. The jeep's frame rattled and shook and bounced over the uneven terrain. Its air jets must have been out of sync, for there was a noticeable dip to the back end. Twice Jamil was bounced off his seat, struck his head on the detachable roof. Both times, when that happened, VanDerGard smiled in rueful apology, just as he might have done in the presence of a real colonel.

Jamil gave up trying to figure what all this was about. No use wasting his energies on guesses. He was stumbling about in the dark and while he might accidentally put his hand on the correct answer, how would he know it? This concluded, he ran quickly through his options. There weren't many. He could, of course, punch VanDerGard in the face, grab his gun (interesting point; the major was wearing a sidearm), shoot the pilot and the driver, and make a run for it.

And go where, exactly? And do what?

Besides, VanDerGard didn't look the type to collapse in a heap at one punch. And if he was armed, the pilot probably was armed, too. Jamil discarded that idea about five seconds after he'd thought it up. Since he couldn't think of anything else constructive, he decided his best bet was to keep playing the game. Besides, by now, he was extremely curious.

His curiosity would probably land him in the brig for about twenty years for impersonating an officer, but he couldn't help it. He was interested to know just what the devil was going on. The only way to find out was to go along with the agenda—whatever that happened to be.

The jeep entered the airfield, the driver looked around for directions. Major VanDerGard pointed, indicated a glistening Stiletto bomber parked at the very end of the tarmac. The tubular fuselage gleamed in the moonlight. Its green and gray camouflage enhanced the sleek look. It was designed for precision bombing, both in and out of atmosphere. The spaceplane sat high on its wheels, indicating that it did not have a bomb load, but the racks of missiles under the wings were real—no practice weapons here. What was known as a wild-weasel pod hung from the central hard-point.

The jeep pulled up beside a refueling bowser. The crew was just finishing refueling the bomber and were starting to replace the hoses back in the bowser.

The pilot jumped out almost before the jeep came to a stop. She began walking around the spaceplane, checking it over to ensure it was sound for flight. Two members of the ground crew were inside the cockpit, readying it for the pilot. The major climbed out of the jeep, walked around, opened the door for Jamil, saluted when he stepped out.

Jamil studied the man's face. If Jamil had seen one flicker of an eyelid, one sardonic curl of the lip, any indication at all that VanDerGard knew he was acting a role, Jamil might have reconsidered and taken on the major then and there.

VanDerGard saluted respectfully, his face grave and solemn as befitted the occasion. Jamil returned the major's salute and stepped onto the tarmac. VanDerGard walked over to the bombardier's hatch, reached inside, pulled out a set of coveralls and a flight helmet, and handed them to Jamil. The major reached back for a set of flight clothes for himself and began to slip the coveralls on over his uniform.

Jamil glanced swiftly around. The pilot had moved on to the back end of the spaceplane. The ground crew were occupied some distance away.

VanDerGard glanced up, noticed Jamil wasn't dressing. "Don't those fit, sir? There's a size larger—"

"Look, Major, let's cut the crap," Jamil said tersely. "You and I both know—"

"—that Katchan is innocent of these charges, is that what you were about to say, Colonel?" VanDerGard shrugged. "I like to think so, sir, but I must add that, from what I've seen, the evidence against him is very strong. You should be getting ready, sir," he advised, seeing that Jamil wasn't moving. "We'll be leaving shortly."

And that was that.

Jamil slid the coveralls on over his uniform, accepted the flight helmet, and waited for the pilot to indicate they were ready to take off. He looked out over the tarmac back to the base, wondered if Xris knew his partner was gone yet, what he was doing about it. Jamil was tense, prepared for action. It was unlikely that Xris would be putting together some sort of rescue attempt, but Jamil had to be alert and ready to react if that happened.

It didn't.

The pilot indicated that all was ready. She climbed up the ladder and took her place in the cockpit.

The two senior officers boarded the bomber by climbing a ladder in the open bomb bay, leading into the crew area. They strapped themselves into the communicator's and the bombardier's chairs. The pilot wound up the engines. To anyone accustomed to flying in the relative comfort of fighter spaceplanes, the engine noise inside the larger and heavier bomber was deafening. Jamil grimaced, wondered how any living being could take this. A hand touched his arm. VanDerGard pointed to a cord with a jack on one end which hung from Jamil's helmet to a socket in the bulkhead.

Jamil plugged in the jack, and all was blessedly quiet. The helmet's noise filters completely removed the engine whine and the creaks and strains of the fuselage. He looked outside the small porthole. A storm was moving in over the desert; lightning shot through the clouds that were building fast in the heat.

Jamil bid Xris a silent and rueful good-bye, wished them both luck, and prepared for takeoff. He was seated in the communicator's chair. A voice came over his helmet.

"Navy Three Five Niner Zircon, you are cleared for priority launch on runway Two Niner. All traffic is cleared of your launch and egress vectors. Have a good flight. Pandor Tower out."

The pilot wasted no time. The spaceplane—clumsy and awkward on the ground, graced with a deadly beauty in space—lurched forward, taxied to the runway.

The takeoff and flight were, in Navy terms, uneventful, despite the fact that lightning struck the fuselage of the spaceplane at least three times that Jamil counted. He expected all sorts of dire consequences, from the engines blowing up to the electrical systems going haywire, but nothing happened. The pilot didn't seem bothered by the strikes. VanDerGard apparently hadn't even noticed. Jamil quit looking out the viewscreen. Gritting his teeth, sweating and nervous, clutching the arms of the seat, he faced grimly forward. He detested space flight. This was exactly the reason why he'd joined the Army. Ninety percent of the time, your feet were on solid ground.

Once into space, the pilot kicked in the radiation drive and exited the Pandoran solar system. Jamil looked out the viewscreen again. A tiny speck of light, no brighter than the stars around it, began to grow larger. Jamil stared at it and, forgetting where he was and under what circumstances, he whistled.

"Never seen a command cruiser before, sir?" Van-DerGard asked.

"Not for a very long time," Jamil answered truthfully. "And they never looked like that! My god, but she's huge."

"The *King James II* is one of the new Septimus Severus Class command cruisers," VanDerGard said with obvious pride. "She was only commissioned four months ago. The king and queen both attended the launching ceremonies."

The ship was larger in area than many cities, held more people. Its blue-gray durasteel hull shone in the reflected light of Pandor's distant sun. Lights from hundreds of portholes sparkled on its surface. Its hull was smooth, sleek, unmarred by antennae, guns, torpedo tubes, lascannons or any other weapon mounts.

But they were there. Harry—who kept up on all the Navy's new designs—had gone on for days about how all the weapons and other instruments had been built into the hull. When the ship went into action, she must be an awesome sight. Jamil imagined gunports sliding open, torpedo launch mounts lifting into place. He was so interested, he almost forgot that he was likely to see more of this ship than he wanted.

Like the brig.

VanDerGard was conferring with the pilot. Probably requesting the armed escort, the leg irons and shackles.

Well, as his old sergeant used to say when they came under enemy bombardment, nothing to do but hunker down, sweat it out.

Jamil hunkered down and began to sweat.

CHAPTER 10

Now is the time for all good men to come to the
aid of the party.

Charles Weller

Customs was not as bad as Darlene had anticipated.
After a critical inspection, she wasn't required to
wear a mask, as were some of her more unfortunate
fellow passengers. The customs agent did recommend,
however, that she do something with her hair. Having
assured the agent that this would be her first priority,
Darlene offered the computer case and her overnight
bag for inspection. The agent cast a bored look at the
computer and a skeptical look at the small and shabby
overnight bag.

"How long are you staying?" he asked.

"A week," Darlene replied. "I'm here for Carnival."

The agent lifted a plucked and skeptical eyebrow.
Opening her carry-on, he peered disdainfully inside.
"You *are* going to one of the nude colonies, I assume,"
he said.

Darlene added hurriedly, "I'm here on a shopping
spree. I plan to buy a whole new wardrobe."

The agent indicated—with a meaningful glance at
what she was currently wearing—that this would certainly be highly advisable. With a languid wave of his
hand, he passed her on through.

Darlene was leaving customs, smiling over this episode
and searching for Raoul, when she encountered a party

of Adonians who were most obviously on their way to visit one of the nude colonies. It was an impressive sight. Darlene was still staring when Raoul and the Little One found her.

Raoul greeted her with a fond hug and kisses, as if they'd been separated for thirty years, not thirty minutes. This was the typical Adonian form of welcome, however, as she learned from the kissing, hugging throng around her.

"You're not masked! Congratulations!" Raoul gushed, then paused—fearful—and asked in a loud whisper, "What did they say about your hair?"

"I'm to have it done," she whispered back.

"Nothing more than that? I thought they might sentence you to ... Well, never mind. They didn't." Raoul breathed a sigh. "We're not out of this yet, though."

He looked around, all directions, scrutinizing the crowd closely. Darlene, assuming he was searching for the Hung assassin, was about to ask him if he had noticed anyone suspicious, when he pulled out a silken scarf from his purse and handed it to her.

"Put this over your head," he said in the hushed tones. "We have to reach my abode safely and the magnet is simply crawling with cops."

Darlene might have welcomed this, had she thought the police were posted in the "magnet" (whatever that was) for the protection of the citizenry. Knowing Adonians, however, she guessed that the cops would be far more interested in outrages perpetrated against fashion than such sordid and distasteful crimes as muggings, theft, or murder. No doubt they would arrest her assassin if he gunned her down in public (especially if he splattered blood on someone's fine white leather shoes). But the police would be apt to arrest the assassin a whole lot faster if he was wearing polyester at the time.

Accordingly, Darlene tied the scarf around her head and accompanied Raoul through the spaceport to the baggage claim, to arrange for the delivery of fourteen trunks—all the clothing he considered necessary for a week's vacation.

"I hope I brought enough," he said worriedly, watching the trunks slide down the conveyer. "Yes, what is it?" he asked distractedly.

The Little One was tugging on Raoul's sleeve. They held one of their silent conversations, then Raoul turned to Darlene.

"The Little One says that no one is following you, that no one is taking the least bit of interest in you. The scarf's working," he continued, and, nodding in satisfaction, he began pointing out trunks to a luggage retrieval 'bot.

"Thank you," Darlene said gratefully to the Little One.

The fedora nodded. The small hands came out of the raincoat pockets, fluttered about the head, which jerked in the direction of Raoul. The small shoulders shrugged.

Yes, thought Darlene, that pretty much says it all.

Having determined that all his trunks were present and accounted for, Raoul entered the delivery data into the 'bot, added a generous tip. ("I forgot to tip once." Raoul sniffed. "Only six trunks made it. The rest of my clothes ended up spending Carnival in Jardina. I trust they had a good time. *I* couldn't set foot outside the house!") The three left the spaceport, headed for the main form of transportation in Adonian cities, known as the magnet.

The magnet was a glistening silver commuter train which ran whisper-soft and extremely fast over magnetized tracks. Magnets went everywhere in an Adonian city, and people went everywhere in them. Driving oneself around in one's own vehic was considered demeaning, not to mention the fact driving was stressful, which caused wrinkles, and being seated in a vehic any length of time was thought to contribute to poor posture.

A short walk through the spaceport—walking was good for a person, developed shapely calves—brought them to the magnet station. Like the spaceport and every other building in Adonia, the station was the epitome of luxury, comfort, the very latest in style and design.

Traveling in the magnet, gazing out the windows, Darlene marveled at the beauty of the world. Every object she looked on—even an object as mundane as a waste container—was elegant in shape, graceful in design, lovely to behold. Mountains, valleys, sky, grass, trees, flowers, rivers, buildings, people, animals—all were comely to look upon, pleasing to the eye.

"I'd probably grow tired of this if I lived here," she said to herself. "Like eating candy. I couldn't make a steady diet of it. But a dark chocolate raspberry truffle now and then is heaven."

Raoul lived in the city of Kanapalia, which was located on the larger of Adonia's two continents. Kanapalia, built on the side of a mountain, overlooking the glittering blue waters of the Bay of Kanapalia, might be described as a resort city. But then so could every other city on Adonia.

Since factories—ugly, dirty, smelly things—were not allowed on the Adonian home world, all materials which required manufacturing were imported. This made the cost of living extraordinarily high on Adonia, but since only those with high levels of income were permitted to remain on-world, the high cost of goods was not a problem. Any Adonian whose income fell below a certain level was deported. Poverty is so unsightly.

Kanapalia, with its year-round perfect climate, its magnificent views of mountain and sea, its picturesque mansions adorning the cliffs, its splendid, sun-drenched beauty, brought tears to the eyes of the off-worlders. As, of course, it should. Most Adonians were well-traveled. They'd been to other parts of the galaxy, mainly in order to reassure themselves that, after all, there was no place like home.

Seated in the comfort and elegance of the magnet, with its wide leather-cushioned seats, its quietly appointed interior that was not permitted to draw attention away from the spectacular scenes of mountain, sea, and clear cobalt sky, Darlene felt herself start to slip under the spell of Adonia. The beauty of the world, the beauty of its people, the air that blew bright and crisp from the sea acted on an off-worlder like one of the mind-altering drugs which were so easy to obtain in this planet of pleasure. Darlene began to feel that nothing bad could happen to her here. Evil—ugly, dirty, smelly—would never be permitted on Adonia.

Darlene knew very well that she was deluding herself. But it was delightful to give in to the delusion. She'd lived in the isolation of safe, sterilized surroundings for too long. She had been afraid for too many years, afraid of the bureau, afraid of the Hung, afraid of co-workers, afraid of friends. No . . . that was not true. She'd had no friends to fear. Her sole refuge was work, her altar the computer. As long as she knelt before it, nothing and no one could drag her out of sanctuary.

At least that's what she'd thought, until Xris crashed through the sealed and locked doors of her sterile world. Intending her death, he'd brought her back to life. And now she meant to enjoy it.

Darlene Rowan quit searching every face on-board the magnet to see if it was the face of an assassin. She quit looking constantly at the Little One, to see if he had tuned in to any hostile thoughts aimed at her. She packed up all her worries and her fears and stowed them away.

Unfortunately, she stowed them in her computer case, which was still carrying, though she didn't know it, the tattle-tell transmitter.

Raoul's chateau was small, by Adonian standards. Gleaming white, with a red-tile roof, it nestled against the mountainside, overlooked the crashing waves of the sea beneath. But the chateau, though small, had all the necessities of life: swimming pool, whirlpool, sauna, ornamental fish pond, ornamental garden, fountain in the courtyard, atrium, aviary.

Considering Raoul's flamboyant taste in clothes, Darlene was pleasantly surprised to find his chateau decorated with taste and elegance. There are strict laws governing interior decorating on the books of every major city of Adonia, however, and this had something to do with it, as Raoul was free to admit.

Left to his own devices, Raoul expressed a longing for an orange crushed-velvet sofa in combination with a hot pink coffee table with gilt edges. This being illegal, as described in the Decorator's Code, Section Twenty-six, Paragraph H, he was forced to make do with mahogany and leather, silk curtains and hand-woven rugs. Sheets were of linen and cambric, edged with lace. Down comforters were warm and would make Darlene feel as if she were going to bed in whipped cream. The first thing Raoul did, on arriving at his home, was to send for the hairdresser.

"I didn't know beauticians made house calls," Darlene said.

"Only in emergencies," was Raoul's reply.

And that was the last she saw or heard of him for the next three days. Raoul entered into the throes of planning his party. Less planning has gone into the taking over of small countries.

"The main objective," Raoul stated, laying out his battle plan for the edification of the Little One, "is to vanquish Raj Vu."

The fedora nodded agreement, the bright eyes beneath the fedora gleamed with fighting fervor.

The enemy, Raj Vu, was an Adonian who lived four mansions and a palace up the road from Raoul and was considered by everyone in Kanapalia, including Raj Vu himself, to be the crowned czar of party-giving. His guest list was highly selective and you knew you were somebody on Adonia if you received an invitation to one of Raj Vu's affairs.

Despite the fact that they were almost neighbors, Raoul had not received an invitation. Raj Vu had once been overheard referring to Raoul as "that grubby little poisoner and his dog-in-a-raincoat toadie." Raoul's friends considered it their duty to tell him this and did so the moment they were sober enough to recall it. Not long ago, however, Raoul had been instrumental in saving the life of the queen; he and the Little One having helped thwart a kidnapping attempt on Her Majesty. Both had been invited to the palace, both had been on galaxy-wide news. Raoul could claim, and often did, that he and the queen were dear friends.

Not long after, Raoul had received an invitation to one of Raj Vu's parties. Though highly incensed by the "grubby little poisoner" remark and hating Raj Vu quite devotedly, Raoul felt it his duty to attend the party on "a reconnaissance mission," as he stated. He expected to have a dreadful time but would suffer through it for the good of the cause. He suffered to such an extent that he was forced to take to his bed three days later, when the party ended, and it was a week before he could lift his head from his pillow or consume solid food. It was at that moment Raoul declared (in a whisper) that he would outparty Raj Vu or perish in the attempt.

The day he arrived on Adonia, Raoul called a meeting of his chiefs of staff, these being the caterer, the hired bartenders, the plant renters, the pool cleaners, the tent makers, the groundskeepers, the carpenters, the wine steward, and the butler. There were the local police to be bribed, the fire department forewarned, the hospital put on alert.

"I'm a nervous wreck," he complained to the Little One the morning of the day before the event.

They were breakfasting on the terrace. Raoul smoothed his hair, which was being ruffled by a mild breeze. He sipped his warm cocoa, tossed bits of his croissant to the swans in the ornamental pond, and repeated his complaint. "A nervous wreck. I don't know whether I'm coming or going." He moved his chair to keep out of the bright sunlight, which would have a devastating effect on his complexion.

"And do I receive any help?" Raoul continued, his tone becoming plaintive. "I knew I could expect nothing from Darlene. I counted on forty-eight hours at least to get her into shape and it looks as if I'm not going to be far wrong. The manicurist left in tears, did I tell you? I had to promise to pay the woman double to persuade her to come back. But I might have expected better from you, my friend. You've been no help to me at all. No help whatsoever."

The Little One growled, hunched down in the raincoat, crossed his arms over his chest, and glared moodily out at the pond.

"If you won't tell me what's bothering you," Raoul

went on, "I can't be expected to sympathize. Here, have a muffin. Perhaps you're hypoglycemic."

The Little One took the muffin and lobbed it irritably at the swan, striking the bird squarely on the beak. The swan swam off in indignation.

"Nice shot," said Darlene, coming to join them. She poured herself a cup of coffee, sat down. "What's the matter with him?"

Raoul shrugged. "He's been in a bad mood ever since we arrived on Adonia. Actually, ever since we left Megapolis. He refuses to discuss the matter. He won't tell me what's wrong. He's going to ruin my party," Raoul concluded in tragic tones. "I just know it."

The Little One growled again, but appeared remorseful at having upset his friend. Squirming about in his chair, the telepath lifted his hands, fists clenched, in a gesture of frustration.

Darlene regarded him in concern. "He does seem upset."

"I understand that something's bothering you," Raoul continued, dabbing at the corner of one eye with the sleeve of his silken bed jacket. He turned a pleading gaze to the Little One. "But couldn't it bother you just as well *after* the party as before?"

The Little One decided, on consideration, that it couldn't.

"It's not me, is it?" Raoul asked, the thought suddenly occurring to him. "*I* haven't done anything to upset you, have I?"

The Little One was emphatic, shook his head.

"I didn't think so," Raoul said complacently, "but it never hurts to ask."

"Not me?" Darlene wondered. "Any assassins lurking about?"

The Little One again shook his head.

"You say he was upset before we left," Darlene said, thoughtful. "Is it Xris?"

The Little One's head jerked up. The bright eyes gleamed at her from beneath the fedora.

"It is Xris!" Darlene was alarmed. "Something's happened to Xris?"

The Little One again shook his head.

"Something's *going* to happen to Xris?"

"The Little One is a telepath, my dear, not a psychic," Raoul said, eating a dish of strawberries in cream.

The Little One did not immediately reply. He stared out from beneath the brim of the fedora, stared into the cloudless sky, stared out farther than that, perhaps, with the fixed, narrow-eyed intensity of someone endeavoring to penetrate the mists of a thick fog.

He failed. His gaze dropped. He pummeled himself on the head, knocking the fedora askew. Then, glowering, he laid his arms on the table, rested his small chin disconsolately on his arms.

"There! You see! He's going to ruin my party. Absolutely ruin it!"

"The hell with your party," Darlene snapped. "I'm worried about Xris. I think— Oh, dear, no! I'm sorry. I didn't mean . . ."

Her apologies were too late. Raoul had fainted dead away.

A glass of champagne, applied swiftly, restored the Adonian, assisted him to recover from the staggering shock of hearing his party consigned to the nether regions.

"I truly didn't mean it," Darlene repeated remorsefully, patting Raoul on the wrist.

"I know you didn't, my dear," he said with a wan smile. "And I forgive you."

"But if the Little One does think that something might be going wrong for Xris, we should try to find out what it is," Darlene pursued.

"I'm certain that Xris Cyborg would not want to ruin my party. He would permit nothing to happen to him that would interfere."

"I'm sure he wouldn't," Darlene agreed gravely. "If he could help it. But what if he can't? Would you ask the Little One to try to describe what he's feeling? Maybe we'll get a clue."

Raoul sighed despairingly, but since it was at least half an hour until the caterer was due to arrive, he supposed he could indulge the odd whims of his guest.

The question being put to the Little One, the telepath concentrated to such an extent that the hat gradually slid down over his eyes, obliterating them completely. At length he shrugged, scratched his head through the fedora, and looked up at Raoul, who appeared slightly perplexed.

"As nearly as I can make out, he says he feels as if he'd been shopping and found this charming blouse, absolutely perfect, lace trim on the cuffs and tiny pearl buttons and it fits like a dream and it's on sale! Well, he gets it home, puts it on and"—Raoul raised his eyes to heaven—"the sleeve falls off!"

"He said that?" Darlene was skeptical.

"Not precisely in those words," Raoul admitted. "He left it to me to translate. But I believe that this accurately describes what he is feeling. Are you going to contact Xris Cyborg?"

"There's no way I can contact him," Darlene said, eyeing the Little One worriedly. "He and Jamil are already on the Army base. We're not supposed to contact them—"

"Except in an emergency," Raoul interrupted.

Darlene thought it over, shook her head. "What would I say? Be careful because the Little One is experiencing strange feelings he can't explain?"

Raoul considered. "You might tell Xris to examine carefully the stitching on any shirts he purchases."

At this, the Little One let out a screech—a startling and unnerving sound, which caused the swan to flutter in the water and head for the opposite shore. Shaking his fists in disgust—perhaps at Raoul, perhaps at Darlene, perhaps at the swan, or perhaps at nothing—the Little One slid off the chair and stomped moodily into the house, angrily kicking the raincoat's hem with each step.

"Oh, God! My party," Raoul moaned, and collapsed onto the table, his head pillowed on his arms.

"Oh, God . . . Xris," Darlene murmured.

CHAPTER
11

"Absent friends."

Toast for the day, Sunday, Royal Navy

On leaving the officers' mess, Xris took a quick stroll to the part of the base located near the construction site. He was pleased to note that, while it was a part of the base in use during the day, it was likely to be deserted at night. This was the base maintenance area; vehics of all sorts, in various states of disrepair, were parked here.

Up against the fence sat three PV-L Devastator light tanks, two with their power packs removed, one with the turret half disassembled. Utility trucks in winter camouflage stood in a line, probably recently arrived from off-world and waiting for a desert paint job. A seventy-two-ton hoverwrecker gleamed at the end of the row. The wrecker was the pride of the workshop and proudly displayed the maintenance symbol on the front bumper. A sergeant was still about. The man glanced at Xris curiously as he sauntered past; the sight of a stranger in this area was enough to arouse his interest.

Xris walked over. "Evening, Sergeant." Xris gazed around the garage with the fond expression of someone who was returned home after a prolonged absence.

"Captain," said the sergeant, glowering and wiping his greasy hands on a rag. This was the sergeant's domain and he was clearly suspicious of high-ranking intrusion. "Can I do something for you, sir?"

"Not at the moment, Sergeant. I've got a warning light on a remote-controlled, temperature-regulated storage crate. I'd like you to take a look at it."

"Pardon me, sir, but ... warning against what?"

"Biohazard. There's nothing to worry about, though. The warning light isn't flashing like it's warning against anything. It's flashing like it's malfunctioning. I can tell the difference."

"Yes, sir." The sergeant was not convinced.

"And there's nothing to worry about unless the crate is opened in an improper manner. Certain systems have to be shut down first, in the correct order. Any mistake there and ..." Xris shrugged, left the details to the sergeant's imagination, which must have been fairly active.

The sergeant backed up a step, glanced nervously around. "Did you bring the crate with you, sir?"

"No. I didn't want to lug the damn thing around with me while I searched for maintenance. I'll drop it off tonight. You can check it out tomorrow. Where should I stash it?"

"How about over there, sir? Next to that hoverjeep with the banged-up fender. No one will bother it, sir. You can bet on that."

"Fine. I'll come around sometime tomorrow, be on hand in case you need to open it."

"Yes, sir. Thank you, sir." The sergeant appeared vastly relieved. Perhaps he had tomorrow off.

"Don't let me interrupt your work." Xris reached his hand to his pocket, automatically, to pull out a twist. He caught himself halfway. "My first assignment was a maintenance troop with the Thirtieth Field Artillery Regiment. Repair and overhaul. We worked on those old modified Devastators. God!" Xris shook his head. "What a bucket of bolts!"

"Yes, sir." The sergeant agreed, more at ease now that he knew the malfunctioning biohazard crate wasn't going to be making an appearance anytime soon. "They were that. But once you got 'em movin', there wasn't much around that could stop them. Why, I remember once ..."

The sergeant related a tale. Xris listened, laughed, and

twice had to stop his hand from reaching for his pocket. The sergeant finished his story, offered to show Xris around the yard.

"Thanks, Sergeant, but it looks like you're closing up shop. Must be past your dinnertime. Or are you in charge of the night shift?"

"Night shift!" The sergeant snorted. "Begging your pardon, sir, what would we run a night shift around here for? It's not like we ever see any action. Busted axles, flat tires, the occasional blown engine, clogged air jets— that's the extent of the work around here. I was staying late to do a little project of my own. If you'd care to see, sir?"

Xris had found out all he needed to know, but he stayed a few moments longer to admire an ancient internal combustion engine which the sergeant had discovered in a corner of one of the storage sheds, resurrected it, and was now in the act of restoring. Xris was properly enthusiastic. He stayed to watch the sergeant lovingly cover the engine in a drop cloth.

"You heading back to the barracks, sir?" the sergeant asked.

"No, not right away," Xris answered. "I thought I'd take a stroll around the base."

The sergeant was regarding him with wry sympathy. He leaned close, said in a low voice, "If you want a smoke, sir, head over by the storage sheds near the fence. It'll be deserted this time of night."

Xris stared at the man.

The sergeant chuckled. "I saw your hand go to your pocket, sir. I'm a smoker myself. Can't beat a good cigar, eh, sir? If there's nothing else—"

"No, Sergeant." Xris smiled. "Thanks. You've been a big help. Uh, which way—"

"That way, sir. Out this door and turn to your right."

Xris nodded. The sergeant pulled shut the door to the maintenance shed, locked it, then saluted and headed back toward the barracks.

"By God," Xris said to himself, walking in the direction indicated, the direction that led him toward the fence, "that was a stroke of luck. Here I was trying to think of some way to get rid of the guy and he sends me right where I want to go. Easiest job ever, so far."

The maintenance shed was a large, hutlike building made of corrugated steel, located only a few meters from the fence, directly opposite the construction site. Walking over by the fence, Xris could see the glow of the security lights illuminating the site of the downed spaceplane. He was almost directly across from it. Little more than a kilometer away.

He couldn't have ordered anything more perfect. Pulling the gold case from the compartment in his leg, Xris took out a twist, lit it, and inhaled deeply, thankfully. After a few puffs, he tossed the butt end of the twist at the fence. The twist struck the metal. Blue light flashed; there was a sizzling sound. Xris grunted. He'd expected as much. Turning, certain now that the sergeant must be long gone, Xris headed back for the shed.

Both maintenance shed and yard were lit by overhead nuke lamps, the only lights around, with the exception of a few security lights above the fence. Xris was satisfied. The yard was the perfect place to stash the storage crate.

Getting off the base was the next problem. Xris strolled back over to the fence, indulged in another smoke. He wasn't planning on going through the fence. It would sizzle his butt as fast as it had sizzled the twist's. In addition, the fence was undoubtedly loaded with sensor devices, including backup sensors if something happened to the first. But Xris didn't need to get over the fence. He could enter the construction site by an easier route. The robot crate needed to get over the fence. It had jets, operated by remote control, and wasn't going to be bothered by a few strands of barbed wire.

The only problem might be some type of magnetic force field radiating up from the top of the fence. Jamil hadn't considered that likely, and Xris, making his inspection, didn't see any indication. He waited a moment and was rewarded by the sight of a low-flying bird skimming over the fence without incident.

It was a sign from the gods. If it had been a dove, Xris might have found religion. As it was, he figured all he had to do was stash the crate in the maintenance shed, come back at o-dark-thirty, when everyone but the guards would be in bed, haul out the crate, place it next to the fence. Once he reached the construction site, Xris would use the remote to hoist the crate up and over the fence. He'd leave the crate by the fence, retrieve the 'bot from the crashed plane, haul the 'bot to the fence, stuff the 'bot in the crate, send the crate with the 'bot back over the fence. He'd return to base, stash the crate in the maintenance yard again, collect it when he and Jamil were ready to leave.

If anyone wondered what he was doing with the crate over near maintenance, instead of at the lecture hall, Xris had already established that the case was malfunctioning; he had brought it over to maintenance to repair.

He took a look at the auditorium in which the phony Colonel Jatanski would be making his speech. Having located the large, empty lecture room, Xris spent several minutes checking out the lighting, testing the sound, putting the podium into place, doing all those chores a captain should be seen to be doing when preparing for a speech to be given by his colonel. When Xris was finished, he walked back outside.

He stood in the darkness, enjoying the warm night air. His next task: to find out how easy it would be to get off base.

Xris sauntered over to the front gate. The lights of the nearby town gleamed in the distance. Must be only a couple of kilometers, a pleasant walk beneath starlit night skies. The gate was wide open; two MPs—a private and a corporal—lounged in the guardhouse, talking companionably. The private's beam rifle was slung across one shoulder. The corporal had leaned his rifle upright against the wall of the guardhouse while he poured himself a cup of coffee. These two were not expecting trouble.

Xris called a greeting as he strolled nonchalantly through the gate.

The private dashed out after him.

"Captain. Excuse me, sir"—the private caught up with Xris, saluted—"but could I see your orders?"

"No orders, Private," Xris answered in a friendly tone. "I'm off duty, thought I'd walk into town, check out the local nightlife."

"Sorry, sir, but the town's off-limits. No one's allowed to leave base without written orders."

"Damn," Xris said. "Town that rough, huh?"

"No, sir. Actually, the town's very nice. We've never had any problem with the locals. It's an agreement between the base and the central Pandoran government. They don't like off-worlders."

Xris considered. He could get nasty, point to his captain's bars, shove his jaw in the private's face, but that would only create animosity, might start raising questions.

"I see." Xris shrugged. "Guess there's nothing much left for me to do but go back to bed."

"Sorry, sir. There's the officers' mess, sir," the private added.

Xris grimaced. "My colonel's in there, if you take my meaning."

The private gave Xris a knowing grin. "Yes, sir. Good night, sir."

"Good night, Private." Xris turned, shoved his hands in his pockets and strolled back in the direction of his quarters.

On to Plan B. He needed orders to leave the base. That should be easy enough to obtain. Pandor was known galaxy-wide for its stout, which was dark, bitter, with a head on it that, according to legend, you could land a spaceplane on. Colonel Jatanski was particularly fond of Pandoran stout, wanted to replenish his supply. Xris headed back toward the mess. He'd have Jatanski give him orders to go into town.

"Pardon me—Captain Kergonan?"

Xris looked up. It was the blond captain, the one he'd spoken to earlier at the bar. She was standing on the sidewalk, had probably just left the officers' mess.

"Captain Strauss," he said, walking over.

"Frances," she said, smiling. "But everyone calls me Tess."

"And I'm Xris." He smiled back. "Everyone calls me Xris."

"I couldn't help noticing you talking to the guards," she said, with a glance in the direction of the gatehouse. "Passing the time of day with the MPs, or did you need something?"

"What I needed was a beer. They said I can't go off base without written orders."

"There's the officers' mess," Tess suggested.

"Too many colonels," Xris replied.

"One less colonel now," she said, smiling in understanding. "What with Jatanski leaving the base."

Xris thought his augmented hearing was acting up on him again.

"I beg your pardon," he said. "I didn't quite catch that. Did you say something about Jatanski leaving?"

"Why, yes? Didn't you know? I'm sorry. Colonel Strebbins sent a messenger to your quarters to inform you. I guess he didn't."

"I didn't go back to my quarters. I took a walk to wake up after that speech, then I checked out the lecture hall." Xris was carefully casual. "Jatanski's left the base, you say? Where's he gone? Into town to fight off six thousand wild-eyed bartenders with a toothpick?"

"No." Tess laughed. "The colonel was called away to attend a court martial. General Hanson sent his aide, a major named VanDerGard. He arrived in a special spaceplane."

An alarm went off on Xris's cybernetic arm, LED lights flashed, a beep sounded, informing him that his nervous system was about to go berserk. He wasn't surprised. The shock had literally rocked him backward on his feet.

"Colonel Jatanski? *My* Colonel Jatanski?" Xris was convinced she must be mistaken. "Tall, good-looking black human . . ."

"I know Colonel Jatanski," Tess assured him. "He is *very* good-looking, isn't he? But a bit arrogant for my tastes." She was regarding Xris with concern. "Shouldn't you do something about that?" She pointed at his arm. The alarm was still beeping.

Xris muttered a curse, rolled up his sleeve. Distracted as he was over the news about Jamil, part of him was thinking it was a damn shame that this attractive woman would now find out he was a cyborg. He braced himself for the look of revulsion, the struggle to remain polite, the sudden recollection that she had to wash her hair tonight.

He was wearing his flesh foam and pastiskin hand. Made from molds of his own good right hand, the fake hand looked, reacted, even felt just like a real hand. It was warm to the touch; had hair, veins, cuticles, and fingernails. For a bit extra, you could add on warts. A fleshfoam, plastiskin, and duramuscle arm went along with the hand. Most cyborgs always wore such "pretty" limbs.

Not Xris. He usually made no secret of his cybernetics, flaunted the steel and wire arm and compartmented metal leg for all the galaxy to see, dared anyone to pity him. Dr. Quong had informed Xris that he did this in order to cover his own insecurity and deep-seated anger at the fate which had turned him in to half man, half machine. He used the blatant display of his cybernetic limbs to repel people at the outset, rather than have to deal with them and their reactions.

Sure. Fine. Xris admitted this to himself, but the knowledge didn't make it easier to see pity in a woman's eyes.

He opened the compartment, made the adjustment that would inject the needed chemical into his bloodstream to correct the imbalance, which was affecting his electronics system. This done, he started to pull his sleeve down. Tess's hand on his mechanical arm halted him. Her touch startled him, almost into forgetting about Jamil.

No revulsion or pity in her eyes. They were bright with interest.

"How fascinating! What did you do there? Correct a chemical imbalance? I've read about limbs with the ability to do this, but I've never seen one this sophisticated."

"Of course not," he retorted. "Who goes around feeling a guy's phony arm?"

Tess flushed, snatched back her hand. "I'm sorry, Xris. I wasn't thinking. Not very tactful of me, was it?" She sighed, smile ruefully. " 'Aim and Fire.' That's my nickname on base and it's not for my weapons proficiency. I'm always shooting off my mouth before I think. It's just that the study of cybernetics was my minor in college. I'm interested in the latest developments in the field. I'm sorry if I offended you—"

"No, no, not at all," Xris assured her. Now it was his turn to be embarrassed. "It's my fault. I'm oversensitive. I have to admit that, well, it's refreshing to find someone who takes such a practical view of my . . . uh . . . alteration."

He finished rolling down his sleeve. "This would be the ideal time for me to say 'I'd love to show you the rest of my body parts' but I really should find out what happened to Jatanski. He left the base, you say? To attend a court-martial proceeding?"

"Yes, I was standing at the bar when the major came for him. Everyone heard. Some lieutenant colonel under Jatanski's command got caught stealing government property. You probably know him. Sorry, but I can't remember the name. He and the colonel must have been pretty close, because the news really caught Jatanski off guard. He looked about as shaken as you did there, for a moment."

"I'll bet he did," Xris muttered to himself. Then he said, "He left the base?"

"About twenty minutes ago. You're on your own tonight, Captain."

"On my own," Xris repeated. He was trying to shift his brain out of neutral, where it appeared to have gotten stuck. Jamil . . . Jatanski . . . court-martial . . . General Hanson . . . Jamil gone. A major . . . escorted him off the base . . . special plane . . .

None of this made a damn bit of sense!

"Odd that Jatanski didn't tell me he was leaving," Xris said. "Or take me with him, for that matter."

"He wanted to talk to you, but the major said there wasn't time. And Jatanski couldn't very well take you along, because you're giving the speech tomorrow."

Xris stared. "I am? Did Jatanski say that?"

"No, it— Oh, here's the messenger. Now you'll have all the answers," Tess said.

Xris wished he could be that confident. A corporal rounded the corner. Tess waved, shouted. The corporal hurried over, saluted. The man was slightly out of breath.

"Captain! I've been looking all over for you, sir. I have a message from Colonel Jatanski."

The corporal delivered the message: Colonel Jatanski had been escorted off base by a Major VanDerGard, taken to General Hanson's flagship, *King James II,* to serve as officer in the court-martial of one Lieutenant Colonel Katchan. Xris only half listened, spent the time attempting to regain his composure, while trying to figure out what the hell was going on. His first thought was that Jamil was trying to put one over on him. If so, by God . . .

Xris abandoned that line of thinking quickly. He and Jamil might goof off on occasion, but Jamil was far too professional—and too mercenary—to do anything to imperil their high-paying job.

". . . carry on in the colonel's absence," the corporal was saying.

Xris started listening again.

"That's what the captain was telling me," he said, interrupting. "What are my exact orders, Corporal?"

"You are to carry on in the colonel's absence."

"Who issued those orders? Colonel Jatanski? Sorry for making such a fuss," Xris added, "but the colonel's a real stickler for detail. And this speech is his pet project. I wouldn't want to screw up."

"He's really keen on the subject, isn't he?" Tess commented. "I could see Jatanski wasn't pleased about leaving. But it was General Hanson who issued your orders. Hanson said that you were quite familiar with the subject material and were capable of handling the assignment on your own. Jatanski argued some, but he didn't get very far."

"The *general* . . . issued my orders . . ." Xris was baffled. This was getting stranger by the minute. "That I was to handle the assignment on my own?"

"That's true, sir," the corporal added. He held out an envelope. "Here it is in writing."

Xris took the disk, stared at it as if he could somehow suck whatever message it contained right off the plastic.

"Is there anything else for the captain, Corporal?" Tess asked

"Yes, ma'am. Captain Kergonan, you are to go to Colonel Jatanski's quarters and pack up his things. The colonel didn't have time."

"Very well, Corporal, I'll do that," Xris said, and remembered to add, "Dismissed."

He stood holding the computer disk. "Maybe I better take a look at these orders now."

"Sure thing. They have 'Sarge' machines over in the rec hall. We're not too far from there. I'll be glad to drive you. You have your ID card with you, don't you?"

"Of course."

Jamil had impressed on Xris that he carry his military ID card wherever he went. They each had one—part of the Mag Force 7 supply of phony IDs, fake passports, falsified visas, and a wide variety of forged citizenship papers, letters of transit, and birth certificates. Darlene had entered all the necessary information into the computer, provided them each with an alias and an ID card to match.

ID cards were the lifeblood of every soldier. Put your card into a slot in a machine and you could issue orders, bank your paycheck, make a phone call home, request a transfer, award someone a medal, send a column of tanks halfway across a continent. Due to restricted access, certain computers on the base only handled certain ID cards, with the exception of "Sarge."

Sarge machines could deal with almost every aspect of military life. So dubbed because they were big and ugly, irascible and ill-tempered, Sarge machines ruled a soldier's life. Frustratingly unpredictable, Sarge had been known to spit the card in the owner's face, to return the wrong card to the card owner (all the while maintaining that Sarge was right and it was the owner who didn't know himself), or simply swallow the card and refuse to disgorge it. Sarge had been physically assaulted on more than one occasion by frustrated victims.

"I'm not keeping you from anything, am I?" Xris asked Tess, on their walk to the recreation center.

She glanced at him sidelong, smiled. "It can wait," she said.

The two entered the rec hall, which was busy this time of night.

Tess indicated the Sarge machines. Xris pulled out his phony ID, hesitated. These orders from the unknown General Hanson might be some sort of trap. Put this card in the machine and the MPs come running. But then, why go to all that trouble? Hanson could already have had both him and Jamil sitting behind a force field, decked out in wrist and ankle disrupters.

All five of the Sarge machines were in use. Xris had to stand in line while a private on a vidphone call was assuring his mother that he was eating right and getting enough sleep, and yes, they'd had to shave his head, but his hair would grow back, and no, they hadn't let him keep a lock of it to send home. When the private finished, Xris excused himself to Tess, who walked away a discreet distance.

Xris swiped the card, punched in his password, and waited, tense, nervous.

The message came up on the screen.

Captain Kergonan,
You are hereby ordered to carry out your assignment as given.
Irma Hanson, General, Commander Zetan Military Sector, Authentication Lima-Two-Five-Niner-Tango.

Xris typed in the authentication code. It came back, a curt *Verified.* The order was straight from General Hanson, all right.

Xris waited hopefully a moment, but nothing more appeared, no clue of any sort as to what was going on, with the single exception that the words "as given" were emphasized, were illuminated in red on the screen. He stood staring at Sarge, wondering what the devil to do now.

A Major VanDerGard—unknown—an aide for General Hanson—also unknown—had nabbed Jamil and, instead of nabbing Xris, too, the unknown general had given written orders for Xris to carry out the job! Carry on with the assignment *as given*. And that in itself was odd. The general did *not* say, "Carry on with the speech."

Carry on with the assignment.

That could mean nothing more than make the speech, but Xris had the distinct impression that whoever had gone to this much trouble hadn't done it for the sheer pleasure of hearing him drone on about "Foreign Object Damage to Spaceplane Engines." The assignment they wanted him to carry out was the job he'd accepted: to steal an antique robot.

Why?

The why didn't matter. Because now it was a hostage situation. They'd taken Jamil hostage in order to force Xris to bring them some old moth-eaten 'bot in exchange. Who were *they*? People with money, power, connections. Some rival archaeologist? Xris pictured academic types dressing up in uniform, impersonating Army majors, complete with military pilot and a stolen military spaceplane.

That would be a job worthy of Mag Force 7. Not the local Space and Aeronautics Society.

What about the Hung? That was much more likely and the thought gave Xris a few very bad moments. Maybe they'd taken Jamil to use as a hostage to get to Darlene. The Hung had the money and the influence to be able to pull something like this off, though it wasn't like them to risk incurring the wrath of an organization as big and powerful as the Royal Military.

Still that theory made more sense. And if so . . .

No, by God, there was the damn robot again. What would the Hung want with the robot? And this General Hanson had said explicitly that Xris was to carry on with the assignment *as given*, which meant steal the robot.

He'd come back around full circle and he had to admit he was rotating completely in the dark.

The only thing he knew for sure was that someone had Jamil. Xris had to assume that Jamil's life was therefore in danger, and if they wanted the robot in exchange, Xris wasn't about to argue. It meant letting down a customer, but the team came first. Especially—

"Xris! Xris?" Tess's voice and the touch her hand on his good arm jolted him out of his troubled reverie. "If you're finished, there's someone waiting."

Xris hadn't realized he'd been standing, doing nothing, in front of the machine. He apologized to the lieutenant who was next in line, turned and headed toward the entrance.

Steal the robot. Right. But—now that Jamil was gone—how was Xris going to get off base without orders? He supposed he'd have to risk cutting the fence.

"You seem really upset." Tess interrupted his thoughts. "What's the matter? It's only a speech, isn't it?"

Xris was making too much out of what must seem to her a trivial incident. He shrugged, managed a weak smile. "Stage fright. I've had it ever since I was a kid. I passed out during show-and-tell in kindergarten."

"I've heard that it helps if you imagine your audience is sitting there in the nude," Tess suggested.

"Only if *you* were in the front row," he said.

"Ah." She grinned, linking her arm with his. "But then I'd be sitting next to Colonel Strebbins."

Xris shook his head. "That's one fantasy I'll pass on."

They walked out of the rec hall. Xris was silent, preoccupied, considering his options. The fence. He'd have to use the sensor bypass relay to isolate a section of the fence. Such a bypass would route the electronic signals around the fence area. The fence could be cut, and the sensors would not register it. Quong had developed the device, though the doctor had warned Xris it wouldn't work on certain types of sensing equipment. Still, the bypass was the only way.

Tess gave a polite cough. "Pardon me, but have we

been introduced?" She extended her hand. "My name's Tess."

Xris looked up, smiled. "Sorry. I guess I'm not very good company tonight."

"You're really shaken up over this, aren't you?" Tess lowered her voice. "Are you still interested in going into town?"

"Sure," Xris answered promptly. "But I'm not allowed off base without orders and my colonel's not here to give me any. What do I do? Tunnel my way under the fence with a teaspoon?"

She shook her head. "Solid bedrock. It would take you a good three years."

"I'm too thirsty to wait three years. I'd like to buy you a beer tonight. And *not* in the officers' mess."

"You're on. It's twenty-two hundred now. I'll meet you back here"—she looked at her watch—"in fifteen minutes."

Xris did some fast thinking. "Make it thirty, could you? I noticed one of the warning lights on the exhibit crate is flashing. It's probably nothing. Just a malfunction, but I'd like your maintenance people to check it out first thing tomorrow. Especially since I'm the one slated to give that damn speech. I don't want to accidentally gas everyone. I'll haul the crate over to maintenance, then meet you back here."

"Do you need help?"

Xris shook his head. "No, thanks." He paused, then added casually, "You know of some way to get us off the base?"

"Yes," she said, with an impish grin.

"Am I going to enjoy it?"

"Not particularly. But the beer'll be worth it, I promise."

Xris grunted, waved his hand, and was off.

Five minutes later, Xris left his quarters. He steered the robot's crate on its air cushion in front of him. Clouds had rolled in, covering the stars. On the horizon, lightning flared; thunder rumbled. He guided the 'bot over to the maintenance building. It was locked up tight, his friend the sergeant off having dinner and probably a

well-deserved cigar. Xris eyeballed the distance between
the shed and fence; less than twenty-five meters.

He positioned the crate right outside the main door,
shut it down. It settled on the ground with a thump. No
need to worry about anyone walking off with it. Not
with those biohazard warnings and the fact that the thing
weighed in at about a metric ton. He tested the remote,
just to make certain, touched a button. The crate's lights
flared. He touched another button. The crate's jets
kicked in. The crate started to rise into the air.

Satisfied, Xris touched the first button again. The jets
shut down, the lights winked out. He looked at his
watch. 2230. He'd be a few minutes late. He started back
at a run.

As it was, he was ahead of Tess. Xris loitered near
the rec hall, wondering if he'd been stood up, when a
staff car drove in front of him. The air from the car's
jets washed gently over his feet and legs, stirred up small
clouds of the fine Pandoran sand which covered the
streets.

The window slid down. Tess leaned out.

"Hi, Captain. Need a lift?"

She parked the staff car out of the bright lights of the
rec hall, in dark shadows between two buildings. Xris
walked over to meet her.

"Now what?" he asked.

In answer, she hit a button. The trunk lid flew open.

Tess climbed out the car, walked back, pointed.
"Climb in."

"You're kidding."

"Climb in, Captain. That's an order. And hurry up.
Someone'll see us."

"Yes, ma'am." Xris squeezed his bulk into the trunk—
a tight fit. He had to lie sideways, draw his legs up almost beneath his chin. "I feel like I'm back in college.
How far do I have to ride like this?"

"Six or seven hundred kilometers," Tess said, her
hand on the trunk lid. "Don't worry. I'll hire a crane to
lift you out. Not claustrophobic, are you?" She prepared
to shut the trunk.

"You *are* kidding . . ." Xris eyed her.

"Sure." She grinned. "It's not far, really. Just keep thinking about that beer. We'll drink to absent friends."

"Make that absent colonels," Xris said.

Tess slammed the trunk shut.

Xris squirmed around to try to get into a more comfortable position, realized eventually that there was no such thing, and gave up. He heard and felt the vibrations of the engines, the gentle jolt as Tess drove forward. The car stopped, presumably at the base entrance. No use even trying to hear what was being said, what with the noise of the engine and the whoosh of air from the car's jets.

Lying cramped and contorted in the dark, sweating in the heat, with what felt like a jack or a crowbar poking him painfully in the back of his ribs, Xris made a decision.

"I'll carry out this assignment *as given*," he said. "But I'll be damned if anyone gets anything—including the robot—until Jamil's back safe and sound."

Chapter
12

Except Thyself may be
Thine Enemy—
Captivity is Consciousness—
So's Liberty.

Emily Dickinson, "Life," No. 384, stanza 4

Xris's ride in the trunk of the staff car was mercifully brief, although it seemed to him that he must have spent hours cooped up in the darkness with a wrench poking him in the back. Tess assured him—as she helped him out—that he'd only been in there ten minutes. He surveyed the area. Red sand, scrub pines, some sort of scraggy flora—he wasn't up on Pandoran horticulture. He could see the lights of the Army base in the distance, guessed they must be about five kilometers away.

He drew in a deep breath, grateful to be out in the open. The air was spiced with the fragrance of desert plants, tinged with the smell of coming rain. The storm clouds were closer; lightning flickered on the fringes.

"Did you have any trouble getting through the gate?" Xris asked, trying to rub the feeling back into his numb right arm.

Tess shrugged. "Why should I? I leave base all the time. Most of the officers do. I stopped at the gatehouse, of course, but the guards never looked at my orders, just waved me on through. You see—"

"Hush!" Xris cautioned. "I hear an engine. Some-one's coming."

"Are you sure?" Tess regarded him quizzically. "I don't hear anything."

"I'm sure." He tapped his left ear. "Augmented hearing. The sound's coming from behind us, the direction of the base."

Tess wasted no time. "Get into the car!" She hopped into the driver's seat.

Xris dashed around to the passenger side, jumped in. Anticipating a wild ride, he started to strap on his seat belt. To his astonishment, Tess shoved the seat belt to one side. Sliding next to him on the bench seat, she threw her arms around his neck and kissed him.

"Uh, Captain," he murmured, not quite knowing what to do with his hands. "This is all very enjoyable, but that car's getting closer and—"

"Shut up, Captain," she returned in a throaty whisper, "and kiss me back. I know what I'm doing."

"Yes, ma'am," Xris said meekly, and obeyed her order to the letter.

Headlights flared. A vehic pulled up alongside. Xris couldn't see it, due to Tess's hair being in his eyes, but by the sound of the engine, it was a hoverjeep. Nuke lamps beamed in through the car window. Tess pulled back from Xris, turned her head slightly. Xris kept carefully hidden in the shadows.

Tess blinked at the bright light. "Jeez, guys, shove off, will you? Give a girl some privacy!"

"Sure thing, Tess. Sorry," came a female voice. "Just wanted to make certain you weren't having car trouble."

Another woman in the car laughed. "She probably fed him the old line about being out of gas. You heading out to Jake's later?"

"Maybe," Tess answered. "Maybe not. I've got plenty of gas! So just clear out, will you?"

The women laughed again. The jeep whizzed off, its jets sending up clouds of sand. "My roommates," Tess explained, turning to Xris.

"They didn't seemed surprised to see you here."

"No," she admitted, snuggling back into his arms. "The area around here is known unofficially as Lover's

Lane. My," she added, putting her hand on his chest, "your heart's pounding. Real or artificial?"

"Artificial," Xris said, "but the hormones are real."

Tess slid her hands up around his neck. "Is that it?" she said, teasing, "And I thought you were just nervous about getting caught."

He was going to make a suitable rejoinder, but found something better to do with his lips.

After a few highly enjoyable moments, Tess drew back away from him, regarded him speculatively.

"You weren't, were you, though?" she said.

"Weren't what?" Xris asked.

"Worried about getting caught." Tess's tone was serious, thoughtful. "Most colonel's aides I've known would have been sweating their captain's bars. But then, you're different from most. You're a bit too old to be a captain. And, this may sound odd, but do you know that if I'd just met the two of you—you and Jatanski—and you were both out of uniform, I would have guessed that you were *his* superior officer."

Damn, this woman was sharp! She was peeling off layers faster than Xris could glue them back down.

"You nabbed me," he said. "I used to be a general. Got busted to private for fraternizing with ... what's your job classification?"

"Special projects officer."

"For fraternizing with special projects officers. I'm working my way back up the ranks. I expect to be a general again in about a year. When that happens, I'll come back here and propose to you and we'll get married and have ten kids and you can teach them all how to shoot straight. We'll name our firstborn Jatanski."

"You!" she said, shoving him away. "You're incorrigible."

"Is that a good thing?" Xris asked.

"Look it up," she retorted. "You must be thirsty after that long speech." She slid across the seat, over to the controls. "Ready to go to town, Captain?"

"Drive on, Captain. Where are we headed, by the way? The place your roommate said? I forget the name—"

"Jake's." Tess nodded.

The staff car whirred off, heading for the distant lights. The two inside were both silent, enjoying the ride, enjoying the sparks of electricity still lingering in the air, savoring what had passed, anticipating what was to come.

What was to come. Yeah, Xris coldly reminded himself—you've got to steal that damn robot. You're here on business, not pleasure.

"What is Jake's? A local bar?"

"Yes, it's on the edge of town."

"I thought the nasty off-worlders weren't supposed to mingle with the home folk."

"We're not supposed to, and we don't, for the most part," Tess said. "Jake's is different. I guess you could say we have an arrangement. Strictly off the record, of course."

"Of course," Xris said. "Which is why you often smuggle men off base in the trunk of the staff car. My guess is that you're a serial killer. You prey on innocent male officers. Maybe that's what happened to Jatanski."

"I confess. I lured him off base, had my way with him, then bashed him over the head with a beer bottle. You're next, you know."

"You may find the bottle-bashing difficult in my case. My head's mostly steel. What do you do with the bodies?"

"I have them stuffed," Tess said, grinning. "You'll look great in my museum. I'll put you next to Jatanski."

"No, I want an entire wing to myself," Xris stated. " 'Creative Things Done with Metal.' "

"You never let people forget, do you?" Tess glanced at him sidelong.

"*I* can't," he said. "Why should anyone else?"

He stared straight ahead, across the red Pandoran sand that shone with a faintly phosphorescent gleam. Beneath the cloud-dark sky, the softly glowing sand, dotted here and there with black clumps of plants, made for an eerie landscape. His fingers itched to take a twist from the case in his pocket. He tapped his hand moodily on the armrest.

"You can hate me all you want, but don't dare pity me. Is that it?" Tess said archly.

"Something like that." Xris settled back, faked a relaxed

pose. "Look, if you dig any deeper, you're going to strike oil. Tell me about this bar. What arrangement do you have? The only people who get busted are privates?"

"You can't brush me off that easily," Tess said, shaking her head. Her blond hair fell over her shoulders. Her hands on the staff car's steering controls were supple, capable. She filled out her uniform well—the latest fashion would have said too well, but her ample figure was toned, firmly muscled. Laughter and intelligence made her features attractive. "I can't hate you and I refuse to pity you, so where does that leave me?"

"I don't know, Captain," Xris said, smiling in spite of himself. "Where does that leave you?"

"Liking you," said Tess softly. "Liking you very much. Now," she added, tossing her head, flipping the blond hair back, "what do you want to know about Jake's? It calls itself a bar. I suppose most people would call it a dive. It's run by a Pandoran who likes money more than he hates off-worlders. The beer's cold and the whiskey's okay and the place isn't raided oftener than once a quarter. The restrooms are filthy—at least the women's is, I wouldn't know about the men's. Every so often we girls get sick of it and go in and clean it up. Anyone who can get off base—legitimately or otherwise—goes to Jake's. And that's about it."

"Does the colonel know?"

"Sure he does. Like I said, the bar gets raided three or four times a year. They shut the place down. The locals write editorials. Strebbins gives us a lecture. We go thirsty for about two weeks. Then Jake's is back in business and life goes on."

"I'm surprised Strebbins puts up with it."

"You wouldn't be, if you lived here," Tess said, her tone serious. "Duty on Pandor is the pits, a real morale-buster. We're confined to this base, never allowed off it, except when we've built up enough leave time to be able to fly to some more hospitable planet. I have leave coming up in a month. Got any suggestions?"

She looked over at him. It was his cue to say that he had leave coming up in about a month, too, and that he knew a planet where the water was blue and so was the moon and they could admire them both together. It would be easy enough. He could drag Captain Kergonan out of the closet every few months, have himself a good time. Hell, he was due.

Xris said nothing, stared out the window at the flaring lightning.

You're a fool, he told himself. This attractive, vibrant woman actually thinks you're something special. She's made it plain that she doesn't mind hearing your insides whir and hum while you're making love. Jamil's got two wives on two different planets, for God's sake. Tess's a career soldier. She knows it's not going to be anything serious. . . .

"I've got a wife," Xris said.

"Ah, well, that's different," Tess said quietly, with a half smile, a shrug.

Xris nodded. He was watching the storm, watching the lightning flash and spread in sheets over the bottoms of the clouds. A few drops were starting to splatter on the windshield. He'd meant to use that as an excuse, a way to get them both off the hook. It hadn't quite come out right.

"It doesn't have to be different," he said. "But it is. We've been married a long time. Since before the . . . accident. I should have died. I was left to die. Marjorie was the one who made the decision to turn me into half man, half can. She couldn't let go. And then, when I came home . . ."

Xris stopped talking. He'd give his life for a smoke about now.

"When you came home?" Tess prompted gently.

Xris shrugged. "I should have expected it. She realized that she couldn't live with a husband who had to have an oil change and a lube job every ten thousand kilometers."

"Xris, I'm sorry," Tess said. They had reached Jake's Bar, or so the glaring neon sign informed them. She parked the staff car in the shadow of an adjacent building, shut off the engine. She turned to face him. "You'd rather be hated than pitied. I guess I understand now."

"She gave me one look," he said. "That's all it was.

But it was enough. I turned around and walked out and I've never been back. That was ten years ago or thereabouts."

"You haven't seen your wife in ten years?" Tess was amazed.

"I've seen her," Xris said. His hand went to his pocket.

"For God's sake," Tess said, laughing, "if you've got 'em, smoke 'em! You're making me nervous, diving for your pocket like that all the time."

Xris hesitated, then reached into his pocket. He drew out the gold cigarette case, took out a twist, put it into his mouth. There was a lighter in the staff car (so much for regulations). He drew in the smoke gladly. "I've seen her," he repeated.

He had seen his wife just about a year ago. He'd rescued her from a Corasian meat locker—a terrible prison in which the aliens kept their victims until they were needed for food. Marjorie had looked at him a lot differently then. She'd been grateful. Very, very grateful. Gratitude was the reason why, on the trip back, she'd told him she still loved him. Told him that she had always loved him. . . .

Xris opened the window, tossed what remained of the smoldering twist out, closed the window again. He reached over, took hold of Tess, pulled her close. She hesitated just a moment, not to make it look good, but studying him intently. Then she slid into his arms and they got to know each other a little better.

"Now I *am* thirsty," she said, drawing away.

"We better go in before the storm breaks," he said in agreement.

She tilted her face for one more kiss, then they climbed out of the car and walked—arm in arm—to the bar.

As they drew closer to the bar, Xris reconnoitered. Jake's was nothing special. A dilapidated, run-down building made of the Pandoran stone that must be used to build everything on this planet. It was large, two-story—the owner probably lived on top—and was located outside of town, probably not even in the city limits. Windows ran the length of the front and the sides, showing those outside what a good time everyone was having inside. He could see people dancing.

As he stood in the road, the bar was on his left. Straight ahead was the construction site. He could probably follow the same road to reach it. He could see the green lights of the force field surrounding the downed spaceplane containing the robot easily from this distance, calculated that it was probably about two kilometers away.

He would welcome the exercise, a nice jog. Too bad it was raining. He'd have to come up with some excuse to ditch Tess. It could be done, but it wouldn't be pleasant. She'd be hurt and angry, figure he was a jerk, a cad.

That's what you want, isn't it? he asked himself. Better to be hated ...

"They're planning a new shopping mall there. First they're going to build a wall three meters high to separate us," Tess informed him, noting his unusual interest in the construction site.

"Yeah," he said, "so I heard."

"That's what they were going to do. But now it's turned into—of all things—an archaeological dig. You see that green glow? They found an ancient spaceplane—"

"Let's go get that beer, shall we?" Xris said, rudely cutting her off. He started walking toward the bar. He was sorry—damn sorry—he'd gotten her involved.

"Sure," Tess replied, giving him a puzzled glance. She pulled her arm away from his and he didn't make an effort to get it back.

The rain spit and spattered, the storm was still some distance away. The thunder rumbled over the ground. They walked the rest of the way to the bar in silence. Xris opened the door, Tess walked past him into an entryway. Raincoats hung on pegs, umbrellas stood in a stand, hats lined a shelf. A newsvid machine—broken—stood in one corner, along with a bubble gum machine. It, too, appeared to be broken. Through the glass window in a second door, Xris could see the bar. It was packed with people, most of them in uniform, laughing, dancing, having a good time. He reached for the inner door. Tess blocked his way.

"Look, Xris," she said coolly, "don't think you're obligated to go through with this. We can just call it a night and drive back to the base, if that's what you want."

No, that wouldn't work at all. He still had to get that damned robot. And he didn't want the evening to end, not yet.

A couple, giggling and kissing, staggered out of the bar. The entryway was small, and the coats, the vid machine, and more people made it smaller. Xris and Tess were forced back against the wet coats on the wall to let the other couple pass. On his way by, the soldier stumbled into Tess. She fell against Xris.

Xris caught hold of her, steadied her. Tess tried to pull away, but he didn't let go. The other couple lurched out the door. It slammed shut behind them. Xris still didn't let go.

"You said you studied cyborgs," he said to Tess.

"Yes," she replied.

"The psychology as well as the physiology?"

"Some, not much," she admitted. "Xris, if I said anything—"

"No, you didn't." He drew in a deep breath. "You've been great. And that's the problem. If you've studied cyborgs, you know that it's difficult for people to relate to us in any sort of romantic way. When most women hear my arm start beeping, they don't ask me if I'm suffering from a chemical imbalance. They usually just turn pale and walk off."

Tess was smiling at him. She pressed closer, took hold of his hand—his "bad" hand, his phony hand.

"I'm going to leave base tomorrow," Xris continued, "and maybe we'll see each other again and maybe we won't. Let's not look past tonight. All right?"

To his surprise, she didn't badger or tease or argue. She was grave, thoughtful.

"I understand," she said.

And Xris had the odd feeling that she really did.

CHAPTER
13

Thus it is said that one who knows the enemy and knows himself will not be endangered in a hundred engagements.

Sun-tzu, *The Art of War*

The Pandoran stout was as good as its reputation. Xris regretted he couldn't enjoy it to its fullest, but he had work to do that night and needed a clear head. He sipped slowly at his, explained—when Tess asked him if he wanted another—that the delicate chemical balance of his body didn't deal well with alcohol.

Tess's roommates spotted them, came over to take a good look at Xris, exchange a few bantering remarks with Tess, then left to return to the dance floor.

Xris and Tess sat side by side in a high-backed wooden booth next to a window. They had to sit practically chin to chin to hear each other over the roar of the music, which was provided by a couple of soldiers on portable synthesizers. The soldiers had more enthusiasm than talent, but they knew enough to lay down a steady, thumping beat, which was all the dancers wanted. Xris and Tess shouted companionably at each other, enjoying the stout and the company.

Xris's earlier half-formed plan of ditching Tess to flirt with another woman—maybe one of her own roommates—was out. Tess would know it was an act, she wouldn't believe it for an instant. And, Xris had to admit to himself, he just wasn't the type. Women weren't exactly doing nosedives over the bar to get close to him. He had about decided that the best policy was honesty—perhaps not complete honesty, but as honest as he could be. He would simply tell her to drive back to the base without him. He wanted to be alone, to do some thinking. Maybe he wanted to be alone to rehearse his speech. That was it. Rehearse his speech.

"Want another?" Tess asked, indicating his empty glass.

"No, but you go ahead. I'll get it."

"That's all right. I need to stand up for a while."

Tess joined the line at the crowded bar, waiting to place her order for another glass of stout. Xris glanced at his watch. 0100. The rain had quit, but, judging by the flashes of the lightning on the horizon, the storm had been the first in a long series. If he was going to make his move, he needed to make it soon. He stood up, started to go over to Tess, to feed her his line, when something large crashed into the door with a thud that was audible even over the raucous music.

A soldier, seated at a table near the front windows, sprang to his feet.

"Raid!" he bellowed.

The Pandoran police smashed through the front door.

People scattered every conceivable direction. Xris looked at Tess. She turned to look at him. Flailing, pushing, and shoving bodies churned between them. Xris's instinct was to fight his way to Tess's side. His second thought was more rational. *This is it, fool! This is your chance!* Still, he might have ignored the rational, gone for the instinctual, if Tess hadn't made the decision for him. She pointed urgently behind him, directing him to the windows.

"What about you?" he mouthed.

She jerked her thumb in the direction of the women's restroom and, in the same motion, turned and ran that way. Xris hesitated one more instant, saw Tess's two roommates making a dash for the lady's room, as well.

Xris lost sight of her then. A large Pandoran cop loomed in front of him, yelling something unintelligible and swinging a nightstick at Xris's head. Xris caught the nightstick in his cybernetic hand, squeezed. The night-stick crumbled into small particles. The cop stared, open-mouthed, then backed away.

Xris wasted no more time. He smashed into one table, leaped onto another, aimed a kick at the window with his steel leg. Glass exploded outward. Xris dove through, headlong. Two more soldiers were right behind him, and more were coming after them.

Xris landed heavily on one shoulder, rolled across concrete, bumped against a curb. He picked himself up, brushed off the broken glass, and took a quick look around.

The Pandoran police, in unmarked squad cars, had the front covered. More were arriving, lights flaring and sirens wailing. A large van—presumably to be used to haul away the unfortunates who got caught—drifted ponderously down from the sky.

Tess's staff car was fenced in, fore and aft, by two Pandoran cop cars. If she managed to escape, she'd be traveling back to the base on foot.

Xris fretted over this, reminded himself that she knew the territory. She was quite capable of taking care of herself. Still, he hazarded a few more seconds he couldn't afford, hoping to catch sight of her. That proved useless. Bodies were diving through the windows. Fights had broken out. The Pandoran police surged through the parking lot, attempting to cordon off the back of the building. Xris didn't dare wait any longer. He ran.

His running style was clumsy, awkward. His physical side seemed always to be in competition with his mechanical side, giving him a peculiar, swing-legged, lopsided gait. But he could move fast and most of him didn't tire. The parts that did grow weary or started to hurt or cramp he ignored.

He found the road leading to the construction site, discovered that it was also, unfortunately, the main route the cops were taking to reach the bar. Headlights caught him. He made a mad dash to a culvert on the other side. Someone shouted, and one car swerved to try to catch him, but he put on some speed, headed straight into the desert. The cops gave up the case, went after easier prey.

Xris loped through the desert, slogging over the shining Pandoran sand that had now—after the rain—turned into mud. A particularly clinging, sticky mud that caked on his boots and made running difficult.

He kept to the desert until the cop cars and the lights of the bar and the sound of shouting and swearing were behind him. The city proper was off to his left. The lights of the construction site shone ahead of him. The base lights were to his right. This part of the road was deserted since it went essentially nowhere. The pavement ended in ruts left by the heavy dirt-moving equipment.

More mud, and puddles of water. Xris had to stop every half a kilometer to clean the gunk off his boots, which had become so caked with the gooey gray muck that they were slowing him down.

Lightning flared. Thunder crashed. The next storm in line chose this moment to dump on him. Rain slashed down in torrents, typical of desert storms. He was soaked to the skin in seconds. This did nothing to improve his spirits, which were as dark, gloomy, and thunderous as the weather.

He hoped Tess had escaped the police. He felt rotten enough about using her as it was. If she was caught in a raid, ended up in a Pandoran prison cell, she'd probably be a private in the morning. He tried to sell himself on the fact that she would have gone to Jake's with her roommates anyway, but he wasn't buying it. If anything happened to her, it would be his fault.

And there was tomorrow to look forward to.

He'd say good-bye to her. They'd exchange a few wisecracks. He'd promise to vidphone—a promise that he would never keep. He couldn't tell her the truth. She'd assume then that he had only been using her to get off base and she'd assume right. When you peeled back the layers, the ugly truth was there, like the ugly mechanics in his arm. All the foamflesh and plastiskin in the galaxy couldn't hide it. Far better to cut the arm off clean, never see her again. He might spare her some pain. She'd be left with the memory of a few laughs, a few kisses, a pleasant evening.

At least, Xris hoped, that was how Tess felt about

their time together. As to *his* feelings, he continued to pummel himself mentally all the way along the road. This blasted job. It had come wrapped in brown paper, looked so plain and simple on the outside, and when he started to cut the tape, it had blown up in his face. For a single plastic credit, he'd call the job off, return Sakuta's money, let the Pandorans keep the antique robot. It was theirs, by rights.

Unfortunately, Xris couldn't do that now. He had his orders. And someone had Jamil.

He stopped running, bent down once again to clean the mud off his boots and—now that he was alone—to equip himself for the job ahead.

Xris detached his fleshfoam hand, replaced it with his working hand. His fingers were now tools: drill, cutting torch, screwdriver. The hand that had appeared ordinary had suddenly become something monstrous. Tess wouldn't be so eager to jump into his arms if this steel hand was attached.

Sure, he could always take off that working hand, replace it with the fleshfoam hand, replace the steel with Captain Kergonan.

But he wasn't Captain Kergonan.

This hand would always be steel, cold, without life, designed to do a job.

That was all it was good for.

All he was good for.

Xris began to run again.

CHAPTER
14

This living hand, now warm and capable
Of earnest grasping, would, if it were cold
And in the icy silence of the tomb,
So haunt thy days and chill thy dreaming
    nights . . .

John Keats, "This Living Hand"

Xris jogged along the road until he reached the rusty
barbed-wire and wooden plank barricade that had
been erected to protect the construction site. A security
light illuminated the gate, probably for the benefit of the
night watchman. Xris saw no hut, however, no lights
behind the gate. The guard was probably inside the area,
closer to the heavy equipment, the building materials.
Xris glanced behind. He could still see, off in the distance, the flashing lights of the police cars. He could
hear the wail of sirens.

Xris leaned down, picked up a good-sized rock, and
heaved it at the light. He missed. He tried another. The
third time, glass shattered. The light went out.

Crude, but effective. Anyone discovering the broken
bulb would probably put it down to vandals. Now that
every movement was no longer in the spotlight, he
walked over to the gate, studied the padlock. It was a
cheap hardware store lock with a dial on the front. With
his mechanical hand, he gave it a healthy yank. The lock
popped open.

He entered the construction site, paused to look and

listen. The workers were still in the digging stages; no one had started building anything yet, though the metal forms into which they'd pour the concrete for the foundation were stacked in long rows. He could now see, some distance away, a small shed with a light in it, and figured he'd found the night watchman. Would the watchman be making routine inspections of the site? Doubtful, considering the rain, but Xris was prepared for that eventuality. He had a tranquilizer dart positioned in the projectile firing digit of his tool hand. He checked to make certain all his systems were functioning properly, then set off at a lope for the crash site.

It only took him about five minutes of running to reach it. He saw no one on the way and trusted that no one had seen him. The rain continued to pour down; his clothes were soaked, the night air was chill. He'd slipped and fallen once, done no damage.

Arriving at the crash site, Xris stopped to catch his breath, clean the mud from his tool hand, and inspect the downed spaceplane.

The force field had one advantage: It lit the place bright as day.

The old spaceplane was only partially dug out. The Pandorans had found enough to determine what the plane was and then had called a halt to the project, fearful—according to Sakuta—of contamination. The spaceplane had apparently plunged nose-first into the ground, probably long before anyone had come to colonize this planet. Since then, the shifting desert sands had washed over it, buried it, obliterated all trace of its existence.

Xris studied what he could see of the plane. Sakuta had provided him with old photographs and vid footage of this particular type of craft, known as a Pelican light utility plane, which had been mainly used for long-haul, light cargo loads. It had also proved excellent for unmanned exploratory missions.

According to Sakuta, in the early days of human space colonization, robots like the one Xris was supposed to retrieve had been sent out to various sectors of the galaxy to do mapping and surveying, searching for planets that would be suitable for human habitation.

Crashes were relatively commonplace; the robot-controlled planes would venture too near a system, get caught in its gravitational pull, and, being unable to break free, would be pulled down to the surface. The shielding on the old planes was highly inadequate. Most failed to survive the entry through the atmosphere and burned up, which was why finding one in such well-preserved condition was extremely rare.

Xris surveyed the angle of entry into the ground, assessed the amount of damage to the portion of the spaceplane that he could see, and calculated that the crash had been a controlled one. Whoever had piloted this craft had stayed with it all the way, must have used every bit of ingenuity and skill possible to land this plane and keep it in one piece. This didn't exactly fit in with Sakuta's description of these robots as plodding, noncreative space-traveling dummies who did what they were told, but no more. Such a 'bot would have accepted the inevitable, plunged to its death without a struggle. Whoever piloted this plane had fought hard to survive—almost as if it had been human.

Xris considered the point as being of mild interest, but nothing more. There were various explanations—perhaps a human *had* been aboard, for one reason or another. Maybe the Pandorans had discovered skeletal remains. That might be why they thought the plane could be contaminated. Not logical—if there had been any germs or viruses on that plane, they would have all died centuries ago. But then any government that would go to the expense of building a wall to shield a shopping mall from off-worlders didn't score high marks on logic.

Xris glanced over the spaceplane—what he could see of it that wasn't buried in the gray dirt. The fuselage stuck out of the ground at a shallow angle, with the tail and thrusters pointing at the sky. The wings were gone, probably sheered off in the crash. The nose was mostly buried, as was the forward cargo area. The only access was through the top emergency hatch. No windows were visible. He couldn't get a look inside.

According to Sakuta's colleague, the hatch controls were not working. The hatch itself had been discovered partially opened; it had probably sprung open during the crash-landing. The Pandoran government had ordered the hatch sealed shut, in order to keep any stray viruses from sneaking out into the atmosphere. The seal was a standard restraining bolt; shouldn't present any problems. Xris's main concern was getting past the force field. He walked over to inspect the machine being used to project the field.

The device was one of the latest designs for portable force field projection. The field it generated not only repelled physical objects, but redirected energy that it encountered. The machine itself was made of tempered durasteel, was smooth-sided, no controls on the outside, except for one and that was an alarm. Touch that box and the whole planet would know he was here.

Xris was, for the moment, confounded. He studied the force field device and it occurred to him that it must be sucking down one hell of a lot of electricity.

Xris walked around to the other side of the device, found what he was looking for, shook his head. He could use his tool hand, but why bother? Keep the impression of vandals. A pile of steel bars stood to one side, ready to be used for reinforcing rods in concrete. Xris picked up one, balanced it on its end, and directed its fall—straight onto the portable generator. The top of the generator caved in, sparks flew, and then all went dark.

So much for the force field, which *might* have kept out a troop of Cub Scouts.

"Once I finish this job, I think I'll offer the Pandorans my services," Xris muttered. "Someone needs to teach them a few things about security."

He walked unimpeded over to the hatch, inspected the restraining bolt. A flick of his wrist and the bolt came off in his hand. Xris paused again to listen, look around. The rain was letting up; the night watchman might decide to make his rounds. Xris heard nothing, saw nothing. Switching on a hand-held nuke lamp, he crawled inside the downed plane.

The storm had passed. The lightning and thunder had

moved on, rumbled far away in the distance, and could not be heard inside the spaceplane. A light rain fell. Drops splatted against the plane's hull, but that was the only sound and Xris couldn't even hear that as he moved deeper into the plane's interior, searching for the robot. The silence was thick and old, dry and oppressive.

Xris flashed the light around the dusty and cobwebbed control panels, with their ancient and archaic instruments. The leather on the seats for pilot and copilot was cracked, split. Bits of stuffing mixed with rodent dung lay scattered all over the deck. No robot here. And why seats for pilots? If this ship was robot-controlled, seats shouldn't be necessary.

Xris gave a mental shrug. Sakuta would probably spend years researching that one. The cyborg flashed the light to the other side of the plane, played it over more instruments, metal storage containers, dangling ropes of electrical wire, the smashed front viewscreen. Parts of the control panel were blackened, covered with soot.

Xris crossed the deck, bent down over the damaged panels, rubbed off the dust to take a closer look. He smiled at the crudeness of the instruments—kids' toys were using more sophisticated hardware these days. That wasn't what he found interesting. Damage like this might have been done on entry. But it was far more consistent with damage done in battle.

Xris wished Harry were here. An expert pilot, Harry would have recognized the signs, been able to confirm Xris's suspicions. Too bad most of the spaceplane was buried under half a hill. Xris would have been interested to see if he could find evidence of damaged shields, carbon scoring along the sides, all of which would go to prove his theory.

This plane hadn't been sucked into the atmosphere. This plane had been deliberately shot down.

Why? Why shoot down a harmless mapping and surveying, robot-controlled spacecraft? And who had fired on it? If he remembered clearly his Earth history, this had been a period of peace.

" 'Curioser and curiouser,' as Raoul would say," Xris said aloud, and it was good to hear a living voice. The silence and the dust and his speculations were all starting to act on his nerves. Despite the fact that he couldn't see any bodies, he felt as if he were violating the sanctity of a tomb.

Which was nonsense. No skeletons in flight suits sat in the pilots' chairs. No one had died in this crash. It was a robot-controlled craft, remember? Xris left the control panel, continued his search for the robot.

No sign of it. He was heading deeper into the plane's interior, back into what would be the cargo portion of the spaceplane, when his weight and movement caused the unstable craft to shift, settle. The door to one of the metal storage compartments came unlatched, swung slowly open.

Eyes, caught in the beam of his light, stared out at Xris from inside the compartment.

Childhood memories of ghost stories of pharohs' tombs, wild thoughts of dead people come to life leaped from his subconscious and ambushed him. Xris had heard of being paralyzed with shock and now he experienced it. Lights flashed on his arm, alarms went off. One more jolt like that and he'd have to go in for a complete overhaul. He drew in a deep, shivering breath, let it out in a curse.

The eyes belonged to the robot, of course.

Xris focused the light beam directly on the 'bot, studied it, waited for his heartbeat to return to normal, and wondered if it was racial memory that caused him to feel the grip of cold, bandaged mummy hands closing around his throat.

Examining the robot, Xris let himself off the hook.

"No wonder you scared the hell out of me."

The 'bot had eyes, real eyes—or rather, eyes whimsically designed to resemble human eyes, with white eyeballs, blue irises, and black pupils. Sakuta hadn't mentioned anything in his description about eyes, and Xris wondered if the eyes worked or if they had been built in for show. Nothing else about the robot was the least bit human—nothing except those staring, unblinking, and unaccountably sad eyes.

The robot itself reminded Xris of a gigantic jellyfish.

Its head was saucer-shaped, made of metal, about a meter in diameter. A blue light flashed intermittently on the top. The eyes were located in what Xris presumed to be the front. The rest of the head was covered with instruments and small antennae, projecting outward at odd angles.

Dangling down from the head were at least twenty—by quick count—reticulated arms. These arms were of varied length. Each arm ended in a "hand." Each "hand" was different, each obviously designed to perform different functions aboard the spaceplane.

The robot huddled in a heap on the closet floor, its arms all akimbo, and gazed at him with its sad eyes. Xris had the strangest impression that the 'bot had been frightened by the crash, had run into the closet to hide.

"Watch it," Xris cautioned himself in disgust. "Next you'll be giving it a name!"

He took off his tool hand, replaced it with a large clamp, providing himself with a grip that was—literally—a vice. He reached into the closet, took hold of the 'bot beneath the head, and tried to lift it. He managed to drag it about five centimeters before he was forced to admit defeat and let it fall back to the deck.

"Damn!" He grunted, straightening and massaging his back.

The 'bot must weigh in at about half a metric ton. Sakuta hadn't mentioned this little fact, either.

Xris considered making adjustments to the load-bearing portion of his cybernetic arm, but doubted that would help him much. The arm's designers had not intended him to go around hefting small trucks. He'd have to go out, retrieve the crate, and bring the crate to the robot, instead of the other way around.

All of which would take up more time—

"Central," came a voice, barely heard. "This is Mike. That blasted generator's shut down again."

Xris switched off the nuke lamp, froze where he stood. He could have sworn, in the last seconds before he turned off the light, that the robot's eyes had widened in alarm. He slid into the closet next to the 'bot, closed the door behind him all but a crack, and readied the tranquilizer dart. The watchman was speaking Pandor, presumably. Xris had activated his built-in translator while he was in the bar and now he heard pretty much what he might have expected to hear.

"Must have been the storm. Steel bar blew over, bashed in the generator," the voice was continuing. "Guess you better send out the repair crews. No, morning'll be fine. It's darker'n the inside of a cow's belly around here."

A pause in the conversation, then, "Yeah, I'll look the place over. I'm not goin' near that plane, though. I ain't gonna risk catchin' some alien disease. Plus I got to make the rest of my rounds. Mike out."

Xris smiled to himself. He shifted position slightly, to get better leverage in case he needed to leave the cramped confines of the closet in a hurry. Moving his shoulders, he jostled the robot.

Something went *snick*.

Lights began to glow in the robot's interior. It started to hum.

Xris cursed Sakuta long and bitterly. The professor had assured Xris that the robot would *not* be in working condition. Its systems must have failed long ago, corroded over time. It was just Xris's luck on this blasted job that the closet had kept the robot in a hermetically sealed environment, the low humidity of the desert had prevented the 'bot from rusting.

Xris glared at the thing, wondered if he should try to shut it down, though he had no idea how it worked, or let it be and hope like hell it wasn't equipped with bells, whistles, wouldn't start singing "God Save the King."

For the moment, the robot was quiet, except for that low hum. Its systems were warming up, apparently, for its interior lights, which Xris could see reflected off the metal arms, were growing brighter. And, of course, its manic designer had put lights in the eyeballs. The eyes began to shine with a luminescent luster, rather like a girl attending her first prom.

The 'bot's arms twitched.

Xris listened to the footsteps of the night watchman crunch through the wet sand. The man was walking around the crash site's perimeter. The rain would have washed away any tracks Xris had made. He tormented himself by wondering if he'd left the hatch open, when he knew perfectly well that he'd shut it.

The footsteps came to a sudden halt.

Xris swore silently. He knew what was coming.

"Central, Mike again." The voice was tense. "The restraining bolt's been removed. Send someone out right away. Hell, don't worry about me. I ain't bein' paid enough to be a hero. Mike out."

Xris heard the footsteps, heard the screech of the hatch being tentatively lifted. Light stabbed inside.

"Hey! Anyone in there?" the watchman called nervously, adding in firmer tones, "I got a gun."

"*Mrp,*" said the robot. The humming sound was replaced by the distinctive whoosh of air jets.

"Hey! Halt! Stop!" Xris hissed at the 'bot, hoping it would respond to verbal commands.

Apparently it didn't. Either that or it didn't understand the language.

The robot clanged and clattered its metal body parts against the side of the metal closet. One of its arms shoved on the closet door, opened it. Eyes glowing, the robot rose into the air, started to float out the door.

Xris made a grab for one of the reticulated arms with his vice-grip hand, intending to hang on to it, keep the 'bot inside the closet.

The arm detached, came off in his grasp. Remaining nineteen arms dangling beneath it, the 'bot drifted across the deck of the spaceplane, heading for the hatch. Xris stood clutching the robot's arm, felt an absolute fool.

"Come on out," the watchman was saying. His voice cracked. He cleared his throat. "I got a big gun."

And he probably had his shaky finger on the trigger. Xris had no idea how to stop the 'bot, but at least he might stop this blaster-happy watchdog from turning the robot into scrap metal. Xris activated the sleep dart in his metal hand and chased after the robot.

As he exited the closet, the metal door banged against the bulkhead. He stumbled over wires and crates that he couldn't see in the dark, his feet thudded against the metal deck plating. With his crashing and the robot's whooshing, they were making enough noise for an army—a thought that must have occurred to the watchman.

"Come out with your hands up! You hear? I got a gun!" The watchman's voice shook.

The robot, humanlike eyes glowing, arms wiggling, floated out the hatch.

Xris heard a gasp, a high-pitched shriek, then the sound of feet scrabbling in wet sand.

He reached the hatchway in time to see the watchman disappearing into the darkness. Remembering his own feelings on encountering the robot with the strange eyes in this tomblike spaceplane, Xris felt a certain sympathy for the man.

Xris could have felled him with the sleep dart easily, but decided against it. If the watchman didn't report back, this was the first place security would come searching for him. As it was, security would find Mike running through the desert as if ghouls were after him. They'd have to stop to listen to his ghost story first. And that might take them a while.

"Minx-not," said the robot, gazing after the watchman with its unblinking eyes. It sounded extremely puzzled.

Xris took a moment to determine his next move. He had a lot of things to do and very little time in which to do them. He had to get the robot away from the crash site, safely stowed in its crate, and the crate back on the base, and he had to do all of that in—he figured—the next ten minutes.

The 'bot shifted its gaze back to him, was looking at him expectantly. Green lights flashed on its head. The pupils of the human eyes opened wide, as if absorbing him. A tiny beep sounded in Xris's ear—a warning that he was being scanned. Xris held still, hoped the robot wasn't going to take long in its investigation.

It didn't. The light shut off, the eyes returned to normal. It had learned something about him, apparently. Xris reciprocated. He studied the 'bot.

Considering how much the thing weighed, the fact that it was up and moving was a distinct advantage. If he

could persuade it to accompany him, his problems would
be solved. He wondered what the 'bot was thinking, if
anything. It appeared to be extremely intelligent, but
that may have just been the impression given by the
humanlike eyes. Xris was about to reach out his hand,
to see if he could give the robot a gentle shove in the
right direction, when it spoke again.

Its voice was a recording of a human voice, but there
was no doubt it was a machine speaking; the words
lacked all inflection or emotion. It rattled off what may
have been three sentences, since it paused at certain intervals, then it fell silent. The human eyes were solemn,
grave, and, again, expectant. It appeared to be waiting
for him to do or say something in return.

Which was going to be difficult. He hadn't understood
a single word. His translator was able to translate a few
hundred thousand languages, but not, apparently, this
one.

"Sorry," Xris said shortly. "I don't understand. Now
here's what we're going to do."

He raised his hands to indicate he meant no harm.
Moving slowly, as if approaching a fearful child, he extended one hand, his flesh-and-blood hand, and kept
talking. If he couldn't understand the 'bot, it wouldn't
be able to understand him, but it might pick up from
his tone that he wasn't threatening.

"Don't be frightened. I got a job to do. You and I—"
Xris stopped talking.

The blue light had begun flashing again on the robot's
head. The light stopped when he stopped talking and he
halted all motion. He waited tensely a moment, but he
didn't dare wait long.

"We're just going to take a little walk."

The blue light began to flash again. Xris experimented,
watched the light. Sure enough, the light's flashes were
pulsing in time to his voice. When he quit talking, the
light quit flashing. It was probably recording his voice.
He'd have to remember that. He had a few choice com-
ments to leave with it, remarks the 'bot could relay to
Professor Sakuta. Xris again extended his hand toward
the robot.

The 'bot extended one of its hands to him.

Xris gingerly touched the metal hand, which had two jointed "fingers" and a "thumb" and had undoubtedly been designed to perform tasks a human hand could perform. Xris gave the hand a gentle tug, hoped like hell it wouldn't come off.

"Follow me," he said experimentally, watching the light, which pulsed three times, for the three syllables. "This way."

The 'bot's hand did not come off this time. Xris gave the 'bot a gentle tug, motioned with his other hand that they were going outside the hatch, indicated that they were leaving the spaceplane.

The robot obeyed, floated silently after Xris. It even switched on a beam of bright light to illuminate the way. Xris had his doubts about the light, which could probably be seen on Pandor's moon, but he had no idea how to shut it off and no way to command the 'bot to do so. He increased his speed. The 'bot kept up with him.

They reached the fence. Xris could hear the sounds of some sort of heavy-duty vehicle approaching, but it was heading for the crash site and he was a good two kilometers away from the site by then. From this position, he could see the back end of the maintenance building. He fumbled for the crate's remote, switched it on, waited tensely.

At first, nothing happened. He was just thinking up some truly unique and imaginative swear words—words he intended to make certain the robot recorded—when he saw the crate float out from around the corner of the maintenance building, drift slowly down the alley toward the fence.

The thing had only one speed, and that was glacial. Nothing he could do to hurry it. Xris kept one eye on the 'bot, kept his ears tuned. He heard voices now. They sounded excited. They were too far away for his translator to pick up, and so he had no idea what they were saying. He could guess, however. He mentally urged the crate to move faster.

At last the crate reached the fence. Xris touched another button on the remote. The crate's jets fired. It soared up and over the barbed wire effortlessly, settled down on the ground right in front of him. He opened the lid.

This was going to be the tricky part—getting the 'bot inside the crate.

The robot was regarding the crate with interest and, by the green light flashing on its head, Xris guessed it was scanning the crate as it had scanned him.

"Inside," said Xris, pointing to the crate. "You go—inside."

The voices were coming closer, within range of the translator. He had deliberately left tracks for them to follow. They had spotted the indentations of his boots and had figured out quickly enough that they weren't dealing with some sort of space ghost.

"Go. Inside," Xris repeated, more urgently.

The robot completed its scan. It drew its nineteen arms into its interior, flew over to the crate, and nestled down into it.

"Grnx," it said, and then all its lights blinked out.

The robot had shut itself down.

"Sleep tight." Xris breathed easy for the first time since he'd entered that tomblike spaceplane. He placed the robot's missing arm gently next to it and shut the lid of the crate. He even took time to make sure all the instruments were reading correctly. After all the trouble he'd gone through to get this 'bot, he didn't want anything happening to it during transit. Everything checked out.

Using the remote, Xris sent the crate back up and over the fence. It drifted effortlessly to the ground. He ordered it back to the maintenance shed, told it to shut down.

The voices were headed his direction, following his tracks. Keeping near the fence line, staying well clear of the road he'd taken into the construction site, Xris returned to the main road, loped back in the direction of the town. He took care to keep his tracks visible, stepping in muddy patches, crashing through undergrowth.

He soon outdistanced the voices, but they were hot on his trail. When he reached the outskirts of town, he stopped, cleaned the mud off his boots, and after that took care to leave no trail at all. He circled back around to Jake's Bar.

He'd left security a nice puzzle to solve. He hoped security would read it this way.

The night watchman catches a thief looting the spaceplane. He scares the thief away. The thief flees across the desert, only to run smack into the fence which surrounds the Army base. The thief spends a few panicked moments trying to figure out how to climb the fence, gives it up, and follows the fence line back into town. This scenario should draw suspicion away from the Army base.

Of course, the charade might be completely useless, given the fact that whoever had snatched Jamil knew about them, the robot, everything. But Xris figured he should at least make the effort. He took a few moments to detach his tool hand, replace it with the "pretty" hand.

Captain Kergonan returned and began to wonder just how the hell he was going to get back on base.

Xris turned his steps that direction.

The rain continued to fall. He reached the main road, decided to take it, not risk getting himself lost in the unfamiliar territory. He hadn't been on the road long when car lights beamed in the distance. They were coming from the base, not from the town. He could hide in the ditch. . . .

The hell with it. Jail would be dry. And warm.

Xris stopped, waved his arms.

The hoverjeep pulled over. An MP climbed out.

Xris put on his best contrite, shamefaced air. "Good to see you fellows," he said.

A nuke lamp flashed in his eyes.

"Captain Kergonan?"

"Yeah, that's me. You must be wondering—"

"Excuse me, Captain. We were ordered out to search for you. Captain Strauss told us that your colonel had sent you off base. You probably don't know this, sir," the MP continued, keeping a straight face, "but there was some trouble at one of the local taverns tonight.

Captain Strauss was worried that you might have accidentally become involved. Maybe ended up in a Pandor jail."

"Well, yes, as a matter of fact, I did happen to be in the vicinity. In all the confusion, I guess I got turned around. I've been roaming around this damn desert half the night."

"Yes, sir," said the MP. "If you'll climb into the car, sir, we'll take you back to base."

Xris climbed in, settled down in the seat. Tess again. He'd have to send her something. A present. He had no idea what she might like, but Raoul would know. He'd get Raoul to pick out something nice. . . .

It was after midnight when Xris arrived back on base. The MPs drove him to his quarters, gave him a brief scolding on letting someone know when he left base, let him go. He headed for his quarters, just in case anyone was watching, then—halfway there—he took a detour.

Arriving at the maintenance shed to check on the 'bot, Xris felt like a parent going to a child's bedroom to check on its slumbers. After some searching in the dark, he discovered the crate nestled between a hoverjeep with a banged-up fender and a light truck with a recoilless launcher on the fritz. He opened the crate. There was the 'bot.

Xris debated briefly hauling the 'bot's crate back to his room. The sound of measured footfalls decided him against it. He could not have explained to anyone's satisfaction what he was doing taking his crate for a walk at this time of night. Patting the 'bot solicitously on the head, Xris shut the crate, returned to the transient officers' quarters.

His clothes were soaked. He was cold clear through to his bones. He had aches in muscles he hadn't even thought were real muscles. He was dead tired—a reaction to spending half the night living off adrenaline. He would have given six robots in six fancy crates to be able to go to his room, lie down and relax. Unfortunately, he still had more work to do.

He went to Jamil's room, packed up Jamil's gear, and

hauled it back to his own room, Xris still had to get ready for that damn speech tomorrow.

He luxuriated in a hot shower. Lying down on his bed, a twist in his mouth. Xris took out Jamil's electronic notepad, brought up the file on "Foreign Object Damage to Spaceplane Engines," and began to read.

Within five minutes, Xris was asleep.

CHAPTER
15

'Tis an ill cook that cannot lick his own fingers.

William Shakespeare, *Romeo and Juliet*, Act 3,
Line 198

Nightfall on Adonia. This was the evening that was to
see the vanquishing of the enemy—Raj Vu. Raoul's
party commenced precisely at 1800 hours. That is to say
the party began then. The guests did not start to arrive—
nor were they expected—much before 2200 hours. Most
would show up after midnight and more than a few
would appear the next day, somewhere around the dinner hour. Adonians take a very relaxed view of time.

Raoul was up early, however, as are all generals on
the day of the big battle. He crawled out of bed around
noon, applied a cucumber mask to alleviate the effects
of the stress of the last few days on his complexion,
soaked in a seaweed bath to boost his metabolism, and
confided to Darlene that he'd taken only the mildest of
artificial stimulants, in order to keep his thinking clear.

He spent the rest of the afternoon shampooing and
styling his hair, applying his makeup, took two hours to
decide what to wear—this crucial decision had been
preying on his mind for days—and finally, at about 1800,
appeared clad in a black unitard trimmed with black
sequins, accompanied by a white and black feather cape,
sequined black high heels, and an armload of red ruby
bracelets.

"I'm dressing down, my dear," Raoul said to Darlene. "It's impolite for the host to outshine his guests."

Darlene, in a simple silk suit devoid of decoration, hoped she could stay awake for the guests to arrive. The Little One kept to his room, partly in order to spare Raoul's nerves and partly to avoid being trampled by the armies on the side of good.

Off-worlders often expressed sympathy for those on Adonia who were forced to work for a living, those who were the props and mainstays of the decadent lifestyle of the other Adonians. What off-worlders failed to realize was that most Adonians work for a living; it just doesn't show.

Work takes second place to pleasure. Office hours do not exist. If there is ever anything on Adonia that has to adhere to a schedule, has to be done on time—the taking off and landing of spaceplanes, for example—the Adonians hire off-worlders to see to it.

The caterer was actually early, but she compensated for this marvel by bringing the wrong food. This occasioned a fight in the kitchen, which ended with Raoul pink-cheeked and overheated but victorious, a cherry torte on the floor, and the caterer made to deliver the layer cake made with nine different flavors of chocolate as she'd been ordered.

"I can't believe she thought I wouldn't know the difference!" Raoul sniffed.

The two bartenders arrived on time, which proceeding made Raoul suspicious, but they assured him it wasn't intentional. The bartenders were extremely handsome young men, tanned and muscular and highly ornamental. Raoul tasted the champagne—just to make certain *it* had not been replicated. Finding the bubbles genuine, he forgave the bartenders and, after an exchange of kisses all around, showed them where to set up the bars—one in the atrium amid the orchids and one by the side of the swimming pool.

The pool cleaners arrived with the first of the guests, who were highly entertained by the proceeding and stood around sipping champagne and offering helpful suggestions. The people hired to pitch the tent never came at all, but since it wasn't raining, Raoul didn't miss them. The orchestra began as a soloist, grew to a trio, expanded to a quartet, and by the end of the night had almost enough members to play the Mozart symphonies that had been commanded, if you weren't picky about lack of violins.

Darlene sat outdoors at a table near the swimming pool, drinking champagne, enjoying the pageantry, the beauty, the splendor. And that was just the pool cleaners.

Raoul was the perfect host, relaxed, charming, unperturbed, unruffled, no matter what the emergency (such as when a group of guests set the deck on fire). He was wherever he should be and wasn't where he was not wanted. He mingled and chatted and kissed and hugged, he welcomed Raj Vu as one long-lost brother might have welcomed the twin he hadn't seen in twenty years. And if Raoul made a disparaging remark about Raj Vu appearing at an evening affair in blue jeans—though they were decorated with rhinestones—this was only after Raj Vu had been heard to make cutting remarks about the food.

Breathless and panting, the Little One planted himself in front of his friend and made wild gestures with his hands.

Raoul, preoccupied with his insult, could think of nothing else. "Did you hear what Raj Vu said? That my truffles were ... were ... were mushrooms!" Raoul was faint from the shock, forced to fortify himself with champagne. "That man may be a swine, but he wouldn't know a genuine truffle if it bit him in the snout!"

The Little One flung himself on Raoul, began to pummel him on his shapely legs. "Forget the truffles!" The frantic command made its appearance in Raoul's head, seeming to flash on and off in bright colors, like a neon sign.

This, at least partially, captured Raoul's attention.

"Forget the truffles?" he repeated, dismayed. "But Raj Vu said—"

"Boil Raj Vu's liver in vinegar!" was the next remark, pertaining perhaps to some quaint Tongan custom of which Raoul was not, thankfully, familiar. He was about to remark that, although the man undoubtedly deserved it, this operation might be somewhat messy, when the Little One interrupted.

"What do you know about the bartenders?" The question jabbed Raoul's brain.

"Well"—Raoul was thoughtful—"they're both quite good looking and very charming, especially the blond. He's invited me to his gym to work on my triceps. I don't know what they are, but he says they need developing. I said that I was looking forward to whatever developed and he—"

The Little One took off the fedora, flung it to the floor, and stomped his foot emphatically. Raoul was struck dumb, stared at his friend in astonishment. The Adonians are noted for their beauty and so, since every action requires an opposite and equal reaction, it is not surprising that there existed a race known for its ugliness. The Little One belonged to such a race.

It is difficult to describe his physiognomy, except to say that once Xris had come across the Little One after he'd been attacked by members of the now defunct Knights of the Black Earth. It was the first Xris had seen of the face beneath the fedora. He had thought, in horror, that the Little One's face and head had been smashed into a bloody, misshapen mass of bone, blood, and brains, only to find out that his injuries were relatively minor. The Little One's face normally looked like that.

Raoul averted his head, shaded his eyes. He had gone quite pale. "Please, dear friend, you know how this affects—"

The Little One lunged, grabbed hold of Raoul's wrists, forced his friend to look at him. "The bartenders are assassins! They're here to murder Darlene!" The thoughts, materializing in Raoul's head, were tinged with blood.

Raoul stared, aghast. "Here? Now? During my party?"

"Yes! Any moment!" This flashed red with alarm.

"But ... someone dropping dead at my party! That

would ruin it!" Raoul clung to the kitchen counter for support. "Absolutely ruin it."

The Little One's thoughts became very black and savage. "It won't do Darlene a whole hell of a lot of good, either!"

"Oh, yes. Quite," Raoul murmured, and after some consideration, he added, "I see your point. Where is she? Is she all right? We should warn her—"

He started to leave, was accosted by his small friend, who grabbed hold of a handful of unitard and jerked Raoul back. The Little One pointed out the kitchen door.

Raoul looked.

Darlene was seated on a wicker settee in the atrium, near a group of Adonians—Raj Vu among them—who had gathered together to exchange the latest gossip. She was listening to their conversation and, judging by her wide-eyed and slightly shell-shocked expression, she was eavesdropping on a lifestyle that she had probably only previously witnessed under the rating of Triple X. She appeared amazed and bemused but, otherwise, quite healthy.

Raoul breathed a sigh of relief. Perhaps his party could be salvaged, after all. "How do they intend to perpetrate the crime?"

The image of a vial appeared in Raoul's mind, a vial filled with a clear substance and marked with a label. Raoul was familiar with the chemical composition.

Recovering his composure, he sniffed, disapproving. "How gauche. How unimaginative. Putting the poison in her champagne. Not to mention risky. What if she decides to quit drinking? Or takes it into her head to leave? Now, if they had only consulted with me, I could have told them fifty far more reliable ways to poison her. Ah, yes. Pardon me. I am forgetting myself. It's the professional in me. I do so hate to see a job bungled."

He continued to keep watch over Darlene, who did not, Raoul noted, have a glass in her hand. One bartender had set up his bar in a picturesque area near the smaller of the two waterfalls. He was pouring champagne into a number of fluted glasses on a silver tray.

Every so often, a guest would come to the bar, take a glass, walk off with it. The bartender was smiling at Darlene, who so far had not noticed him. He was obviously trying to catch her eye.

"Cheap little tart," Raoul remarked, favoring the bartender with a scathing gaze. "After going on about my triceps. He can't be certain she will actually ingest the poison. What is his backup plan?"

An image of a nasty-looking weapon blew apart the other assorted bits of irrelevancies that had drifted into Raoul's mind. He shuddered. "What *is* that thing?"

"A scrambler," was the Little One's reply, which filled Raoul's head with hideous reds and oranges.

"Ah, yes. I remember our former employer, the late Snaga Ohme, had a number of those weapons in his keeping. Rather nasty devices. As I recall, they used some sort of random alpha wave transmitter to foul up everyone's brain processes. However," Raoul added, looking puzzled, "I seem to recall from our time spent with our former employer and from certain facts I have since picked up during our sojourn with our present employer—referring to, of course, Xris Cyborg—that these 'scramblers' were designed for crowd control and that they are not lethal. Also that they affect everyone in the vicinity. Their range is quite extensive.

"I do say, dear friend," Raoul added plaintively, "would you mind putting on your hat?"

The Little One picked up the fedora, thrust it on his head, pulled it down low over his face. He made a fist, smashed himself on the forehead several times.

"Ah, I see," Raoul said quietly. "The weapon can be altered so as to be lethal, which is what they have done. I begin to understand their plan. If they do not manage to kill Darlene this night, or if their plot is discovered, they will activate the weapon and scramble the brains of everyone at my party! How ghastly!"

The Little One made a comment.

"Well, certainly I think they'd notice!" Raoul dabbed at two tears with the corner of a cocktail napkin, taking care not to smudge his makeup. "And I could do without the sarcasm. I am having trouble enough as it is.

Instead of being heralded in the society pages as the host who gave the best party of the season, I shall be mentioned as the one with the highest death toll!"

Raoul gave a sob, hid his face in the napkin. The Little One gave him a punch in the thigh.

"I know," said Raoul, gulping down his tears. "This is no time to fall apart. I'm calm now. Very calm. Let's see. What can we do to stop this?"

The Little One patted the inside breast pocket of his raincoat, where he kept his favored weapon—a blowgun filled with poisoned darts.

"Yes, we could kill the two bartenders—you say they're both assassins?"

The Little One nodded.

"But," Raoul continued reflectively, "we would have a difficult time explaining their deaths to the police without revealing the truth about Darlene, destroying her cover, and thereby exposing her to even greater danger. Not to mention the fact that it would be most difficult for me, in the future, to hire a bartender. No, there must be a better way."

Raoul was thinking this over when the Little One suddenly began jumping up and down.

"*Now* what?" Raoul demanded in despair.

The Little One pointed frantically into the atrium. Darlene was on her feet, approaching the bar. Either the bartender's smile had won her over or she was thirsty.

Raoul and the Little One exchanged glances. A plan flashed between them. The Little One didn't appear to like it. He shook his head vigorously.

"My friend," said Raoul gently, "we have no choice. If Darlene does not die this night, everyone will die this night. You know what I need. You know what you must do."

The Little One shook his head morosely, but then gave the fedora a nod and, after grabbing Raoul's hand and squeezing it tight, the Little One dashed off. He ran from the kitchen into the atrium, pushing and shoving his way through a jungle of plants and legs. He hurtled past Darlene, wringing his small hands, and headed for the living room.

Raoul turned to an ornate wooden rack that occupied one corner of the kitchen counter and was marked SPICES. He selected a vial from among the extensive collection and, after taking a brief moment to ensure this was the vial he wanted, he slid it up the sleeve of his black unitard.

Moving swiftly but unobtrusively, Raoul left the kitchen, walked through the crowd, dodging those who wanted to engage him in conversation—or any other acts—with a charming smile, a kiss for the air, a wave of his hand. On his face, the vacuous, vague, and euphoric look of the Loti. His eyes, hidden beneath blue-shadowed lids, glittered clear, keen, focused. Their gaze was fixed on the bartender's hands, never left them.

Darlene started to reach for one of the glasses of champagne on the silver tray. The bartender intercepted her. Raoul couldn't hear their conversation over the music of the orchestra, but he could guess what the bartender was saying. "The wine's been sitting there too long, ma'am. It's far too warm. I'll pour you a chilled glass."

Raoul watched closely the man's every move.

Darlene was not watching the bartender. She had no fear. She was completely unsuspecting. Swaying slightly on her feet in time to the music, she leaned her hands on the bar, looked back at Raj Vu and his friends. The bartender said something to her, reached one hand under the bar. Darlene glanced at him over her shoulder, laughed appreciatively, looked away.

For an instant, both the bartender's hands disappeared beneath the bar. He brought forth a fluted crystal glass seconds later.

"The clean glasses are on the table *behind* him," Raoul murmured. "That's it, of course. He put the poison into that glass while he had it under the bar."

The bartender was pouring champagne into the glass. Raoul observed the glass closely, but could not see any other substance in the glass itself. Not unusual, he reflected. The poison, according to the Little One, was a derivative of a lilylike plant which grew on Adonia and, though it had a formal, scientific name, was more commonly known as the Good-bye Kiss. The poison was said to have a faint and not unpleasant taste, as of camellias, and produced death by causing every cell in the body to view all other cells as the enemy and immediately launch an attack. The body, essentially, rejected itself.

The poison came in many forms, including clear liquid, and a single small drop was enough to start the cellular chain reaction, enough to kill.

Lifting a glass of champagne from the hand of Raj Vu—ignoring that gentleman's indignant protest—Raoul glided forward. He deftly fingered the vial that he had positioned up his sleeve. Removing the cork, he passed his hand over the champagne glass, shook out a fine white powder into the glass. He deposited the vial in a nearby orchid plant, continued on.

The champagne poured, bubbled, and sparkled. The bartender handed the glass to Darlene, with some comment that made her laugh again. She took the glass, turned away, was bringing the glass to her lips.

"My dear!" Raoul called out. "A toast!"

Darlene was right-handed. She was holding the glass in her right hand and, at Raoul's call, she lowered the glass from her lips.

Raoul's mincing footsteps carried him to her side. He observed, as he approached, the bartender frown. The bartender put down the champagne bottle. He was keeping both hands free. The weapon, the scrambler, was probably located underneath the bar.

Dancing up on Darlene's left side, Raoul raised his arm, slid it around Darlene's shoulders, turned her so that her back was to the bar. Raoul's white feather cape blocked the bartender's view. As he turned Darlene, incorporating the move into an elegant waltz step, Raoul slipped his right hand over her right hand, lifted the glass from her fingers. He shoved his glass, which he was holding in his left hand, into her right hand. Giving her a dazzling smile, he lowered his arm, stepped back away from her, providing the bartender with an unobstructed view.

Raoul touched the glass to his lips, but did not drink. He noted the lipstick—his own special Rogue Red

color—on the rim. He then plucked the first glass from
Darlene's hand, gave her the original glass back, and
then—before she could take a sip—he cried, "Switch
glasses. Whatever your neighbor's drinking, you drink!"

Darlene's neighbor was Raj Vu, who was ingesting
some sort of syrupy red concoction adorned with a
bunch of fruit on a stick. Noticing this, Darlene grimaced. "I'll stick to champagne," she said and, once
again, raised her glass.

Raoul leaned over and, under cover of the music, said,
"An Adonian party game, my dear. Don't be a stick-in-
the-quagmire."

Before she could protest, Raoul removed the champagne glass from Darlene's hand and gave it to Raj Vu,
who—most obligingly—handed the fruit drink to
Darlene.

Just as Raj Vu was starting to drink, Raoul snatched
the glass from the hand of his rival. Handing Darlene
the champagne glass that he'd been holding, Raoul took
the fruit drink away from her, handed it to back Raj Vu,
and, lifting the glass of champagne to his own lips, Raoul
drank it down.

"Can I drink this now?" Darlene asked, amused.
"You're not going to take it away from me again, are
you?"

"Drink up, my dear," said Raoul complacently. He
raised his empty glass. "To your health."

Darlene raised her champagne glass in return, toasted
Raoul and the highly annoyed Raj Vu, who pronounced
it a "stupid game" and tossed his red concoction into a
fish pond. Darlene took two swallows of her champagne.

Raoul stole a glance at the bartender. Obviously confused by all the shifting of glasses, the man was watching
them closely. He might have been extremely suspicious
and figured his plot had been discovered, had not Darlene ended up with a champagne glass. As it was, he
would wait to see the consequences.

Those should not be long in coming.

Darlene was about to take another swallow when the
expression on her face altered. Her features contorted,

her eyes widened. Sweat broke out on her forehead and lips.

"I ..." she began faintly. "I don't ..."

The glass fell from her nerveless hand, smashed at her feet. She made a choking, retching sound and suddenly slumped to the floor. She lay there, unconscious, amid the spilled wine and broken glass.

Raoul promptly screamed. Raj Vu turned. He and the rest of the guests in the atrium looked over to see what had happened. The bartender poured someone a whiskey.

Raoul, hands fluttering, bent over Darlene. "She looks ghastly!" he cried.

"It's the dress," said one woman, standing nearby. "She should never wear that color."

"I don't mean that!" Raoul returned indignantly. "I mean that she appears to be very ill. Someone call a doctor!"

"I'm a doctor," Raj Vu announced.

"You would be," Raoul muttered.

Taking care to keep his designer jeans out of the spilled wine, Raj Vu crouched down beside Darlene. He lifted her wrist in his hand, held it a moment. A crowd had gathered. They awaited the verdict in breathless anticipation.

"This woman's dead," Raj Vu pronounced.

She did look extremely dead.

Raoul had a moment's misgiving. Perhaps he'd truly gotten the glasses mixed up. Then he felt a sudden tingling in all his nerve ends, a jabbing pain in his head. He relaxed.

Despite the pain, he had the sublime satisfaction of hearing a guest remark, "I say, Raj Vu, no one ever died at one of *your* parties!"

And though the pain was now intense and he was having difficulty breathing, Raoul smiled.

CHAPTER 16

What is food to one, is to others bitter poison.

Lucretius, *De Rerum Natura*

Raoul held a vial under Darlene's nose. She breathed deeply, choked, coughed. Her eyelids fluttered, opened. She stared at him bleary-eyed.

"What . . . the hell . . . happened?" she demanded dazedly. "Where am I?"

"In your room," Raoul replied. "I had them carry you up here. I know one isn't supposed to remove the body from the scene of the crime, but after the initial excitement of the murder, your corpse was casting rather a pall over the party. I'm sure the police will understand. Particularly when they learn that it was all a hoax."

The Little One tugged on Raoul's sleeve, motioned at the French doors, which led from the room to a deck with a seaside view.

"Ah, yes, speaking of the police"—Raoul put his arm around Darlene's shoulders, helped her sit up in the bed—"they'll be here any minute. You should really be leaving."

"Tell me what happened," Darlene said, clutching Raoul and giving him a shake. "I have to know what happened! It was the Hung, wasn't it?"

"They tried to poison you."

"In the champagne. That's why you switched . . ." She paused, stared at him. "Good God! You drank it!"

"One of us had to," Raoul said simply. "The Little

One read their minds. The assassins were prepared to kill everyone here in order to make certain of you. They had with them devices known as scramblers."

"Yes, that would have done it," Darlene said. She was regarding Raoul anxiously. "Are you sure you're all right?"

"Don't worry. I— Whatever is the matter?" Raoul demanded.

The Little One had gone stiff, rigid. Suddenly he threw himself down face-first on the floor, began to kick his feet and beat his fists into the carpet.

"What is it? What's wrong?" Darlene asked, alarmed. She stared at him. "I've never seen him behave like that. Have you?"

"Well, yes, but not generally when we have company. Don't worry, my dear, I've taken the antidote." Raoul pointed to a hypo lying on the nightstand. "And, really, considering the number of chemical substances of which my body is the humble repository, I am not certain I needed the antidote at all. The poison, once it reached my bloodstream, must have been in a highly confused state of mind."

"You could have been killed!" Darlene said, shuddering. She put her arm around Raoul, hugged him close. "And you know it." She kissed him. "You saved my life!" She looked over at the Little One, who had rolled over onto his back, was beating his heels on the carpet, pounding himself on the head.

"Just ignore him," Raoul said lightly. "And now, my dear, the police are notoriously slow to respond to calls during Carnival season, but the prospect of a murder to investigate might give them some incentive."

"Yes. You're right. I'm going." Darlene rose hurriedly to her feet. She staggered, swayed, sat back down just as hurriedly on the bed. She put her hand to her forehead. "Whoo, boy. Just a minute. What was that stuff you gave me? No, on second thought, I don't want to know. There." Taking it slower, she stood up again. "That's better."

"Here's your overnight bag." Raoul handed it to her. "I packed it."

"Where am I going?" Darlene asked, taking the bag without being cognizant of either the fact that she'd taken it or the bag itself.

"Out the French doors. Across the deck. Climb over the railing. Descend the stairs down the cliff side to the beach. Once you reach the beach ... reach the beach—that rhymes," Raoul added, charmed.

"Yes?" Darlene prompted.

Raoul recalled himself to the task at hand, though he could not forgo repeating his ascension to the poetic. "Once you reach the beach, take the boardwalk to the magnet, the magnet to the spaceport. Cruise ships leave from there all the time."

Darlene opened the French doors, looked out into the night, which was beautiful, as are all nights on Adonia. The sounds of music, voices, and laughter wafted in from the garden. A splash and another splash. People were jumping into the pool. She paused, her hand on the ornate door handle. "I wonder how the Hung found me. The Little One was positive no one was following us."

The Little One let out a savage howl. Jumping to his feet, he raced across the room, shut himself up in the closet.

Darlene gazed after him in astonishment.

"He admits that he is sometimes mistaken," Raoul said quietly. He edged her out the French doors. "But at least now they will think you are dead. This should effectively throw off all pursuit."

"Yes ... good-bye. And thank you." She started out the doors. She halted, looked about vaguely. "My computer."

"Leave it," Raoul said, shoving her along. "You have your clothes, that's most important."

"Hang the clothes!" Darlene dropped the bag on the floor. "Hand me my computer."

"You can't go on a pleasure cruise without clothes!" Raoul stated firmly. "Not, that is, unless you're planning on taking one of the nude—"

"No, no," Darlene said hastily.

"I packed them all specially."

"Very well, then," she said, knowing that she'd never

get away otherwise. "I'll take my clothes *and* the computer."

Raoul picked up the computer case. Regarding it with distaste, he handed it to her. "I packed all your new clothes. Your old clothes, I'm sorry to say, met with rather an unfortunate accident. Here you are."

Darlene grabbed the bag, clutched at her computer case. She kissed Raoul again on the cheek. "Thanks again, for everything. You and the Little One. Tell Xris I'll be in touch."

"Yes," Raoul said, smiling airily. "I'll tell him."

Muffled howls and thumps could be heard coming from the direction of the closet.

Darlene gave it a worried glance. "Are you sure he's all right?"

"Positive. Don't worry. Take care of yourself." Raoul had hold of the French doors. He was drawing them shut when he recalled last-minute instructions. "Remember to smooth the blush in the hollow of the cheek. Use that cream I gave you to get rid of those lines around your eyes. Keep the bangs soft and don't wear red. It makes you look anemic."

Darlene waved from the deck railing. She climbed up and over and, the next moment, had vanished from Raoul's sight. He could hear her footsteps as she ran down the wooden stairs. He shut the doors, an unusually thoughtful expression on his face. Ordinarily, Raoul took care not to think—it was damaging to the complexion—but matters had taken a serious turn. A knock came, the bedroom door opened. The butler entered.

"Pardon me, sir, but the police have arrived."

"Have they?" Raoul asked, preoccupied. He waved a negligent hand. "Give them something to eat."

"Very good, sir," the butler replied. His gaze shifted to the bed. He raised one eyebrow. "I beg your pardon, sir, but where is the corpse?"

"Corpse," Raoul repeated vaguely. His gaze was fixed on the closet, which had suddenly fallen silent.

"The young woman, sir, who collapsed and died in the atrium."

"Ah, that corpse." Raoul shrugged. "I assume it must be around somewhere."

"Am I to understand, sir, that you have misplaced it?"

"Yes, that's it," said Raoul. "We'll hold a scavenger hunt. The first person who finds the corpse wins a prize."

"Very good, sir. Oh, and I should inform you, sir, that the bartenders say their time is up. If you require them to stay longer, they are to be paid triple."

This caught Raoul's attention. "Indeed? Their time is up? I should say that it very well might be. Send them to me." Reaching for his handbag, Raoul took out a tube of lipstick. "I have a little something to give each of them."

He walked over to the mirror, began to carefully apply the lipstick to his lips, taking care not to touch his lips with his tongue.

"Very good, sir. And, in the interim, sir, I am a bit concerned about that missing corpse. . . ."

"Don't worry," said Raoul. "I'm certain it will turn up. If not that particular corpse, then some other. I suppose the police are not fussy?"

"I'm afraid I couldn't say, sir."

"Discuss the matter with them while they are dining," Raoul instructed. "Give them some champagne. Show them the scene of the alleged crime. Let them question a few witnesses. See to it that they are occupied for the next thirty minutes. By that time, I'm certain a corpse—or maybe even two—will have surfaced."

The butler lifted a second eyebrow to match the first, but he said nothing. He had his orders. Bowing, he withdrew, shutting the door softly behind him.

Raoul went immediately to the closet.

The Little One was sitting on a hat box in an attitude of the deepest dejection. His head clutched in his hands, he rocked back and forth, making small feral sounds. Raoul put his arm comfortingly around his friend's thin shoulders.

"It's not your fault. How were you supposed to have known?"

The Little One pulled his fedora down over his head, shook it vigorously.

"We don't have much time," Raoul said. "The bartenders are coming to be paid. After that, I suggest that we embark on a cruise ourselves. The Adonian police are generally fair and open-minded, particularly to those who have contributed to their association generously in the past, but with one corpse gone missing and a couple of new ones showing up in its place, this is likely to tax the sheriff's patience. While we're waiting for the bartenders, fill me in on the details. Xris and Jamil are in danger, you say?"

The Little One shoved his hat back; his eyes gleamed from beneath the brim. Lifting his hands, he pointed to his head, described circles with his fingers around his temples.

"A telepathic scrambler! That's what has been bothering you, ever since we visited the museum. The name of the weapons known as scramblers. That made you realize what had happened. Professor Sakuta is not what he seems. He was lying to us all the time. Have I understood you?"

The Little One gave a gloomy nod.

"I don't suppose," Raoul said, "that you have any idea what Professor Sakuta's true thoughts were?"

The Little One shook his head morosely, beat himself on the forehead with his small fists.

"It's not your fault," Raoul repeated kindly. "No one blames you. Don't blame yourself."

Raoul was again thoughtful, again risking damage to his complexion. The urgency of the situation appeared to warrant the sacrifice.

"There is only one thing to be done," Raoul decided. "Darlene is safe, for the time being. The Hung thinks she is dead and we'll make certain that they don't find out otherwise. It seems to me, therefore, that our next priority must be to rescue Xris Cyborg and Jamil from whatever it is that threatens them. We could undertake to do this ourselves—"

The Little One growled.

"No, you're right," Raoul agreed. "We must assemble the team." The idea appealed to him. He smoothed his hair. "*I* will assemble the team. I've never done that before. It should be quite thrilling. Well, of course they'll listen to me," he added, offended. "Why shouldn't they? I—"

A knock on the door interrupted him.

Raoul rose to his feet. Opening the door, he saw the two bartenders—handsome, charming, smiling, confident.

"Dear boys," Raoul said. "Do come in."

He greeted them each with a kiss.

CHAPTER

17

"I can't explain myself, I'm afraid, sir," said Alice,
"because I'm not myself, you see."
"I don't see," said the Caterpillar.

Lewis Carroll, *Alice in Wonderland*

"*King James* Control, this is Navy Three Five Niner
Zircon. Please clear for priority landing."

"Navy Three Five Niner Zircon, you are cleared for
immediate landing in Bay One Forward. All other traffic
is diverted. Do not exit your spaceplane until the Marine
Guard is in place. Understood, Navy Three Five Niner
Zircon?"

"Roger that, *King James* Control. Beginning landing
sequence now. Navy Three Five Niner Zircon, out."

The bomber cruised toward the massive ship. Jamil
studied it, memorizing detail for possible use later. The
aft engines were modular in design and were fitted out-
rigger style, so that they could be jettisoned in case of
an engine overload. Below the engines, the hull formed
a flight deck and landing platform.

The bomber gracefully arced toward the platform, and
gently touched down. Maneuvering thrusters kept the
spaceplane from bouncing off the deck, until the magnetic clamps took hold and trundled the spaceplane
along the deck into the hangar.

The hangar's blast doors did not shut behind it, once
they had cleared the atmosphere shields. The pilot did
not leave her seat. The bomber would not be staying

here long. Once the bomber was stationary, the ground crew scrambled over the wings and up the side of the spaceplane for servicing. The hatch popped, and both VanDerGard and Jamil exited, climbing down the ladder to the deck.

A colonel, accompanied by two Marines armed with beam rifles, awaited them. Behind the colonel, a platoon of Marines were assembled.

"Oh, God. This is it," Jamil said to himself, blinking in the bright lights.

The colonel stepped forward, extended his hand.

Jamil stared at the hand in astonishment—he'd been expecting a rifle in his gut, not a handshake. Belatedly, awkwardly, he reached out, shook hands.

The colonel had a firm, confident grip. He was in his early forties, freckled, with buzz-cut red hair, a warm smile, and a friendly manner.

"Colonel Jatanski, I'm Colonel Michael Ponders, General Hanson's chief of staff. You're to come with me."

Ponders had to nearly shout to be heard in the hangar bay, which was echoing with the banging and clanging and swearing of maintenance crews at work on the spaceplane. He and Jamil started walking, heading for the blast doors that led off the hangar deck. Major VanDerGard fell unobtrusively into step behind them, as did the two armed Marines.

The doors opened, slid shut. Jamil and the Colonel, the Major and the Marines entered a corridor that was sleek, carpeted, quiet. They could talk normally now.

"Where are you taking me, Colonel?" Jamil asked, figuring he knew the answer but thinking it was about time somebody said it.

"To meet with General Hanson, of course," Ponders said, looking surprised that Jamil would even ask. "She'll be briefing you on the Katchan case."

"Oh, ah, I see," Jamil said, just for the sake of saying something.

He was starting to wonder if he'd slipped through a worm hole and had ended up in an alternate universe where he really *was* a colonel. He tried to think of what might be a logical question to ask that would clarify this bizarre situation, but he was so confused that nothing came immediately to mind. He was like an actor in a play who's not only forgotten his lines, he's forgotten the plot as well. Fortunately, Ponders was the gossipy, sociable type, who carried on without prompting.

"Yes, I'm afraid it looks bad for the lieutenant colonel. Katchan must have stolen some pretty sensitive material. I guess you can't tell me what he was working on, eh?"

"Well, actually, uh, n-no. I can't say," Jamil stammered. "Security, and ... all that."

"Right, right. I understand. It must be top-level, though." Ponders glanced over his shoulder. "These two Marines have orders to accompany you wherever you go. General Hanson's direct command."

"I see," Jamil said, eyeing the Marines, who were regarding him with the impassive detachment of men who have been ordered to shoot to kill. Jamil experienced an odd sense of relief. This—at least—made sense!

"I sure would like to know what this poor bastard Katchan did. You two in some sort of Special Ops? No, don't answer that." Ponders raised his hand. "Listen, when the General's finished with you, give me a call on the comm and we'll go grab a bite in the Senior Officers' Wardroom. A pity we can't get you something to eat now, but I'm supposed to take you straight to your briefing."

Jamil glanced at the Marines and the eyes of one man flicked over to meet his. The eyes were cold, did not blink. Jamil could have sworn he saw the man's hand on the beam rifle tighten.

"Sure thing. Thanks," Jamil said, and accompanied the colonel down the corridor. The Marine guards marched behind.

Three times he, Ponders, and the Marines had to stop, identify themselves, show ID cards, and submit to retina scans, all before proceeding to the next level of the gigantic cruiser. Jamil's ID card stated he was Colonel Jatanski, his retina scan matched that of Jatanski—all thanks to Darlene Rowan and her skill at breaking into computers. Security passed him without a murmur. The

Marines proved a comfort. They continued to give him
the fish-eye. *Someone* on this ship knew Jamil was Jamil
and not Jatanski. At least he hoped so. He was starting
to doubt it himself.

Ponders talked the entire time, trying to elicit information without really trying to elicit information. He was
either a very good actor, truly endeavoring to make
Jamil incriminate himself, or he was what he appeared—
a gregarious man who made himself popular on board
ship by spreading the latest rumor, dishing the latest dirt.

They passed through a fourth set of guards, who stood
with their backs against yet another set of closed blast
doors, and again they all presented their ID cards. The
blast doors opened onto another corridor. Ponders
walked up to a door, punched in a code. The door slid
open.

"Here's where I leave you," Ponders said regretfully.
"Good luck with Katchan. It sounds like he's in one hell
of a mess. Give me a call later—we'll do that dinner."
He nudged Jamil. "You can fill me in on everything
then. After your meeting with the general."

Ponders left. Jamil entered the room. The door slid
shut behind him.

He might have been in the waiting room of the office
of some high-priced attorney. The room was small but well
furnished, with expensive-looking leather-upholstered
chairs, carved wooden end tables, a coffee table with a
few slick mags arranged artfully upon it. Ambient lighting from the ceiling softened the fact that the room had
no portholes. A smaller door opened to his touch, turned
out to be the head. He made good use of it, studied
himself in the mirror, did what he could to smooth out
the rumples in his uniform, then returned to the waiting
room. There were even a few paintings—spacescapes by
Gutierrez. Jamil was impressed. Someone who designed
this room had good taste in art.

All in all, it was a comfortable waiting room and only
the fact that the paintings were bolted to the wall and
the furniture was bolted to the floor gave any indication
to Jamil that he was on a ship of war, which might be
called to go into action at any time.

He sat down in a leather chair, fidgeted, stood up, fidgeted, sat down, flipped through a mag. He stood up again, walked over to the door. A touch of his own on the keypad and the door slid open. The two Marines stood there, one on either side of the door.

Colonel Jatanski had every right to leave. Jamil, confidently, stepped out.

Two beam rifles snapped up in front of him so fast they nearly clipped him in the nose.

"Sorry, sir. General Hanson's orders," said one of the Marines.

"It was a long flight," Jamil said in iced tones. "I have to use the head."

"In there, sir," said one of the Marines. "Touch that panel on the wall on the far side."

Jamil muttered and stalked back inside. The door slid shut behind him.

He now knew all he needed to know. Sitting on the couch, he picked up one of the mags—this one on golf, his favorite game—and settled down to read how to improve his putting.

Some of these minimum-security prisons had pretty good golf courses.

He had just finished the article and was on his feet, an imaginary putter in his hand, testing what the author had said about wrist action, when the door opened. One of the Marines looked in.

"They're ready for you, sir."

Jamil was about to make some suitable remark, but his throat was dry, he suddenly couldn't talk. He was surprised. He hadn't thought he was nervous. He drew in a deep breath, stepped into the corridor. Another officer was waiting for him, a black-skinned human male who said something—Jamil didn't hear for the blood pounding in his ears.

The officer led Jamil into yet another room. This room was plush—carpeting wall to wall. A large round wood table stood in the center of the room. Crests of all the ships serving in the fleet the *King James II* commanded lined the bulkheads. A man and a woman sat on the opposite side of the table. The officer saluted smartly.

"Here is the prisoner, my lord. Jamil Khizr, of Mag Force 7."

"Thank you, Commander," said the man behind the table.

Jamil stared, sucked air.

The commander made introductions. No need. Jamil knew one of these people by sight.

"General Irma Hanson, commander of the Second Armored Drop Corps. Lord Admiral Sir John Dixter, commander-in-chief of the Royal Military."

"Holy shit," Jamil said softly.

"You could say that, Khizr. And—holy or unholy—you're into it up to your armpits." Dixter issued orders. "Tusk, reseal the doors. Post the guard. No one without authorization has entered this room since we did the last security sweep, have they?"

"Yourself, myself, General Hanson, and the prisoner are the only three to be admitted. The prisoner was scanned, my lord. He's clean."

"Fine, carry on."

Tusk saluted, turned on his heel, walked out the door.

The prisoner—that's what they'd termed Jamil.

He cleared his throat. "My lord, General Hanson, it is an honor to meet you both."

Dixter grunted. "An honor I'll wager you wished had been deferred, right, Khizr? Or perhaps I should address you as 'colonel'?"

Jamil felt his face grow warm. "My lord, I can explain—"

"And you will," Dixter said gravely. "General, hand me the file."

General Hanson passed over an electronic file viewer. Dixter took it, instructed it by voice to bring up the information on Mag Force 7.

"You may be seated," he told Jamil, adding dryly, "This could take a while."

A chair had been placed for him in the center of the room. Jamil sat, hunkered down, and waited for the barrage to start.

"First," said the Lord Admiral, reading from the file, "there was the raid on a company known as Olicien Pest

Control, the theft of a spaceplane belonging to that company, and the deliberate drugging of the employees by the admittance of a sleeping gas into the air-conditioning system."

Jamil shook his head. "My lord, I've never been near—"

"We have positive IDs," Dixter said. "That job could get you twenty years. Next file," he told the computer.

"The assault on RFComSec, a secret naval base. Disguised as exterminators for Olicien Pest Control, you and your accomplices lied your way onto the base. Once there, you sabotaged the robots designed to rid the base of its flea infestation. You then proceeded to kidnap a Naval officer, one Darlene Mohini, and take her off the base, meanwhile disrupting base communications and its computer system, putting at risk the entire Royal Navy, not to mention the people of the galaxy, whom we are responsible for protecting. Again, we have positive IDs."

Jamil settled into his chair, maintained silence. The shells were falling thick and fast, the flak was flying. He had one small bit of hope to cling to in his exposed position, and that was the fact that he was sitting here, right now. Ordinary prisoners headed for the disrupter were not brought before the Lord of the Admiralty to hear their cases reviewed. This barrage was simply clearing the way for the main advance. He had only to endure it, wait it out.

"Then," said Sir John, referring back to the file, "there is the attack on an unarmed research vessel known as the *Canis Major.* You were acting under the belief that one of your comrades was being held prisoner aboard that vessel. As it turned out, you were correct in your assumption. The *Canis Major* was afterward proven to belong to the terrorist organization known as the Knights of the Black Earth. But," Dixter added, his voice cold, "you had no way of knowing this at the time. You took the law into your own hands. No positive IDs on this one, but that's only because the knights are no longer around to press charges.

"To continue. There is next the matter of the hijacking of an Army Special Forces drop ship from a

NOROF rebuild and overhaul facility. Not only do we have positive IDs on this, your leader, Xris, actually had the nerve to send me a message. As for the rest of your adventures after that, they were recorded and broadcast by every news station in the galaxy!"

"Yes, my lord." Jamil was on secure ground here. "I assume Your Lordship is referring to the time we saved His Majesty, King Dion Starfire, from the assassin. And, my lord, may I respectfully point out that we *did* give back the drop ship."

He'd meant that as a little joke. Neither the Lord Admiral nor General Hanson was amused. Dixter put the file down, folded his hands on the desk, and regarded Jamil with an intense gravity that was more disturbing than the previous accusations. It was like the period of eerie silence which comes when the artillery barrage has ceased and you know that the enemy is preparing to advance. Jamil braced himself.

"Jamil Khizr," said the Lord Admiral, "I have, right here, warrants for the arrest of"—he read the list— "Xris, a cyborg, Harry Luck, Dr. Bill Quong, Raoul de Beausoleil—which, by the way, is just one of his aliases—a being of unknown origin known as the Little One, Tycho, a 'chameleon,' and you, Jamil Khizr." Dixter taped his hand on the computer. "I can issue these warrants in a single second, by simply pressing 'Enter.' The charge is murder."

"Murder, my lord?" Jamil shrugged. "If you mean the assassin, yes, I admit we were responsible for his death, but—"

"You saved the life of His Majesty. I'm well aware of that," Dixter said coolly. "And that is not it."

"Then what?" Jamil was truly puzzled.

The Lord Admiral was grave. "Jamil Khizr, you and all the rest of the people previously mentioned are charged with the kidnapping and murder of Naval officer Major Darlene Mohini."

CHAPTER
18

Crime like virtue has its degrees.

Jean Racine, *Phèdre*

The bombshell landed squarely in Jamil's foxhole, burst above his head. He was stunned from the concussion, could only gape at the Lord Admiral, while trying to gather together the scattered bits and pieces of his brain.

"The game's up, Khizr," said John Dixter. He lowered the file, looked over the top at Jamil. "We have you on vid at RFComSec. We have vids of Xris and Major Mohini together; Xris is holding the major hostage at gunpoint. That was the last time anyone ever saw Major Darlene Mohini alive. An excellent case, don't you agree, Khizr? Men have gone to the disrupter on less."

Jamil leaned an elbow on the armrest, shifted his weight in his chair. He crossed one leg over the other, tapped the fingers of one hand lightly on his knee. All the while, he kept his gaze fixed on Lord Admiral John Dixter. The dust had settled. Jamil had to figure out now how to escape from the wreckage.

He didn't see much hope. In fact he was in one hell of a mess.

The major picked up me alone, Jamil reminded himself. They left Xris behind. They ordered him to "carry on." They wouldn't have done that if they seriously thought we'd murdered someone. They're after something, but what? How should I answer this?

Advice once offered by Raoul came to mind: "Try the truth. . . . But only as a last resort."

Jamil uncrossed his legs, sat up straight. "My lord, Darlene Mohini is alive and, as far as I know, she's well."

Dixter raised an eyebrow. "Is she? That's good news—for everyone. If you'll tell me where she is, how to contact her, we'll clear the record of this matter."

"I'm sorry, my lord," Jamil said. "But I can't do that."

"And why not?" the Lord Admiral asked grimly.

"I think you know the answer to that, my lord," Jamil said, taking a big risk, but figuring he had nothing to lose. "It's because Darlene Mohini isn't really Darlene Mohini. She's someone else and that someone could be in serious danger if her true identity ever became known. If she came forward now, there'd be all sorts of publicity. Her face would be transmitted from one arm of the galaxy to the other. The people who are searching for her would recognize her from the news reports. She'd be dead before the first break to go to the local sponsor."

"We could guarantee her protection."

Jamil decided this had gone far enough. He was tired of playing blind man's bluff, of fumbling around in the dark.

"Begging Your Lordship's pardon, but that's a crock of bullshit. His Majesty the King rides in an armored limo, he's surrounded by the best-trained bodyguards in the business, and if it hadn't been for us *and* Darlene Mohini, His Majesty would be dead right about now."

Silence settled over the room. General Hanson, a stringy, scrawny, tough old bird in her sixties, who was not known as Iron Guts for nothing, tightened her lips, cast a sidelong glance at the Lord Admiral. Dixter gazed steadily at Jamil.

"You won't tell us where Major Mohini is."

"No, my lord," said Jamil respectfully.

"You and Xris have been caught impersonating officers in the Royal Army. You finagled your way onto a military base. You were on that base with the intention of stealing an object which, if it falls into the wrong hands, could endanger the lives of every person living in this galaxy, not to mention disrupting trade routes, destroying the economies of hundreds of worlds, and very possibly plunging this galaxy into chaos and anarchy."

Jamil shook his head. "You've got it all wrong, sir. We weren't hired to steal anything like that. We were hired to steal some moth-eaten old robot."

Dixter was grim. "Moth-eaten old robot. You and the rest of Mag Force 7 are in trouble, Khizr, more trouble than you can possibly imagine. There are only six people in the universe who know about the existence of this robot—myself, General Hanson, His Majesty, the prime minister, the head of Naval intelligence, and one of our operatives on the Pandoran military base. This is so god-damned classified it's not even classified. We couldn't risk it. Nothing's been written down about it, nothing's been entered into any computer. Hell, I don't even let myself dream about it!"

Dixter leaned forward, hands on the table. "Imagine my surprise when you and Xris suddenly show up on base with a container that just happens to be the right shape and size for transporting one moth-eaten robot!"

"My lord, I can explain. . . ." Jamil began, then hesitated, wondered if he could.

"You better," said John Dixter, his tone cold with fury. "I can't charge you with anything concerning this case. I don't dare risk any hint of this robot's discovery leaking out—at least any more than it apparently already has. But I can and I will bring you up on charges of murdering Major Mohini, which puts you in one hell of a fix. Either you produce her alive, in which case you blow her cover and the Hung will find out that she was, once upon a time, Dalin Rowan, former FISA agent who was personally responsible for the downfall of the Hung . . . or you refuse to admit you know anything about her, in which case you and Xris and everyone else involved on that raid on RFComSec are convicted of kidnapping and murder and you end up on death row. And you wouldn't be there long," Dixter concluded, his mouth twisting.

Jamil listened in silence; then, with dignity, he stood up. "You don't need to threaten us, my lord. Like I said, we didn't know anything about this 'bot, except that some museum wanted it and was willing to pay us to snatch it. If that robot's as hot as you say it is, we don't want any part of it. You can have it and we'll forget we ever heard of the damn thing. But first I want two things from you, my lord.

"One, I want assurances that Darlene Mohini is taken off the record books, that as far as the Navy's concerned, she never existed. Second, I want to know why—after all this—you gave orders that Xris was supposed to continue with the plan. That he was supposed to go ahead and steal that robot. You've set him up for something and I want to know what. Otherwise," he continued coolly, forestalling an attempt by General Hanson to intervene, "the only words you're going to hear from me after this are: 'Where the hell's my attorney?' "

Dixter eyed Jamil narrowly.

Jamil held the man's gaze, didn't flinch beneath the intense scrutiny.

The Lord Admiral let out a deep breath. "I didn't think Xris would take on a job like this if he knew the whole story, but ... I had to be sure."

He closed his eyes, wiped his hand over his face. General Hanson asked him in a low voice if he needed something, started to pour him a glass of water. Dixter shook his head. Opening his eyes, he gazed steadily at Jamil.

"I can't promise you anything regarding Major Mohini, but I'll take the matter under advisement. At least I can promise that I will keep her identity secret. As for setting up Xris, I'm giving both him and you a chance to try to repair some of the damage that you two have done. Inadvertently, perhaps," Dixter added, seeing Jamil about to protest, "but Xris knew what he was doing was breaking the law."

"In the interests of science, my lord," Jamil protested.

"In the interests of your bank balance, is what you mean. You'll pardon me if I don't feel particularly sorry for you. Sit down," Dixter concluded wearily, waving his hand. "You're not going anywhere. Not for a while, at least."

"Yes, sir." Jamil sat down again, breathed a careful sigh. Sweat trickled down his back, beaded on his brow. That had been close. Really close. But they weren't out of this yet. Which brought up an important point. "One thing I need to know, my lord. Is Xris in any danger? If he is—"

"No, he's not. In fact, our operative reports that he was successful in removing the robot from the crash site. He is, I presume, at this moment boning up on his notes for his speech. What was that topic again? 'Foreign Object Damage to Spaceplane Engines.'" Dixter shook his head.

"It's a serious problem," observed General Hanson, looking quite fierce. "Tears the hell out of them. Some bonehead leaves a Coke can on the runway, it gets sucked into the engine of a Claymore bomber, and you can kiss sixty billion eagles good-bye. I wouldn't mind hearing that lecture myself."

John Dixter's face relaxed in a smile. "Xris is safe and sound, Khizr. Set your mind at ease on that point. You'll be rejoining him—soon, in fact. We wouldn't want anyone on the base to miss that lecture."

"And after that?" Jamil was tense, wary.

"You're going to deliver the robot to the man who hired you, to 'Professor' Michael Sakuta."

"I take it he's no professor."

"Oh, yes, he is. But he's *not* connected with any Space and Aeronautics Museum."

"That's funny," Jamil said warily. "Because he had an office in the museum on Megapolis. Xris met him there."

"And if Xris had bothered to check, he would have discovered the business offices of the Space and Aeronautics Museum on Megapolis had been closed for a week in order to remodel."

"Oh," said Jamil. He squirmed in his chair. "What do you want us to do, sir?"

"Deliver the robot as agreed. Collect your paycheck and leave. That's all you have to do. We'll handle it from there."

"Begging your pardon, my lord, but if this job is as hot as you say, what's to keep Sakuta from spending his money on our funerals, not our paychecks?"

"There is always that possibility," Dixter conceded, "but I assume you knew that was a risk when you undertook this job. Xris *must* have known Sakuta was a phony."

"Well, no, my lord, we didn't," Jamil admitted, his face burning. "We thought he was an egghead—a cracked one, at that—but not dangerous. The Little One—he's our telepath—he verified that Sakuta's thoughts matched up with his words."

"Telepathic scrambler," Dixter said succinctly. "He's used it before."

"But how would he know about the Little One? Xris never said—"

"Sakuta did *his* homework. He learned all about Mag Force 7. He learned all about Xris. He knew what type of jobs Xris would take, what kind he wouldn't. Sakuta's a skilled actor. I've no doubt he played the role to perfection. And, of course, he was just exactly what Xris expected an 'egghead' professor to be. Khizr, I'm going to level with you."

"Begging your pardon, my lord, but it's about time," Jamil said bitterly.

"No apologies, Khizr. You're damn lucky—you and Xris both—that you're not sitting behind a force field about now. You came that close to blowing this case all to hell. Instead, I'm going to give you a chance to set it right."

"We'll be glad to help you out, my lord," Jamil said respectfully. "How much does the job pay?"

"What?" Dixter was incredulous.

"How much does the job pay, my lord?" Jamil repeated. He leaned back, crossed one leg over the other. "I figure, say ... twice what Sakuta was prepared to pay us...."

"Don't bother with the brig. Throw him out the air lock, John," General Hanson said.

"Calm down, Irma," John Dixter returned. He put the tips of his fingers together. "There's the small matter of kidnapping and murder charges. The small matter of impersonating an officer in His Majesty's Army. The small matter of working for an enemy of the state. What do you think this job is worth to you, Khizr?"

Jamil sat up straight. "My skin, sir?"

"Your skin, Khizr."

"Plus expenses," Jamil added.

Dixter stared, then he started to chuckle. He caught himself, rubbed his eyes, drew in a deep breath. "All right, Khizr. Plus expenses. Tell Xris to send me a bill." The Lord Admiral activated the commlink.

The door slid open. The admiral's adjutant entered, saluted. "Yes, my lord."

"Take Khizr and get him something to eat and drink. Fill him in on all the details of this job, tell him what he's supposed to do. Good luck, Khizr." The admiral rose to his feet. He was no longer laughing. "I can't begin to tell you how critical this assignment is. If you fail, God help you."

"God help us all," General Hanson intoned. She no longer looked fierce. She looked just plain worried.

"Yes, my lord. Yes, ma'am," said Jamil, subdued. He stood up, started instinctively to salute, as Sir John and General Hanson departed. He stopped himself just in time, changed the salute to an awkward scratching of his jaw.

He remained standing until the Lord Admiral and the general had left the room through a side door.

"If you'll come with me, Colonel Jatanski," Tusk said, motioning Jamil toward the open door, where stood the two armed Marines.

Jamil had had enough. "Look, I'm not—"

"Not ready to leave yet, sir?" Tusk interrupted. "Sorry, colonel, but I'm afraid your time's up."

Jamil sighed. He knew when he was licked. "Very well. Carry on, Commander."

Tusk was grave. "Yes, Colonel, sir. This way, sir."

Jamil walked out the door. The armed Marines fell in behind.

CHAPTER
19

. . . the articulate and audible voice of the Past . . .

Thomas Carlyle, *The Hero and Hero Worship*

At just about the time Xris was dreaming of robots with human eyes doing irreparable damage to spaceplane engines, and Jamil was sweating it out with Lord Admiral Dixter, a human named Jeffrey Grant, who lived in another part of the galaxy and who had never heard of the planet Pandor and who only knew the Lord Admiral from the news vids, was taking his usual morning stroll to work.

Grant lived on a world known as XIO, short for some number that had been assigned to it by ancient explorers. It says a great deal for the creativity and originality of XIO's inhabitants that they had never bothered to come up with anything different. The planet was rich in mineral resources and was therefore heavily industrialized. Factories belched untold poisons into the air, the people breathed them and breathed money. Profit was king. Pollution laws were nonexistent and, to be honest, XIO polluted wasn't much worse than XIO in pristine condition.

Its people were hardworking, no-nonsense, solid union, and almost predominantly members of the middle class. The few wealthy business magnates who ran XIO did not live there. As for the poor, XIO was proud to boast that, like Adonia, their world did not have any poor. On XIO, if you were union, you had a job, or you were retired and living off your pension. If you were not union, you didn't belong on XIO.

Jeffrey Grant had been a union worker for thirty-five of the fifty-five years of his life. Now he was retired and, because he had no family, was able to live quite well on the generous pension plan his union provided. He was a gray man in appearance. His hair was gray, he wore gray off-the-rack suits. His eyes had probably started out blue but had now faded. His complexion had a grayish tinge to it, but that may have been due to the dust and soot of his environment. He was short, inclined to be tubby around the waist, with a preoccupied smile and a benign expression. A gray, ordinary man, you would guess.

You would be wrong. Jeffrey Grant was a man with an obsession.

He was obsessed with space flight.

Grant had been a pilot of sorts, his job having consisted of flying an orbital shuttle from one side of XIO to the other. Lesser minds might refer to Grant as more bus driver than pilot. Grant never argued the matter, but merely responded with a secret smile which implied a wealth of adventures equivalent to those of any Royal Navy hotshot and known only to Grant himself. Such secret adventures did exist, if only in the head of Jeffrey Grant.

A quiet, somewhat shy, and retiring man, Grant had entertained himself on the long shuttle flights by imagining his Ladybird orbital transport was a sleek fighter and that he was the flying ace of every major space combat battle from the time of the Black Earth forward. His shuttle bus never deviated from its set course, its fixed speed. It was run by computer. Grant had little to do but watch the stars flit past him.

Jeffrey Grant saw more than stars. Jeffrey Grant saw squadrons of Scimitars swooping in to attack the planet in the name of some rogue dictator. He saw Claymore bombers fly off to do battle for the new king. He saw deadly dogfights between Flamberge bombers and Corasian fighters. He saw Jeffrey Grant, in his Scimitar or his Claymore or his Flamberge. He saw Jeffrey Grant, the wing commander.

Since the hated Corasians—who were on the other side of the galaxy—never attacked XIO, Grant never had a chance to put his dream into action. Considering that his shuttle bus was not armed, this was probably just as well. He didn't really want the Corasians to attack, nor did he particularly want XIO to fall to a bloodthirsty dictator. But he did admit to a feeling of disappointment that the most exciting thing to have happened to him in thirty years of space piloting was the malfunction of the toilets on the shuttle bus, which had resulted in a flood of a most unpleasant nature.

He spent thirty-five years piloting the shuttle bus by day, piloting Scimitars on his flight simulator by night. When retirement was forced upon him at age fifty-five by a benevolent union, which needed to make room for younger employees, he was provided with an adequate pension. In addition, Grant had quite a tidy sum of money saved, all of which enabled him to make at least one of his dreams come true. He opened a space museum.

His museum was as different from the Megapolis Space and Aeronautics Museum as Grant's shuttle bus was different from a sleek Katana fighter prototype. The museum was located in a dusty storefront on a side street in a part of the city that no tourist in his right mind would have any inclination to visit. This was perhaps just as well, since Grant neither liked nor trusted tourists, and if any happened to wander into his museum—perhaps to use the bathroom—he did his best to get rid of them.

He had on display in his museum various antiques from bygone eras of space travel which he had collected over the years. These included boost engines from an original Arc-Class Terraforming Transport, two small Type F-66 fighter spaceplanes with no guns. (Originally in service with the Galactic Express, the spaceplanes had been painted bright orange. Grant had repainted them their original gray.) He was the proud possessor of a jump-juice distillery (not in working order) and owned innumerable flight and computer instruments from very early space flight in various stages of disrepair.

Grant spent his days dusting his treasures, poring over

his books and old papers, playing games on his flight simulators (he owned forty-seven), and browsing through vid antique catalogs, searching for material to add to his collection.

A new arrival was expected today, in fact. A gun site simulator for a Scimitar Type A, still in working condition. Grant smiled in pleasant anticipation.

The morning was fine—a rare commodity on XIO. The sun struggled to shine through a haze of smoke and fumes, but at least the sun was shining. Grant enjoyed his short stroll between his small brownstone and the museum. He nodded the usual greetings to his neighbors (he'd never spoken to any of them in the twenty-five years he'd lived in the neighborhood, except once, when the house next door caught fire, and then he felt compelled the next day to politely inquire if anyone needed a blanket).

His part of the city was a very old part, containing crumbling brick buildings that had once housed important firms, but were now reduced to selling adult vids and renting out clown costumes. It was the last place one would have expected to find a museum. Grant considered himself lucky to have discovered it.

He inserted the key into the lock of the wooden door, pausing as he paused every morning to admire the gold lettering on the glass pane which read: GRANT'S AIR AND SPACE MUSEUM: AN OUT-OF-THE-WORLD EXPERIENCE. Pleased with the sign and himself and the sunshine, looking forward to a day filled with dusting and puttering, unpacking and perusing, Grant opened the door and switched on the overhead light.

Something was wrong.

Jeffrey Grant didn't know quite what yet, but he was so attuned and accustomed to the atmosphere of his quiet little museum that the slightest change registered instantly. He stood in the door, nervous and wary, trying to figure out what was disturbing him. A first cursory glance around the room seemed to indicate that all was exactly as he had left it the night before.

Of course, he couldn't see every part of the museum from where he stood; the one-room museum was filled from floor to ceiling with his collection, and what portion the helmets and gloves and hull plates from rocket boosters and instruments did not take up, his books and papers did. The book he'd been reading was still on the vidscreen; his prized artifact—a graduation ring from the Mars Terran-Command Flight School—was still in its glass case. He hadn't been robbed.

Yet something was most definitely wrong.

Standing, alarmed and troubled, in the open doorway, Grant deliberated his next move.

He decided, on consideration, to shut the door.

This done, he was immediately cognizant of a strange sound, a high-pitched and annoying hum that had not been there yesterday, nor any days prior to yesterday.

He relaxed, relieved, no longer alarmed, merely annoyed. The furnace was old enough to have almost qualified as an exhibit. It required constant attention and was a considerable source of trouble to him. True, the furnace had never made a sound like this before, but Grant was confident that it could if it truly put its mind to it. Muttering mild imprecations, he made his way through the clutter to the back of the room, opened a door, and began to descend to the cellar, where the furnace was located.

He stopped halfway down the stairs, puzzled. The sound, instead of growing louder, as it should have if the furnace was the source, was growing softer. Grant paused on the staircase, head cocked to one side, listening intently. Yes, the hum was not nearly as pronounced down here as it had been up above.

Grant experimented, walked down to the bottom of the stairs. He could not hear the hum at all. He checked the furnace, just to be certain. The furnace was not at fault.

"I see," said Grant to himself. "Sorry," he apologized to the furnace, then turned and went back up the stairs. "It must be one of the computers. Or maybe I forgot to shut off the flight sim."

He knew that wasn't the case. Grant was a creature of habit. (It had taken him a week, following his retirement, to break himself of the habit of going work. He'd finally accomplished this only by writing the words NOT

NEEDED on a large placard and posting it on his refrigerator.) Grant habitually turned off the flight simulators every time he was through with them. If not, his electric bill—already substantial—would have been astronomical.

He stepped out into the museum. The hum was distinctly audible.

Methodically, Grant checked all the computers, then began walking down the line of flight simulators that took up one entire wall. He turned each one on, listened to it, turned it off, and moved to the next. He was fairly certain that they were not to blame; he had excellent hearing and the hum seemed to be coming from another part of the room. It was best to rule out the obvious, however, before investigating further. He was switching off the twenty-third simulator when it occurred to him—rather uncomfortably—that the hum might be the prelude to something nastier. An explosion, perhaps.

Grant wavered in his determination to check out all the rest of the flight simulators. He looked about fearfully, thinking he should carry all his valuables out of the building, but that would take days. Then he thought he would only carry out his most valuable artifacts, but that meant choosing between them, and that was impossible. Then he thought that perhaps he should call in an expert. But ... an expert in what? Annoying hums? Perhaps he should call the police, firemen. He had a vision of the firemen, with their laser cutters and foam canisters and water hoses, entering his beloved museum, and he shuddered. He'd rather be blown up.

It was at this point, during his dithering and his fitful darts to grab something beloved, only to put it down distractedly to pick up something else, only to put that down and finally head for the phone in back, only to reconsider and pause in confusion, that Jeffrey Grant saw the light.

It was a blue light and it was flashing on an antique machine, an ancient antique machine, a machine that was one of Jeffrey Grant's most valuable artifacts, a machine that—as far as he had been able to ascertain—had not worked in centuries. This was the machine that was flashing. This was also the machine that was humming.

Grant stared, began to tremble, as if an icon of a dutifully worshiped saint had suddenly begun shedding tears of blood. He approached the machine—which had a corner location of honor all to itself—with timorous footsteps, regarded it with reverential awe.

He had acquired the machine several years previous. It was very old and had run off electrical power supplied by lines run through the walls. No building on XIO operated with such antiquated equipment; Grant was forced to hook the machine up to a nuclear-powered battery. The cost of the battery had been considerable, but Grant deemed it worth the price. The machine had a large text screen on the front, and though it had never displayed any information, Grant kept it turned on. The screen cast a soft glow which bathed the back portion of the room in white luminescence. In other words, Grant used the machine for a lamp.

The machine was truly antique. It had a keyboard interface on the front with a track-ball built into the keyboard. The central memory and functioning hardware were housed in a small box attached behind the keyboard. The front of the box was a vid unit that provided the wonderful white glow. Along the side were six small lights, about two centimeters in diameter. One of these lights was flashing a bright blue this morning.

Grant was careful not to touch the machine; he was afraid he might do something wrong, might cause it to shut off. He examined the machine closely, intently, studied every part of it, rotating it by turning its stand in order to see the back.

Finished with his inspection, he regarded the machine in doubt. He had read up on the machine, knew all about it, what it did, why it did it, was completely familiar with its workings, and there was only one logical explanation as to why it had suddenly begun, after all these years of silence, to speak.

But that explanation was so bizarre, so strange, so impossible, that Grant had to consider some other cause.

More practical, less wonderful: a malfunction, a short in the wiring, a lightning strike.

He wanted so much to believe. He wanted to fall down on his knees and give praise. And therefore he knew he had to consult some higher authority. He had to prove the saint's tears were blood, as it were, not streaks of rust.

Leaving the machine to hum to itself—a hum that was, for Grant, no longer annoying, but a chorusing of angels—he headed for the reference library part of his museum. He was forced to stop, however, to calm himself. His heart was racing in a most unhealthy fashion, his hands shook, the palms were clammy with sweat. He began to see spots in his vision and was horribly afraid he was going to pass out.

"Get hold of yourself, sir," he counseled himself sternly. "I expect you to set the example for the younger pilots. Enemy sighted. Lock onto target."

Since the only people with whom Grant communicated were the fellow pilots and commanders inside his space games, he was used to talking to them and interacting with them. He took all the parts and, in this instance, considered himself as being chewed out by his commander.

The momentary dizziness passed. Grant felt better. He locked onto his target—the bookcase—and proceeded toward it. Once there, he studied the shining metallic disks in their plastic cases, selected three, pulled them out and carried them to his computer. He inserted the first, brought up the file.

He spent the remainder of the day in study so intense and rewarding and exalting that he lost all notion of time, forgot even to eat his baloney and mustard sandwich for lunch, something that had not happened in thirty-five years. He ascended to a higher state, reveled in the ecstasy of his discovery, forgot everything on the more mundane levels of existence.

How long he would have remained at his work is open to question. Mankind being heir to the weaknesses of the flesh, Jeffrey Grant was brought back to this realm rather abruptly by the rude insistence of his bladder that he go to the bathroom and that he go now.

Returning from the communal bathroom he shared with the other tenants of the building (or would have shared had there been any other tenants), Grant glanced out a window and was astonished to see the sun was sinking low into the smokestacks. The machine was still flashing, still humming. Grant knew that it would continue to flash, continue to hum. He knew that it was not going to explode. His faith had been rewarded.

"Good work, men." He congratulated his squadron of research material.

Walking over to the machine, with which he now felt sufficiently aquainted to be able to call it by its correct name: Collimated Command Receiver Unit. Grant gave it a moment of reverent, silent respect. His research had proven that the miracle wasn't so miraculous, but this had not lessened his awe. If anything, it had enhanced it. He had formed a theory as to why the unit had suddenly been activated. His theory was perfectly sound, borne out by his research, and if what he theorized was true, then he stood a chance of making one of the greatest scientific finds of this millennium.

First, Jeffrey Grant must find the courage inside himself to touch the unit. He must type in the correct command sequence to engage the Command Decoder. Just placing his fingertips on the keys of the machine, such an old machine, was a sin of immeasurable scale, but Grant reminded himself that this was for a greater good. This was a Command Receiver Unit. It was now receiving. The manuals described the method by which Grant could ask the unit for the coordinates of the device which was sending the signal which had caused his Collimated Command Receiver Unit to flash its message-received light.

What Grant was about to do was something he had never before done in his life, something he had never considered doing, something that, with all his imagining, he'd never imagined himself doing. Picking up the machine, handling it with extraordinary care and gentleness, Grant rested his trembling fingers on the keyboard.

After a few moments of impotence, when his fingers refused to obey the admittedly weak orders coming from his brain, Grant regained hold of himself. He typed in the requisite series of commands. The screen went dark.

Grant experienced a moment of fear that would have served him well had he ever faced any Corasian fighters.

And then the screen returned to life. Information scrolled rapidly past his wondering gaze. The scrolling stopped.

He didn't understand most of it, but he didn't need to understand most of it. All he needed was a number, and there it was, at the bottom of the screen.

Grant copied the number onto a pad, took the pad to his personal computer, pulled up a stellar map, and typed in the numbers he had on the pad. The computer gave him his answer.

He then placed the unit in the old worn leather container in which it had been originally found, strapped the straps, made certain the unit was still humming. He slid the three disks into a pocket of the leather case. After a moment's consideration on proper wording, he wrote a note stating: "Closed. Indefinitely."

He put on his hat and coat and left the museum—a full half hour ahead of his usual time. Shutting the door, he locked it, slid the key into his pocket, and posted the note on the glass.

This done, he stood a moment on the sidewalk, feeling tense and light-headed and buoyant and nervous and, above all, determined.

"You can do it, Captain," he said to himself. "The admiral has every confidence in you."

Tightening his grip on the machine's case, which was heavy and rather awkward to carry, Grant walked down the sidewalk. In the distance was his home.

He took a right—not a left—at the corner.

He did not go home. He went to an automated bank, removed his entire life savings from his account, indulged in a taxi ride to the nearest spaceport, and rented a spaceplane.

"Destination?" the attendant asked Grant, handing back his pilot's license.

"Pandor," said Jeffrey Grant.

CHAPTER
20

Now the dang robot's a-wearin' my shoes.
I got the robot blues . . .

Anonymous, "Robot Blues"

The robot was no longer confused. It had received an answer to its signal. The Doctor had responded. Directions were given. The robot knew now what it was supposed to do, if not necessarily how to go about doing it.

The robot had been busy during the night it had spent in the packing crate. It had taken the opportunity provided it by the Rescuer to assimilate the situation, determine what had happened in the past, decide how best to proceed in the present. Also, during this time, the robot set its programming to work, studying the unknown speech pattern of the Rescuer in an attempt to open channels of communication, should that eventuality become necessary.

The robot did a complete scan of its own memory banks, starting from the time that memory had been initiated, up to the present. It had a memory of the Doctor, whose commands must be obeyed without question, although the 'bot was free to use its own determination on how best to carry out those commands. It had a memory of its spaceplane—a nonentity, as far as the robot was concerned; a mindless machine that did what it was told to do in a plodding manner, had nothing to say for itself, and was incapable of acting on its own. The robot also had a memory of that spaceplane being shot down.

The Doctor had Enemies. Information on the Enemy had been entered into the robot. Information on evading the Enemy had been entered into the spaceplane.

If approached, retreat.

If fired upon, retreat.

If hit, self-destruct.

At all costs, avoid capture.

The robot had no difficulty with these orders, but the spaceplane did, apparently. The plane had been both approached and fired upon. The spaceplane had been unable to retreat and should have blown up itself and the robot. Destruction had not occurred, with the result that the plane had plummeted down through the atmosphere, ended up by burrowing nose-first into an enormous sand dune. To give the plane credit, it had attempted to self-destruct, but something had gone wrong. The robot did not know this, however, and had, in its report—recorded on the way down—castigated the plane quite severely.

At this point, the robot noted a blip in its memory. Nothing really very serious, rather like a hiccup, but there was definitely a segment of time missing. The robot determined that this blip must have been due to damage sustained in the crash. It had detected a loose connector in its neural pathway circuitry. Logic dictated that the loose connector had been put back into place by the first Rescuer, when that Rescuer found the robot in the storage closet.

As to what the robot had been doing in the storage compartment—that was uncertain. The 'bot's last memory before the blip was of the plane descending at a steep angle, the robot sliding across the deck, the storage closet door flying open, sudden darkness, and nothing.

Until the Rescuers.

In the event that any of the robots ran into trouble, the Doctor had provided them with a "help" signal. The cry for help was not general, it would not bring ships from all over the quadrant to the rescue. The cry was specific, would reach only the Doctor and his team. The robot sent out its call for help as the spaceplane descended.

Then came the slide into the closet, the crash, the momentary blank-out. Then the Rescuer, with repairs.

The robot found it impressive that help arrived so quickly. And it noted, in its report, that haste was probably the reason the Rescuers acted in such a peculiar and illogical manner. The robot also noted, for future reference, that it would be useful if the Rescuers spoke a language which the robot was programmed to understand.

Looking back on its encounter with the Rescuers, the robot could make very little sense out of what had happened. However, since the incident involved humans, this was only to be expected.

Rescuer A had discovered the robot in the closet, repaired the robot, and then, instead of bringing the robot out of the closet, had entered the closet with the robot.

When Rescuer B had arrived on the scene—standing outside the damaged plane and yelling something unintelligible—the robot had started to leave the plane to go to the Rescuer—as it was programmed to do. Rescuer A, for some unknown reason, had attempted to keep the robot inside the closet.

This was illogical. The robot was not going to be able to perform its functions inside the closet. And so it had left. Detaching the arm onto which the Rescuer was holding, the robot had floated through the damaged plane, had reached the open hatch. The robot had confronted Rescuer B, who had then behaved in the most illogical manner thus far recorded.

Rescuer B had screamed and run away.

Really, the Doctor needed to hire better help.

The robot had spoken to Rescuer A, who did not understand. Rescuer A had spoken to the robot, who did not understand. The robot had scanned Rescuer A, discovered it to be a mixture of human parts and machine parts—a cyborg. The robot had set about recording the cyborg's speech, storing it away, analyzing it in order to learn the language.

The Rescuer had been able to communicate his wishes

to the robot by means of gestures. The robot was able to deduce that the Rescuer wanted the 'bot to accompany him. The logic for this move became apparent when the robot saw the storage crate.

Which was where the robot was now.

But not for long.

Safely tucked away inside the storage crate, the robot assumed it would be placed aboard a plane in order that it could, once more, commence with its duties.

The robot was extremely discomfited when it found its crate being deposited in what its scanners revealed to be some sort of storage facility for broken-down machinery!

The robot was willing to give the Rescuer the benefit of the doubt. The Rescuer obviously thought the robot was in need of repair, did not realize that the robot was designed to repair itself. Which reminded the robot—it was missing its #20 arm. It needed to make a note to have the arm replaced. This accomplished, the robot beamed its customary signal to the Doctor. Do I have my orders straight? Am I supposed to return to duty?

Ordinarily the response was immediate. This time, the wait was rather longer and, when the response came, it was extremely weak. Investigation revealed that the signal was emanating from a different portion of the galaxy. The signal was clear, however. The robot was to carry on.

Escaping from the storage crate was easy. The robot selected a tool built into one of its many arms, adjusted a valve, which caused the air pressure inside the compartment to increase. The pressure grew until the lid on the storage container popped loose. Using a second arm, and a levering device, the robot pried the lid of the container open. Activating its air jets, the robot floated out. The 'bot reattached its arm, then closed the lid to the crate. The crate had been really quite comfortable. The robot did not want all these strange-looking machines sitting around the crate to contaminate it.

Once free of the crate, the robot began its search for a suitable transport spaceplane. The robot's spectrum analyzer isolated no less than forty different space-to-tower communications. A launch facility must be nearby.

The robot tucked its twenty arms up inside its head and soared off in the direction of the communications tower of the spacefield.

CHAPTER

21

Grasp the subject, the words will follow.

Marcus Porcius Cato, *Ars Rhetorica*, I

"The topic of this lecture is 'Foreign Object Damage to Spaceplane Engines.' I regret"—Xris paused, repeated himself, with emphasis—"I *truly* regret the fact that Colonel Jatanski, who is an acknowledged authority on this subject and who was supposed to be here today to deliver this lecture, was called away last night to serve at a court-martial proceeding. It has fallen to me to carry on in the colonel's absence. I'll . . . do the best I can," Xris concluded, and, because he'd moved his head too close to the antiquated mike, the last statement was lost in ear-piercing feedback.

"Oh, sorry."

Xris stepped back hastily from the mike, nearly fell off the rostrum. He caught himself by grasping hold of the podium. In the audience, Tess ducked her head, put her hand over her mouth to smother her laughter. Xris recalled what she'd said yesterday about imagining the audience completely naked. Contrary to popular opinion, this did nothing to help his composure.

Unfortunately for Xris, the turnout for the lecture was quite good. He'd been nursing a secret hope that no one would show up. He couldn't understand why anyone would want to attend who wasn't ordered to do so. A few whispered words exchanged with Tess prior to the speech gave him the explanation.

"Life is so boring on Pandor that any break in the routine, even a speech on foreigners stuck in spaceplane engines"—she had grinned at him—"is a welcome change! I predict a sellout crowd."

"Wonderful," Xris had muttered. "You know what I said yesterday about fainting during show-and-tell, that wasn't exactly the truth. I didn't faint. I threw up."

"You're not joking, are you?" Tess had regarded him in concern. "You really hate this. It'll be over soon. I'll buy you a drink later."

"After last night, I may never drink again. You made it back okay? The MPs didn't stop you?"

"No, but then they weren't trying real hard. How about you?"

"They had me surrounded," Xris had told her. "Brought me in at gunpoint. I asked to be locked up in the brig for life, but they said no, my sentence was to give a speech."

Tess had laughed, kissed him lightly on the cheek "for luck," and had gone to sit next to her roommates.

The small auditorium held about two hundred people and, as Tess had predicted, it was practically a sellout. Someone in back shut the doors leading into the auditorium. The crowd settled down, if not to enjoy the speech, at least to find some amusement in the discomfiture of the speaker.

Xris opened his mouth. His voice cracked. He coughed, cleared his throat, and looked around nervously. "If I could ... uh ... have a glass of water?"

Colonel Strebbins himself rose from the seats in the front row to pour Xris a drink, placed it next to him on the podium. He patted Xris on the back, said gently "You're doing fine, Captain," and resumed his seat.

"Thank you, sir," Xris mumbled. He looked down at Jamil's notes, which now appeared to have been written in hieroglyphs. He could make nothing of them.

Lifting his head, he looked again out into the audience and was immediately sorry he'd done so. His panicked thoughts flitted to the time he'd gone behind enemy lines, sneaked into a Corasian "meat locker" to rescue his estranged wife. He was being hunted by the deadly, flesh-devouring aliens. Breaking out of their robotic cases, the fiery orange blobs oozed across the floor toward him. He fired at them, but they kept coming. . . .

Xris stared into the flesh-devouring eyes of his audience and would have liked to do now what he had done then.

Run. Run like hell.

Colonel Strebbins gave a polite cough. "Anytime you're ready, Captain."

Xris gulped down more water, sucked in a breath, activated the holographic display, and launched into his speech.

"Er, um, as you well know, the delicate Clormin Turbocharged Hyper Velocity Spaceplane Engine used on the lighter spaceplanes can be a difficult maintenance job. Even when working correctly, the engine can act up for a variety of reasons. Now let's imagine . . ."

Xris paused, fumbled with the controls, and finally brought up the first holograph—a beautiful human female clad in the uniform of a maintenance worker, holding a soft-drink can. A Dirk fighter was warming up in the background.

"Let's imagine," Xris continued, "what would happen if our corporal here were to let go of that Coke can. . . ."

Xris shifted to the next holographic image, which showed the same Dirk fighter, smoke billowing out the engine port, and the beautiful woman running for her life. The audience was highly amused, and someone in the back gave the holographic woman a cheer to spur her on.

Colonel Strebbins turned, glared at the unknown offender. The audience quieted.

Xris lost his place. By the time he found it, he had decided that the best thing he could do was get this over with as quickly as possible.

"Just imagine what a plasma retainer screw or . . ."

Proceeding at a rapid pace, without any real idea of what he was saying, he tried, at all cost, to avoid looking at his audience. He kept his gaze fixed on his notes in order not to lose his place again. But the sound of the door opening at the back of the auditorium drew his attention. A man in uniform was attempting to sneak in quietly.

The door shut behind the man. Xris went back to his notes. Suddenly he realized who the man was. Xris looked up in astonishment. What he had been going to say dribbled away to an incoherent burble.

Dr. Bill Quong, wearing the uniform of any Army medical officer, attaché case in hand, was seating himself in the back row. Quong might have made some hand sign to Xris, but at that moment Colonel Strebbins, attracted by the sound of the door opening, again whipped around to glare at whoever was interrupting.

Seeing a strange medical officer, Strebbins stared, turned to his aide, whispered something.

The aide glanced back, spotted Quong, who gave a slight nod of apology and subsided into a seat. Shrugging, the aide turned back to the colonel, who shrugged and turned back to Xris.

Xris had no idea what Quong was doing here. Why had he come? How had he known that the job had gone sour? Xris wasn't at all sure he was glad to see him. The fewer of them involved in this mess, the better.

The audience began to stir restlessly. Xris tried to remember where he'd left off, didn't have a clue. In attempting to bring up the next holograph image, he accidentally shut off the machine and had no idea how to start it again. Choosing a place in the notes that looked as good as any, he began to speak. By the time he'd reached the third sentence, he realized he was repeating himself. At that point, it didn't matter. He floundered on.

"Uh, oh, yes, sorry, I said that already. Yes. Um, now, about those pesky turbine blades twirling around to keep the reactor core, um, well, cool, and then this object comes hurtling in, sucked in by the air intake, and striking the blades. Catastrophic results would occur. The object might glance off the blades and impact the plasma bottle, causing . . ."

The door opened again. Xris continued talking during this second interruption, fighting gamely to retain his hold on his audience. He had no idea what he was say-

ing, but it didn't matter, because no one was listening to
him. The colonel had again turned to see who was entering late and this time his stare attracted the attention of
everyone in the room.

An excessively tall and extremely thin humanoid,
whose skin had assumed the same gray shade as his uniform, stood just inside the door. Tycho spotted Quong,
pretended not to see him, took a seat at the aisle. The
people next to him immediately moved a seat or two
away. Not because they were prejudiced against aliens,
but because Tycho wore the gray uniform of the branch
of the military known as Unconventional Warfare. The
insignia on his shirt identified him as a SyOps with
BCW—Biological and Chemical Warfare.

BCWs were notoriously unpopular, being generally
suspected of harboring all sorts of deadly viruses.

Tycho folded his long body into the chair, which was
not made for "chameleons," and sat, arms and legs
akimbo, his knees practically up to his shoulders.

"What the hell is *he* doing here?" Colonel Strebbins
demanded of his aide in a voice that was meant to be
low but—due to the excellent acoustics—carried
throughout the auditorium.

"Possibly something to do with contamination . . . the
crash site . . ." his aide was heard to respond.

Xris plunged loudly forward. "And, um, then there is
always the problem of indigenous life acting as foreign
objects being ingested into the intake of a spaceplane.
One small sakira lizard sleeping in the engine cowling
could cause . . ."

Tess was gazing at him. She wasn't smiling; she looked
. . . bemused.

Xris was feeling bemused himself. Fortunately, due to
unintentionally cutting out three paragraphs, he had arrived at the halfway point. The end in sight, he was
racing on to the finish when he heard several members
of the audience start to snicker. A faint scent, as of orange blossoms, wafted through the air.

Xris jerked his head up. The door at the rear remained shut. No one had walked in. But the audience

was now chuckling. People pointed to something happening on the stage behind Xris.

Colonel Strebbins, eyes bulging, gaped.

Xris turned to look over his shoulder.

Raoul was mincing across the stage on tiptoe. Seeing himself noticed, he halted, waved a delicate hand. "Don't mind me."

"Who the devil are you?" Strebbins demanded.

"Ah, Colonel, darling." Raoul advanced to the front of the stage. He was dressed in a uniform that, by its tailored cut and elegant material, was obviously not Army issue. His hat sat at a jaunty and strictly nonregulation angle on his head. His salute, accompanied by a wiggle of his hips, brought down the house.

"Corporal de Beausoleil. Morale Troops. Here for next week's show. Just thought I'd sneak a peek at the stage. I had no idea anyone was in here. Silly me! Carry on, Captain," he said to Xris. "So sorry to interrupt. Bye."

With a kiss of his hand, he left the stage, to the accompaniment of whistles and cheers. Colonel Strebbins's aide rose to his feet and turned to face the crowd, which suddenly fell silent.

Xris sought refuge in another glass of water. He had seen, in the wings, the Little One peering at him from beneath the fedora. Xris opened his mouth when the door at the rear of the auditorium banged open.

At this point, Xris wouldn't have been surprised if His Majesty the King had entered. The sight of Harry Luck, wearing a Naval pilot's flight suit, his helmet dangling by a strap from his hand, his flight suit torn and ripped, a trickle of blood running down his face, didn't phase Xris in the least.

Harry dashed in, saw Xris, saw the audience—every one of whom had turned at the sound of the door banging to stare at this new arrival.

Harry's jaw sagged; his mouth fell open. He flushed a deep and unhealthy shade of red. Dr. Quong was on his feet, taking charge of the situation. Grasping Harry firmly by the arm, the doctor led the big man to a seat, shoved him into it.

"Even the Navy showed up to hear this speech," Strebbins said, awed.

The audience was having a hard time settling back down. Judging by their grins, this was the most fun they'd experienced in a year. Under cover of the whispers, coughs, and muffled laughter, Dr. Quong frowned, leaned over to Harry, said something on the order of "What the devil do you think you're doing?"

Harry, looking aggrieved, responded. Xris knew exactly what the big man was saying.

"But I heard Xris was in trouble . . ."

Xris pitched out two pages of notes, found the ending, delivered it.

"And, in conclusion, I just want to apologize for the fact that, due to the lack of time, I am unable to show you the exhibits I brought with me. I leave you with this important reminder: FOD, or Foreign Object Damage, cannot only kill you, it can ruin an otherwise clean maintenance record!"

The audience, in a good humor, gave Xris a rousing round of applause. Most even remained in their chairs a few extra seconds, obviously hoping for more.

The colonel ascended the stage, congratulated Xris on a fine job, shook his hand. "Sorry about the interruptions," the colonel said. "I had no idea this topic would prove so popular!"

"Me either, sir," Xris said with heartfelt sincerity.

He tried to catch Quong's eye, but the Doc was deep in a low-voiced conversation with Harry. Tycho was on his feet, moving to the back of the auditorium. Xris had no idea where Raoul and the Little One had gone, though obviously not far. He could still smell orange blossoms.

"We'll have you back next year," the colonel promised.

Turning on his heel, he walked up the aisle, headed for the door. The other officers filed out behind him. The enlisted personnel were on their feet, waiting their turn. Xris cast a quick look about for Tess, but couldn't find her.

The colonel had just reached the back of the auditorium when the door opened yet again.

Jamil walked in.

Xris didn't know whether to kiss him or slug him.

"Colonel Jatanski!" Colonel Strebbins was enthusiastic. "You just missed it. Captain Kergonan did a fine job. A fine job. I guess the court-martial proceedings were pretty rough, huh? You don't look as if you'd slept much. You can tell me all about it at dinner."

Jamil mumbled something unintelligible. The colonel took a close look at the new arrivals. Dr. Quong and Tycho both saluted smartly. Harry saluted, but only after Quong elbowed him in the ribs.

The colonel made a short speech of welcome, walked out.

Jamil, carrying a metal briefcase, shoved his way through the departing audience, continued down the aisle. Handsome, suave, urbane, Jamil invariably looked as if he'd just stepped through the doors of a modeling agency. Now he looked as if he'd just stepped through the gates of hell. His handsome features were soft and blurred from fatigue, his eyes were bloodshot. His uniform was rumpled and sweat-stained. He didn't see Tycho, though he walked right past him; didn't notice Quong and Harry.

Xris waited, tense and nervous, beside the podium. Whatever had gone wrong had obviously gone wrong big-time. The auditorium was emptying out. Quong, Harry, and Tycho lingered behind, watching for a sign from Xris, who—not knowing what was going on—decided to leave them where they were, for the present.

He would have given anything for a twist now, was wondering if he might not be able to slip one into his mouth when he felt something cold and hard press into the small of his back.

"This is a .10 decawatt lasgun," said a voice.

Xris went rigid.

"Continue to act naturally, Captain," the voice went on. "Keep your hands where I can see them. You and your friends are going to join me for a nice, quiet little chat. But first you're going to answer one question."

Tess jabbed Xris painfully in the back with the gun. "What the hell have you done with the robot?"

CHAPTER
22

The past is but the beginning of a beginning and all
that is and has been is but the twilight of the
dawn.

H. G. Wells, *The Discovery of the Future*

"All right," said Xris, keeping his hands in plain sight,
"I think it's about time someone tells me just what
the hell is going on!"

"Isn't that a coincidence," Tess said coolly, making
certain he continued to feel the pressure of the gun in
his back. "I was thinking the same thing. We'll wait right
here for those men of yours to come up to be introduced. Oh, and don't worry about your pretty boy and
his funny little friend. I have them tied up at the back
of the stage."

"What men? What pretty boy?" Xris asked in-
nocently.

"Nice try, Captain. I've got files on all of you."

The last of the base personnel were leaving the auditorium. Xris motioned. Harry, Quong, and Tycho started
to walk down the aisle toward the stage.

Jamil arrived first. He looked at Tess, standing behind
and to one side of Xris, and put on a charming smile,
only slightly frayed around the edges. "Captain Strauss.
Good to see you again. If you would excuse us, Captain,
I'd like to talk to Captain Kergonan—"

"Forget it," Xris said laconically. "She's got files on
all of us. Not to mention a gun in my back."

Jamil dropped the smile. He eyed Tess. "She does, huh?"

"Yes," Xris said, shrugging. "Though I don't really think she'd use it."

Jamil grunted. "Yeah, well, think again. She's not regular Army. She's NI. Naval Intel. You're one of Dixter's people, aren't you, Strauss?"

"That's right," Tess returned crisply. "The first move you make I don't like and I'll shoot. Nothing personal, Xris," she added, her voice softening. "I had a lot of fun last night."

"Yeah, me, too," Xris said bitterly. "For someone who was set up, I had a great time!"

Tess shifted her attention to Jamil. "I take it you just came back from your 'briefing' on board the *King James*."

Jamil nodded, wary. "My orders are to grab the robot and be on the first spaceplane out. Take it straight to Sakuta."

"And, of course, that's what you were planning to do," Tess said, her lip curling.

"Certainly!" Jamil returned, scowling.

"Sure you were. You called for all this backup to help you carry the 'bot to the staff car. I think you're trying to double-cross us. I think you're going to take off with the 'bot yourselves. Make a tidy profit putting it up on the open market."

"Look, lady," Jamil growled, "after what I found out about that 'bot, the only thing I want to do is fling it out the air lock! As for calling in the team, how could I? I've been on that mother of a command cruiser with two trigger-happy Marines breathing down my neck the entire time."

"And I'd like to remind everyone that I still don't know what's going on!" Xris said savagely. "Why would *I* call in the team?"

"Because you want the robot," Tess returned.

"I don't even like the damn robot! It's got eyes. It gives me the creeps. Look," Xris said, "there's a real easy way to solve this." He glanced over his shoulder at Tess. "You know everyone from our files, so that will save long introductions. Tycho, Harry Luck, Dr. Bill Quong.

"Doc," Xris continued, as the rest of the team gathered around him, "this woman, who is currently holding a gun to my back, would like to know who told you to come here and why."

Dr. Quong raised an eyebrow. "I am with the Army Medical Corp. I was told to report—"

Jamil shook his head. "On the level, Doc. She has files."

"Oh. I see." Dr. Quong made Tess a formal bow. "I was told to report to the military base on Pandor by a colleague of mine, Raoul de Beausoleil."

"Raoul called me, too, Xris," Harry offered. "He said you were in some kind of trouble. I crashed my plane getting here to rescue you."

"You crashed the plane," Xris repeated. He knew the answer, but he asked the question anyway. "Why?"

"I had to, Xris. They weren't going to let me land."

Xris sighed, glanced at Tycho. "What about you?"

"I spoke to Raoul. He stated that there was an emergency and we were to meet here on the Army base on Pandor."

"Now, I wonder why Raoul—" Xris realized suddenly that they were minus one team member. "Darlene! Something's happened to Darlene!" Forgetting about the gun, he started to turn, only to feel the barrel gouge him painfully in the ribs. He held still, but he was rapidly losing patience. "Look, Captain Strauss, the only way to clear this up is to talk to Raoul."

Tess hesitated, then said, "Come on. Back of the stage. The four of you"—she motioned to Quong, Harry, Jamil, and Tycho—"first. Remember that I have the gun."

Tycho gave Xris a look that said as plainly as if he'd spoken through his translator. *There are five of us. We can take her out.*

Xris shook his head emphatically. The agents for NI— Naval Intelligence—were highly trained and dedicated to their work. Tess meant what she said; she'd kill him without hesitation. And then, of course, she'd be the next to die. If everyone kept cool, they might all get out of this alive.

"Start walking," Tess ordered. "And you still haven't answered my question about the robot."

"It's someplace safe," Xris said.

"Where?" Tess demanded.

Xris shrugged. "After all, Captain, how the hell do I know I can trust *you*? I don't suppose you have any identification on you. Or maybe you could kiss me again. Then I'll tell you all my secrets."

"Just keep walking, Captain."

Tess herded them all to the rear of the stage. Parting the back curtains, they found Raoul seated in chair, his wrists and ankles locked in disrupters, a gag in his mouth. The Little One crouched on the floor beside his friend. Disrupters were too big to fit on the small wrists and ankles. His hands and feet were tied with what appeared to be nylon stockings.

Dr. Quong, on Tess's command, removed the gag from Raoul's mouth, the disrupters from his hands and feet. Quong untied the Little One.

Raoul drew in a deep breath, let it out in an indignant explosion. He pointed a quivering finger at Tess. "She wiped off my lipstick!"

"She's read your file," Xris said grimly.

"Oh." Raoul thought this over, was considerably relieved. "I'm glad it's that. I thought perhaps she was making some sort of fashion statement. Which, considering her choice of—"

"Can it!" Xris said irritably. "In case you haven't noticed, she's holding a gun on me!"

"Oh, I noticed," Raoul said, taking a mirror from his handbag and attempting to assess the damage. "I thought perhaps you were enjoying it."

"Where's Darlene?" Xris asked nervously.

Raoul glanced sidelong at Tess. His eyelashes fluttered. "She decided to take a pleasure cruise. I believe she's heading for Moana."

"You let her go? By herself?" Xris was furious.

Raoul looked up at Xris. The Loti's eyes widened. "I am sorry, Xris Cyborg. I did not realize that Darlene was my prisoner. She was not having fun on Adonia and so I suggested that she try a pleasure cruise. I would have accompanied her, but at the time I was somewhat occupied."

"She's all right?" Xris asked, tensely.

"She's all right," Raoul said, his voice quiet.

Xris relaxed. He wasn't being told the whole story, but he didn't dare ask for more, not with an NI agent listening in. Tess was suspicious as it was.

"Who is this Darlene?" Tess asked.

"What's the matter?" Xris retorted. "Don't you have a file on her, too?"

"I'm asking the questions." Tess smiled at Raoul. "Who told you to come to this base, Adonian?"

Raoul gave her a charming smile. "I guess that would be me."

"You told yourself."

"I suppose I must have. I told everyone else. That meant I was next in line. May I touch up my lipstick?"

Tess shook her head.

Raoul sighed bleakly. Looking at himself in the mirror, he shuddered and snapped the compact shut.

"All right," Tess continued, "why did you tell yourself to assemble the team here?"

"We thought that perhaps Xris Cyborg might be in trouble." Raoul glanced at the Little One, who nodded. "Considering that Professor Sakuta was not what he claimed to be. And he was so perfectly beautiful, too." Raoul sighed again. "Beauty is as beauty does, however."

"What's this? How could he be someone else?" Xris asked, puzzled. "The Little One read Sakuta's mind. The Little One told me—"

"Wait a minute," Tess said. "As you say, I have files. The Little One. He's supposedly the telepath?"

"He is a telepath, Captain," Xris said.

"It comes with age to certain members of his race," Dr. Quong added didactically. "I am writing a paper on the subject, which I plan to present at the next Conference of Surgeons. If you would be interested in reading it, I could make a copy available—"

"Yes, I would be," Tess said softly. She frowned, stared intently at the Little One, who stared just as intently back at her.

"Anyone can claim to be a telepath," she said finally. "Let's see how good he is. He couldn't have heard us talking out front. What organization do I work for?"

The Little One tilted his head back, to see her better from beneath the brim of the fedora. Then, making a snorting sound, he rubbed his hands together and, folding his short arms across his chest, he turned his back on her.

Raoul nodded in approval. "The Little One says that he doesn't need to prove his talents to anyone, particularly a woman with little or no fashion sense. That last bit," Raoul added unnecessarily, "was mine."

"Uh-huh." Tess smiled wryly. "Go on with your story, then, Adonian. Your friend, the telepath"—she lifted an eyebrow—"was supposed to read Sakuta's mind. And he failed."

"It was not his fault!" Raoul rushed to the defense, put his arm protectively around the Little One. "You cannot blame him! Sakuta used a telepathic scrambler on him."

"Oh, a telepathic scrambler." Tess rolled her eyes.

"There are such devices," Dr. Quong stated. "They use a high-frequency resonator that produces alpha waves. The mind targeted wanders but does not notice anything wrong. As it detects an anomaly or error, another random alpha wave interrupts it, and so on."

Tess shook her head, unconvinced.

The Little One, when he thought the woman wasn't looking, jerked his head toward Xris, sniggered, reached out a small hand, and made a swipe at Raoul's upper arm. Raoul's lashes fluttered; a side of his lipstick-smudged mouth twitched. He nudged the Little One in the ribs with an elbow.

Xris figured he could guess what that charade was all about. He'd have a talk with those two later.

"Let's say that Sakuta *did* use a telepathic scrambler." Xris looked at Tess, who shrugged. "If that's true, this is finally beginning to come into focus. This whole job is a setup. Sakuta hires us to steal this 'bot, tells us it's worthless except to a museum. And we fall for it." Xris reached for his pocket, took out a twist. He didn't give a damn who saw him anymore. He put the twist in his mouth, bit down on it, hard. "He played us for suckers."

Xris was silent, chewing. Then he demanded, "All right. Who the hell is Professor Sakuta?"

"His real name is Nick Harsch," Tess answered.

"According to Tess, Harsch's a Corasian agent, Xris," Jamil finished.

"Son of a bitch," Xris said, soft, bitter.

"I didn't know who he was," Raoul stated. "But I reasoned that anyone who would use a telepathic scrambler was doing so only because he desired to hide his thoughts. And if one is hiding one's thoughts, one must be thinking bad things. Bad thoughts in such a lovely head."

"Son of a bitch," Xris said again. "And I fell for it. One of the oldest con jobs in history. All so damn obvious! The museum offices are being renovated, so everyone takes the week off. Sakuta and his people show up to do the work. They slap paint on the walls, no one asks questions. One afternoon, Sakuta cleans the paint off his hands, dresses up in a suit and tie, and meets with us for an hour or so, gets rid of us, goes back to painting. The job's done. Everyone goes home. Son of a bitch."

"You're saying that's what happened?" Tess sounded skeptical.

"Look, Captain, you can contact the Lord Admiralty," Jamil offered irritably. "They'll tell you we're acting on Dixter's orders."

"I've been in contact with the Lord Admiral," Tess returned. "You and Xris . . . yes, you have your orders." She waved her hand. "It's the rest of the floor show I wasn't expecting. But, just to prove we're all on the same side, tell me this. Where is the robot?"

"In a crate in the maintenance shed," Xris said. "For repair."

Tess eyed him, smiled. "I think you're telling the truth."

"I don't much give a damn what you think, sister," Xris returned. "Go check it out, if you don't believe me."

Tess regarded him intently. Her expression softened. She lowered the gun, tucked it into the holster on her belt. "Don't beat yourself up, Xris. Nick Harsch is slick. You're not the first person he's fooled. If it's any comfort, you've managed to come closer to him than any of *our* people."

Xris snorted. "Just tell me what the devil's going on. What does a Corasian agent want with an antique robot?"

Tess glanced around.

They stood in the wings to the left of the stage. Anyone approaching would have to climb the stairs leading up to the stage from the side. The back of the stage was accessible only by a door leading into the wings.

"This is as good a place to talk as any." Tess touched a button, lowered the stage curtains. "We're not likely to be interrupted here. You'll find more chairs in the back. I think they're props."

Raoul cast himself on a love seat, hid his lipstick-smeared face in his arms. The Little One stood by his friend, patted his shoulder in a conciliatory manner. The rest of the team took their seats in the semidarkness.

Xris drew out another twist. "This robot must be pretty damn important."

Tess drew in a deep breath, let it out with her words. "It is. There's a possibility that it's a Lane-laying robot. And if it is, it will be the first one we've ever found with all its programming and memory intact."

Harry's eyes widened. He gave a low whistle. "I'll be swizzled," he said, awed.

Quong evinced interest by sitting up straighter in his chair. "It is in working condition?"

"We think so," Tess replied cautiously. "We can't be certain until we run tests on it—"

"It works," Xris stated. "At least it lights up and talks. And it's mobile. And it may or may not lay lanes. What does that mean? It works in a bowling alley? I still don't get it."

"Space Lanes, Xris," Harry said, eager, excited. "We studied about these robots in school. I did a report on them in sixth grade. I got an A. Hey, I think I've still got the report back home. I could ask my mom to send it—"

"How is your mother?" inquired Quong.

"Oh, she's fine. She sends her best."

"A very gracious lady," Raoul murmured, his voice muffled in his arms.

"Yes, our best to Mrs. Luck," Xris said through clenched teeth. "Now, if we could return to business? Fine. Now that you mention it, I do remember hearing in physics class something about Lane-laying robots. They built the hyperspace Lanes, or some such thing."

"Yes, indeed," said Tess. "And if this robot is, in fact, one of those very same robots, and is in working condition, then this discovery is of monumental importance. And it could be very dangerous if it fell into the wrong hands."

"Why? I admit it would be interesting from a scientific standpoint. A real museum piece, but—"

"It's like this, Xris," Tess explained. "Back in the early days of space travel, about the time of the Black Earth wars and the ecological disaster which followed, these robots—or rather, the scientist who created them—"

"Professor Colin Lasairion," Harry interjected, proud of his knowledge. "He discovered how to warp space in order to form the hyperspace Lanes that let us move through space but not time. That was always the main problem with faster-than-light travel. Professor Lasairion was of Irish descent and he—"

"Save it for the term paper," Xris snapped. "Go on, Captain Strauss. The short form."

"The short form is Tess," she said.

"I meant about the robot."

"Oh, that. Well, Pilot Luck is right," Tess continued, "Professor Lasairion built over one hundred of these Lane-laying robots, sent them out in unmanned spaceplanes to 'build' the Lanes. For forty years, the robots traveled throughout the galaxy, using the Lanes they'd built in the beginning to reach other Lanes, expanding ever outward. The professor kept an enormous and complex map of all the Lanes, ensuring that no Lane would intersect with another or travel too close to another because, of course, any ship moving that fast colliding with another ship . . ."

She shrugged. "They'd both be vaporized. The professor also developed the scanning devices that ascertain whether or not a Lane is clear before a ship makes the Jump into it. Professor Lasairion made it possible for thousands to flee a dying Earth, find new lives on new worlds in outer space."

"Throw the man a fish," Xris stated. "He was a genius and now we're left with an old robot. I still don't see what makes this 'bot valuable—outside of the science fair at Harry's grade school."

"Lasairion was a genius. He was ahead of his time," Tess said gravely. "So far ahead, in fact, that no one since has ever been able to duplicate his work."

"I can't believe you don't know about this, Xris!" Harry was shocked. "Didn't you ever wonder why no one's ever built any new space Lanes?"

"Yeah," Xris said, taking out another twist. "I lay awake nights worrying about it."

"That is because you are not a pilot, my friend," Dr. Quong said. "Or a merchant in one of the newly emerging planets that are light-years away from the Lanes. If you were, you would know that the need for more Lanes is critical. This robot could provide us with the basics scientists could use in order to duplicate the professor's work. I congratulate the NI, Captain," he added, making Tess a small bow. "This was excellent detective work."

"We've been searching for such a robot for years," she said. "Every time an ancient crash site is uncovered, we always hope that this will be the site to contain one of the Lane-lying robots—one that either crashed or was shot down—"

"Shot down?" Xris halted her story. "You said the planes were unmanned. Someone went around shooting down Lane-laying robots? What for? Some crazed 'bot-hater?"

"The professor had enemies. A *lot* of enemies. Religious fanatics, who believed that man was not meant to leave Earth, travel among the stars. Despots and dictators, criminals and corporations, who wanted the professor to work for them, give them control over the Lanes. One or more of these groups tried at various times to buy him. They offered him fabulous amounts of money. He accepted only public funding. He allowed no one government or person or corporation to control the Lanes. The Lanes were free for anyone to enter; they were dedicated to the service of mankind and, later, to other races living in the galaxy.

"When it was clear that the professor couldn't be bought, someone tried to kill him.

"It was only by a stroke of luck that the professor escaped his assassin. He fled Earth, sought refuge on an unknown planet. His enemies couldn't find him, but they could find the robots. They tried to capture the robots, in order to study them, emulate them. The robots were programmed to destroy themselves if capture appeared imminent. Many of them did so, which is why they are so rare and valuable.

"When the professor died—of natural causes, I'm happy to say—his family, acting on his orders, retrieved those robots that were left and destroyed them. The family trashed all his notes and files, making it impossible for anyone to duplicate his research."

"What about that rumor that one of his children stole some of the equipment and sold it?" Quong asked.

"That was never verified," Tess answered. "I tend to doubt it. The equipment would have been useless to anyone who didn't have the background information on how to operate it. Why waste your money?"

Quong nodded in understanding.

"I would have," Harry said in a low voice. "Just to have something that was once touched by Professor Lasairion."

Tess smiled. "Yes, me, too. You can imagine our excitement when this ancient spaceplane actually proved to be one of those used by the professor in his work. A Pandoran NI operative was able to verify the fact that a robot was inside the wreckage and that the robot was intact and, apparently, in working condition."

Dr. Quong's expression altered. No much. Probably no one else noticed. But Xris had been watching Quong closely, to see his reaction to Tess's words. Something was eating the Doc now, to judge by the narrowing eyes, the deepening frown line between the brows. Xris made a mental note to talk to Quong somewhere in private.

"We immediately went to work, through diplomatic channels, to recover the robot," Tess was continuing. "The Pandoran government was a pain. We thought that they were just being reactionary. They're always difficult to deal with. They have an overinflated view of their own importance. They're convinced that there is some giant conspiracy at work in the galaxy. That the king and his ministers do nothing all day long but plot to seize Pandor. If it wasn't for its strategic location near the Void and the Corasians—"

Xris interrupted, "Save it for *your* thesis, Captain."

Tess glanced at him, looked away. "Sorry. I get a bit carried away," she said coolly. "Suffice it to say the Pandoran government used every legal manuever in the book to keep us from taking the robot."

"Maybe they weren't being difficult just to be difficult," Xris suggested. "Maybe they were being paid to be difficult."

"By Nick Harsch, you mean. Yes." Tess nodded gravely. "Yes, that's what we now believe. We thought we kept the lid on—"

"He did his homework," Tcyho said. "Like friend Harry here."

"He did his homework, all right. Sakuta—I mean Harsch—told me he had an informant on Pandor," Xris said. "He provided me with detailed information on the 'bot. Either he's got someone on his payroll or he came to take a look at it himself."

"However he found out about it, he found out. And we found out that he found out." Tess spread her hands. "Don't you see? This was our chance. We've been trying for a long time to catch Nick Harsch. We know he has sold information, weapons, and technology to the Corasians.

"The Corasians have used his information to launch attacks on the outer systems. Harsch has been responsible for the deaths of hundreds of thousands. I think you all know how horribly those people died, too," Tess added somberly.

"I saw Chico die," Harry said. "They ate him. Started from the feet up. He—"

Xris interrupted, not liking to think about Chico. Xris had been the one forced to put his friend out of his misery. "So you figured that when Harsch showed up to steal the 'bot, you'd nab him. That's why NI posted you here."

"A little more complicated than that, but something like that, yes. To be honest, I figured one of you"— Tess's gaze went from Jamil to Xris—"for Harsch."

"You don't know what he looks like?"

Tess shook her head. "We know very little about him at all. He's good, really good. That's why we decided to use the robot as bait. We figured that this was so important, he'd come himself. We were wrong. Your photos were picked up on security cams when you landed, sent to the Admiralty. They spotted you immediately. I believe the Lord Admiral's response was, 'Oh, shit! Aren't we in enough trouble?' "

"Nice to know we're appreciated," Xris growled.

"At that point," Tess continued, "it was either have you both arrested and locked up or use you to get to Harsch."

"You pick up Jamil and haul him off on some phony court-martial scam—"

"—to meet with Dixter," Jamil said. "That's where I've been for the last twelve hours."

Xris cast his friend an interrogative glance.

Jamil nodded. "Yeah, she's telling it straight. At least, she's telling it the same as the Lord Admiral's adjutant told me. We deliver the robot as planned—with one exception. This." Jamil reached into the metal briefcase, brought forth a small object that looked rather like an ordinary writing pen, except that it had magnetic grapples at both ends. He held it up. "Tracking device. We insert this in the robot's innards. The device leads the NI to Harsch."

"Our orders are—"

"Deliver the robot and collect our payment. That's it. The tracking device"—Jamil slid it back into the case—"does the rest."

Xris snorted. "Who's the bright person thought this one up? What happens if Harsch decides to run a scan on the 'bot? He finds out it's wired. The man is understandably upset and, to even things out, he blows our heads off! Has NI considered this little possibility? Or don't they give a damn?"

Tess was attempting to be patient. "It would take a very sophisticated scanner to detect the tracking device. And I doubt if he's going to have such fancy equipment with him. Where are you supposed to rendezvous?"

Xris muttered something.

Tess leaned forward. "What was that?"

"Hell's Outpost on the frontier. Near the Void."

"Near the Corasians," Tess said, exasperated. "And didn't you think this was a strange place for a rendezvous with a professor?"

"I was the one who suggested it," Xris snapped. "How the hell was I supposed to know any different?" He shook his head. "I'm still not keen on this. What happens if we refuse?"

"Go to jail," Jamil said. He flicked a glance at Tess, looked back at Xris. "Go directly to jail. After we stand trial, of course. For the abduction of Major Darlene Mohini."

Raoul lifted his head, stared. The Little One shivered all over. Harry's forehead creased in puzzlement.

"But Darlene isn't—"

"Ahem!" Xris coughed loudly, interrupted.

"Uh? Oh." Harry blinked. "I get it." And he scratched his head.

"Quite the nice little setup," Xris said quietly. "What did you tell the Admiralty?"

"To go play with themselves." Jamil was blunt. "No offense, ma'am," he added, his brow dark, "but I don't like threats. I told them we'd take the job, but we do it for our own reasons, on our own terms. *Not* because we're being blackmailed."

"Good man." Xris smiled, took out a twist. He glanced at Tess. "What happens if that fancy gadget of yours doesn't work? Suppose you lose track of the 'bot or Harsch or both?"

"Oh, did I forget to mention?" Jamil was grim. "The tracking device is also a remote-controlled bomb." He patted the briefcase. "Touch a button in here and *boom*."

"We don't want to destroy the robot, of course," Tess said. "We'll do everything possible to keep it intact."

"And us along with it, I hope," Xris said dryly.

Tess nodded absently. "But we're prepared to destroy it, rather than allow the robot to fall into enemy hands."

In Xris's view, a lot of things weren't adding up. He tried an experimental question, waited to see the reaction.

"Seems to me that the Navy's making a hell of a sacrifice just to take out one Corasian agent. *If* this robot's all you say it is."

Xris wasn't watching Tess. He had his eyes on Quong.

The Doc lifted his hand and rubbed the side of his nose.

I was right, Xris thought. Something smells. And it isn't Raoul's perfume.

Quong suddenly began to cough. He coughed until he was red in the face. Harry reached around, gave him a sound slap on the back.

The doctor glared at him. "What are you trying to do?" he demanded, in between hacks. "Dislocate my spine?" Choking, he turned to Tess. "Excuse me, ma'am." He jumped to his feet, headed for a drinking fountain at the far end of the theater.

"Why don't you build a fake robot?" Harry asked. "Pull the old switcheroo."

"We considered trying to replicate the robot," Tess answered, "but it's just not possible. Some of the materials—metal alloys, for example—used in that 'bot can't be re-created today. Harsch is intelligent. One look would tell him he'd been double-crossed. As for the robot, NI intends to retrieve all the information stored inside the 'bot first, before you take it to Harsch. The information is what's most important. Not the robot itself. I have with me all the equipment necessary to download . . ."

She continued talking, but Xris had stopped listening—to her, at least. Quong's voice was in Xris's ear, coming over the commlink that was part of the cyborg's inner workings.

"She is not telling us the truth, my friend. The robot would be worthless to the Corasians and my guess is that she knows it. Even if the 'bot is in working condition, it would not be able to perform its function of laying space Lanes. Professor Lasairion equipped all his 'bots with fail-safe devices. Before the robot could go ahead and lay a space Lane, the professor sent the robot a confirmation signal. If it did not receive confirmation, it would not lay the Lane."

"Uh-huh," Xris said aloud, as if talking to Tess. "Thanks. That clears a lot up."

He could hear the sound of Quong noisily gulping water. The doctor, his coughing fit eased, returned to the stage.

So, reasoned Xris. This whole scheme is a bait to trap Harsch. The Navy makes a big commotion over this 'bot, stirs up the political hornets, attracts Harsch's attention. He figures there's something to this, sends in his agent, who confirms that this robot must be highly valuable because the Navy is making such a fuss over it—top-level security, all that. When, in fact, the blasted 'bot couldn't lay a Lane if its life depended on it.

"As for killing Harsch," Tess was saying, "don't waste your pity on him. He intends to sell a Lane-laying robot to the Corasians. Can you imagine what that would mean? It has always been difficult for the Corasians to mass their forces due to the lack of space Lanes within their own galaxy. They would now have the capability to lay Lanes wherever they wanted. They could send immense armadas to attack us.

"Once here, the Corasians could continue to build

their own Lanes, travel unimpeded to any portion of the galaxy. They could also disrupt our Lanes, making it difficult, if not impossible, for the Navy to come to the defense of planets under attack. The death and devastation would be incalculable."

Tess was pale and serious and earnest. And it was all a lie. You're good, sister, Xris told her silently. You're real good. I wonder what else you're not telling us.

"I know there are rotten people in this galaxy," Harry Luck was saying, "but I can't imagine how anyone could be twisted enough to work for the Corasians."

"Money has a lot to do with it," Tess said. "But it's more than that with Harsch. Or so we think. He could make a fortune—hell, he cold make a hundred fortunes—by selling the robot to any number of people in our own galaxy. Our people believe that he has some sort of weird fascination with the Corasians."

"Probably sexual," Raoul commented.

"Sex?" Harry guffawed. "The Corasians are big blobs of molten lava—"

"Not technically." Quong, having returned from the drinking fountain, interrupted. "The Corasians are actually a protoplasmic mass that is about ninety percent pure energy with just enough fleshy matter to ensure that they can interact with the material world."

"So they're not lava," Harry carried on, undeterred. "They're fiery, flesh-eating blobs of goo that haul themselves around in plastic cases. I don't see anything so very sexy about all that."

"You have no imagination," Raoul stated loftily. His eyes grew dreamy, unfocused. "Think of being consumed by flames, of tongues of fire licking your loins . . . of the sweet, terrible pain . . . ."

"That's sick!" Harry protested, disgusted.

Raoul gave a delicate shrug. "As I said, you have no imagination."

Jamil rubbed his eyes, flexed his shoulders. "Could we get on with this? All I want to do is go to bed and sleep for about twenty-four hours." Yawning, he shook his head to clear it, then hunched forward on his chair. "It seems to me that this is all settled. We deliver the robot to Harsch. We get paid. That's that."

"Speaking of payment, since the government now knows about this job, we'll have to declare it as income," Tycho said in gloomy tones.

Xris eyed Tess. "I don't understand, Captain. Why don't your own people deal with this? If this robot's so damn dangerous and so damn valuable, why didn't *you* just snatch it?"

Tess made no answer. She merely smiled.

"Ah," Xris said in sudden understanding. "I interrupted something, didn't I? Of course. You had that raid on the barroom planned in advance. That was the diversion *you* were planning to use to sneak off base! Until I wandered onto the set. Worked out great for you, didn't it? You let me go pick up the robot. If I get caught, I take the fall. You bat your innocent eyes, give a little horrified scream—"

"Cut the self-pity," Tess snapped. "You were operating on the edge, and you knew it. You were happy enough to use *me* to get off base. You took off like you had a missile up your ass when that diversion came down. You thought you were so smart! Thought you were in control of the whole situation! If you could have seen your face when you heard Jamil had left the base . . ."

Xris took out a twist, but he didn't put it in his mouth. He held it in his hand, stared at it, tapped it against the gold case. "Yeah, I guess I must've looked pretty funny at that."

In the silence, Xris could hear the whir of the machinery that kept him alive. Everyone in the place could hear it. Great acoustics, this theater.

Tess's hand touched his shoulder. His good shoulder. "Look, we both know that this is a hell of a way to earn a living. But I think we'd both have to admit we enjoy it." Her hand slid gently around to his back. "And if it's any comfort to your poor bruised male ego, those kisses were on my own time. They weren't government-issue."

Xris tried hard to stay angry, but he couldn't. What she said was absolutely true. She had used him. He had used her. She had lied to him. He had lied to her. And he'd known all along those kisses hadn't been bought and paid for. He lifted his head, looked up at her, and smiled.

"So we've managed to prove that each of us is a sneaky, conniving liar and a cheat. Sounds like the basis of a great relationship to me. Where do we go from here?"

"To bed," Jamil muttered, yawning again. "I meant to sleep," he added.

"No imagination," said Raoul, sighing. Once again he regarded himself sadly in his mirror. "I, for one, am going to have to find someplace to repair the damage."

"Me, too," said Harry. "My plane's a mess. I've got a broken front gear and number two engine is out. Something flew off the tarmac, ripped up the turbines. Don't the people here know that FOD can ruin an engine?"

Harry was incapable of being witty. Xris could only assume he was serious—which was even more frightening.

"Well, Captain, what are our orders?" Xris turned to Tess.

"Bring the robot to me. I have the equipment needed to download the data. When that's finished, you fly off."

Xris chewed on the twist. "We're taking a hot robot wired with explosives to a guy who turns people into Corasian lunch meat." He glanced around at the team. "Everyone got their life insurance paid up?"

"Harsch won't figure it out," Tess said firmly. "He couldn't possibly. We've kept the lid on this, tight. No one else knows about this robot. No one."

Xris grunted. "Whatever you say."

He had another problem to solve, and that was the disappearance of Darlene Rowan. He hoped twenty-four hours would give him time to establish contact with her, make sure she was all right. He turned to Raoul. "Mind if I come along? Watch you put on your lipstick?"

Raoul was pleased, flattered. "If you truly think you would enjoy it, Xris Cyborg. So few people realize that it is an art form—"

The Little One nudged his friend. Raoul's eyelashes fluttered. "Oh. Yes, well." He gazed at Xris from beneath lowered lashes. "If you would accompany me to the little boys' room ..."

Tess suddenly put her hand to her ear. She listened a moment, said "Excuse me, gentlemen," and walked to the back part of the stage.

"Implanted commlink," said Harry knowingly.

"Gee, you're a scientific wonder today," Xris remarked caustically.

He was watching Tess. He didn't like the way her shoulders slumped, the way she slowly lowered her hand from the commlink implanted beneath her skin behind her ear, the way she stood a moment, as if trying to sort out what to do next.

"Something's gone wrong," said Jamil in an undertone.

"Surprise, surprise. Look, next time you hear me say 'This is the easiest job on record,' just shoot me, will you?" Xris returned. "Point-blank. Through the heart. Get it over with."

Tess began to walk. She was headed off the stage, moving rapidly.

The entire team was on their feet.

Xris was the first to catch up with her. He grabbed her elbow. "What gives, Captain? Where are you off to in such a hurry? We're on the same side, remember?"

Tess shook him off, glared up at him. She was clearly furious. "Mag Force 7. And there's only *six* of you. What a chump I am. Let go of me."

Xris didn't. "What are you talking about?"

"Your number seven just showed up."

Xris silenced the others—particularly Raoul—with a flashing glance.

"And," Tess continued, "he's raising one hell of a row. He's blabbing his head off about the robot!"

CHAPTER
23

And trust me not at all or all in all.

Alfred, Lord Tennyson, *Idylls of the King*,
"Merlin and Vivien"

"Here goes my nap." Jamil groaned.

Tess fixed them all with a grim stare. Her hand rested on her holster. "You want to tell me what you're up to?"

"I don't know who this guy is. He's not one of ours. Maybe," Xris said, "he's one of *yours*. Maybe this is something *you've* cooked up for us?"

Tess flushed in anger. She started to retort, caught herself, swallowed her words. After a moment, she was calm again. "I suppose this is inevitable. We neither of us can trust the other."

She looked narrowly at Xris, at the rest of the team. "You're saying that this man isn't one of your team?"

"Yes, that's what I'm saying. Is he one of yours?"

"No, of course not! But then who? . . . How? . . ." Tess sighed, put her hand to her forehead. "I don't believe this."

"Maybe it's Harsch?" Jamil suggested. "Or one of his agents? Maybe he got suspicious, decided to check things out himself."

"That was the first thing I considered," Tess said, "but NI doesn't think so. He calls himself Jeffrey Grant. He flew to Pandor in a rent-a-plane. He requested clearance to land. When that was refused, he said he had to see someone about the 'old robot.' The Admiralty's been monitoring all air traffic on this planet. They stepped in at that point, ordered that Grant be allowed to land. He was immediately taken into custody. He hasn't been permitted to leave his plane. He's being held incommunicado at the airfield.''

"Harsch wouldn't be likely to broadcast the fact that he knows something about the robot," Jamil pointed out.

Tess was silent, thinking. She glanced at Xris. "You've seen Harsch. Could you say for certain whether or not this might be him?"

"I might not be able to," Xris said. "I saw Sakuta, remember? He may or may not have been Harsch. But the Little One could. He could also tell if this guy is Harsch or is working for Harsch."

"And I'm supposed to rely on what he says? Oh, very well. You and the hat come with me."

"Sure," Xris answered. He rubbed the right side of his nose. "But what about the robot? I don't *think* anyone will bother it, not with all those biohazard warnings decorating the crate's exterior. But you never know—"

"Tycho and I could go collect the robot," Quong offered, picking up on the cue. "Our friend is also decorated with biohazard warnings—so to speak." He indicated Tycho's biochemical warfare patches.

"And it would be consistent with my story that I suspected something was wrong with the crate," Xris said.

Tess was regarding him with renewed suspicion. "You know, I might almost think you had this planned."

"Yeah, I'm a genius," Xris returned, shrugging. "I'm such a genius I get taken in by a Corasian agent posing as a museum curator and an NI agent posing as a human."

Tess contemplated him a moment longer, then smiled a half smile. "The number-one rule for someone in my business is don't get personally involved—"

"—because you may have to shoot the involvee," Xris finished. "Yeah, I know. You've got a job to do. And so do we. Why not let us do it? Quong and Tycho collect the robot. You can send an armed escort with them if you want. Harry, you go make certain the Claymore's in shape to fly us out— What's the matter, Harry?" Xris interrupted himself. "You *do* remember where you left the bomber, don't you?"

"Uh? Oh, yeah, sure, Xris. I remember *where* I left it. It's just *how* I left it—sort of sudden-like. You see, I really wasn't supposed to have left it at all, only I said I had to go to the can and— For God's sake, Xris," Harry expostulated. "I heard you were in trouble!"

Xris thrust a twist into his mouth. "Still think I planned this?" he asked Tess in an undertone. Aloud he said, "Jamil, go with Harry. See if you can keep him out of the brig. Doc, you and Tycho meet us at the airfield with the 'bot. I'll take the Little One with me."

Xris turned to the small raincoated figure. "Would you know this time if Harsch was using a telepathic scrambler?"

The Little One nodded emphatically, smashed his two small fists together.

"And if the Little One comes along with you, Xris Cyborg, I come along in addition," Raoul announced. "*After* I repair my makeup, of course."

Tess glanced sidelong at Xris.

"I'm afraid he's right. He has to come," he said, grinning. "They're a team. We all are."

"God help us," Tess muttered.

She left to arrange for an armed escort for Tycho and Quong and the robot. ("It's not that I don't trust you. Let's just say that I don't want anything else to go wrong.")

Jamil and Harry left to try to retrieve Harry's spaceplane. ("I know where I left it. It's sitting right on the tarmac. Jeez! I wish you guys would forget about that other time....")

Once Tess was gone, Raoul drew out a pocket mirror, began redoing his lipstick. Xris bent down, said quietly, "What about Darlene?"

Raoul answered in the same soft tone, pausing at intervals to examine the tracings of the lavender-colored pencil around his lips. "It was close, Xris Cyborg. Very close. The Little One discovered the plot and warned me in time."

Xris's stomach clenched. "The Hung?"

Raoul looked not at Xris but at Xris's reflection in the mirror. "Yes, my friend. That is what the Little One says. They were Adonian assassins, hired by the Hung. Third-rate, mind you." Raoul sniffed and concentrated on his work. "No delicacy. No finesse. And they used a poison to which there was an antidote. Still, I suppose that a mob can't be all that selective—"

"She's all right," Xris repeated urgently.

"She's fine. She left on a pleasure cruiser to Moana. She chose that planet because it is near Pandor. I have . . . somewhere"—he glanced at his handbag—"exactly where and when we are supposed to meet her. She sent it in code. She said you would know how to decode it."

"How the devil did they track her?" Xris demanded angrily. He grabbed hold of Raoul's arm roughly. "Stop painting your face and listen to me. Damn it! You and the Little One were supposed to be on the watch—"

"We were, Xris Cyborg," Raoul interrupted. He regarded Xris with mild reproach and put his arm around the Little One, who shrank into a heap of wrinkled raincoat at Xris's furious tone. "No one followed her. We kept close watch. We would have known. After all, we are fond of Darlene, too."

The Little One darted forward, grabbed hold of Xris's pants leg, tugged on it fiercely, and pointed a jabbing finger at Raoul. The Little One put his finger to his mouth, pointed at Raoul again, repeated this gesture twice. Raoul had returned to his interrupted beauty regime, was again complacently regarding himself in the mirror.

Xris suddenly understood the pantomime. "You ingested the poison."

Raoul gave a delicate shrug. "My body is able to adapt. Hers might not have been." He searched through his purse, found the note with the coded message. It was scribbled on the back of a shopping list.

"I'm sorry." Xris took the list, tucked it carefully in his pocket. "It's not your fault. I brought this on her.

This is my fault. If I'd left her alone, she would have had the whole goddamn Royal Navy protecting her!"

"Like they protected her from you?" Raoul asked, with a slight, sweet smile.

Xris stared at him.

"*You* found her," Raoul continued. "It would have only been a matter of time before the Hung accomplished the same task. She would have died at their hands. And she would have died alone."

"She's alone now," Xris muttered.

"No, Xris Cyborg. For you are in her thoughts. And she is in yours."

"A lot of help *that's* going to be."

"There is nothing you can do, my friend. The matter is out of your hands, beyond your ability to control. And that, of course, is why you find it frustrating. It is very presumptuous, not to mention egotistical, for you to take responsibility for the odd quirks and twists of fate. Only the Creator—should He, She, or It exist—may lay claim to that, for which blessing we should all be extremely thankful."

"You've been hanging around Quong too much," Xris snapped. He was silent a moment, brooding, then said abruptly, "Anyhow, thanks for what you did for her. And, again, I'm sorry I yelled at you."

"No thanks are needed, Xris Cyborg," Raoul returned. He shut the compact, placed it back in his purse, along with his makeup kit. "Although the apology is accepted. As you said, Darlene is one of the team. One for all and damn the torpedoes, as our friend Tycho has been known to say. And here comes that wretched woman!" He glanced at Xris from beneath lavender eyelids. "I can't think *what* you see in her!"

Xris patted reassuringly the pocket where the coded message resided. The first moment alone on Harry's spaceplane, he would try to get through to Darlene

Tess motioned them to join her. She was brisk, cool, a demeanor put on—Xris guessed—to conceal her nervousness and anxiety. This job had every prospect of blowing up in *her* face now. He should have felt a little vindictive satisfaction, but he was gloomily aware that—

if the bomb went off—he was standing right beside her. Tess managed a smile for Raoul.

"You look lovely," she said sincerely.

"No thanks to you!" Raoul sniffed, tossed his hair, and—well-groomed head held high—flounced past her.

Jeffrey Grant sat in his spaceplane, eating a chocolate bar and watching the two armed MPs standing guard outside the hatch. He wasn't surprised at the reception he'd received. He was actually pleased. It restored his faith in his government. He was glad to think that they were on top of this matter, that they were treating this with the respect it was due. He'd been worried that no one here would understand the danger, that he would have to be firm and persuasive.

If there were two things he was *not* good at, it was being firm and persuasive.

As it was, obviously these people knew the treasure they had and were guarding it carefully. Grant settled back and finished the chocolate bar.

He had enjoyed the trip. It felt good being at the controls of a spaceplane once more, even if it was a rental, and a cheap one at that. He threw the candy wrapper in the trash compactor, took another look at the antique machine that he'd brought with him. He'd strapped the unit into the copilot's seat to keep it from being jostled. The machine was still humming, loudly, contentedly. Grant found himself humming, too. A tuneless song, a song whose words he'd long since forgotten . . . or had never known. Something about robot blues.

He puttered around the plane, tidying up, for he knew he would be receiving visitors. This done, he went back to his chair and amused himself by watching the comings and goings of the squadrons, naming each type of plane as it landed or took off, imagining himself at the controls, wondering what missions they were flying. He was so absorbed in watching and imagining and wondering that he didn't, at first, notice the rather odd procession advancing across the tarmac toward his plane. When he did, he glanced at them, said to himself "Time for your debriefing, Captain," and returned to revel in the glorious sight of a Claymore bomber thundering into the Pandoran sky.

The MPs saluted. Grant was quick to open the hatch, so as not to annoy anyone. He met his guests at the entrance to the small plane.

"Please come in, Captain, sir, Captain, ma'am," he said shyly, speaking ·standard military, to put them at ease. "You, too, uh . . ." He was momentarily stumped on the lovely personage with the lipstick, long hair, pants, and an Adam's apple. He finally gave up and coughed to cover his embarrassment. As for the small figure in the fedora and the raincoat, Grant looked at it with interest. Turning to the female captain, he said politely, "Your child, ma'am?"

"Uh, no," the woman replied, taken aback. "He's—"

"A spy," said the lovely long-haired person. "He's incognito. So am I." The lovely person sat down, crossed his legs. "You won't tell, will you?"

"No, certainly. Of course not," Grant murmured.

The female captain appeared to be under considerable strain and this exchange did nothing to relax her. She frowned and bit her lip and shot an irritated glance at the male captain.

"Won't you all please sit down?" Grant said, recalling the duties of a host. "Would you care for refreshment? I have soft drinks and chocolate bars."

"No, thank you," the male captain said, smiling politely. "My name is Captain Xris Kergonan. This is Captain Tess Strauss. This is my aide, Corporal de Beausoleil, and this person"—he indicated the small being in the raincoat—"is known only as the Little One. I can't tell you his real name. Military security."

Grant nodded. "Very sound."

"What?" Captain Kergonan appeared confused.

"I said, 'Very sound,' " Grant reiterated. "In light of the circumstances. Now"—he clasped his hands together, to keep from wringing them, which would have looked undignified—"please tell me. Where is the robot?"

"Robot?" Captain Kergonan leaned against the control panel. "I must tell you, Mr."—he lifted his hand, glanced at the pilot's license he held; the MPs had con-

fiscated the license immediately upon Grant's arrival—
"Mr. Grant, that you are in very serious trouble. The
people of Pandor do not like off-worlders. They have
laws which prohibit them from visiting this planet—"

"Oh, dear," said Grant, truly distressed. "I didn't
know. I'm terribly sorry. Will this cause an ... an ..."
Momentarily he couldn't think of the word. "An incident, do you suppose?"

"That's why we're here," said Captain Strauss. "We're
going to try to smooth this over. I'm sure you don't want
to cause trouble."

"I really didn't mean to violate any laws," Jeffrey
Grant said, worried. "I suppose I should have checked
first, before I came, but I was so upset about the robot,
you see. I didn't know who had it and I was afraid they
might damage—"

"Excuse me. What robot?" Captain Kergonan asked
mildly.

At this point, the lovely person—Grant couldn't recall
his name—reached out with a delicate hand and tugged
on the back end of Captain Kergonan's uniform.

"Give it up, Xris Cyborg," said the lovely person. He
indicated the small being in the raincoat. "The Little
One says to inform you that this drab gray person is not
Sakuta or Harsch or anyone else except himself. And"—
dramatic pause—"he himself knows more about the
robot than anyone else here in this spaceplane."

Jeffrey Grant smiled shyly, proudly, glad to be
appreciated.

CHAPTER
24

Hope is a good breakfast, but it is a bad supper.

Francis Bacon, "Apophthegms contained in
Resuscitatio" No. 36

Dr. Quong and Tycho, accompanied by two MPs, walked over to the maintenance shed. The MPs had been briefed by Tess, who told them that a problem had developed with the colonel's exhibit materials; the crate appeared to be malfunctioning. Although it presented no threat at the moment, Dr. Quong and Tycho, expert on biochemical warfare, were going to check the crate out, remove it to a place of safety. The MPs were ordered to show Quong and Tycho the way to the maintenance shed, go along to see that no unauthorized personnel obstructed the proceedings.

Not being required to strictly guard the two, the MPs walked several paces ahead, clearly not wanting to come any closer to Tycho than was necessary. The "chameleon," for his part, altered the shade of his skin to a sickly bluish gray, which, with his excessive thinness, made it look as if he were in the last stages of some wasting disease. He and Quong were able to talk freely without fear of anyone overhearing.

"Why is it," Tycho grumbled, his translator giving his voice a tinny, mechanical sound, "that no one ever hires us for a normal job?"

"Define *normal*," Quong said.

"I could if I wanted to," Tycho said, taking offense. "In several different languages."

"No, no. That's not what I meant. What do you consider to be a normal job for people such as ourselves?"

"Ah, I see. Yes, well . . ." Tycho gave it some thought. "Not the job itself so much as the fact that it should have a clear-cut beginning, a clean middle, and a swift and satisfactory finish. And the money should be good and in no way traceable. With us, it's always the same. Either the job gets screwed up somehow or we end up having to report the income. Or both."

"Friend Tycho, as a citizen, it is your duty to pay taxes," Quong said seriously.

"And who tries, every year, to take the payments on his sports runabout as a medical deduction?"

Quong bristled. "Driving the runabout is a reliever of stress, as I have several times informed you. I have a written medical opinion—"

"Of your own writing."

"—that it is necessary for my mental well-being— Ah, I think we have arrived at our destination."

The MPs had stopped, were talking to a sergeant, who was wiping greasy hands on a rag and looking considerably alarmed.

"The crate is over there in the corner, sirs," he said as Tycho and Quong approached. He nodded in the general direction, apparently had no intention of getting any closer. "There's nothing wrong with it, is there?"

"We certainly hope not, Sergeant. Now, have you or any of your people come within a three-meter distance of the crate?" Dr. Quong asked crisply.

"Three meters." The sergeant ruminated, shook his head. "Nope, sir. Why? What would happen if we did?"

Tycho produced a strange-looking instrument from his briefcase. Activating it, he pointed it at the sergeant and touched a button, producing a slight whooshing sound. A series of lights began to flash different colors.

"What's that, sir?" The sergeant eyed it suspiciously.

"Have you experienced any of the following in the past twelve hours: dizziness, nausea, trouble swallowing, fever, swelling of the hands or feet, bloody stools, coughing, vomiting, or premature ejaculation?" Dr. Quong asked, electronic notebook in hand.

"Huh?" The sergeant blinked at them, backed up a pace. "I—"

"What about tenderness of the stomach, swelling of the head, skin eruption, or attention deficit disorder?"

The sergeant, looking worried, put his hand to his brow. "Now you mention it, I—"

"Thank you!" Tycho said abruptly, switching off his toothbrush and inserting it back into his briefcase. "All appears normal, Doctor. He has not been contaminat—er—affected."

"Excellent, excellent," Quong murmured. "Now, Sergeant, if you could show us the crate . . ."

"Over there, sir, next to the Devastator. You can't miss it." The sergeant stood his ground, was apparently not going anywhere near the crater.

"Thank you, Sergeant," said Dr. Quong, and turned to the other mechanics. "Perhaps you gentlemen could wait outside."

This request was obeyed with alacrity, most of those within the work area having already sidled over near the door. When everyone was outside the shed, the MPs took up a position in front of the door, a completely unnecessary precaution.

"See, friend Tycho?" said Quong, as they walked over to find the robot crate. "This was easy."

They discovered the crate leaning up against the Devastator, just where Xris had described it. Tycho bent his long, thin frame, crouched down to peer at it.

"You are being overly pessimistic," the doctor continued. Quong remained standing, keeping an eye on the MPs.

"Am I?" Tycho straightened. His expression was grim. His skin had flushed to a fevered orange. "Take a look at this and tell me if I'm being a pestilence."

"Pessimist," Quong corrected; Tycho's translator occasional lapsed into incoherence.

The doctor walked over, bent down to study the robot crate. He took a good, long look. Quong raised his gaze.

"Oh, shit," he said.

"Without a paddle," Tycho added gloomily.

CHAPTER
25

Yet, ah! why should they know their fate?
Since sorrow never comes too late,
And happiness too swiftly flies,
Thought would destroy their paradise.

Thomas Gray, "Ode on a Distant Prospect of
Eton College"

Ignorance is bliss and Xris was, for the moment, blissful. Or rather, he had his own set of problems and was operating under the assumption that these problems were his most urgent problems. Which meant that he was currently blissful, if only by contrast.

He and Tess, Raoul and the Little One were all crowded together in the front of the rent-a-plane, discussing Jeffrey Grant. Grant hovered near, shy, uncomfortable, and persistent.

"You're saying that the Little One figured this all out telepathically." Tess cast a scornful glance at the raincoated figure. "And that's how he knows that this man knows about the robot."

"Of course," Raoul said loftily. "How else would he know?"

"Oh, maybe because this man works for you. That he showed up right on cue—"

"For what reason?" Xris asked impatiently. "To do what?"

Tess lifted her hands helplessly. "I don't know! I don't know anything anymore. I don't know who to believe.

All right. Let's say, for the sake of argument, that the Little One is right. That this man does know something about the robot. How?"

"Maybe he's Harsch," Xris suggested. "Maybe he's using the telepathic scrambler."

The Little One opened his small palms, slapped himself on the forehead several times.

"No. He could tell," Raoul stated flatly.

The Little One put his head between his two hands, heedlessly smashing the rim of the fedora, and rocked his head back and forth, rolling his eyes.

"He said that the entire time we were with Sakuta, he"—Raoul gently touched his friend on the shoulder—" felt dizzy and sick. He thought it was some sort of flu and he said nothing about it, for fear Dr. Quong would start poking at him again. No offense to the good doctor," Raoul hastened to add. "But you must admit that his bedside manner is somewhat abrupt—"

"The telepathic scrambler," Xris reminded Raoul. The iridescent-winged mind had fluttered from one flower of conversation to another, required netting.

"Ah, yes." Raoul had to pause to think of where he'd been. "The Little One thought he was coming down with the flu. He didn't, however. His health has been excellent, as you know. The strange feeling passed, but it left him rather out of sorts. In a bad mood. He kept thinking that something was wrong and he should know what, but he couldn't figure it out. And then, during the party, when I mentioned to Darlene that the assassins had scramblers, he put two and whatever that other number is together and came up with—"

"Assassins? Scramblers?" Tess looked from Xris to Raoul.

"Not important," Xris said. "Another case we were working on. I know one thing. This isn't the same person I met at the museum. Not by a long shot. Of course, Harsch might be a master of disguise."

"The Little One says that this is *not* Harsch," Raoul reiterated. "The Little One is of the opinion that this Grant person is precisely the Grant person he claims to be. He has acquired knowledge about the robot from years of study of ancient space flight, with particular emphasis on ... on ..." Raoul waved a vague hand. "Professor Lasagna ..."

"Lasairion, sir," Jeffrey Grant corrected. He had been listening to the conversation with the befuddled gaze of someone whose translator is on the fritz. He could understand a few words from time to time, but most of the talk was meaningless. Now, however, he had heard something he understood. He rose to his feet, literally trembling with excitement. "Do you know about Professor Lasairion?"

Raoul bowed from the waist. "God forbid. I am merely the translator. And then, of course, there is his machine."

"What machine?" Tess demanded, clearly rattled.

Raoul pointed to the copilot's chair. They all trooped around to look. In the chair, strapped in lovingly with extreme care, was some sort of strange-looking machine. A small electric backlit screen tilted up from an ancient computer keyboard—the kind with all the letters in the most inconvenient places. A blue light flashed intermittently on the side of the machine. An odd, yet not unpleasant humming emanated from it.

"Please don't touch it, Captain," Grant begged, as the entire contingent stared at it. "It's very old and delicate."

"Another antique," Xris said. "With a few more of these we could hold a garage sale."

"It is very special," Raoul said, with a knowing flutter of his eyelids. "This machine is in communication with the robot. According to the Grant-person, that is why it is making that tooth-grating sound."

Jeffrey Grant gazed at the Little One in astonishment. "That's *exactly* what I was thinking! He's quite remarkable, isn't he, sir? As for the humming sound, I know it *is* a bit irritating. I'm really sorry, but there's nothing I can do to stop it. I'm not completely certain how it works—"

Tess interrupted him. "This machine's in communication with the robot. ... Good God!" She bent down, peered at it intently. "Are you telling me that this machine is a . . . a Collimated Command Receiver Unit?"

"Yes, ma'am!" Jeffrey Grant clapped his pudgy hands together. "Absolutely correct! And may I say, ma'am, that you're the first person I've ever encountered who has studied the work of Professor Lasairion. How did you—"

"I'm asking the questions," Tess snapped, and then she didn't ask anything. She stood in silence, frowning deeply at the humming machine.

Xris took advantage of the lull in the conversation to have a private talk with Raoul.

"What's going on with this guy?" Xris asked quietly, keeping his back to Grant. "What's the Little One picking up?"

Raoul shook his head—carefully, so as not to muss his hair. "You know how the Little One feels about technology, my friend. He doesn't understand it. He doesn't like it. He finds that it frightens him. This man's mind is a technological jungle. The Little One says that looking inside the Grant person is akin to looking beneath the hood of a hoverjeep. It is filled with objects that make no sense to him."

"No sign that this is all a put-on? An act?"

The Little One, crowding beside Xris to hear, shook his own head emphatically.

Tess had apparently thought out what she wanted to say. "Where are you from, Mr. Grant? How did you come into possession of the Collimated Command Receiver Unit? When did the unit start to . . . uh . . . hum? How did you know to come to Pandor to find the robot?"

Grant looked somewhat confused, decided to take the questions in order. "I'm from the planet XIO, Captain. I run a museum there—"

Xris snorted.

Grant paused, regarded him anxiously. "Did I say something—"

"I've had it up to here with museum curators, that's all. Never mind. Go on."

"I have been a collector of space memorabilia for over

fifty years, sir," Grant said with quiet pride. He seemed to feel better, talking about himself. "Ever since I was a child. This"—he laid a hand lovingly on the Collimated Command Receiver Unit—"is my most valued possession, though not, I must say, my most valuable. The unit was offered for sale over one of the computer bulletin boards. Its owner obviously had no idea what he had. I recognized it immediately from his description. He wanted a lot for it, mainly because it was old, not because he knew its true worth. After a month of delicate negotiations, during which I had to appear interested, but not too interested, I drove down his price and finally acquired the Collimated Command Receiver Unit. It has resided in an honored place in my museum for the last twenty years. Beneath it is a plaque that reads: ONLY KNOWN RELIC OF THE LASAIRION PERIOD." He was wistful. "I only need the robot to complete my collection. I have a special place all ready to house it."

"I'm sorry, Mr. Grant," Tess said, firmly but kindly destroying all hope. "That robot is government property."

"Yes, I know," he said softly. "But I would take good care . . ." His voice trailed off.

Xris took a twist out of the gold case, studied it longingly, glanced out the window at the MPs on guard outside the spaceplane. He put the cigarette back in its case, the case in his pocket. He looked at his watch.

"Captain Strauss," he said. "Could I have a word with you?"

Tess glanced uncertainly at the machine, then at Grant. Keeping them both in sight, she walked over to where Xris was standing. "What is it?"

"I know that this is all very fascinating from a scientific point of view, but we're running out of time," Xris said in a low voice. "I arranged to meet Sakuta at Hell's Outpost tomorrow. How long will it take you to debrief the robot?"

"You mean download the information? Several hours, maybe all day," Tess said. "I'm going to have to experiment; finding the correct interface could prove difficult.

And now there's this unit. This makes everything a lot more complicated."

"Yeah. Just answer me one question: Do I or do I not take the robot to Sakuta?"

"Harsch."

"Whoever!" Xris was losing patience. "Look, you've got the robot. Let's take it *and* the unit back to the command cruiser and let the admiral deal with it."

"What about Grant?" Tess asked. "He may be as innocent and naive as he looks, but he may also be one hell of a good actor. Suppose he is an agent for Harsch? He comes to get the 'bot, discovers that we already have it. So he plays stupid."

"And brings along an antique machine as a prop? Well, I suppose anything's possible." Xris was edgy. He wanted to get this job over with, fast. He didn't like the idea of Darlene out there somewhere on her own. "Look, you can shoot him, for all I care—"

"I can't do that!" Tess was shocked. "He's a civilian!"

Xris grinned. "So am I. And you were ready to shoot me."

Tess ignored him. "I'll go back to HQ, relay all this to the Admiralty. You stay here with Grant."

"What about the unit?"

"The unit comes with me for safekeeping."

"Still don't trust me, huh?"

"Sure I do," Tess said, patting him on the shoulder. She returned to Jeffrey Grant. "I'm afraid I'm going to have to confiscate your Collimated Command Receiver Unit, Mr. Grant. Don't worry. The government will compensate you."

Grant looked stricken, moved to stand protectively in front of the unit. "But I don't want to be compensat—"

Xris heaved a sigh, glanced again at his watch. He should have heard from Tycho and Quong by now, wondered what they were doing.

Tess attempted to soothe the distraught museum curator. "Please, Mr. Grant, I don't want any trouble. The government has the right to confiscate any equipment that might affect national security."

"Don't worry, Grant. We'll give it back," Xris said.

"Thank you, Captain Kergonan." Tess shot him a warning glance. "But I'm perfectly capable of handling this."

"By this time next year," Xris muttered.

Jeffrey Grant was looking from Xris to Tess to the unit and back to Xris again.

"The Navy just wants to study the unit," Xris explained. "We'll make a few vids of it. Then we'll give it back. *If* that's what you want."

"Personally," Raoul offered his opinion, "I'd take the money. Buy a new wardrobe," he hinted.

"I don't want the money, sir. Or a wardrobe. I want my Collimated Command Receiver Unit." Jeffrey Grant was firm.

"Fine. No problem." Xris was eager to please.

"Captain ...." Tess was beginning to get irritated.

Grabbing hold of her hand, Xris gave it a squeeze.

"This is for your king, Mr. Grant," Xris said solemnly. "For your king and your galaxy."

"For the king," Grant murmured.

Xris could have sworn he saw the man's hand start to lift in a salute. "Very well, sir." Jeffrey Grant altered his move, put his hand lovingly on top of his humming Collimated Command Receiver Unit. "You can take it, ma'am. But I insist on coming with it."

"We'll see," said Tess, in a tone which meant *Not on your life.* "I'll have to clear that with the Admiralty."

Grant slowly nodded. His eyes blinked rapidly. "The unit has a traveling case. I'll get it." He went to the back of the plane, began to rummage around loudly in a storage bin.

Tess sidled over near Xris. "You know he'll never see that machine again."

"I know that. You know that. He doesn't," Xris said.

Tess sighed. "Sometimes I really hate this job."

Grant returned with the case. Fussily, refusing all offers of assistance, he packed the unit securely inside the case, closed it.

Xris stepped politely around Grant, bent down, lifted the case. It wasn't particularly heavy, though somewhat awkward. He handed it to Tess.

"Good-bye, Mr. Grant," she said. "Thank you."

Carrying the case, she left the spaceplane. Xris watched her walk across the tarmac. Grant was watching, too, his face and hands pressed up against the steelglass, his expression that of a parent who's lost a custody battle.

"She'll take good care of it," Xris said. "I promise you."

"I wish I could see it. The robot, I mean," Grant said softly.

"So do I. Before they blow it up," Raoul added offhandedly.

"What?" Jeffrey Grant turned. He had gone a sort of sickly wax color. "What did you say, sir? Blow it up!"

"Yes, we have a bomb. It's in Jamil's briefcase. We're going to plant it in the robot and detonate it."

Grant's mouth opened and shut several times before he could make anything coherent come out. "Why ... why ... why would they do such a terrible thing?"

Xris was grim. This was just all he needed. "Raoul, you and the Little One go see if you can find out what's keeping Quong."

Raoul cast a horrified glance out the window onto the baking tarmac. He looked back at Xris, reproachful. "You know how bad the sun is for my complexion. Do you want to see me covered with freckles?"

At the moment, Xris would have liked to have seen Raoul covered with blood-sucking leeches. Grant was breathing funny, quivering all over, and making odd gasping sounds.

"I'll risk it," Xris snarled. "Go. Go on. Both of you. Beat it."

Hurt, Raoul rose majestically to his feet and swept out of the spaceplane, the Little One trudging behind. Outside, Raoul put his hand over his forehead in a vain attempt to shield himself from the ravages of UV rays. Taking the Little One by the hand, he ran as fast as the Little One's short legs would carry him, heading for the nearest shade.

Xris assisted the stricken Grant to a chair. "I'll get you some water. Are you on any type of medication?"

"No, no, sir. I'm fine." Grant was bewildered. He clutched at Xris. "Why are you going to blow it up?"

"We're not. Raoul misunderstood. We'll keep the robot safe. I promise you." Xris was making a lot of promises. Maybe someday he could actually keep one. "Just relax, Mr. Grant. Don't worry. Perhaps if you told me a little more about this professor—"

Xris's built-in commlink, located in his left ear, buzzed—a bad sign. It meant that one of the team had something to communicate which was strictly private.

"If you'll excuse me, Mr. Grant? I ... uh ... gotta go ..." He motioned in the direction of the head.

Grant nodded vaguely back and whispered, "Blow it up! ..."

Xris left the bridge.

The head in these rent-a-spaceplanes was small for a normal-sized person. Xris, with his large shoulders and broad chest, was a tight fit. He had to work to shut the door, and then was forced to straddle the toilet. One elbow was in the sink.

"Xris here. What is it?" he said, keeping his voice low.

"Quong here. Bad news, boss. The robot's gone."

"Gone?" Xris protested. "What do you mean, gone? Someone stole it? That's impossible! The case itself weighed in at about a metric ton, not to mention the robot! It'd take a crane to lift it—"

"Hold on, boss," Quong cut in. "The case is still here. From a preliminary investigation, I'd say the 'bot freed itself. The case has been popped open from the *inside*."

"I'll be damned. . . ." Xris was awed, stunned, amazed, and in a hell of a lot of trouble. "Find it!" he ordered, squeezing the words out of his constricting chest. "Don't say a word to anyone, just *find it*!"

"Sure, boss." Quong was confident. "What does it look like? There's a lot of robots working around here."

"Not like this one. Picture a metal jellyfish with sad eyes. Once you've got it, sit tight and get back in touch."

"Yes, boss. Quong out."

Xris took a twist, chomped down on it savagely, chewed it, and swore, briefly and bitterly. He indulged in one of his favorite pastimes—beating himself up. He should have anticipated this. He should have taken precautions. He should have this. He should have that.

But the damn 'bot had seemed so meek and compliant. . . .

"Fuck it!" Xris said loudly.

He slammed open the door to the head, walked to the bridge and right on past. "Please stay here, Mr. Grant," Xris said. "I've got to leave for a few minutes. I'll send someone for you shortly."

On his way out of the spaceplane, Xris picked up the two MPs.

"Come with me," he ordered.

"Yes, Captain." The MPs obeyed with alacrity.

Xris was, after all, still in uniform.

CHAPTER
26

Opportunity makes a thief.

Francis Bacon, "A Letter of Advice
to the Earl of Essex"

Jeffrey Grant, left alone in his rent-a-plane, was barely cognizant of the captain's departure. The shock had left Grant dazed.

Blow up the robot!

Why? It wasn't harming anyone. Didn't they realize how ... how wonderful this was? To be able to touch, to speak, to listen to an entity that had been touched, spoken to, and listened to by Lasairion—the great Lasairion—himself!

And then came a cheering thought.

"Perhaps," Jeffrey Grant said to the console, "if they don't want the robot, they would give it to me."

The female captain had said the robot was government property. But surely, if he talked to the right person ... perhaps his planet's representative in Parliament. Or the prime minister. Or—Grant seemed dimly to have heard of an important talk show host ... Jeffrey Grant couldn't say. He had never been much involved or even interested in politics. His union had told him how and where and when and for whom to vote and he had gone and voted that way for as long as he had been eligible to do so. The universe had seemed to run along very satisfactorily in this manner. If only he could remember a name. . . .

Grant closed his eyes and tried to think back. He re-called a billboard for a political candidate. Grant could see the face; he could, after a short struggle, remember the woman's name. But had she won? Had that even been the current election, or was he thinking of a bill-board from ten years ago? He had no idea and eventu-ally he gave up worrying about it. He formed a vague plan of writing a letter to the king. Perhaps His Majesty could persuade them not to blow up the robot, but to let Grant have custody of it.

"I suppose they're worried about maintenance costs," Grant said to himself. "The upkeep might be a bit ex-pensive, but I'd handle all that myself. I wouldn't ask the government for a single credit."

With that thought, Jeffrey drifted into a happy daydream.

"I would put it . . . where? Over by the bookcase. Yes, that's the place. It has the best light. I'll move the display case that's there now into the back of the room. The robot will be the first thing people see when they walk into the door. And they'll be amazed. They'll be over-whelmed. I'll be the only museum to own one. Scholars will travel from all over the galaxy to study it. They'll ask questions."

Jeffrey Grant's blissful contemplation of the future was suddenly interrupted. He was seated in the pilot's chair, looking out the viewscreen. He leaned forward, stared, openmouthed.

They were hauling a Claymore bomber onto the tarmac.

One of Jeffrey Grant's favorite space simulator games was Wing Commander MCIII, in which he flew a Clay-more bomber on various glorious missions to keep the galaxy safe for commercial traffic. Grant had played this game a few hundred times and had won every time ex-cept the first, which he counted as just learning. And here was the Claymore—a real Claymore—not fifty me-ters away.

A hauler dragged the Claymore to a cleared area on the tarmac. Once in place, the crew detached the hauler and drove it off.

"I'm certain they won't mind if I just take a closer look," Grant said to himself.

He walked to the hatch of the rent-a-plane, opened it, and climbed down the ladder onto the hot tarmac. He looked about for the MPs, planning to shyly ask for permission to walk over and inspect the Claymore. He couldn't find the MPs.

Grant searched vaguely around, even glanced under the rent-a-plane's belly. No, the MPs were gone.

They must have left with Captain Kergonan, Grant reasoned.

He was a little uncertain about leaving his plane. If he had been the cause of an interplanetary incident, he certainly didn't want to escalate it. He wished the MPs were still here. They would have been able to advise him. He looked across the tarmac to a large building, the control tower. He glanced back toward the Claymore.

Grant could either walk over to the control tower—a long walk in the hot sun—and ask permission to go look at their Claymore or he could walk over to the Claymore. He didn't intend to stay long. He just wanted to see it close up.

"What harm can there be?" Grant asked himself. "I'll take a quick peep. That's all."

He started off across the tarmac.

Something wasn't quite right.

Grant halted, pondered, then knew what he should be doing. Returning to his own plane, he picked up his helmet. As the pilots did in his simulator game, he tucked the helmet under his arm and, attired in his union flight suit, he ran across the tarmac toward the Claymore.

He wasn't running to evade pursuit. In his mind, Grant could hear the sirens blowing, the order shouted, "Man your planes!" He was one of an elite group of brave men and women ready to risk their lives for whatever cause was on today's plate. His white silk scarf trailed behind him as he ran. He reached the bomber. His crew chief was there, waiting for him.

"*Minx noggle,*" said the crew chief.

Grant blinked away the daydream. He stood beneath

the belly of the Claymore, sweating in his hot flight suit, breathing heavily, trying to catch his breath.

Confronting Jeffrey Grant was a robot.

It took Grant only a few seconds to realize that this was *the* robot.

He had, of course, seen old vids. One in particular came to mind. Professor Lasairion in his laboratory, exhibiting one of the Lane-laying robots. This robot would, the professor said, "take humankind into the stars, where, I trust, humans will have learned from their past mistakes and will use this opportunity to carry civilization forward into the twenty-second century."

This robot was the robot of the vid—dangling reticulated arms, saucer-shaped head, humanlike eyes. Those eyes were regarding Grant with interest. A green light began to flash on the robot's head. The pupils of the eyes widened.

Grant felt funny, as if the robot were able to see inside him.

"*Reep glut?*" The robot had a questioning tone.

Grant glanced about nervously. He expected Captain Strauss or Captain Kergonan or perhaps the short spy in the hat to appear and take the robot away.

No one was in sight.

Grant waited a few more moments, standing on the broiling hot tarmac in the shadow of the enormous Claymore, watching and listening.

Nothing.

And then Grant knew what had happened. The robot had escaped.

"Run away!" said something inside Jeffrey Grant, something strange and foreign and alien. "Take the robot and run away! Save it from being blown up! Now! Quick! Before they come back!"

Grant trembled. He knew that voice. He'd heard it before, on occasion. It was always trying to get him to do wild and daring things. "Tell Ms Kline next door that you've always loved her!" "Tell the boss it was your idea!" "Tell the guys you'd like to join them for a drink!"

No, I can't. . . . I couldn't possibly. . . . Leave me alone. I'm fine the way I am.

Grant had always before been able to tune out that rabble-rousing voice. He could shut it off, as he occasionally shut off the sound on one of his vid games. He hadn't heard the voice much in his later years (it had bothered him excessively when he was young), and he was rather hoping it had retired. He was considerably disturbed to hear it, irritating and insistent as ever before.

"Save the robot! If you don't, they'll kill it!"

"This is outrageous, sir!" Grant returned, flustered. "You're insane! You are seriously contemplating stealing government property and making off with it! This is a capital crime, sir. An offense against the Crown. They might consider it kidnapping. They might consider it treason!"

"It's murder, Jeffrey Grant," said the inner voice. "They're going to kill it."

Grant's imagination was, from long practice, extremely vivid. He saw the robot sitting in some disintegrator chamber, saw the female captain sealing up the door and walking away. He saw and heard the cyborg give the order to detonate. He saw, he heard, he felt the robot explode, arms torn asunder, fluid spattering against the walls, eyes popping out. . . .

"I'll do it, sir!" said Jeffrey Grant firmly, and he astonished the inner voice so much that it shut up.

"*Mrft,*" said the robot. The green light had ceased to flash. The pupils returned to normal size. The robot turned away, began to drift off toward the front of the Claymore.

Grant followed it, wondering how he was going to get hold of it, haul it back to his rent-a-plane. He glanced around the airfield, fearful that someone would see them.

No one did. No one was around.

Grant trailed after the robot, who was now examining the Claymore, the green light on its head flashing again.

"Of course!" Grant said, watching the robot with interest. "It's scanning the plane. Just as it must have scanned me. I wonder," he wondered wistfully, "what it thought of me."

Not much, apparently. The robot didn't give him a second look. Grant followed it, cobbling his plan together.

Once he had smuggled the 'bot onto his spaceplane, he would have to hide it somewhere.

The bathroom. It would fit nicely into the shower stall.

"Then I'll take off," Grant said. "I'll have to request clearance, of course. This might prove to be a problem. But I've given them the unit, after all. They don't seem to be interested in me now. Perhaps they'll be glad to get rid of me."

He felt a pang of regret, leaving the unit behind. But it was either that or lose the robot, and the robot was far more important. Besides, Captain Kergonan had promised to return the machine once they were finished with it.

"I'll simply explain to the people in air traffic control that I have to get back home. To . . . to . . ."

What were people always going home to do? Feed the cat. See the wife and kids. Water the plants. Any or all of the above.

Grant was certain the Army would let him go.

Fairly certain. Almost certain.

"I won't worry about that now," Grant said to himself.

The important thing was to smuggle the robot aboard his spaceplane.

"Excuse me," Grant said shyly, speaking to the robot.

It had reached the open bomb bay. The robot's eyes focused on the hatch. It paid no attention to Jeffrey Grant. He recalled the old vid of Professor Lasairion. That vid had been subtitled.

The robot didn't understand Standard Military! But it could learn. He recalled this fact from his studies. Lasairion had believed in life on other planets. He hoped that his galaxy-traveling 'bots would encounter other life-forms and that, when they did, they would communicate with them. The professor had therefore given the 'bots the ability to record the spoken language of other beings, with the instruction that they bring the recordings back for study. The robot was also, by means of auto-event comparison and frequency-of-sound analysis, supposed to have the ability to "learn" languages.

Grant needed the robot's attention.

"Lasairion," Jeffrey Grant said shyly, experimentally.

At the sound of his voice, a blue light began to flash on the top of the robot's head. It pulsed four times, to the syllables of the professor's name.

The robot turned. The sad eyes were suddenly bright. It reached out one of its arms. Metal fingers took hold of Jeffrey Grant's sleeve, gave it a gentle tug, then let loose.

"You," it said.

"Me?" Grant was momentarily confused, then realized what was being asked. "No, I'm not Professor Lasairion."

But, of course, the robot must know this. It had scanned him and evinced no sign of interest in him until he spoke the professor's name.

Obviously, the 'bot was trained to search for alien life-forms. Grant was nothing new. He was merely human. But now that he'd mentioned the professor, the robot was interested in him.

"Watch it," said the robot. "Next you'll be giving it a name."

The robot was speaking Standard Military as well as anyone in the military. As well as Captain Kergonan. In fact, the robot sounded a great deal *like* Captain Kergonan. Of course! Grant realized, excited. That was because the robot must have been speaking to Captain Kergonan. The 'bot had recorded the captain's voice and was using its programming to try to make sense of the words. Either that or it was selecting phrases at random. Grant didn't think that likely.

"Name," he repeated, then added, "Jeffrey Grant."

The blue light pulsed and Grant realized that the robot must be recording *him*. Grant was pleased, flattered . . . touched.

The robot's sad, humanlike eyes gazed at Grant steadily. The 'bot appeared to be considering. "You and I— we're just going to take a little walk."

"Yes," said Grant eagerly. He half turned, pointed to his spaceplane. "Over there." He took a few steps in that direction, hoped the robot would follow.

Such a method was, he believed, supposed to work with dogs.

"Halt! Stop!" the robot commanded.

Grant stopped, turned around, pleaded, "Please, you *must* come with me. Now! Quickly! Before someone finds you!"

The robot lifted one of the metal arms, pointed toward the hatch of the Claymore. "You go inside."

Good grief! The robot was going to save itself! It was going to hide in the Claymore. And it wanted him to come along.

Why? Grant stared at the robot. The robot stared back. Grant saw his reflection in the metal saucer head. . . .

"Of course! I'm wearing a flight suit!"

He almost shouted, he was so enthused. Communicating with the robot was exhilarating, fun! It was like trying to solve a crossword puzzle.

"And I'm carrying a helmet. Which means that the robot has mistaken me for the pilot. The robot doesn't want to hide in the Claymore. It wants me to fly the Claymore! The robot is trying to save itself!"

"Do it!" said that troublemaking voice inside him.

"I couldn't," Grant whispered, suddenly appalled at his temerity. "Could I?"

"Don't be frightened," counseled the robot in Captain Kergonan's voice.

Grant had the feeling there were three people lined up against him, urging him on: the robot, Captain Kergonan, and the inner self.

"No, no, I won't be frightened," Grant promised. He looked up at the hatch, looked at the bomber, which was really much larger than it had looked in virtual reality.

After all, he'd flown a Claymore a thousand times.

And they were going to blow up the robot.

The robot floated effortlessly into the bomb bay and then turned to examine the hatch. Grant had to climb the ladder to the hatch quickly in order to keep up.

The robot used one of its attachments on its tool arm to force open the hatch.

Grant dropped down inside the bomber, looked around. He was terrified, excited, and exalted all at the same time. It was different from the flight simulator. These controls were real, not portrayed on a screen. It was ... well ... grayer than he'd pictured. Dirtier. Not that the inside of the bomber was dirty; it was kept in good condition. But the real thing was different from the simulation. It wasn't pristine, wasn't perfect. One of the steelglass faces on a dial had a crack in it. He touched the instruments, felt hard edges, smooth surfaces beneath his fingers. The metal was hot, from the sun shining in through the viewscreen. The interior smelled of metal and of stale sweat and musty webbing, warm plastic and a brown, shriveled apple core that someone had tossed toward the trash compactor and missed.

Grant sat down in the pilot's seat, studied the controls, and panicked.

The controls were not the same. They were similar, but not the same. Of course, for security reasons, the makers of the game wouldn't be allowed to replicate exactly the insides of a Claymore. He recognized a few: atmospheric pressure, airspeed, space speed, vector controller. But what were those blue baubles that sat in some sort of liquid with silver reflectors, or the myriad of computer consoles with keys hanging just above their banks of switches?

This was a mistake. A very bad mistake. Grant had always known he would get into trouble listening to that inner voice.

He had to leave, before someone caught him! He tried to stand up, but his legs wouldn't support his sagging body.

The robot shut the hatch, sealed it.

Grant gasped and gulped, then stared, baffled, at the myriad controls.

"I'm sorry ..." he began faintly.

The robot tapped him on the shoulder. Its arm pointed to a berth at the back of the crew's living quarters. Claymores were equipped to make the Jump to hyperspace, which meant that they could take journeys which might last days or weeks.

"Don't be frightened," the robot said again.

Grant pushed himself up from the pilot's chair, tottered on unsteady feet. Hesitantly, he moved away.

The robot floated over to the bomber's controls, studied them—green light flashing. It reached out one of its arms, plugged the attachment on the end of the arm directly into the console.

Minutes ticked by. Grant, sweating, stared out the viewscreen, waited—hoped—someone would come.

The robot spoke again. "I understand, computer. We can communicate. Command Sequence Request, stand by to receive."

The computer responded. "Protocol low, require authorization and voice print."

"Voice print negative," returned the robot. "Protocol low for security. Analyze feature packet sending . . . now."

"Unknown packet type."

"Your request was garbled, please resend."

"I didn't send anything," said the computer. "I request that you send authorization."

"You are responding to my request for authorization," the robot returned. "Last command was garbled. Please resend your authorization and command structure information."

"Sending," said the computer. "Please stand by."

"The robot doesn't need me," Jeffrey Grant realized out loud. "Then why am I here? And where is it going?"

The robot shifted around, looked back at him.

"I've got a job to do," it said in Captain Kergonan's voice.

Jeffrey Grant blinked. "Oh, my," he said softly. "Oh, dear."

He laid down on the berth. He was dizzy, having difficulty breathing.

"Oh, my goodness," he said again.

"Sleep tight," said the robot.

CHAPTER
27

The optimist proclaims that we live in the best of
all possible worlds; and the pessimist fears this
is true.

James Branch Cabell, *The Silver Stallion*

A corporal drove Harry Luck and Jamil over to the airfield. Jamil, sleepy, grumpy, and irritated, threw himself in the back, crossed his arms over his chest, and
glowered at the back of Harry's head.

Harry, seated in front, chatted with the driver, who
happened to be a redhead. Harry had a weakness for
redheads.

"You ever flown in a Claymore bomber, Corporal?
What did you say your first name was? Janet? Is it all
right if I call you Janet? Oh, officers aren't supposed to,
huh? Fraternization. Whatever that means. Who made
up these dumb rules anyhow? I— Yeah?" Harry turned
around in response to Jamil kicking the back of the seat.
"You want something?"

"Do you want something, *sir*?" Jamil growled.

"No, I'm fine, thanks. It's just—"

"I suggest, *Captain* Luck," Jamil said in loud and fro-
zen tones, "that you keep quiet and permit the corporal
to do her job."

"Yes, sir." Harry appeared properly chastened, but
when he turned around, he winked at the corporal, who
was having difficulty controlling her smile.

Jamil shut his eyes, sat back in his seat, and decided the hell with it.

The next thing he knew, Harry was shaking his shoulder.

"Jeez! I thought you'd never wake up! You feeling any better?" Harry asked.

"No, I don't." Jamil growled. "I feel groggy and thick-headed. We'll make a perfect team."

"We always do," Harry replied, flattered. "That hangar's where they towed the Claymore."

"You better fill me in on your story," Jamil said beneath his breath as they walked that direction.

Harry nodded. "I flew into Pandoran airspace. I'd spotted that mother of a command cruiser on my way in, so I sort of implied that I belonged to them. Said I was on a routine scouting mission and that I'd developed problems with the stabilizer. Now, if you got stabilizer problems, they don't particularly want you attempting to make a landing on a ship in space. Oh, sure, they can tractor you in, but what happens when you reach the docking bay?"

"I give up," Jamil said grimly. "What does happen?"

"Mostly they wash what's left of you out with a hose," Harry said, grinning. "It can be done, but it's a real tricky maneuver and gives everyone a lot of tense moments. No one likes it, and they'd much rather you make a land-based landing if possible. You got long runways, lots of space to wobble around, and if you veer off you'll end up in a cornfield, not the Lord Admiral's dining room."

"I understand. So you informed Pandoran air control that you had stabilizer problems."

"Yeah. They turned me over to the base airfield, who checked me out, but only sort of. After all, that mother-cruiser is floating around up there and everyone knows it."

"What do you mean, they 'sort of' checked you out? Either they did or they didn't."

The two were drawing near to the hangar. Ground crewmen were eyeing them curiously.

Jamil halted.

Harry pretended to point out the interesting features of a Stiletto fighter to the Army colonel.

"They said they were going to check with the cruiser, to verify that I was one of hers. I gotta admit that gave *me* a few tense moments," Harry commented, squinting into the Pandoran sun, shading his face with his hand. "But I guess they must've received verification, 'cause they came back and said I was cleared to land."

"What name did you give?" Jamil asked.

"Harry Luck," said Harry. "Why? What name was I supposed to give?"

"You ninny!" Jamil snorted. "The Lord Admiral was the one who gave you clearance to land. Dixter recognized your name, of course. Otherwise you'd have been given clearance to land on the nearest prison planet."

"Oh, well." Harry shrugged, not much concerned. "As long as it worked. Anyway, the landing looked real good. I was all over the sky. And I bet I bounced sixty meters back into the air when I hit the ground. That's how I got the cut on my head. I don't suppose many pilots could have brought that plane in—damaged like that," he added with simple pride.

"You mean," Jamil said slowly, his brain sleep-befuddled, "that you actually sabotaged the stabilizer *before* you came in for a landing?"

"Well, sure!" Harry returned. "I'm not *that* big a dunce. Of course, I knew that they'd be looking for a busted stabilizer and that they better find it. . . . Oh." He paused, his face crinkled.

"Yes," said Jamil. "Why didn't you fake the landing, *then* damage the stabilizer? You could have been pretending to try to fix it."

"Yeah," Harry said thoughtfully. "I see your point. It would have been a whole lot safer, huh?"

"A whole lot," Jamil concurred.

"I'll remember that." Harry nodded to himself.

"How did you manage to walk away from the airfield? I presume they told you to stay here."

"Oh, yeah. They did." Harry grinned. "But I said I had to pee and the head of the ground crew said he bet I did, after a landing like that. So I took off for the john, walked in the front, out the back, and just kept on going."

Jamil rubbed his neck. The Pandoran sun was baking the tarmac, and him right along with it. He would have given half of his not inconsiderable wealth (he'd been making sound investments—with Tycho's help) for a cool shower.

He reflected, as he stood there, sweaty and bone-tired and miserable, on the fact that he and Xris had spent long hours devising an intricate, complex, involved plan for sneaking onto the base.

When all they would've had to do was say they had to go pee.

He knew it was more complicated than that, but his weary brain couldn't handle the details. He was far more content to be bitter over the injustice of it all.

"Where the hell's your damn plane?" he grumbled.

"In here. At least, that's where they towed it." Harry led the way to the hangar, where he and Jamil were met by the crew chief.

"Hey, Captain. That was one long trip to the can." The crew chief winked.

"I had a lot on my mind," Harry replied.

The crew chief raised his eyebrows, seemed about to laugh, caught sight of Jamil's thunderous expression, and played it straight.

"Yes, sir. Is there anything wrong, sir?"

"No," said Harry breezily, glancing around the empty hangar. "I was just looking for my Claymore. Is she fixed?"

"Why, yes, sir. You must have walked right past it. We had it fixed not long after you left. A busted stabilizer controller. And you must've sucked a bird into your number two engine on the way down. We hauled the Claymore out to the tarmac."

"Which one?"

"We only have one tarmac, sir." The crew chief walked to the hangar entrance. "It's right over . . . mmmmm. Now, that's odd."

"What's odd, Chief?" Jamil demanded.

The crew chief was gazing at the tarmac in puzzlement. "The Claymore, Colonel. It should be right over there. Hell, it *was* right over there. Not an hour ago!"

Harry squinted, took a good look, shook his head. "It's not there now."

Jamil felt the beginnings of a splitting headache.

"I was gone for a little while," the crew chief said. "Turning in my daily report. Just a minute. I'll ask the guys." He disappeared back into the hangar. They heard his voice. "Hey, any of you fellows see what they did with that Claymore?"

"It took off," was the answer.

"What'd he say?" Harry asked.

"He said it took off," Jamil repeated.

"But I'm the pilot." Harry was baffled.

"Apparently not anymore," Jamil replied.

"Son of a bitch." Harry swore. "Some bastard stole my plane!" He thought a moment, then said, "Xris isn't going to be happy about this, is he?"

"Oh, sure," Jamil snapped. "Xris is going to hop around singing and dancing when he hears this one! There'll be an investigation. Which is just *all* we need. Not to mention the fact that it cost us a year's profits to find and refit that Claymore and ... Oh, skip it!" He massaged his pounding temples.

"Yeah. You're right." Harry considered the implications, then, face flushed, he tromped into the hangar to angrily confront the flustered crew chief. "What the hell did you guys do with my plane?"

Jamil should have gone with him, but he didn't. He stood in the hot sun, his head pounding, staring at the empty place on the shimmering tarmac.

And he wondered just exactly when the command cruiser was going to fall out of the skies and smash down on top of them. Everything else had gone wrong. There was nothing left except that.

Which only went to prove that, by nature, Jamil was an optimist.

CHAPTER
28

This is the third time; I hope good luck lies in odd numbers.

William Shakespeare, *The Merry Wives of Windsor*, Act 5

Xris found a hoverjeep parked on the tarmac near the air traffic control building. He was in the act of climbing into it; the MPs were scrambling in behind, when they were accosted by Tess. She cast an amazed look at the MPs, then confronted Xris.

"Excuse me, Captain Kergonan," she said mildly. Lowering her voice, she added in a furious undertone, "But just where the hell do you think you're going? Where's Grant? You're supposed to be watching him!"

"Grant's not important. I had word that the ro—"

"Just a minute," Tess interrupted him. Turning to the MPs, she said, "Thank you, gentlemen, but we can handle this. Return to your post."

The MPs saluted, departed, walked across the tarmac to stand guard at the rent-a-plane.

"You know that *no one* is supposed to know about the robot," Tess said angrily.

"Yeah, well, I think the whole damn base is about to find out about the robot, Captain Strauss," Xris returned, settling down into the driver's seat. He switched on the ignition. "The robot's missing. It popped out of its case and escaped. My guess is that it's wandering around the base somewhere."

She stared at him, stunned.

"You want to get in?" Xris shouted over the roar of the engine.

Wordlessly, Tess circled around the jeep, climbed in next to Xris. The air jets lifted the jeep off the ground.

The comm tickled the inside of his ear. Xris answered, yelling, "Quong? You find it?"

"Huh? Found what? This ain't the Doc, Xris. It's me. Harry."

"Look, Harry, whatever it is, it can wait. I—"

"No, it can't! Some bastard stole my bomber, Xris. Our bomber. The Claymore." Harry was plaintive. "Someone flew off with it and it wasn't me."

Xris knew. He knew exactly what had happened. He didn't know how or why he knew. It was one of those flashes of intuition that come sometimes, striking suddenly and unexpectedly like lightning from a cloudless sky. He felt the bolt sizzling behind his eyeballs.

"Did you talk to the air traffic control?"

"Yes."

"What did they say? Who was pilot?" Xris waited tensely.

"Pilot? What's going on?" Tess shook him by the arm.

He waved his hand to quiet her. "What did you say, Harry? I didn't hear."

"The computer on board the Claymore performed the takeoff. And that's really weird, Xris, because I had shut the computer down during that phony landing. Control refused to give it permission, but the spaceplane flew off anyway. They sent a couple of fighters up to try to force it back down, but whoever is flying that plane has balls."

After meeting Grant, Xris would have voted, odds on, against it. Apparently he'd misjudged the little gray man.

Harry continued, "The computer didn't pay any attention. The Claymore just kept going."

"Did they shoot the plane down?"

"Shoot what plane down?" Tess demanded, exasperated.

"No," Harry answered. "The *King James* gave orders not to shoot. The fighters fired one of those tracking missiles into it and let it go. And you want to know another weird thing? They scanned the bomber and found a life-form aboard. But they couldn't establish contact with whoever it was."

"Shit," Xris said with feeling, and he struck the two sides of the jeep's steering mechanism. The entire left side crumpled beneath the blow of his cybernetic hand. His right hand hurt like hell.

"What do we do, boss?"

"Hold on a minute. I've got to think."

"You have three seconds to tell me what's going on," Tess said grimly, "or I *will* shoot you."

Xris stared out over the tarmac. Harry and Jamil, standing near the hangar, were two small figures distorted by the heat waves roiling up from the red surface. He should have known. But Grant seemed so meek and compliant. . . .

"Jeffrey Grant found the robot," Xris told Tess. "He took it on board our Claymore bomber and flew off with it."

Tess regarded him warily. "You're joking."

Xris shook his head.

"This is some sort of ploy to make me give him back his machine, isn't it?" Tess said hopefully.

Xris continued to shake his head.

"All right. Let's suppose for a minute that this is on the level." Tess was trying very hard to remain calm. "Why would the man do such a crazy thing? Does he plan to take the robot to Harsch?"

"No," said Xris. "He plans to save its life."

"Save it— Someone told him about the bomb. Great!" Tess said bitterly. "That's just wonderful!" Flinging open the door, she started to jump out.

Xris tried to stop her. "Wait till I set the hoverjeep down! You'll break your neck."

Tess ignored him. Leaping nimbly over the side, she dropped to the ground, set off at a run toward the air traffic control building.

Xris swung the jeep around, caught up with Tess. Driving the jeep in front of her, he slammed on the brakes. The air jets shut down. The jeep plunked to the ground.

"Remember me?" he shouted. "I'm the guy who's supposed to deliver this robot to Harsch!"

Tess was breathing fast, her face flushed. "Tell me— did that pilot of yours really fake a crash-landing in a Claymore?"

"Yes."

"Is he that smart? Or that stupid?"

"You don't want to know the answer. Either way, he's the best damn pilot in the galaxy."

She considered, then nodded her head. "Fine. Meet me at the hangar. Be ready to fly."

She turned, started off. Xris jumped out of the jeep, followed.

"Wait just a goddamned minute, Captain! I'm not in this man's Army. I admit I screwed up taking this job. Boy!" Xris shook his head "Did I screw up! And I'm willing to take the robot to Harsch—"

"You're willing to get paid!" she cut in.

"Damn right. I've earned it. But this is more than I bargained—"

"Darlene," Tess said loudly, clearly. She frowned, concentrating. "Your Adonian friend mentioned the name Darlene. Could that be Darlene Mohini? Major Mohini? There are a lot of people who'd like to know where she is."

Xris glared at her.

"Let go of my arm, Captain"—Tess lifted her chin— "and carry out your orders."

"Yes, ma'am," Xris said coldly. Straightening, with a snap, he saluted. "Go to hell, ma'am."

Turning on his heel, he left her.

Muttering imprecations on everything from women to robots to Naval Intelligence and meek, mild museum curators, Xris climbed back into the hoverjeep, slammed it into gear, and roared off toward the hangar.

On arrival, he found Harry standing in the spot where his Claymore had been parked, staring wistfully at a grease spot. "I can't believe it's gone," he said, as Xris walked up.

"Believe it," Xris snapped. "Where's Jamil?"

Harry waved in the general direction of the hangar.

"Asleep." He shook his head admiringly. "That man can sleep anywhere. I never saw nothing like it."

Xris walked over to the hangar. Jamil sat in a folding chair, his arms and head draped over an oil drum. His eyes were closed, his breathing deep and even. Xris started to touch him, to wake him.

He changed his mind. Let him sleep. Odds were, he was going to need it. Xris twitched his jaw in a certain way. The comm channel in his subcutaneous transmitter came on.

"Doc, Tycho, you both hear me?"

"Yes, Xris. No sign of the 'bot. One guy thinks he saw it, but he isn't sure if it was the 'bot he saw or if he was experiencing flashbacks from a bad acid trip—"

"Skip it. New developments. Report back to the airfield. ASAP. Xris out."

He next tried Raoul.

"Raoul, this is Xris. Over."

No response, although he did hear a startled "Mmmm?"

"Raoul, this is Xris. Over."

"Xris?" Raoul was tentative.

"Raoul, this is Xris. Over."

"It sounds like Xris," he heard Raoul say, probably to the Little one.

"It *is* Xris!"

"Where are you?" Raoul's voice had a hysterical edge. "I can hear you, but I can't see you!"

"I'm on the comm, Raoul," Xris said patiently. "The comm. You remember. Left ear. Put your hand up, touch the skin. You'll feel a bump."

"Ah!" Raoul sighed deeply. "I thought you were a disembodied spirit. Or perhaps one of those other voices I sometimes hear. . . ."

"Where—"

"Isn't that redundant? Disembodied spirit? Aren't all spirits disembod—"

"Never mind!" Xris seemed to always get sucked into these weird conversations. "Where are you?"

He could practically hear Raoul's head swiveling.

"We are in an establishment which maintains that it

serves food. Personally, I have my doubts. The man behind the counter asked me what I wanted. I said something light—crackers and pâté fois gras, with a glass of
white wine, dry, chilled to the correct temperature. I
did not specify the vineyard, because I could tell it was
hopeless. The man was extremely rude anyway. He
said—"

"Report to the hangar!" Xris was finally able to get a
word in. "We're leaving."

"Not a moment too soon." Raoul was emphatic. He
was silent a moment, then asked, "Where, exactly, will
we find the hangar?"

"Ask someone. Xris out."

He slumped down in a chair in the empty hangar, felt
the sweat pool in a damp patch on the back of his uniform. He could guess what Tess had in mind—she was
going to go chase after this blasted Grant and his blasted
robot. And what about Darlene? They were due to meet
her when her ship docked on Moana. He wanted someone there with her. He didn't like the idea of her being
alone, not now. Not since the Hung knew who she was.
The Hung may have lost her for the moment—at least
he hoped that was the case. But they'd find her again.

Maybe he could shake loose Doc and Tycho, Raoul
and the Little One? Xris had never planned to have
every last one of them involved in this job. He'd send
the others off to guard Darlene. Yes, that was a good
plan. He'd send them off. He'd stay with Tess and
Harry, help capture Grant and the kidnapped robot.

That settled, Xris tried to relax, but he only grew more
fidgety. When he caught himself thinking that, yes, the
term "disembodied spirit" *was* a redundancy, he angrily
shoved himself to his feet and stomped outside to see
what the devil was keeping everyone.

"Please hurry, gentlemen," Tess said crisply. "The
Claymore has a head start on us. Climb on board and
take your seats. Pilot Luck, what's the matter? I assume
you can fly a PRRS?"

"I can fly anything, ma'am," Harry said. He was being

honest, not bragging. "But ... we're going to chase the Claymore in this?"

"Yes, Pilot Luck," Tess's voice hardened. "What's wrong with this spaceplane?"

"Nothing, ma'am," Harry replied seriously. "Except when do you want to catch the Claymore? Sometime next year?"

Tess's cheeks reddened. She reached for the comm in the hoverjeep. "I'll get another pilot—"

"Take it easy." Xris intervened. "Harry's just being honest. And he's right. This clunker"—he made a disparaging gesture—"will never catch up with a fighter-bomber."

Tess frowned; her eyes glinted. "I'm open to suggestions. Just how did you plan to stop the Claymore and recover the 'bot?"

"Send the command cruiser *King James* after it."

Tess hesitated, then said, not looking at Xris, "Something I didn't mention. We're convinced that Harsch has high-level contacts in the Navy. A flagship command cruiser goes tearing after one insignificant Claymore. A strange-looking robot is captured and brought on board. It would be the talk of the ward room for a week. If Harsch found out, that would be the end of our operation. We might never have another chance to catch him. No, we can't risk it."

"But you'll risk losing the Claymore and the robot?" Xris raised an eyebrow, or what would have been an eyebrow if he'd had any eyebrows. "That doesn't make sense."

"It's not much of a risk," Tess argued. "The Claymore is being flown by an inexperienced novice. We checked Grant's records. He has a pilot's license, but he only ever flew corporate shuttles. As for this 'clunker,' as you term it, the PRRS may not look like much, but she's faster than she looks. She has a tractor beam and, as her name suggests, the PRRS is built specifically for this type of operation."

"PRRS?" Dr. Quong said. "The name doesn't suggest anything to me, except maybe a cat with a lisp. Purrs. Get it? Cat with a—"

"PRRS. Pilot Recovery and Rescue Ship," Jamil informed them. "If a pilot's plane is disabled or damaged in space or if the pilot is forced to eject, the PRRS can tractor home the crippled plane or pick up the life pod. These spaceplanes aren't real pretty to look at, but when you're marooned out there in the endless night with your fuel running low and the black cold creeping into your bones, nothing looks more beautiful than this old girl coming to take you home."

Harry only shook his head gloomily. He clumped up the ramp, entered through the enormous, gaping hatch.

The PRRS was a converted Flamberge medium bomber. Its bomb bay and weapons mounts had been removed to add a tractor beam and a much larger cargo section. The gun turrets had been taken off, replaced with grappling equipment.

Dr. Quong and Tycho boarded, carrying with them the equipment Tess had stowed in her jeep. This included Jeffrey Grant's Collimated Command Receiver Unit, which was still humming to itself.

Jamil lingered a moment to take a long, nostalgic look, then he walked up the ramp. He patted the hull affectionately as he entered.

That left Xris and Tess and Raoul and the Little One. Raoul was hovering, obviously had something urgent to impart. He had probably lost an earring.

Xris shook his head. "Later."

He turned to Tess. "You're chasing after the Claymore. Do you mind telling us what *we're* doing here?"

"Just what you're being paid to do," she said coolly. "Once we catch it, you're going to deliver the robot to Harsch."

"It doesn't take all of us," Xris said. "Harsch isn't expecting an army. He'll get suspicious if seven people descend on him. Harry can fly the plane. Once we catch the 'bot, Jamil and I can handle the delivery. You don't need Quong or the others. I want to send them—"

"Xris Cyborg." Raoul plucked at his sleeve.

"Just a minute," Xris said impatiently. He faced Tess. "Well? How about it? You've got me. You've got Harry and Jamil. Let me send the others on their way."

"And I'm sure the others would go right straight home. No little detours?" Tess smiled. "Nice try, Xris. But no. You're all coming."

Xris gritted his teeth to keep back the words that would have made her furious, accomplished nothing. With any luck, this job would go fast. They'd finish it on schedule, meet Darlene as planned.

Luck. They'd had none so far. They were due.

"Yes, what is it?" He turned to Raoul.

"You said something about the Grant person flying the bomber."

Xris nodded.

Raoul was grave. "He is not the one flying. He is not, *per se*, the pilot."

"Then who the hell is?"

"The robot."

Tess had started to walk up the ramp. Hearing this, she paused, half turned. "What did he say?"

"Jeffrey Grant did not run off with the robot," Raoul repeated his information. "The robot ran off with Jeffrey Grant. The robot is piloting the bomber."

"How does he know that?" Tess had gone extremely pale. "I don't believe it."

Xris motioned. "The Little One. That's my guess. He must have read Grant's thoughts before the plane got off the ground."

Raoul confirmed this. "The Grant person is a very easy subject. His thoughts are simple, colorful, close to the surface, and tinged with whimsy."

"Oh, God!" Tess gasped. "If he's right . . . Oh, dear God! Hurry!" She beat on the railing with her hands. "Hurry! Get on board! There's not a moment to lose! We have to stop the robot!"

The PRRS gave a shudder. Whatever else Tess said was lost in the whine of the turbines cranking up. Xris dashed inside as the hatch slammed shut. The whine reached a painful level, changed to a thunderous roar. The ex-bomber's dual engines began sucking in ionized air faster than the speed of sound, dumped it out just as quickly. Harry released the magnetic brakes and the bomber bucked and bounced down the tarmac.

"Stop the robot?" Xris yelled over the din. He dropped himself into his seat, strapped himself in. "Stop it from what?"

"From doing its job!" Tess shouted back.

CHAPTER
29

Marriage and hanging go by destiny; matches are
made in heaven.

Robert Burton, *Anatomy of Melancholy*

The interior of the PRRS was cramped and crowded,
being essentially a spacegoing ambulance. Living
space was divided into three major areas: the bridge,
crew quarters, and two treatment rooms. The plane's
most prominent features were a docking and recovery
bay, designed to accommodate life pods and the tractor
beam, extremely powerful for a spaceplane of this size.

"The tractor beam could take a small-sized fighter in
tow," Harry advised them. "If it had to. But that's not
what it's designed to do. If a plane is disabled, for whatever reason, it's generally drifting helpless in space. Crippled planes can perform some pretty wild gyrations,
making it dangerous for other planes or ships to venture
near. The tractor beam locks on to the crippled plane,
clamps it down, and holds it in place until the medics
can go aboard to check on the condition of the pilot."

Several enormous, pressurized spacesuits, standing in
a corner of the docking bay, their inflated arms outstretched, their helmets balanced on their shoulders, suggested one way the medics could board a disabled
spaceplane. The arms swayed and bounced with the
movement of the PRRS, the helmets nodded. The sight
was unnerving. Xris, investigating the ship's interior,
caught sight of these apparitions out of the corner of his

eye, thought at first someone else was with him in the docking bay.

Dr. Quong was impressed with the equipment in the treatment facilities. Raoul, investigating the medicine cabinet, was obviously impressed as well. He disappeared for about half an hour, returned smiling, dreamy-eyed, and hungry. Jamil appropriated one of the beds, stretched out, and was immediately asleep. Xris sent Tycho forward to act as copilot.

Tycho protested. Harry was in a bad mood. Disconsolate over the loss of the Claymore, frustrated over the real or imagined inadequacies of the PRRS, he whined and complained, ranted and swore and generally made life hell for anyone in his immediate vicinity.

"Turn off your translator," Xris advised, when he sent Tycho into the lion's den.

The advice obviously worked, for the next time Xris went onto the bridge, he found Harry bitching and moaning and Tycho concentrating on his instrument readings, obviously not understanding a single growl or mutter.

"How's it going?" Xris asked. "You got a fix on that Claymore?"

"It's going okay, I guess," Harry said. "Yeah, I got a fix on the Claymore. The Navy sent in the latest coordinates. They're keeping an eye on it, but they got orders to back off when we get there."

"What's it doing?"

"Damned if I know. The Claymore's just ambling along, taking its own sweet time. Not a care in the galaxy. It's like it's sightseeing. Cruising, surveying the territory. At this rate we're due to catch up with it in the next two hours."

"You know, Harry, you might be right," Xris said thoughtfully.

"Huh?" Harry looked up. "I am?"

"What is this phenomenon?" Quong walked onto the bridge. "Harry is right about something?"

"He may be. He said the Claymore acted like it was surveying the territory. According to the Little One, the robot is actually in control of the Claymore. Is that possible? Could an antique robot fly a modern spaceplace?"

"Certainly," Dr. Quong said promptly. "The robot doesn't have to know anything about the Claymore. All it has to know is how to communicate with the onboard computer. They talk to each other using machine language, which essentially has not changed since the dawn of object-oriented machine language."

"Okay. Tess thinks the robot may be on its way to continue its work—laying Lanes. After all, the robot has no concept of the passing of time. It doesn't know it was sidelined for a good two thousand years."

"And the Collimated Command Receiver Unit belonging to this Mr. Grant has reinforced this idea."

"Did you get a chance to study that thing, Doc, when you brought it on board? Is it really talking to the 'bot? And if so, what're they saying to each other?"

"Yes, I examined the unit. I understand how it works, but not—I am afraid—why. In other words, I do not precisely understand what it was designed to do. And therefore I have no way of knowing what they are saying to each other."

"Do you agree with Captain Strauss? Is it likely that the robot is simply carrying on with its assignment? Getting ready to lay more Lanes?"

"Conceivably," Quong said, sounding dubious. "But I doubt it. I hate to break this to the Admiralty, but I don't believe that this robot will provide them the answers for which they are searching. Yes, it is a Lane-laying robot, but, as I told you before, these robots were in constant communication with Professor Lasairion. He undoubtedly fitted them with a fail-safe device. They would have had to receive a confirmation signal before laying a Lane."

"Wait a minute." Xris raised his hand. "What's this 'undoubtedly' business? Back on base you told me that the professor *had* fitted the robots with such a device. Did he or didn't he?"

"I looked it all up for my report. According to the *Encyclopedia Galactica* ..." Harry began.

Xris and Quong both glared at him. Hurt, Harry fell silent.

Quong answered. "Research exists which indicates that the professor did indeed install such a device."

Harry was shaking his head.

"Suppose the unit is sending out that very signal," Xris suggested. "The one telling the 'bot to go ahead."

Quong was decisive. "The professor himself was the only one who could have done so. The signals were undoubtedly coded. He was the one—the only one—who had the code. The robot might try to lay the Lane, but if it did not receive the correct confirmation signal, it would not go ahead."

"Sure it would, Doc!" Harry protested. "The professor stored all his knowledge in the robots and sent them off. That's according to the *Encyclopedia Galactica*. You can look it up."

"I realize that this is the popular theory," Quong said. "I happen to believe it is in error and I am not the only one. There have been a great many papers written on the subject—"

"Like mine," Harry interjected, with pride.

"Precisely," Quong said dryly.

"Then if we shut down the Collimated Command Receiver Unit, maybe we stop the robot dead in its tracks," Xris suggested.

"Perhaps," Quong said, "perhaps not. Perhaps shutting the unit down might make matters worse."

"How could they possibly get worse?" Xris demanded, exasperated.

"They could." Quong was ominous. "Believe me."

"Tell me."

The doctor shook his head. "No, I do not have enough data."

"Then at least you can tell me what you think it's doing out there. Is it sightseeing? And why steal the Claymore? And Jeffrey Grant? And why is Captain Strauss lying to us? Tell us how dangerous this robot would be if it falls into Corasian hands."

Dr. Quong started to reply, checked himself. He

pursed his lips, shook his head. "No. I do not have enough data."

"C'mon, Doc," Xris ordered. "Cut the 'enough data' crap. At least tell me what you're guessing."

"Crap!" Quong repeated, incensed. "It is not crap! I do not have enough data to make an informed determination of the robot's activities and I will *not* guess. When I acquire more information," he added, bowing stiffly, "I will let you know."

Clearly angry, he left the bridge.

"He said the encyclopedia was wrong." Harry was shocked. "The encyclopedia's never wrong. You want me to look it up for you, Xris? I'm pretty sure the encyclopedia's on file in the research section of the ship's computer."

"No, I don't want you to look it up!" Xris snarled. "Just catch the damn Claymore, will you?"

He turned to leave the bridge, swore savagely when he clipped his elbow—his good elbow—against the bulkhead. Banging the blast door shut, he stomped off, rubbing his elbow and muttering to himself.

"Geez, everyone sure is in a bad mood," Harry commented.

Tycho, not understanding a single word, nodded and smiled and agreed.

Xris headed for the galley. He had two things to do, one of which was to try to contact Darlene on board the cruise liner, find out if she was all right. First, however, he needed to talk to Raoul. And the Little One.

Walking past the crew quarters, Xris glanced in. Tess was seated in a chair, her gaze fixed on the unit, which was blinking its blue light and humming in its monotone voice. She had taken off her shoes, sat with her legs outstretched, her head resting on her hand, her arm leaning on the arm of the chair. Her expression was unreadable. She looked tired, but then they were all tired. She also looked thoughtful, abstracted, worried.

She's got good reason to be worried, Xris thought. The Lord Admiral would not smile favorably on a captain who had not only lost a prize robot, but had let it hijack a plane, kidnap a civilian, and go wandering about the universe, perhaps getting ready to carry on with an assignment it had been given two thousand years previous.

Dixter might be holding a court-martial on board the *King James,* after all. A real one.

Xris shook his head, continued on his way without speaking to Tess. He felt sorry for her, but not as sorry as he might have felt, given the circumstances. If what Dr. Quong theorized was true—and Xris had been with the Doc long enough to trust his opinion—then Tess had lied to them. The robot was not A Danger to All Humanity. It was more like a juvenile delinquent, taking Dad's vehic out for a joyride. So what was Tess up to? Xris needed to find out.

Raoul and the Little One were in the galley. Raoul had ten slices of bread laid out on the counter, was adorning each slice with a vivid yellow substance that Xris recognized (every space traveler recognized) as the durable and nutritious, if not particularly tasty, delicacy known to its detractors as plasticheese.

Raoul was making sandwiches—nibbling as he concocted them. The Little One, standing on a chair at his friend's side, assisted by closing up the portions of bread as Raoul completed placing the slices.

Xris grimaced. "Is that all there is to eat aboard this thing?"

Raoul nodded gravely. "Apparently no one thought to advise the cook that we were taking off. I discovered several bags filled with a supposedly edible commodity made of wheat paste laced with artificial meat flavoring. It goes by the name of W-ham. If you would like, I could add a slice of W-ham to your sandwich. However, if such is your inclination, I feel it only fair to advise you that I have poisons which act much faster and probably taste better."

"Give it to Harry. Tell him you found the recipe in the encyclopedia. Now"—Xris leaned against the counter—"if you and the Little One could halt your culinary endeavors for a moment, I need to talk to you."

The two exchanged glances. Raoul laid the alleged cheese on the counter, turned, regarded Xris with a hazy, dreamy-eyed attention that did not bode well for the lucidity of the conversation. The Little One rotated slowly and carefully upon his chair, his feet shuffling beneath the raincoat, his hand on Raoul's shoulder for balance. The eyes beneath the fedora were hooded, shadowed.

Xris hit the controls. The door slid shut. He locked it.

"This is the first time we've had a chance to talk privately. I want you to tell me about Tess. Captain Strauss. What's she thinking? What's going on inside her?"

Another exchange of glances. The Little One put his hands over his mouth. His small shoulders heaved with what for him were apparently giggles. Raoul smiled a knowing smiled.

"She is very much attracted to you, my friend."

Taking out a twist, Xris thrust it into his mouth. "Yeah, I know. Poor kid. She never had a chance. Let's move past that. What's her angle? I know she's lying about the robot and maybe a few other things."

Raoul was apparently in deep concentration. He actually permitted his smooth brow to furrow slightly— something he never would have done under any less serious circumstances. The plucked eyebrows drew closer together. He stared fixedly at a point somewhere around Xris's uniform breast pocket and observed, "You have not had sex in a long time, my friend."

Xris attempted to be patient. "Outside of the fact that this is none of your goddamed business—"

"Lack of sex over a prolonged period of time is not healthy," Raoul continued, grave and solemn as a biology professor. "I believe I heard that you can go blind. It also makes you irritable."

Xris chomped down hard on the twist, reminded himself that Raoul was a valued member of the team and that it would be counterproductive to wring his neck. "Tess is lying," he said, clearly and deliberately. "Either that or she's not telling us all the truth. Why? And what is she holding back?"

"We have witnessed your deprivation with a keen amount of sympathy," Raoul carried on. "What you can possibly see in a woman who wouldn't recognize the need of a lipstick tube from a guided missile is beyond me. Still, she is genuinely fond of you, Xris Cyborg and"—Raoul and the Little One exchanged sly glances—"we know that you are fond of her. There should be no barrier to your happiness. Go forth, my children," Raoul said solemnly, with a graceful gesture, "and procreate."

Xris went forth, but not to procreate. Thoughts of pulverizing Raoul and stuffing him into a bag with the W-ham were far too tempting. Xris headed for the comm room on his next mission: to establish contact with Darlene, assure himself that she was safe and likely to continue that way.

Yet deep down, down somewhere around Xris's gut, in parts of him that were still human, was a warm glow of pleasure. It was nice to be wanted. Granted the woman who wanted him was lying to him, had been prepared to shoot him, and was quite possibly leading him into a very ugly situation.

But, hell, no one's perfect.

In the galley, Raoul put the finishing touches on the sandwiches, all the while holding a seemingly one-sided conversation with his mute friend.

"Should we tell Xris Cyborg the truth, do you think? It seems to me"—Raoul tilted his head to one side, to view the sandwiches from a different angle—"that this could be rather important."

The Little One agreed that this might be so, then presented his argument.

Raoul had a clear vision of a flower, wilting.

"True. It would take the bloom off their budding relationship. You are right. In point of fact, such a thing could blight the rose of love forever."

The Little One snorted, wiggled his small fingers in the air.

Raoul sighed deeply, relieved. "Right again, my friend. As long as *we* know the truth, we can be prepared to do whatever must be done. And perhaps *she* will tell him herself. I have always heard that good relationships are founded on honesty. I, personally, have other criteria, but most people lack my imagination. So we will hope, for the sake of this relationship, that she tells him the truth. As for the rest, what we do, we do for Xris Cyborg's own good. Someday he will thank us. It would be terrible if he went blind."

The Little One gave an emphatic nod, such that his hat almost fell off into the sandwiches.

CHAPTER
30

For solitude sometimes is best society,
And short retirement urges sweet return.

John Milton, *Paradise Lost*

Darlene was lonely. The feeling startled her, for she was used to being alone.

She'd always been considered odd, even as a child, when she had startled her teachers by being able to provide the correct answer to any math problem almost the second she saw it. What made this more unique was that she was a very mediocre math student. She was rarely able to show her work or explain how she arrived at the correct answer.

Tests indicated that she was a genius, possessed extraordinary capabilities in linear thinking. The teachers, never quite trusting her after that, let her alone.

She made few friends in school. Dalin Rowan never went out for sports or enjoyed hanging out with the guys. Darlene Rowan was still asleep inside Dalin's psyche. It wasn't until Rowan went to work for FISA and met her partners, Xris and Mashahiro Ito, that she found two people who were not intimidated by her. Two people who admired and respected and, better still, just plain liked her.

And then Ito had died, horribly, in a Hung trap. Xris had been supposed to die, but he survived—more machine than man. A part of Darlene died in that explosion, too, though she hadn't been anywhere near it at the time. She spent the next year of her life working under cover, working to destroy the Hung, who had destroyed her life. She was successful. Most of the top people in the Hung were now busting rocks in penal colonies.

But the Hung's reach is long and their memories longer. They are not the type to forgive and forget. Agent Dalin Rowan was a marked man. When his job was finished, he disappeared.

Darlene Mohini was born. Shortly after her birth, she joined the Navy.

A few hints dropped into the computer along the way prompted the top brass to post her to a secret Naval base located in the absolute center of nowhere. Here she was safe—at least for a little while. Here she could perform good work, be of benefit to someone. Here she could be eccentric and no one would mind.

It was considered part of her odd nature that she liked to work at all hours of the day and night, never kept to any sort of routine schedule, frequently requested a change of location for her office and her living quarters, rarely left the base, rarely requested leave.

She never went to visit anyone on base, never invited people to visit her, could be found working in her office over major holidays. She ate alone and at varied hours. She jogged alone. Eccentric, people said. She's a genius, people said. What can you expect?

They never knew she was hiding. They never knew that she took these precautions because she feared for her life.

And then Xris found her anyway.

She was lucky it had been Xris and not the Hung.

During that time, she had become accustomed to a solitary life. She told herself she actually enjoyed it and had gone out of her way to avoid the vid parties and volleyball games and other social contact. Darlene had made of RFComSec a womb—warm and snuggly and soothingly dark. She was fed, pampered, housed, and clothed in her embryonic sac.

The birth process had been violent; she hadn't wanted to leave. But her first gulp of fresh air had brought back to her everything she was missing. Having come to kill her, Xris had ended up giving her back her life.

And now, on this so-called pleasure cruise, Darlene was once again isolated, alone. She didn't know any of the two thousand people on board and none of them knew her.

At least she hoped none of them knew her.

The passengers were intent on having fun, enjoying the major pastimes aboard an Adonian cruise vessel, these being sex and food. Several Adonians—men and women—had indicated that they found Darlene not quite repulsive (which was high praise from the beauty-addicted Adonians), and that they found her company not quite boring.

Then a handsome Adonian gentleman smiled and handed Darlene a glass of champagne. She was immediately back at Raoul's party, seeing again the smiling, handsome face of the Hung assassin.

And though Darlene told herself repeatedly that she had thrown off her pursuers, that the Hung must think her dead and that she was safe, she pleaded space sickness and took her meals in her stateroom.

Darlene thought a lot about Xris and Jamil, wondered how their job was going. They must be finished with it by now, she reasoned. She would have liked to have seen that antique robot.

Surely I've thrown off the Hung. Surely I can go back. When we stop at the next port, I'll—

A mellow tone sounded. A call coming through.

Darlene had been lying on her bed, trying to read an improving book and not making much headway. At the sound—which she admitted to herself she'd been waiting to hear ever since she came on board—she jumped up, ran for the vidphone so fast, she knocked over a chair. She punched the answer button, crouched down so that she could see and be seen on the screen.

"Hello?" she said eagerly. "Hello? Xris?"

Righting the chair, she sat in it, waited to see Xris's face, waited to hear his tobacco-shredded voice.

He came on screen, wearing an Army uniform and hat. Xris detested hats.

"Xris, how nice—" she began.

"Darlene?" Xris smiled at her, casually straightened his shirt collar, tugged at the captain's bars. "That you, sweetie?"

"Yes, it's me, dear. How is everything at home? Nothing's wrong, is it? How are all the kids? Are they okay?"

"Sure, sweetheart. The kids are fine. They send their love. You having a good time?"

"The best," Darlene said dryly. "But I really miss you and the kids, honey."

"Yeah, me, too." Xris was grim. "You're not having any trouble with that one fellow who was trying to hit on you, are you?"

"No. I think he got the message. I hope so, at least. Say, dear, are you and the kids still planning on meeting me when the ship docks at Moana?"

"That's why I'm calling." Xris made a face. "My leave was canceled. We'll make it, but we may be late. I've got a new assignment and my new commanding officer's a royal pain. Very demanding. But, with any luck, we should be on Moana a day or two after you arrive. We're operating in the same sector of space. That's the one good thing about this assignment. Check into a good hotel and wait for us."

"I will. Is . . ." she hesitated, "is there anything I can do?"

"Take care of yourself," he said with a smile.

"You, too," she said. "My love to the kids. I'll see you all in a couple of days. Oh, you won't be able to reach me after midnight, SMT. We'll be making the Jump then. We'll be out of communication range for forty-eight hours."

"Fine." Xris nodded. "Have a good trip, sweetheart. By the way, I ran into one of your old college profs. Lasairion. Professor Colin Lasairion. You remember him? He said to tell you hello. He wants you to look him up sometime."

"Sure! Yes, I remember him," said Darlene, not having a clue. "Say hi back for me."

"Will do. Love you." Xris grinned, winked.

"I love you, too," Darlene said. "Kiss Jamie and Little Harry for me."

Xris rolled his eyes, made a face.

His image faded.

Darlene sat staring at the empty screen. Something had gone wrong. She wondered what and how badly. Xris didn't seem all that stressed and he'd been free to contact her, so he wasn't in dire straits. And he might have kept the disguise more for her safety than his own. Still, she couldn't help wondering.

And worrying.

Professor Colin Lasairion.

Darlene left the vidphone, went to her computer. She knew the name, someone from history. She tapped into the shipboard computer, searched through the ship's archives, which included an *Encyclopedia Galactica*.

"Oh, *that* Lasairion. Damn, I *really* would have liked to have seen that robot. But why would Xris tell me to look all this up?"

She didn't know, but at least now she had something to do.

CHAPTER
31

The boundaries which divide Life from Death are at
best shadowy and vague. Who shall say where
the one ends, and where the other begins?

Edgar Allan Poe, "The Premature Burial"

Jeffrey Grant sat disconsolately on the bunk and
watched the robot pilot the spaceplane. The robot was
doing a very good job. Rather, the Claymore's computer
was doing a very good job, but it was the robot that was
in command. The two rarely spoke to each other, audi-
bly. One of the robot's reticulated arms remained
plugged into the instrument panel on the console. Grant
assumed that they were communicating machine to
machine.

At length, finding the bunk uncomfortable and feeling
sort of silly and undignified, rather like a child that has
been sent to bed while the grown-ups party, Grant ven-
tured forth onto the bridge.

The robot hovered over the control panel. Grant considered seating himself in the pilot's chair, but feared
this might irritate the robot. He sank down meekly into
the copilot's chair.

The robot's sad eyes shifted to him. "Talk to me,"
said the robot, and this time it was not using Captain
Kergonan's voice.

The voice was human, had been prerecorded, and,
from the distinct and separate and uninflected intona-
tion, Grant guessed that the robot had recorded various

vowel and consonant sounds and was stringing them together.

It occurred to Jeffrey Grant, and the knowledge gave him a little thrill, that the voice might well be that of the late Professor Lasairion, dead these past two thousand years.

"What would you like me to say?" Grant asked.

He studied the instrument panel. The comm unit was located in the same place as it was on his simulator game. His game often required him to communicate with Command Central. Grant thought he might know how to use the comm. But he wasn't certain if the robot would let him.

"Your words," said the robot. "I must know your words. It is my job."

"Ah!" Grant was enlightened. "Is that why you brought me along? You want to study my language?"

He felt considerably deflated. He'd been going to rescue the robot, to save it from death, to escape with it into the stars. Instead, it had flown off with him, wanted to use him as a sort of linguistic guinea pig.

Grant talked to the robot. He didn't know what else to do and he hoped, rather bleakly, that by talking he might be able to find out what the robot was intending. It had some purpose. It had to have a purpose. Unlike humans, robots did not act aimlessly.

Grant told the robot about his childhood, which, being relatively happy, had been singularly uninteresting. His teenage years had been unremarkable and those were dispatched in a few sentences. He expanded more on his job, which he had enjoyed, but he talked most about his beloved museum.

The robot was an attentive listener. It never interrupted. The blue light atop its head pulsed and flashed with every word. It evinced little or no interest in what he was saying, until he came to the museum. Then it seemed to Grant that the blue light was a little brighter, that it pulsed a little faster. And once the robot actually repeated a word—an ancient word, referring to some piece of equipment—and it had a very natural sound to it. As if Professor Lasairion had spoken it whole and intact, not just a compilation of meaningless syllables.

As they talked, the Claymore cruised slowly through space. And then Navy fighters dove into view.

"Unknown Claymore, this is Navy Dirk Two One. Shut down your engines and prepare to be towed."

Grant heard the pilot's voice clearly. The robot apparently heard it, too, for the blue light flashed in time to the orders. But the robot ignored it.

"Continue talking," it said to Grant.

"Shouldn't we obey them?" asked Jeffrey Grant. "Or at least acknowledge their instructions? After all," he added with a sudden qualm, "they might shoot."

"They will not shoot us down," said the robot. "The professor has told us this. The enemy will try to capture us whole and intact in order to use us."

Grant didn't know what to do. He knew he should attempt to talk the robot into surrendering, but if he did that, the Navy was going to destroy the robot. Still, if he didn't, the Navy was likely to destroy the robot anyway and end up destroying Jeffrey Grant in the process.

"Unknown Claymore, if you don't shut down your engines, we will be forced to open fire. Stand by for towing."

"Do you understand what they're saying?" Grant asked, a tremor in his voice. He had never played poker, nor ever even heard of the game. He didn't know a bluff when he heard one. "They're going to shoot us!"

"Very possibly," said the robot with the professor's calm voice. "That is not my concern. I am ordered to do my job."

Grant could see the fighters maneuvering into position. Very much like his simulator. In the game, when the enemy shot you down, there was a bright flash on the screen and the enemy voice either saluted you as a worthy opponent (if you had fought well and honorably) or sneered at you as you went down in flames (if you'd fought dirty). Grant wondered what they did if you didn't fight at all. He supposed nothing. They sounded very businesslike.

"Couldn't you just talk to them?" he pleaded. "Explain the situation."

"I am not allowed to talk to them," said the robot. "I am waiting for the professor to respond. When I receive the professor's response, I will continue with my job."

Grant didn't know how to handle this. He supposed he should tell the robot that the professor was dead, but he feared the news might cause alarm or distress and then he had no idea what the robot would do. The 'bot seemed genuinely attached to the professor. Grant decided he would break the news gently, gradually.

"Um, suppose that the professor doesn't respond. Suppose that something happened to the professor. So that he ... er ... couldn't respond." Grant was floundering. It was not easy, talking to those sad, intelligent eyes.

"Nothing has happened to the professor," stated the robot.

Grant was taken aback. The robot was so extremely certain. "How can you be sure?"

"Because I received a signal from him."

Grant thought guiltily of his Collimated Command Receiver Unit. "How ... how did that signal work ... exactly?"

"Whenever one of us has been shut down for a length of time, we are programmed, on awakening, to send a signal to the professor, letting him know that we are back on line. He then sends a corresponding signal to us. If we do not receive that signal, we are to shut ourselves down again and take no further action. I received the signal. Therefore the professor is still functional."

You received that signal because I thought the Collimated Command Receiver Unit made a nice table lamp! Jeffrey Grant groaned and stared bleakly out the vidscreen at the menacing fighters.

This is all my fault! I am the one responsible. If the robot and I get shot down, it will be my fault.

He gazed at the commlink controls. They were very complex, far more complex than those on his rent-a-plane.

"Would you mind if I talked to the fighters?" Grant asked meekly.

"As long as your actions do not hinder my actions, I have no authority to stop you."

Grant reached for the comm. He had no idea how to tune to the correct frequency, but if the Dirks could talk to them, he reasoned that he could talk to the Dirks. He hit the TRANSMISSION—HANDS FREE button. He spoke very rapidly.

"This is the unknown Claymore bomber do you read me over."

And, while he listened for a reply, a thought occurred to him. "What are you waiting for now?" he asked the robot. "Another sort of signal from the professor?"

"Yes. I am programmed to warp space, to lay space Lanes. According to my records, I have laid twenty-five Lanes in this sector. I performed this function prior to the plane crashing. I have transmitted the information on the Lanes to the professor. I am now awaiting his approval."

Grant considered this. He and the robot were cruising slowly through space, awaiting approbation from a man who had been dead two thousand years.

They weren't going to get it.

"What will you do," Grant asked hopefully, "if you don't hear from the professor?"

The robot told him.

Jeffrey Grant's hope drained. He listened in horror. His hand on the controls of the commlink went limp. The pilot of the lead fighter was responding, but Grant did not reply.

It would be better if they did shoot them down.

CHAPTER
32

For the sins of your fathers you, though guiltless,
must suffer.

Horace, *Odes, III,* 6:1

The chase after the robot was very strange.

The Claymore bomber meandered sluggishly through space. The PRRS lumbered along behind it. They knew they were nearing the Claymore when Harry reported sighting the two fighters that had fired the tracking missile, were now keeping an eye on the errant bomber.

The fighter pilots reported in. Tess took the call.

The pilots had not been able to establish contact with the bomber, although they thought someone on board was trying to do so, but was having difficulty using the equipment.

When the pilot of the lead fighter replied, either the robot was cutting him off or something had happened to the person making the attempt to contact them, because the pilot hadn't received a response.

"Most likely he's frightened. I'll try talking to him," Tess said. "You guys back off." She added, in an undertone, to Harry, "Get ready to lock onto the Claymore with the tractor beam."

Harry nodded. The fighter planes fell back, almost out of sight, but within call if they were needed. The PRRS slid forward, into range. Xris was on the bridge, right behind the copilot's chair, where Tess sat. Dr. Quong was standing by in the infirmary, in case Grant was injured. Jamil and Tycho were manning the controls of the docking bay, ready to bring the Claymore alongside. Raoul and the Little One were also on the bridge; Xris suggested that perhaps the Little One could make some sort of telepathic connection with Grant.

Raoul was not confident.

"I do not believe they formed a close enough bond prior to the Grant-person's departure."

"Mr. Grant, this is Captain Strauss." Tess's voice was calm, soothing. "Do you read me, over?"

No response. Tess glanced at Harry. "Do you think he can hear me? Or could the robot be cutting us off?"

Harry considered. "My guess—he can hear you. And he could respond, if he wanted to. The comm isn't tied directly into the ship's computer. The 'bot would have to shut it down independently. Grant sent out a message once and the 'bot didn't try to stop him. He knows how to operate the equipment. He's clammed up for some reason."

"Either that or the 'bot clonked him over the head," Xris said grimly.

Harry's eyes opened wide. "The robot would never do such a thing, Xris. Not one of the professor's robots! They held life sacred."

"Yeah, but this one's got a screw loose. How long until we're in range?"

"About fifteen minutes. Sooner, if you can convince Grant to shut down the engines. It'd be safer, too. Otherwise it's gonna be one hell of a jolt for them when we lock on."

Tess tried again. "We know that what happened wasn't your fault, Mr. Grant. We know it was the robot who stole the Claymore. You're not in any trouble. We understand that you're not in control of the spaceplane, but if you could manage to shut down the engines—"

"Tell him to give the robot something to do to keep it busy," Xris suggested.

Tess nodded. "That's a good idea. Mr. Grant. Tell the robot to ... uh ... run a detailed analysis on all of the Lanes in this sector. While it's busy doing this, Mr.

Grant, Pilot Luck will instruct you in the correct procedure for shutting down the engines."

"No," came the unexpected response, "no, I can't do that." Grant's voice quavered. "I think it would be better if you just went ahead and . . . and shot us."

"Mr. Grant—" Tess began.

"I'm sorry for all the trouble I've caused," Grant went on, his voice growing firmer. "The keys to the museum are in the mailbox. I've left my collection to the Aeronautics Institute on XIO—"

"Mr. Grant!" Tess was finally able to cut in. "We don't *want* to shoot you. We have no *reason* to shoot you. Look, I understand that you may not want to risk interfering with the robot—"

"It's not that. It's what the robot plans to do. It's going to— Oh, dear! You better hur—"

His voice was cut off.

The Claymore made what appeared to be a convulsive leap and then it vanished.

"Damn," said Harry, impressed. "I didn't see that coming! They made the Jump to hyperspace," he added, for the edification of those on the bridge.

"No kidding," Xris snapped. "Can we catch them?"

"Yes," Tess said. Back on the comm, she hailed the fighters. "Did the tick tracking device pick up on their coordinates?"

Xris was familiar—all too familiar—with how the tick devices worked. He'd had an unfortunate experience with one not long ago, in fact. Just before a plane entered one of the space Lanes, the tick would transmit the coordinates of the Lane. The pursuer would know exactly where and when the Claymore would emerge from hyperspace.

"Yes, we have them, Captain," reported the fighter pilot. "Feeding them to you now."

"Can we catch it on the other side?" Tess asked anxiously.

"No problem." Harry was confident. "We wait until the instruments indicate that it's safe for us to make the Jump and then we Jump. We use the same Lane, come out the other end, not far behind them."

Harry stared at the nav computer. "All right, they're in the Lane. This is a real short lane. They're in there, all right. They're ... out. They're out of the Lane.

"Okay, the coordinates of the Lane have been fed to the nav, and we're preparing to make the Jump." He was on the comm. "Strap yourselves in! I repeat, strap ... Oh, shit!"

The words echoed through the spaceplane.

"What do you mean, 'Oh, shit'?" Xris demanded. "Look. This is no time to be reading the goddam instruction manual."

Harry was flipping hurriedly through the nav computer manual. "I know. But this damn nav computer doesn't show that Lane anymore. The computer's on the fritz. Must be. I gotta recalibrate the whole damn thing."

Tess was fuming. "God! I knew I should have brought my own pilot. This—"

Xris was on the comm. "Doc, get up here, right now!"

Harry was reading aloud from the "If This Goes Wrong" chapter of the manual. Quong entered the flight deck, followed by Jamil.

"What's going on?" Jamil demanded. "Where's the plane we're supposed to catch? We lost it on our instruments."

Raoul and the Little One flattened themselves against a bulkhead to make room.

"The plane made the Jump," Xris informed them. "We were going to follow it, but the blasted computer's gone haywire. Doc, help Harry fix the nav computer."

Tycho entered the flight deck. He had to nearly fold in half to squeeze in. The deck was designed for three, and now seven were jammed into it.

"Son of a bitch," said Harry softly, slowly. "There's nothing wrong with the computer, Xris."

"Come off it, Harry. There must be. Doc, take over."

"Harry is right, my friend," Quong announced. "The nav computer is functioning perfectly. It is the Lane that is gone."

Tess paled. "What do you mean . . . the Lane is gone?"

"It's just gone!" Harry was starting to sweat. "I swear

to God, Xris. It *was* there and now it's . . . it's gone! I've never seen anything like this before," he added, his gaze searching space, as if he could find the missing Lane. "I've never heard of such a thing happening before! It ain't natural!"

"The Lanes aren't natural, you idiot," Xris returned. "The robot laid them and— By god!"

He and Tess and Dr. Quong reached the same conclusion at the same time. They stared at each other, appalled.

"Is that possible?" Tess asked, awed.

"The robot giveth and the robot taketh away," Dr. Quong murmured. "Yes, that is eminently possible. In fact, I would say that is what has occurred. I suspected something like this might happen, but I didn't have enough data."

"*That's* why Grant told us to shoot the plane down," Xris said. "He knew. The robot told him. He realized the danger."

"Knew what?" Harry asked. "What are you three talking about? You're always doing this to me—"

"The robot isn't laying Lanes," said Xris. "It's taking them out."

Harry blinked, dazed. "The robot's taking Lanes *out*. Do you know what that means? If there was a ship or a plane in one of those Lanes . . ."

"R-r-r-rip," said Raoul, with a roll of the tongue.

CHAPTER 33

"Excellent!" I cried.
"Elementary," said he.

Sir Alfred Conan Doyle,
The Hound of the Baskervilles

Darlene Mohini sat in front of her computer, which was on the desk in her small stateroom, staring out the window directly opposite. She was staring at nothing, really. The black void, with its pinprick stars, held no interest for her and thus she used it as an artist uses a canvas, painting her own thoughts, her own musings onto what was an essentially blank and uninteresting surface. Having lived in that black void for many years, she had long ago outgrown the wonder and awe felt by the first-timer space traveler.

Actually, if Darlene had been paying particularly close attention to one tiny spot in the dark and star-pocked vista in front of her, she would have seen several of those bright lights moving, for this sector of space was well-traveled. It was a major trade route, and it was also popular with the luxury cruise ships that sailed to the resort world of Moana, a world which was ninety-percent water, a world in which cities floated both on top of and beneath the surface, a world of spectacular beauty and amazing aquatic life-forms and some of the best surfing in the galaxy.

Darlene didn't see ships or stars. She was thinking about her "old college prof," Professor Lasairion.

The information she had on the professor was sparse and not very helpful. She knew enough to guess that the 'bot Xris had been hired to steal was probably one of the professor's Lane-laying robots. Such a find would be very interesting, if you were an archaeologist or a devotee of space flight history, neither of which described Xris. Darlene was wondering why he'd asked her to study up on the subject, when the vidphone buzzed.

Darlene swiveled in her chair to face the screen.

It was Xris, still in uniform. "Hi, dear," she said to him. "I enjoy hearing from you, but twice in one day? I hope nothing's wrong. Little Harry didn't get his head caught in the banister again, did he?"

Xris smiled—the smile that was rarely a complete smile, involved one side of his mouth only and sometimes glimmered in his one natural eye.

"The kids are fine. We're all fine, including Professor Lasairion. The reason I called is that a message just came in for you. From your old job. They said it was urgent. Amy Dixter wants you to get in touch with her. She's got some computer files she wants you to download. She says she's sorry it's your vacation and all, but that you're the only one who can handle this."

Amy Dixter . . . Darlene was momentarily baffled, then she caught on. Or thought she did.

"Amy Dixter? Are you sure? We had a little disagreement, you know."

Xris waved away that consideration with a motion of his hand. "Completely forgotten. Call her at the old number."

"I'd love to, dear," Darlene returned cautiously. "But the last time I tried to call, the number had been disconnected."

"It's hooked up again," Xris said. "Amy Dixter needs to talk to you as soon as possible. You can get through on the old number. You'll log on right away, won't you?"

"Sure. If you're certain that the old number works. . . ."

"I'm certain. I have go now. Love you!" Xris waved at her.

"Love you, too, dear," Darlene said.

The transmission ended.

Darlene sat, mystified, staring at the vidphone screen, playing both conversations over again in her mind. The first she'd figured out easily. A new boss, Xris had said. One who was a royal pain and very demanding. That could only be His Majesty, translated: Xris and the team were working for the government. But now—*Amy* Dixter. A. Dixter. Lord Admiral Dixter. The team was working for the government, specifically the Royal Navy. The old number. That would have to be her files at RFComSec.

The last time she'd tried to access those files—admittedly by going through a "back door"—the computer had turned on her, sent a "worm" after her. But then, at that time, the Navy had been acting under the assumption that Major Darlene Mohini was a traitor. Now . . .

Darlene went to the computer, sat down. She rested her fingers on the keys. This would be a typed transmission. Voice wasn't approved, wouldn't be recognized. She wondered, at first, if she could remember her access code, had a momentary flutter of panic when it didn't immediately come to mind.

Panic eased. The code was there, inside her fingertips, if nowhere else. She'd typed that entry at least once a day, every day, for years. She wasn't likely to forget—ever.

The Royal Navy would dearly love to get their hands on her, erase from her mind all the information on codes, secret bases, classified plans, classified weapons, on all the other interesting and dangerous material that she carried in her head. The Navy had some hold over Xris and the others, but they were able to operate freely. No one was asking her to give herself up in exchange. Xris was smart enough and savvy enough and suspicious enough not to let the Navy make a monkey of him, trick him into revealing Darlene's location.

Darlene was weighing her options when she had a momentary image of Xris stomping around, seething with impatience, waiting for word that she had logged on. She grinned, shook her head. He was the one who had always liked to kick the door down, rush in, guns blazing. She was the one to stand out in the hall and say, "What if ..."

What if ...

Oh, the hell with it!

Darlene typed in the code.

It took the usual amount of time to get through the passwords, the counter-passwords, the genuflecting, the performing of the ritual sacrifices necessary in order to propitiate the Security Gods, gain admittance to the secret temple.

Once there, she did her business swiftly—got in, got out. Only one file was listed. She downloaded that file in microseconds, logged off, assuming—probably correctly—that "Amy" Dixter would get peeved if Darlene made any attempt to roam around the sacred grounds.

The file was safely in her computer.

Now intensely curious, Darlene brought it up.

Xris was on screen.

She grinned at him, though she knew he couldn't see her. He was just a prerecorded image.

"Well, at least now we can talk like regular people," he said. "None of that husband/wife crap. First, I heard about the poisoning from Raoul. I'm sorry it happened, friend. I hope it won't happen again, that you're safe from them. But you and I both know the Hung. Don't let down your guard. Not for a minute."

"I won't, Xris," she promised, though he couldn't hear her.

He went on. "You probably thought one of my circuits had come unplugged when I asked you to find out whatever you could about Professor Lasairion and his robots. The 'bot Jamil and I stole is one of them. God knows now I wish I'd never seen the damn thing. We stole the robot, but it paid us back. It ran off with our Claymore."

"Good grief!" Darlene exclaimed.

"Yeah," Xris said, as if he had heard her. "It's a long story. You'll find it all in here, including my own personal log. It'll make for entertaining reading. To put it briefly: As you probably found out, this 'bot is a Lane-laying robot."

"Oh, my . . ." Darlene exhaled in a soundless whistle. She thought she guessed what was coming. "The 'bot has the Claymore, it's going out to lay Lanes."

"The 'bot has the Claymore," Xris was saying. "The damn thing's out there removing Lanes."

"Removing!" Darlene repeated, trying to assimilate this new and unforeseen information.

"It's taken out only one Lane so far—a Lane we tried to Jump into. Fortunately, the Lane was gone before we leaped into it. If not . . . if we'd been inside that Lane when the 'bot took it out . . . well, as Raoul put it, 'R-r-rip!' "

"Dear God," Darlene murmured.

"We know where the 'bot is," Xris continued. "The Navy fired a tick into the Claymore. The problem is, we can't catch it, because we don't dare Jump into a Lane anywhere near it. The Navy's sent planes, but they've got the same problem we have."

"Why?" Darlene said to herself. "Why is the robot taking *out* Lanes? There must be some reason."

"Dr. Quong, our resident robot expert, thinks that the 'bot must be operating on a preprogrammed pattern. We know what Lane the 'bot has taken out. What we need now is for someone to determine what Lane the 'bot is *going* to take out next. The Navy can safely send fighters to intercept it. We need to do this fast. Next time the robot strikes, it might take out a Lane when there's a ship inside.

"I've given you all the data we have on the robot and the Collimated Command Receiver Unit."

Someone said something in the background. Darlene thought she recognized Dr. Quong's voice.

"Oh, yeah," Xris said, taking out a twist, "I guess I forgot to tell you that part. A fellow named Grant has this Collimated Command Receiver Unit. It's been talking to the robot.

"As you can see from the coordinates, the robot is still in the same sector of space we're in. It's still relatively close. We might be able to reach it before it Jumps again *if* we can figure out what Lane it's going to Jump into. Anticipate its next move.

"The Navy has its top people working on this. You used to be one of them and the Lord Admiral hopes that you'll look all this over and see what you come up with. Use the same log-on if you find anything. RFCom-Sec will patch you through to me. Good luck and take care of yourself."

Xris's image flashed off, to be replaced by a screen full of text—everything Darlene had never wanted to know about an ancient Lane-laying (and Lane-removing) robot and Collimated Command Receiver Units.

Darlene leaned her arms on the table, drew closer to the screen, began to read.

She completed studying the data the Navy had accumulated on the robots, much of which was classified. They had found several of the 'bots, over the years, and had studied them, in an attempt to try to learn how to lay Lanes. The studies had not been fruitful. Apparently the robots on their own had not been able to lay Lanes. The professor had given them instructions, which they had then followed. It required the Collimated Command Receiver Unit, every time, for a Lane to be laid.

"That's it," Darlene realized. "The robot sends a message to the professor saying that it has found an ideal location for a Lane. The professor sends the signal via the Collimated Command Receiver Unit, which activates the robot's Lane-laying programming. It lays the Lane. The professor checks the Lane out, determines if it meets his criteria for space Lanes—whatever that may be—and then sends a signal to the robot telling it that the Lane is okay and that it should go on to the next. But what if the professor didn't like the location of the Lane? He would communicate to the robot that the Lane was faulty and that it should be taken out.

"Let's see." Darlene replayed the situation as she knew it, both from Xris's log and the Navy's files. "The Collimated Command Receiver Unit is stashed away in Grant's museum. He leaves it turned on, plugged in, uses it for a high-tech table lamp. The Navy finds the robot. They can't recover it, due to the bad relations with Pandor, but they send one of their intelligence people—Captain Strauss—to investigate. She sneaks onto the downed plane, finds the robot, reports that it doesn't work.

"Odd," Darlene muttered to herself. "Of course, Strauss didn't have any sophisticated equipment, but if Xris caused the robot to turn on just by jostling it with his shoulder ... mmmmm. Oh, well. Maybe she was interrupted. Security came around or something.

"Anyway, Strauss reports back to the Navy that the robot is not in working condition. The Navy wants it anyway, of course. Meanwhile, the Corasian agent Harsch hears about the robot. How? Good question. Most likely his contacts in the Navy. He wants the robot to sell to the Corasians.

"Now, why would he do that," Darlene asked herself, "if he knew the robot didn't work? That wouldn't make any sense. But suppose he knew the robot *did* work. Then it would be highly valuable to the Corasians. Especially if he knew about the existence of the Collimated Command Receiver Unit. It would be interesting to ask this Grant fellow if anyone ever offered him a lot of money for his machine or maybe tried to steal it. . . .

"Anyway, let's say Harsch knows that the Collimated Command Receiver Unit exists and that he can get his hands on it. All he has to do now is find one of the antique robots. He does and it's in the ideal place, the ideal time for him to snatch it.

"It *is* in an ideal place, isn't it?" Darlene said, now talking to her reflection in the window. She had fit the corner pieces of the puzzle together, put together the outer rim. Now she could start on the interior. The complete picture was staring emerge. "A little too ideal. This was all a trap! The Navy set a trap for Harsch. Except it was Xris and Jamil who walked into it. The robot was the bait. What the Navy didn't count on was the fact that the Collimated Command Receiver Unit still existed. Harsch didn't count on the fact that Grant would take the machine and skip town with it. . . .

"No! Wait! What if Grant is linked in with Harsch? Xris says Grant is a mild-mannered, intellectual type, but then so was Clark Kent. Maybe Grant's trying to double-cross Harsch. Or link up with Harsch. . . . Bother.

That piece doesn't quit fit. Grant told Xris to blow the plane up. He wouldn't say that if he were one of the bad guys. Unless Grant knew that Xris knew that Grant knew and he was trying to throw us off. . . ."

Darlene rubbed her temples. This was starting to give her a headache.

"Never mind. That's not important now. What *is* clear is that apparently no one—maybe not even Harsch himself—counted on the fact that the unit and the robot would establish a dialogue, steal a plane, and go around the galaxy taking out space Lanes!

"I don't like this," Darlene said softly. "It all looks very ugly. And Xris isn't being told the whole story. Not by a long shot. There's something I'm missing somewhere. But I can't take time to work on that part of this now. The important thing is to stop the robot before it kills someone."

Darlene brought up the robot's flight trajectory. Its path seemed random, at first glance, but she knew perfectly well that it wasn't. Robots never perform any task randomly.

She punched up a galactic map. A flashing dot indicated the last known location of the robot. Red flashing lines indicated the Lane that had been removed. Yellow steadily glowing lines indicated Lanes in the area that were, as yet, still functioning. Since the robot had only taken out one Lane, the 'bot hadn't established a pattern. Had it taken out that Lane because it was there? It was close? Or . . .

Darlene isolated the robot's particular sector of space and zoomed in on that portion. The Navy had provided her with the coordinates for the space Lanes in that zone. She was studying these when it occurred to her that something about that sector of space seemed awfully familiar.

Much too familiar.

Darlene left the computer, hurried over to the nightstand. Rummaging through the drawer, she came across an electronic circular, which provided travelers with interesting information on their cruise, gave instructions for emergency evacuation, told where to find the

life pods, reminded passengers of the serious nature of
rescue drills, and provided a map and coordinates of
their sojourn through space. She compared that map
with the map on her screen.

"Damnation!" said Darlene.

The robot had entered Lane number Zeta Three Nine
Three Omega. That was a short-hop Lane, a Lane that
took planes from the outer portion of the sector to the
inner. At least that's what it used to do. It wasn't there
to do anything anymore. The Claymore had come out
of the Jump in exactly the same sector of space as the
Adonian cruise ship, the S.S. *Heart's Desire.*

A knock sounded on her cabin door.

Darlene ignored it.

The knock was repeated.

Darlene touched her commlink. "I'm busy."

The knock was repeated again, more insistently.

"I'm not dressed," Darlene snapped. She wasn't planning on opening the door to anyone. "Say whatever it
is you have to say and then leave me alone."

"Captain's compliments, ma'am. We'll be making the
Jump in approximately two hours. I've made a note that
you are in your cabin. Please remain within for the
durat—"

"Fine, thanks," she muttered, absorbed in her
calculations.

Idiots. Why couldn't they leave her alone when she
was working? She frowned at her reflection in the window and put herself into the mind of the robot.

"I've been programmed to lay Lanes," she said. "I lay
them in a systematic manner. I'm halfway through my
assignment—let's say—when I'm attacked. Someone is
trying to capture me. I do what the professor has instructed me to do. I run. I don't get far—this sector of
space is the sector which contains Pandor—and then either my plane is shot down or I cause it to crash in
order to avoid pursuit. I am struck on the head, take a
long nap.

"I wake up. I'm fine. Something's a little wrong with
my internal workings, maybe, but nothing that I can't
self-repair. To me, two minutes have passed, not two

thousand years worth of minutes. I send out my signal, to let the professor know I'm alive and well, and I receive a signal back. I know, by that signal, that I'm supposed to get up and go to work. I have probably been programmed to escape confinement—the good professor being the lovable paranoid that he is. I free myself from the crate, commandeer the first spaceplane I come across. I also end up with a human, one Jeffrey Grant, which doesn't compute," Darlene admitted, "but I'll worry about that later.

"I go back to work. I'm ready to lay another Lane. I send out the signal, expecting to hear the professor's reassuring voice—and I don't. Something's wrong. The professor doesn't like what I've done. I act to correct the situation. I take out the Lanes . . . in the order in which I've laid them! Of course! The next one I take out will be the one I laid prior to the one I just took out. Now . . . how can I possibly figure out which one that will be?"

She went back through all the information she had received on the robot, endeavoring to find some sort of pattern—not easy, since the robot had only removed one Lane. Darlene had to assume that the robot would take out Lanes systematically; that it wouldn't, for example, suddenly jump from one sector to another without reason. If it did that, she was finished before she began. So far, the robot had behaved quite logically. There was no reason to think it would deviate.

But still, there were myriad Lanes in this sector. Darlene fed the information into the computer, started it working. She began work on her own calculations as well, hoping to be able to make an intuitive leap which would arrive at the answer in less time than the computer would take sifting methodically through all the alternatives. Leap taken, she could use the computer to check her conclusion.

In the meantime, she would contact the Navy, have them advise each ship in this part of space that no ship was, on any account—

A voice came over the commlink. "This is your captain speaking. We will be making the Jump in approximately one hour and thirty minutes. Naval regulations require that all passengers return to your cabins at this time. Please . . ."

"Oh, hell!" Darlene stood up, walked to the door, stopped, turned around, walked back, sat down again. "Hell and damnation!"

She'd done it again. Such absentmindedness was a common failing of hers, as Xris would no doubt remind her, if and when he ever heard about this. If she lived to tell him. She had become so absorbed in the intellectual complexities of this problem that she had completely forgotten how said problem might impact on her. Her and about two thousand other people on board this ship.

And what the hell was the Navy doing?

She called up RFComSec, demanded that the computer patch her through to the Lord Admiral's flagship, the *King James II,* asked to speak to someone in command.

"General Hanson here."

"General, this is Major Mohini."

"I must inform you, Major, that you are AWOL and—"

"Yes, yes!" Darlene snapped. "We'll discuss that later, ma'am. For now, I've been assigned to track down that runaway robot."

"I know." The general frowned. "I advised against bringing you in on this, but I was overruled. The Lord Admiral wanted to speak to you himself, but he's unable to get away. What have you found?"

"I'm feeding you coordinates, ma'am. The robot is in the Yanni Two sector of space. I haven't completed all the calculations yet, but I'm certain that the robot is going to stay in this sector. If it takes out another Lane—which I believe it will—the Lane will be in this sector."

The general nodded. "Our experts have reached the same conclusion, Major. Thank you. Now—"

"They have, ma'am?" Darlene slammed her hands on the table. "Begging the general's pardon, but what the hell are you doing about it? I'm on board a cruise ship in this sector, General. They've just announced that we're going to be making the Jump in little over an hour! Why hasn't the captain been informed of the danger? You need to warn every ship in this sector that on no account should they enter a space Lane."

"We have done that, Major." The general's voice was cold. "All military ships and spaceplanes have been advised to refrain from using the Lanes until they receive word that it is once more safe. All private ships, freighters, planes, transports have received the same advisory."

"Advisory! You *advised* them not to use the Lanes! Excuse me, General, ma'am, but you apparently don't realize the extreme danger."

The General was calm. "Major Mohini, do you have any idea of the thousands of vessels of every sort currently plying the Lanes in that sector of space? Privately owned vessels are *not* under our command. The Admiralty can issue advisories. The Admiralty can make recommendations. If the captains of these vessels choose to ignore these advisories and recommendations, that is their prerogative. This is a free society. What would you have us do—send out gunboats and threaten to shoot down every ship that doesn't comply?"

"Did you tell people the reason, General? Surely if everyone understood the danger—"

The general's jaw tightened, one corner of her mouth twitched. "What are we to tell them, Major? That an antique robot, two thousand years old, is going around taking out hyperspace Lanes? How many of them do you think would believe us?"

"Oh, *now* I understand," Darlene said bitterly. "How stupid of me. The robot's classified."

"And it remains classified, Major. Remember that. I suggest that you return to your work and help us catch this robot *before* it takes out another Lane. Contact us if you have anything further to report."

The transmission ended.

"Bitch," said Darlene.

Well, it was not up to her. Somehow she'd have to convince the captain of this ship that he shouldn't make the Jump. She had to think of a plausible reason.

Much as she hated to admit it, old Iron Guts was

right. What captain in his right mind would deliberately disrupt the vacation plans of two thousand passengers? He would incur not only the wrath of the passengers but that of the cruise line, which would be forced to refund millions of credits for ruined vacations. And she couldn't be certain that this Lane was the Lane the robot was going to take out next.

Yet, if the ship jumped into a Lane and the robot *did* take that Lane out . . .

Darlene shivered. There had been hyperspace accidents before. No one ever survived. She remembered reading about a ship once that had been pulled in two. Half of it came out of one end of the Lane, half came out of the other. And with each half, the bodies of the dead . . .

She started for the door again, recalling, as she opened it, that there was always the possibility the assassin was out there waiting for her.

Darlene smiled grimly. That would be the easy way to go.

Picking up a nail file—a gift from Raoul—Darlene walked out the automatic sliding door. Before she left, she slid the nail file under the door. If the door was opened in her absence, the nail file would move along with it. An old trick, but it worked. She performed it routinely, automatically, didn't even give it much thought.

As she walked down the corridor, she noted—because once, years ago, she'd been trained to note such things— that the door to the stateroom six down from hers was slightly ajar. Inside a middle-aged man with graying hair was seated in front of his own vidphone, talking to a little boy of about seven, whose grinning freckled face filled the screen.

Darlene looked at the little boy, at the man. If she couldn't find a way to stop the captain from making the Jump, this child might never see his father again.

Resolve hardening, Darlene increased her pace, hurried to the bridge.

CHAPTER
34

It's all in a day's work.

Anonymous

The gray-haired man in the room six down from Darlene told the little boy on the screen, "Wait just a minute, will you, son?" He stood up and walked to the door. He watched Darlene stop in front of the lift.

She tapped her foot nervously and irritably on the deck, hit the lift button several times in an effort to hurry it along. When the lift finally arrived, she darted into it. The doors shut.

The man waited a moment longer, just to make certain she hadn't forgotten something or decided for some other reason to come back.

Leaving his door ajar, he walked back to the vidphone. "Uh, I gotta go now, Jason. Sorry I can't be there for your big game, but you know how it is. Daddy's work."

"Sure, Dad, I understand," came the cheerful response from a freckle-smattered face. "My new glove'll bring me luck. Thanks a lot, Dad. This was the best birthday present ever."

The man smiled. "You play your best, okay, and remember: Winning's not everything. It's the game that counts. Give your mom my love when she gets home. Tell her I'll call her tonight."

The boy's picture flashed off the screen. The man spent a moment looking at it fondly. Then he picked up a small metal case, tucked it in his pocket, and walked out into the corridor.

He had to wait a few minutes while a couple, clad in wet swimsuits, who had obviously been drinking more than pool water, went giggling and tottering down the hall to their room. The man lounged near an EMER-GENCY EVACUATION PROCEDURE sign, pretending to be reading it carefully. When the corridor was clear, he proceeded to Darlene's room.

He had to figure he didn't have much time. He didn't know why she'd left, she might be back any second.

He didn't need much time.

The door lock was simple. He took out the electronic pass key, which he had purchased for a hefty price from one of the housekeeping staff. He hoped that the key would work. You could never trust Adonians.

The pass key was genuine; the door slid open.

Once inside, he went immediately to the window. Made of steelglass, the window measured about one meter vertically, a half meter horizontally. The advertising brochure stated that the windows in each individual cabin "provided the dazzled traveler with an unparalleled view of the magnificence of space."

The man pulled out his case, took from it a tiny metal device that he could have balanced on the tip of his index finger. The device consisted of two small plates. Inside was a minuscule power cell. Holding the device between his two forefingers, he countertwisted the plates. Feeling the slight vibration in his finger, he knew that the device was activated. He placed the device onto the lower left corner of the window.

This done, he left Darlene's room, returned to his own room, but did not enter. He continued on past his room, walked through the blast doors and into another corridor, kept on going.

He wanted at least one set of blast doors—preferably two—between him and Darlene Rowan.

CHAPTER
35

And then the Windows failed—and then I could not
see to see.

   Emily Dickinson, "I heard a Fly buzz—when I died"

As it turned out, Darlene never spoke to the captain.
   It was now about one hour to Jump. All passengers
were being herded back to their cabins, where they were
ordered to lie down in their beds and strap themselves
in. Those who felt the need could take "Jump sedation"—a mild sedative. Specially built sensor devices in
the beds indicated which passengers were obeying orders
and which were not. Crew members were going from
cabin to cabin checking to make certain that everyone
was tucked in, strapped down, and comfortable.

They found Darlene striding purposefully through the
corridors on the upper levels of the ship, heading for
the bridge.

She was accosted by two stewards—a man and
woman.

"Excuse me, ma'am, but the Jump sequence is scheduled to begin in forty-five minutes. Regulations state that
you must be in your cabin, lying in your bed, with your
webbing strapped securely—"

"I must speak to the captain," Darlene said, trying to
keep her voice calm, level. "It's urgent."

"I'm sorry, Ms.—?"

"Rowan. Darlene Rowan."

"I'm sorry, Ms. Rowan." The female steward smiled.

"But that is quite impossible. No one is allowed on the bridge prior to making the Jump. Regulations."

"Hang regulations!" Darlene snapped. "I have to speak to the captain. He's got to stop the Jump. You must believe me. I have information—"

"Oh, for the love of Elvis," muttered the steward, rolling his eyes. "Another one."

The female steward gave the company speech. "Ms. Rowan, I can assure you that our captain and the bridge crew have the combined experience of over four hundred years of flying these ships. We've made the Jump at least fifty times in this vessel alone and everything's gone smoothly. I understand that you're feeling apprehensive."

"Damn right I'm apprehensive!" Darlene dodged out of the female's grasp. "Look, your captain has received a warning from the Royal Navy advising him that making the Jump in this sector could be dangerous."

"And how do you know this, Ms. Rowan?" the steward asked politely.

"I can't tell you." Darlene pleaded. "I know this sounds crazy. I know *I* sound crazy. But I'm not. I'm telling the truth. If this ship makes the Jump, your captain is putting at risk thousands of lives!"

"Thank you, Ms. Rowan. We'll let the captain know. Now we'll just escort you back to your cabin. . . ."

Accustomed to dealing with hysterical passengers, the stewards took hold of her arms, one on each side, and gently steered her back down the corridor toward the lift.

Darlene had the skill and the training to leave these two lying on the deck in huddled, whimpering heaps. Physically assaulting two members of the ship's crew wasn't likely to advance her cause, however. If anything, it would merely reinforce the idea that she was deranged. She decided to go back to her cabin. By now the computer would have completed its calculations. If she gave the Navy something solid, they'd have no choice but to send out the gunboats.

"I assure you, Ms. Rowan," said the male steward,

arriving at her room, "that everything is going to be fine."

"Are you subject to premonitions?" the female steward asked.

"It's not a premonition," Darlene said, sighing.

Thousands of ships. Hundreds of Lanes. The robot might take out any one of them. Yet our Lane is near Pandor. Our Lane is close to the Lane the robot has already removed. Darlene was starting to feel more certain by the minute. Our Lane is next. The Lane we're going to jump into is next.

"How about a sedative, Ms. Rowan? It will make you feel better."

"No, thank you."

"Do you need any help strapping yourself in?"

"No." Darlene only wanted now to get back into her room, back to her computer. "I'll be fine. I promise. You can leave now. Thank you for all your help."

"We'll be back to check on you," said the steward. He remained standing in the corridor. It was obvious he intended to stand there until Darlene was safely incarcerated.

She started to unlock the door, glanced down and saw the fingernail file moved. It was in front of the door instead of under it.

Someone had been inside her room.

Darlene hesitated, stood outside the closed door.

"What's the matter now, Ms. Rowan?" The steward was struggling hard to remain patient. He must be convinced by now that she was delusional, paranoid.

"Nothing. Thank you, just dropped my file," Darlene said meekly. "I'll be fine now. I'm just a bit nervous. You've been very kind. I know you must have other duties to attend to. Let me give you something for your trouble."

The stewards presented their service pads. Darlene punched in a generous tip for each of them.

"Thank you, Ms. Rowan," said the male steward. "You go along inside. We'll wait out here for a few moments, just in case you need anything."

You mean you'll wait to make sure I don't leave again.

Darlene unlocked, opened the door. She kept to one side, did not immediately enter. Not because she was afraid of being attacked from behind. Hung assassins weren't the type to lurk about behind the door, waiting to knock her over the head with a lead pipe. They were far more sophisticated.

Darlene stared hard at the deck, saw no tiny beam of laser light that she might break as she entered—the high-tech version of a trip wire.

The stewards watched her. Glancing back, she caught the male grinning. He swiftly wiped the smile from his face.

Cautiously, Darlene entered her room.

She cast a quick glance around, saw nothing out of the ordinary. Nothing had been disturbed. She shut the door, shut out the stewards and their amusement. She turned to look everything over once more.

A flicker of light came from somewhere near the window. Darlene tensed, but further investigation revealed nothing. No gun barrel protruding from behind the bedpost.

"You're seeing things," she told herself wearily.

She was suddenly tired of this, tried of jumping at shadows, tired of making what were most likely harmless little molehills into mountains of fear.

Probably the maid had entered the room for some reason. Leaving chocolates on the pillow, turning down the bed. No one was hiding here with the intention of stabbing Darlene in the shower. No one had put black widow spiders in her nightgown.

Just to make sure, she turned down the bed sheets, searched under the bed and inside the bathroom. Nothing. No one.

"By God, I *am* getting paranoid," she said, and returned to the computer.

At least it had been doing something constructive in her absence. It announced that its initial calculations concerning the Lanes the robot might next remove were complete. The computer offered a list of three Lanes and included the probabilities of likelihood of deletion, based on location of the Lanes in relation to the robot at its present location, taking into account certain variables.

Darlene looked over the data. Something clicked in her head, but, at the same time, something clicked in the room. She leaped from her chair, scooted out of the way.

Out of the way of what? Her imagination was offering such bizarre theories now as crossbows in the vidset or termination beams from the smoke detector. Logic told her imagination where to get off. Breathing hard, more from irritation at being interrupted than from fear, Darlene searched the room again, hunting for the source of the *snick*.

The sound had come from in front of her, she recalled, on thinking it over.

In front of her was the computer, the side table on which it sat. The table was bolted to the wall, presumably so that it wouldn't roam around during the Jump.

Well, maybe her computer had gone *snick*. Maybe the drive was going out. Wonderful. Just wonderful. She would never be able to find parts aboard this blasted Adonian ship. Not unless she wanted to try to repair it with swizzle sticks.

Now, what the hell had she been thinking? Something . . . something about the computer's calculations . . .

Mulling over the numbers in her head, Darlene logged on to RFComSec, transmitted the computer's data. She considered requesting a patch-through to Xris. But what would she tell him? That a fingernail file in her door had moved? That something in her room had gone *snick*?

She logged off.

"Fifteen minutes to Jump. All passengers should be in the prone position, their webbing securely fastened . . ."

Darlene tuned the voice out. She ordered the computer to continue working, sat back down in her chair, mulled over the computer's findings in her head. Her abstracted gaze went once more to the window, to the black backdrop of space, the stars slowly meandering past.

That was it! She knew the Lane the robot would take out. She knew why.

Her gaze suddenly fixed, focused, on the window.

A crack.

Darlene jumped up, knocking over the chair, and made a dive for the window. The crack was small, about the length of the tip of her index finger, and located in the bottom right-hand corner of the steelglass.

But it wouldn't stay small. Not in deep space. Not with the pressurized cabin.

As she watched, Darlene saw the crack extend another centimeter.

In that instant, she put everything together. Her first emotion was relief. She wasn't paranoid, delusional, or overdosing on estrogen! Her instincts had been right!

She had time. Not much, but some. She needed evidence.

Thinking back to the moment she'd entered the room, she saw the flash of reflected light. Near the window.

Light reflecting off metal. Not a gun barrel. . . .

The crack had grown to about ten centimeters now; the pressure inside the room causing it to expand rapidly. In the back of her mind was the horrific vision of what would have happened to her if she hadn't noticed that minuscule crack. Of the window blowing from the pressure. Being sucked out into the frigid, deadly darkness.

The crack was about half a meter long now and extending rapidly, insidiously.

Dropping down to her hands and knees, Darlene searched the carpet beneath the window.

She couldn't find it.

It had to be here! She slid her hand over the carpeting on the deck, felt something hard jab into the heel of her palm.

Breathing a sigh, she snatched up the tiny metal object, clutched it tightly. She ran across the room, hit the button.

The door slid open. The two stewards were at their posts, near the door. One was reporting in on the comm.

"Number one-seven-six is still giving us trouble. According to the sensors, she's not in her bed."

Darlene grabbed hold of the nearest arm, shook it.

"There's a crack in my window!" she cried. "You've got to evacuate this part of the ship!"

"Now, look, Ms. Rowan ..." began the male steward, exasperated.

"We've had just about enough, Ms. Rowan," said the female steward.

"Goddammit! There's a crack in my window and it's spreading! It's going to blow! See for yourself!"

Darlene dragged the man inside the room. Marching him over to the window, she pointed.

The steward peered at the steelglass.

"Ms. Rowan, I don't see—" He suddenly went very white. "A crack ..."

He stared at it a disbelieving instant, then he was back on the comm, his voice shaking.

"Emergency! This is Steward Boseman. I'm reporting a crack in the window of one-seven-six. It's spreading fast."

"Exit the room immediately," came the operator's cool, well-trained response. "I repeat, exit immediately. Leave all personal belongings."

Alarms began their pulse-stopping blare. A rumble shook the ship. Blast doors started closing. Metal panels began to slide across the window, coming down from the top—the Jump shields being lowered in an effort to keep the window from exploding. But the shields were moving slowly. The crack wasn't.

And there, on the desk, Darlene's computer. It had arrived at the calculations a split second before Darlene. Taking into account all the variables, it had selected the Lane the robot was most likely to take out next.

"This is *not* a drill. Repeat," came the announcement over the comm. "This is *not* a drill. Put on your pressurized suits and helmets and proceed to the nearest emergency station. Parents, put your own suits on first and then help your children."

Darlene dodged around the steward, who was yelling at her to get out, and picked up the computer. She made a grab for the case, but the steward, catching hold of her around the waist, hauled her out of the room. Outside in the corridor, passengers wearing pressure suits and helmets were being herded toward the blast doors at the end of the hall.

"The white lights on the floor lead to the emergency stations. Keep calm. The white lights on the floor lead to the emergency station. Keep calm. The white lights . . ."

Darlene and the two stewards ran headlong into the arms of the ship's emergency squad. Suited out in pressure suits with helmets and oxygen masks, three members of the emergency team, armed with repair kits and canisters of sealant, dashed into the room.

They dashed out again almost immediately.

"Too late! Get going!"

Two men grabbed Darlene by her elbows and hustled her down the corridor. At the end, they literally threw her through one of the rapidly closing blast doors. The stewards stumbled in behind her. The emergency crew ran in last.

"Is everyone out?" someone asked.

"They better be," said one of the crew grimly.

The blast doors shut.

Out of breath and shaking, Darlene stared at the rest of the passengers. They crouched in the corridor, wearing their protective gear, staring back at her through the bubbles of their helmets. Someone jammed a helmet on her head, hooked her up to oxygen tanks. Someone else told her to sit down. She sat, holding on tightly to her computer.

A muffled explosion sounded from behind the blast doors. The ship rocked as if it had been hit by a missile. The lights went out. For an instant, the ship was horribly, terrifyingly dark. Someone screamed—an odd sound, muffled by the helmet. Then the emergency lights switched on. That was almost worse than the darkness. Harsh white light illuminated frightened faces, casting strange shadows, making the familiar suddenly alien.

The ship listed. Darlene's helmeted head struck the bulkheads. She was flattened against the deck. Someone opposite her was sliding toward her. A hot-water line broke; water spewed from a pipe overhead, pattering down on their helmets, sounding like a rainstorm. Steam filled the corridor, adding to the nightmare quality.

And then the ship slowly righted itself. The captain came over the emergency comm, announced that the situation was under control; all passengers were to remain where they were and follow the directions given to them by the crew.

They would not, he added, be making the Jump to hyperspace.

Darlene edged her way out of the beam of bright light, kept to the shadows. Somewhere in that corridor, perhaps, was the Hung assassin. He would be wondering if he'd succeeded or failed. He couldn't know, wouldn't be able to see her in her helmet in the darkness.

Darlene sat in the shadows, her computer hugged in her arms, and grinned.

The cruise ship limped, wounded, through space. The blast had destroyed Darlene's stateroom and taken out most of the adjoining cabins. The damage extended far into the bowels of the ship, severing the main electronics trunk line, the main power grid, and the water mains. All communications were down, both internal and external. The damage teams acted quickly. The water was shut off. Internal comms were reestablished.

Passengers were permitted to return to their cabins. All but one passenger, who was arrested.

The captain went back on the comm, explained to the passengers what had happened, assured them that the ship was in no danger, stated that the emergency mayday signal had been activated and that they could expect help to arrive within the hour. In the meantime, passengers could remove their pressurized suits and helmets. They were requested to remain in their cabins. The stewards would be around to serve everyone free drinks, compliments of the captain.

Darlene, held under guard in a room off the bridge, was not offered a free drink. His announcement completed, the captain entered the small room. He stood glaring at her.

"I don't know what kind of sicko you are, lady," the captain stated, barely able to talk, anger squeezing his voice tight, "and I don't know how the hell you managed to crack the steelglass in that window, but—by God—I'm going to see that you're charged with sabotage, attempted murder, and anything else I can think of!"

"Yes, sir," Darlene said, composed.

"I'm placing you under house arrest until the authorities arrive. You'll be under twenty-four-hour guard, locked in a cabin *without* windows"—his tone was dire—"and allowed to communicate with no one, not with any member of the crew or passengers."

"Yes, sir. Thank you, sir," Darlene said, then realized—as the man's eyebrows shot up to the brim of his hat—that this probably wasn't the appropriate thing to say. "Listen, Captain, I understand perfectly. You've been in contact with the Royal Navy, of course. You know that this operation is a matter of the highest-level security. I promise to be fully cooperative."

The captain opened his mouth, shut it again. He shook his head in disgust, turned on his heel. "Watch her," he said to the steward. "And don't let her get her hands on any sharp objects."

"Captain," Darlene said, raising her voice as he marched out the door, "check that Lane. The Lane the ship was going to use to make Jump. See if it's still there."

The captain made an obscene gesture with his hand, consigning Darlene to Adonian perdition. The door slid shut. A large female steward—not of Adonian breeding—plunked herself down in a chair opposite Darlene and eyed her suspiciously, obviously considering her capable of ripping out the bulkheads with her bare hands.

Darlene sat in a chair at an empty desk and stared at the bulkhead. When she caught herself staring fixedly at the bare wall—looking for cracks—she forced herself to pick up one the vidmags which they had brought her. They had taken away her computer.

Fifteen minutes later, the door opened. Two members of the crew stood outside. They were, Darlene noted, armed with lasguns. The two stood aside to permit the captain to enter. He walked into the room, came straight up to Darlene, stopped. He thought he was going to say something, for his mouth opened. His mouth closed. He stared at her in baffled, fuming, helpless silence.

Darlene looked up briefly from her vidmag and smiled. She very slightly shrugged her shoulders.

The captain walked out.

Darlene threw the mag back to the desk. She lay down on the bed, kicked off her shoes, stretched, and yawned. For the first time since she'd started her so-called vacation she felt relaxed, comfortable

The Royal Navy was most certainly on the way. They would rescue the wounded ship, escort it to the nearest port, see to it that everyone debarked safely. The Navy would also hustle Darlene off this vessel, take her someplace safe and secure. They'd ask her a million questions, of course, but Darlene had answered a million questions in her line of work and knew how to handle herself.

They could never prove she'd deliberately cracked her own window. Where her room had been was now a gaping hole; where the corridor leading to her room had been was now a gaping hole. They couldn't prove she did. And she wasn't going to deny that she had cracked it. People on board had been badly scared, but no one had been hurt. And that would *not* have been the case if the ship had made the Jump into a Lane that was no longer there.

Darlene wiggled her toes, yawned again. Maybe she'd watch a vid. She hadn't seen one in years and there were a few out she'd heard were really good. Or perhaps she'd read a book. She hadn't done that in years, either.

The Hung assassin wouldn't try again. Not while she was being watched and guarded twenty-four hours, Standard Military Time. No, for the moment she was safe.

She'd have to deal with the Hung sometime soon. But she wouldn't do it alone. She had friends now, she and Xris and Mag Force 7. The Hung had better watch out.

Darlene grinned, giggled, and started to laugh. The female steward was reaching for something, probably a hypo, to administer a sedative. Darlene didn't care. She could see, in her memory, the computer's final calculation, the Lane flashing, the next Lane the robot was scheduled to take out. And projected over that, the Lane into which the cruise ship was scheduled to make the Jump.

The Hung assassin would never know it. He had actually saved her life.

CHAPTER
36

We are star stuff . . .

Carl Sagan, *Cosmos*

The robot was preparing to take out still another Lane. It had taken out two now, so far. It Jumped into the lanes, then removed them. When Grant asked why, the robot's response left Grant sweating and shaking.

"I laid many Lanes in this sector. The professor has undoubtedly decided that there are too many. I have transmitted the data on the Lanes I laid to the professor. I have not received a response. That means I am to continue taking the Lanes out."

Grant attempted to reason with the robot, to explain that what it was doing was wrong, but it was like attempting to reason with a small child. Not that Grant had ever been around many small children, but he had heard his fellow employees talk and he knew that logic and two-year-olds did not mix. Or rather, that two-year-olds had their own particular kind of logic—a simple logic, a refined logic, a distilled logic. A type of logic based on their own view of the world, which was, of necessity, short in stature, confined by immediate surroundings, and centered entirely on themselves.

Add to this toddlerlike perspective of the world an almost certainly damaged logic board and that was the robot. All very frustrating.

"Isn't it possible," Grant argued, "that the professor could be dead?"

The robot was complacent. "That is just what the professor told us his enemies would say, in order to trick us into compliance."

"But there are ships and planes in those Lanes you're proposing to remove!" Grant pleaded.

"That is impossible," stated the robot. "The Lanes were just laid. The professor has estimated that frequent space travel utilizing the Lanes will not occur for another thousand years."

"What do you think we're doing here? All those people on Pandor? Ask the plane's computer, if you don't believe me," Grant cried. "Look in its memory banks! You'll find the date, the time, information on the current political situation, information about all the other inhabited planets."

"Nonessential," the robot returned. "Such information was interfering with the computer's ability to follow my orders. I dumped all such irrelevant material from its memory."

And, at that point, Grant gave up.

He considered sabotaging the spaceplane, but he had no idea how to go about it. The Claymore appeared practically indestructible. He had just about given up on this course of action when a voice hailed him from the comm.

"Claymore bomber One-Oh-Seven-Niner, come in. I say again, Claymore bomber One-Oh-Seven-Niner, do you read me?"

Grant cast a sidelong, nervous glance at the robot. It listened, but it paid no attention. The blue light flashed, which indicated that it was taking note of the words, storing them in its translation program. But it was not taking any interest in what was being said.

The robot was making surveys, performing calculations, reconfiguring the spaceplane's computer programming to function more efficiently for the robot's needs. To take out Lanes more quickly, accurately. As Grant watched, the robot disabled the Claymore's rear guns.

Grant sighed and moved over to the comm. The voice was repeating its call.

"Claymore bomber One Oh Seven Niner, come in.

Claymore bomber One Oh Seven Niner, do you read me?"

"This is Claymore bomber One Oh Seven Niner," Grant replied. "Yes, I read you. Who are you?"

"My name's Harry."

The voice was hearty and friendly and cheerful. Jeffrey Grant warmed to it. He would have been run through the terminator before he said anything uncomplimentary about a woman, but he found Captain Strauss, while undeniably an attractive person, a bit too intimidating, cold-blooded. She struck him as dangerous.

"I'm the pilot of the PRRS," Harry was saying. "That's short for Pilot Rescue and Recovery Ship. How're you doing, Mr. Grant? What's going on?"

"I . . . I told you . . . I mean I told someone . . . to shoot this plane down." Grant was irritated. "You didn't do so and the robot took out two Lanes. Now it's planning on taking out another one. You know that, don't you? You know that the robot removed two space Lanes? Was . . . was a ship in any of them? Do you know?"

"Nothing certain, Mr. Grant." Harry was cautious. "Let's just put it this was: It would be really nice . . . I mean *really nice*"—he emphasized that—"if the robot didn't take out another Lane. We're in a heavily traveled sector, if you take my meaning."

"Yes, I do," Grant said ominously. "And that's why I told you to shoot this plane down."

"Naw, we don't want to shoot nobody down," Harry said. "I take it that since you're talking to me like this, the robot isn't monitoring communications?"

"Yes, it is," Grant said. "I mean, it's taking note of our words, but it's not assimilating them. It's not devoting its energies to understanding us. Why should it? After all, it's in control. It's doing exactly what it's been programmed to do. I think it would try to stop me only if I tried to stop it. From carrying out its programming, I mean."

"Yeah, sure." Harry paused to consider this. "Well, just in case, I'm going to explain to you what a PRRS does, Mr. Grant."

"I know—"

"Let me explain, Mr. Grant," Harry repeated. "We have a tractor beam that is capable of locking onto a life pod, should it become necessary for the pilot to eject."

"Yes, Mr. Harry, I know all that, you see—" Grant was cut off again.

"What you may not know," Harry said in an emphatic voice, "is that when a bomber is heavily damaged and the pilot cannot or will not eject, then it becomes the copilot's job to eject both of them. Did you know that, Mr. Grant?"

Grant paused. "Actually, no, I didn't know that. I've only been in a single-person simulator. Do you mean that the copilot can eject the pilot? Are you, in fact, saying—"

"No need to repeat ourselves, Mr. Grant. We both understand each other. Now, don't you think that you'd feel better if you were wearing your vacuum suit with your helmet fastened and your oxygen attached and on portable power?"

Grant hesitated. He was very nervous. "I don't ... I'm not ... Suppose? ...What if ..."

Harry remained calm. "Mr. Grant, you'll find a vac suit in the closet at the back of the flight deck. Put it on and then contact me. Harry out."

Grant started to get up from the copilot's chair. The robot turned its sad-eyed gaze on him.

Feeling horribly guilty, Grant sank back down.

But this was the way, the only way.

"The odds of you surviving this mission are so small they don't even bear mentioning," said the commanding officer. "Go forth and do your duty. And know that you will be forever honored."

"Yes, sir," Grant murmured, hearing the words of his squadron commander in his head. Tentatively, he stood back up. "Uh, do you mind if I put on something more, that is, more, um, comfortable?"

The robot did not reply. It had swiveled back to complete its calculations.

Grant hurried to the rear of the cabin. "Quickly, there, Captain. Mustn't show fear with the lads about.

Smooth and professional, that's it. Look good for the lads."

He was finding it somewhat difficult to enter his pleasant fantasy. He really was in a Claymore bomber, preparing to eject into deep space, preparing to risk his own life to save countless lives. His dream-world rather paled in comparison. His dream did have one element that the real world did not have, and that was Grant's calm, cool steel nerves. He decided to stay in his fantasy world.

Grant knew all about pressure suits from his days as a shuttlecraft pilot. Bolting on the helmet, he next strapped on the power and air pack. The familiar actions were calming. His hands shook very little. He plugged in the hoses and cords, switched the unit from external power to self-contained. He felt sick, as if his stomach were going to surge up out of his throat and make a mess on the deck. But his squadron commander wouldn't approve.

"Buck up, there, Captain! You've got a job to do. Let's get hopping!"

Grant returned to the bridge, settled back into the copilot's seat. He flipped the communications panel to hands-free again.

"Mr. Harry, are you still out there?"

"Hey, there, Mr. Grant. How're you doing? Are you all dressed up and ready to go?"

"I'm ready, Mr. Harry," Grant said miserably. "Now what do I do?"

"Let's say . . . what would a copilot do in a real emergency?"

"Yes, that's what I meant." Grant started to sweat. The robot had turned to gaze at him again. He gave it a strained smile through the helmet.

"Like I was saying before"—Harry's voice was reassuring—"the copilot's duty is to eject himself and the pilot. To do that, he and the pilot must be securely strapped into their chairs. You securely strapped in, Mr. Grant?"

There was a pause as Grant strapped himself in. "Uh, pardon me, Mr. Harry, but what does the copilot do if the pilot . . . um . . . refuses to cooperate?"

"Would the pilot be somewhere over the pilot's seat?"

"Yes, sir, he—rather, *it*—is hovering there." Grant started to tremble.

"No problem." Harry continued to be reassuring. "All you do is reach between your legs under the seat and pull the yellow handle. Do you see it, Mr. Grant, the yellow—"

"I see it," Grant announced, peering down between his legs. He grasped the handle and gave it a tug, wondering, at the same time, what it did.

His seat exploded.

The rocket beneath the copilot's chair hurled Grant straight up. The top of the chair punched through the canopy covering the cockpit. Steelglass shattered, as it was designed to do, and fell away around Grant in a cascade of glittering shards. The explosion was loud, but only for a split second, and then immense and terrifying silence swallowed him.

Grant's vacuum suit expanded out, swelling like a balloon. He tumbled head over seat, moving ever outward, away from the Claymore. With each revolution, he saw the spaceplane below him, debris streaming out from the cockpit area, moving farther and farther away.

It was only then that Grant realized what had happened.

He had been ejected.

He stared down at his inflated, bloated body. His thoughts were disconnected and floating, much as he was himself.

There is nothing between me and the cold, suffocating blackness of space except plastic and rubber.

I am alone out here. What happens if no one finds me? I can't yell for help. No one will hear me. What a terrible way to die.

And yet, it's quite beautiful. I can see forever. Huge, immense stars are only specks. I am a speck. But at the moment, I'm bigger than the stars. . . .

At least the robot won't take out any more Lanes. The robot. Grant experienced a moment of concern. Where is the robot?

The next revolution, he saw a metallic speck traveling

in the same direction as himself, arms twirling over metal head. Grant felt immediately relieved. He'd been afraid that it might have blown up in the explosion. The robot was safe and they weren't alone. When he rotated back to where he could see the Claymore, he saw the PRRS come up around the disabled spaceplane.

Grant waved his arm, discovered that this slight movement caused a violent shift in his rotation. He wobbled around sideways, catching glimpses of the robot, the PRRS, and the Claymore at different times.

He held himself completely still and gradually his rotation slowed. Grant felt himself being tugged gently toward the PRRS. Glancing around—as best he could, for the view-constricting helmet—he saw the robot being sucked toward the PRRS.

A hatch beneath Grant yawned.

I wonder, he thought, as he sailed gracefully toward the gaping maw of the PRRS, if Mr. Harry will let me keep this vacuum suit for my collection.

CHAPTER
37

... While we think of it, and talk of it
Let us leave it alone, physically, keep apart.
For while we have sex in the mind, we truly have
None in the body.

D.H. Lawrence, "Leave Sex Alone"

"You got a fix on him?" Tess asked.

She stared out the viewscreen of the PRRS, searching for Grant and the robot. Harry had said they would be difficult to see with the naked eye, but that Xris—with his enhanced vision—might be able to pick them up.

"I can't see them. Nothing," Xris reported.

"Not to worry," Harry said softly, his gaze focused on his instrument readings, hands poised over the controls. "I see 'em. I've got 'em. Lock on target," he ordered the ship's computer. "And ... fire!"

No missiles flamed into the darkness, no flashing lethal laser light shot from the guns. An unseen magnetic beam pulsed outward, bringing life, not death, though one might never have guessed that from Harry's orders.

What appeared at first to be nothing more than a red flashing beacon came into sight, very rapidly expanded into the form of a pilot, still strapped into his seat from the Claymore. Grant's face was visible—looking moon-shaped and distorted behind the helmet.

Next, Harry targeted the second blip and brought it in. The robot, with its sad eyes, stared straight ahead.

It looked like a terrified child stuck on a frightening carnival ride.

At least it appeared docile. Xris had been afraid it might attack poor Jeffrey Grant.

"How long?" he asked.

"Another fifteen minutes," Harry said. "We've got to take this slow. Too fast, and we could lose control, end up with them splattered over the hull. Once we get them safely in, I'll lock onto the Claymore."

"I suppose the plane's useless."

"For the time being," Harry conceded. "Hard to fly without a cockpit. But any rebuild and overhaul facility can put it back together."

"For a price," Tycho said gloomily. "You can kiss the ass of any profits we might have made off this business. As for the robot taking that Lane out, have you considered what will happen to intergalactic commerce if word of this leaks out? I have stock in several major shipping companies—"

"Kiss good-bye," Xris corrected. "Not kiss ass. That's something else entirely. And we're not going to make any profit anyway. Tycho, old friend, so just count this as a dead loss."

Tycho groaned.

"The job's finished, huh?" Jamil said.

"For us it is. Tess"—Xris nodded at her—"was on the comm with the Admiralty. This robot's way too dangerous to turn over to Harsch. They don't want to risk it. Our orders are to bring it back to the *King James II*."

Tess was pale, unhappy. She sat with her head in her hand, her elbow on the console. The other hand, resting on her thigh, was clenched to a fist.

Jamil was sympathetic, gave her a pat on the shoulder. "A lot of work down the drain, I'll bet."

"Months," Tess said, sighing. She raked her hair back. "And we'll never have another chance. This was it. Oh, I know they're right. The robot's far too dangerous. It was okay when we didn't think it worked, but now we know that it does ... not only that it works but that it takes out Lanes. But don't pay any attention to me."

She shrugged, looked at them, concerned. "I'm just

babbling. You men are the ones who are out a lot of money. I'll talk to the Admiralty."

"Never mind, it's not important," Xris said. Noting Tycho turning the jaundiced yellow color his people turned when going into sudden shock, Xris added hastily, "I mean, we'll think of something. Maybe we'll ask the Navy to at least pay for repairs."

"Obese chance," said Tycho.

"I will go back to the air lock to meet the robot," Dr. Quong offered. His eyes glistened. He tapped the tips of his fingers together. "And Grant," he added as an afterthought.

"Take care of the human patient first, will you, Doc?" Xris said.

"What? Oh, of course. Certainly I will," Dr. Quong returned stiffly. "The scanners monitoring Mr. Grant's condition indicate that he is doing quite well, considering the fact that he was never trained for such a catastrophic event. His blood pressure is elevated, his heart rate is accelerated, but not beyond an acceptable range. I will administer a mild sedative to calm him. As for the robot"— Quong was intense, eager —"what should I do for the robot?"

"We have to shut it down," Tess said wearily. "From what we've seen, it would be quite capable of taking control of this ship."

"It appears passive enough now," Dr. Quong stated, staring out the viewscreen as the robot and Grant slid past, on their way to the air lock, which was located at the rear of the PRRS. "Still, I will be careful. I believe I know how it can be deactivated. I've been doing some research on it and, as it turns out, I found quite a useful diagram."

"I'll come with you," Tess offered. "Where did you find a picture of the robot?"

"The encyclopedia," Quong said.

"Told you!" Harry glanced around, triumphant.

Xris snorted. He followed Tess and the doctor out into the narrow corridor.

"You go on ahead, Doc. I want a word with Captain Strauss."

"Certainly." Quong chuckled.

Continuing on down the corridor, he ran into Raoul and the Little One on their way to the cockpit. Quong said something in a low voice to Raoul, jerked his thumb over his shoulder.

Seeing Xris and Tess, Raoul raised his eyebrows, smiled delightedly, and, catching hold of the Little One, yanked him out of the corridor with such rapidity that he took the Little One, but left the fedora behind. The hat fell to the deck. A bejeweled and manicured hand appeared, snatched up the fedora, waved it in Xris's direction, and vanished.

Tess almost smiled.

Xris growled, took out a twist. "You want to go to the prom?" he asked her. "My dad gave me the keys to the hover."

This time she did smile. "It's all right. I understand. Your people think a lot of you, Xris. They're not the only ones," she added softly. Her hand twined in his, fingers locking.

Xris pulled her close. "This lousy excuse for a job is just about finished. We drop the 'bot off at the *King James,* and it's over. After that, well, we're meeting a friend on the planet Moana. You know it? It's a paradise."

"The honeymoon planet?" Tess said. "I've heard of it. I've never been there."

"I'd like to take you," Xris said. "You said you had some leave coming. . . ."

She looked up at him, her expression grave, thoughtful, unusually serious. Her hand in his tightened. A small, dark furrow drew her brows together. "I'm not sure . . . You see . . . the job's not quite over yet, Xris. I . . ." she paused, gazed at him intently. Her expression cleared; the furrow was gone. She smiled at him, a true smile. "I'd like that. I'd like that very much. I'll meet you on any planet, any place, anytime. It doesn't have to be a paradise. We can take care of that ourselves."

Xris bent to kiss her, but, at that moment, Harry stuck his head out of the cockpit. "Xris!" he bellowed, as if Xris were at the other end of the ship. "Oh," he said.

grinning. "There you are. Sorry to interrupt, but we've got another message coming through from the Admiralty. For you, this time. Not Captain Strauss. I think it has something to do with ... um ... you know. That Adonian cruise liner." He gave a wink and a nod, probably thought he was being subtle. "And I'll be bringing our passengers on any moment now."

"It sounds like a private conversation. I'll go help Dr. Quong," Tess offered. She slid her hand out of Xris's grasp and was away, walking rapidly down the corridor, before he could stop her.

Xris turned to go back to the cockpit. What, he wondered, had she been *about* to say?

A hand plucked at his sleeve. Xris glanced to his left. Raoul was lurking in a hatchway.

"Well?" Raoul demanded.

"Well what?" Xris glared at the Adonian, silently advising him to keep his mouth shut.

The advice was completely lost on Raoul, who continued on. "Did you ... you know?" He accompanied the words with a salacious wiggle of his hips, making gestures that would have had him arrested on some of the more conservative worlds in the galaxy.

"Not that it's any of your business," Xris said through clenched teeth, "but I was with her for exactly three minutes in a narrow corridor."

Raoul was clearly not impressed. "Unimaginative," was his pronouncement, "and lacking in manual dexterity."

"Xris!" Harry called urgently. His voice cracked.

Xris shouldered Raoul aside, walked into the cockpit. "Yes, I'm here. What is it?"

Harry, seated in the pilot's chair, peered over his shoulder. His ordinarily choleric and cheerful face was blotchy, patches of red mottled with white. He licked his lips.

Xris felt his stomach muscles tighten. "What the hell is it? What's wrong?"

"It's Darlene," Harry began, and had to stop to clear his throat. "Before we caught it, the robot took out another Lane. Her ship. The cruise ship ..."

Xris was in the copilot's chair. "Put me through to the admiral."

"They don't know anything for sure, Xris," Harry said. "Darlene sent them her data on the Lanes the robot might take out next and that Lane was one of them. She knew, Xris. She knew in time to warn the captain."

"Well, did she?" Xris demanded.

"That's just it, Xris." Harry looked sick. "The Navy's lost contact with the ship . . . and with Darlene."

"Damn! Fuck it! Damn!" Xris wanted to hit something, wanted to hit himself.

The "ifs" began their tormenting litany in Xris's mind. If he'd never trusted Sakuta. If he'd never taken this rotten, lousy, fucking job. If he'd kept better track of the goddamned robot. If . . . if . . . if . . .

Not one of them any damn good to him now.

"Xris," Quong's voice came over the comm. "I have recovered Mr. Grant and the robot. Mr. Grant is suffering from shock but is otherwise unharmed. I have given him a mild sedative and put him to bed. As for the robot—"

"Disable it!" Xris said, his voice thick.

"I—"

"Disable the blasted thing!" Xris swore viciously. "If you can't or won't, I'll come down there and crack it apart myself!"

"That will not be necessary." Quong's voice was deliberate, cool. "As I was about to say, the robot is not functional. I'm not certain why; it may have something to do with the ejection. According to Grant, the ride was a rough one. I will, of course, examine it thoroughly."

"Fine. Good. You do that, Doc," Xris said bitterly.

"What is the matter, my friend? You sound—"

"The damn robot took out one more Lane before we stopped it. This time there was a ship in it. An Adonian cruise liner—"

"Oh, dear God," he heard Tess say softly in the background.

"An Adonian cruise ship." Quong was silent a moment, then said, "Have you—has anyone—heard from Darlene?"

"They've lost contact," Xris said quietly. "But it was her ship. The one she was aboard."

"We don't know that for sure," Harry argued stubbornly.

"I'll be right up, my friend," Quong said.

"No. I'm fine, Doc. You stay there, make damn sure that the robot's dead and that it's going to stay dead. Xris out."

Xris sat for long moments in silence. Jamil came in, then Tycho. They'd both caught part of his conversation with Quong, wanted to know what was going on. Harry told them. Xris felt their eyes, felt them looking at him. They were talking to him, too, but he didn't listen.

Raoul came in, with the Little One. "Is it true? I just spoke to Dr. Quong. How very dreadful. And Darlene?"

Everyone looked at Xris, motioned for Raoul to keep quiet. After one more "How very dreadful," Raoul subsided.

Tess arrived. The rest backed up against the bulkheads to make room for her. She leaned down. "Dr. Quong told me you had a friend on that ship. Oh, Xris, I'm sorry. So very sorry."

He ignored her, too. She obviously wanted to say something more, glanced around at the others. They shook their heads. Eventually she, too, backed off.

Xris said, very quietly, "Harry, change course."

"What?" Harry looked startled. "Change course? What about the robot? We're supposed to deliver it to the *King James II* ASAP."

"The hell with the robot," Xris said savagely, glowering at Harry, at them all. "Take us to where that Lane used to be. There might be survivors."

The others exchanged glances. Harry gnawed his lip, stared down at the console. Tess turned her face away. The Little One made a whimpering sound. Raoul put his arm comfortingly around his small friend. Jamil rested his hand on Xris's shoulder.

"Xris, I know how you're feeling. But you have to face the facts."

"I said, change course," Xris said softly. He had to speak softly or else he would start to yell, and if he yelled they would think he was losing control—and he knew what he was doing. By God, he knew what he was doing. There would be survivors. There *would* be survivors. "We're a medical ship. We have a doctor on board. We can tow in life pods."

No time. There would have been no time to get the passengers into life pods. Ri-i-i-ppp. Half the ship could be at the beginning of the Jump, half at the end.

"Change course," Xris said for the third time, and then he was on his feet, getting ready to yank Harry out of the pilot's chair.

"Hold it. Hold it right there," Tess ordered. She held a lasgun in her hand and that gun was pressed against the side of Raoul's head. "Hands in the air. Come on—you, too, Xris."

"Ugh!" Raoul wrinkled his nose. His gaze slid side-long at the lasgun that was pressing against his temple. "She had that thing under her armpit!"

"I said, don't move, Loti!" Tess warned.

"She means it, Raoul," Xris said. "Hold still."

He was starting to figure things out. And if he was right, then he was in line for the Number One Chump of All Time Award.

Raoul's eyelashes fluttered. He was in agony. "Is the gun mussing my hair?"

Xris tested his theory. "Look, Captain Strauss, I don't know what you're in this for. Maybe it's your colonel's bars or maybe the glory. I don't much care. But—"

"It's not the glory, Xris," Tess said. She shrugged, smiled. "It's the money. Harry, back off. The computer will be flying the plane. *I've* changed the course."

"No need," Harry said. "The course is already laid in for the *King James*. Look, Xris, let's go to the *King James* first, drop off the robot, and then we can—"

"We're not going to the *King James*," Xris said.

"Xris, she's gonna blow off Raoul's head."

"Look at your instruments, Harry. What do they read? What's our course?"

"It's . . ." Harry's voice ended in a strangled gargle.

"It's . . . Hell's Outpost!" He twisted around. "The *King James II* isn't at Hell's Outpost, Xris."

"We know that, Harry. Most of us do, at any rate."

"The Navy thinks I work for them, Harry," Tess said. She continued to keep the gun pointed at Raoul's head. "But the Navy's mistaken. In reality, I work for someone else."

"Harsch," said Xris. "She works for Harsch."

"But she's wearing a Navy uniform and everything." Harry was a little slow on the uptake.

"Ever heard of a double agent, my friend?"

"Oh." Harry blinked.

Xris, facing the hatchway, caught a glimpse of movement.

Quong was in the corridor. He had heard what was going on over Xris's commlink. The doctor was padding, soft-footed, toward the cockpit, a lasgun in his hand. He would sneak up on Tess from behind.

Xris saw the Doc, understood the plan, looked away, shifted his gaze so as not to draw Tess's attention that direction.

"That's how Harsch knew about the robot," he said, hoping to distract her. "And that's how Tess knew we were coming to Pandor. Harsch hires us to steal the robot. His agent Captain Strauss is posted on Pandor to keep watch on us and the Navy at the same time. Meanwhile, she plays both ends against the middle, reports on Harsch to the Admiralty.

"Everything goes according to plan. Tess manages Jamil and me. Hell, we fell for her story like a metric ton of bullshit. We were supposed to take the robot to Harsch. The robot has the bomb in it and the transmitter, but my guess is that those 'malfunction.' You see to that, of course. Harsch gets the robot. The Navy gets squat. You roll those pretty blue eyes at the Lord Admiral and say you can't imagine what went wrong.

"Or, hey, here's an idea. Maybe you blame it on us. Make us the fall guys. . . . Yeah, that's the deal, isn't it? Even now. You come out of this smelling sweet and squeaky clean. Who will the Navy believe, after all? One of their own agents? Or us? We're already in trouble with the Admiralty."

Quong, gun aimed, was drawing nearer and nearer. He didn't dare shoot, for fear of hitting Raoul. Or maybe missing completely and putting a lethal hole through the spaceplane's viewscreen.

"She had it planned out well," Xris continued. "But then things started to fall apart. You guys showed up. That really scares her. Captain Strauss here figures that we're about to double-cross her. Double-cross the double-crosser, as it were. And then Jeffrey Grant arrives. The robot takes off. And that leaves you in a pickle, doesn't it, sister? Who was it ordered you to commandeer that plane and take off after the robot? Harsch—of course you reported in to him. Or was it the Admiralty?"

"For once, they were in agreement. I have to admit, things got pretty interesting there for a while," Tess conceded. "Oh, and speaking of that bomb—the one the admiral gave to Jamil. Have you checked, lately, to see if you still have it?"

Xris shot a swift questioning glance at Jamil.

Jamil shrugged, looked helpless.

"Because you won't find it," Tess continued calmly. "I planted it somewhere in this spaceship. It's set to detonate in twelve hours, which is when we're due to arrive at Hell's Outpost. I'm the only one who can stop the detonation. I'm the only one who knows where the bomb is. So I wouldn't try any heroics, Dr. Quong," she added, glancing over her shoulder. "I suggest you put away the lasgun."

The disconcerted Quong looked at Xris.

"She's the boss now," Xris said. "Do as she says."

"Do you believe her?" Quong continued to hold his lasgun, aimed at Tess.

"Believe her!" Raoul said fervently. "Is there grease on the barrel?"

"I don't think we've got much choice," Xris said dryly. "Harry, what would happen if a bomb went off inside this spaceplane?"

"Before or after we decompressed?" Harry growled.

Quong shrugged, tossed the lasgun onto the deck at Tess's feet. "She fooled me completely."

"You aren't the only one, Doc," Xris said. "You aren't the only one."

Tess lowered the gun from Raoul's head. "Okay, Adonian. You're free to go touch up your lipstick."

Jamil was still squirming. "Uh, excuse me, Captain. But I gotta go to the head. Real bad."

"Sure." Tess waved her hand. "Go on. Check the case for the bomb. You won't find it."

Jamil gave Xris a look.

Xris took out a twist. "Go ahead."

Glowering at Tess as he passed her, Jamil left the cockpit.

"Well, you didn't think I was going to spend twelve hours sitting here holding a gun on the Adonian, did you?" Tess asked, amused. "I need my beauty sleep."

"I don't know what for," Raoul said caustically. He cast a reproachful glance at Xris. "And after all the trouble we went to."

The Little One kicked Raoul in the shins.

Raoul groaned, rubbed his leg.

Xris put the twist in his mouth, began to chew it. "I'm beginning to lose sight of what I saw in her myself."

Tess picked up the gun from the deck, shoved it into her belt. "I'm sorry about all this, Xris. I really am. Things were supposed to have worked out differently. You would have never known the truth about me. But first Grant shows up with his machine. We had no idea one of those was still in existence! Then the robot takes off on its own. All of which turned out to be good, in a way."

"Increased the robot's value for your boss," Xris said.

"Yes. And then the robot proved that it was still functional—"

"By taking out Lanes. Boy, I'll bet Harsch pays you a bonus for this one. Of course, that's not going to mean much to the thousand or so people who died on that cruise ship."

"I'm sorry, Xris," Tess repeated earnestly. "I'm sorry about your friend. I know you're not going to believe this, but I wasn't lying about everything. I do really like you, Xris, and maybe, when this is all finished, we can ..."

Xris said nothing. He stared at her and eventually her voice trailed off. Her eyes lowered.

Jamil returned. "The bomb's gone," he reported.

"Sure it's gone," Xris said. "Even if she's bluffing, the bomb's gone. You don't get in the NI by making stupid mistakes." He rounded suddenly on Raoul and the Little One, who were both slipping quietly out the door. "Wait just a goddamn minute!"

He caught hold of the Little One by the collar of the raincoat, dragged him backward.

"What do you mean—all the trouble you went to? I asked the two of you what was going on with Tess. You knew the truth! Damn it! You two knew and you didn't tell me!"

"Do not shake him, Xris Cyborg!" Raoul said worriedly, coming to the rescue of his small friend. "You'll ruin his digestion!"

"Like hell they knew!" Tess said sharply. "I told Harsch that using the telepathic scrambler was a waste of time and money. The little fart's no more a telepath than that girder there. I tested him two or three times and he never once caught on. They've been conning you, Xris. It's all a trick. I've seen better shows in a Laskar nightclub."

Raoul glanced at Xris from beneath lowered lashes. The Little One tilted back his head, peered up at Xris from beneath the brim of the fedora.

No, Xris thought, whoever has been conned, it wasn't me. These two knew the truth about Tess. They've known it all along. And they hadn't said a word, because ... because ...

It's been a long time since I've had sex.

You have to give Raoul credit. He has his priorities in order. They don't happen to be the priorities of anyone else in the known universe, but ... that's an Adonian for you.

"We're going to be making the Jump to hyperspace in about twenty minutes," Tess was saying. "Fortunately, the Lane we need is still there. I'm going to go lie down, get some rest. I suggest that you gentlemen do the same. I'm sure you'll want to be at your best when you meet Mr. Harsch. Unless, of course, you want to spend your time searching for the bomb. If that keeps you happy and occupied, be my guests."

"I'll stay here with Harry, monitor the Jump," Xris offered. "The rest of you—go lie down. Like the lady says, we'll want to be at our best when we meet Mr. Harsch."

Xris shoved past Tess.

She caught hold of his arm, his phony arm. "Xris, I wish . . ." Her eyes were pleading. For what? Sympathy? Understanding?

As Tycho would say, *Obese chance.*

Xris turned away.

Behind him, he heard Raoul wail plaintively, "I can't think *where* we went wrong."

CHAPTER
38

You must be generous to double agents.

> Sun-tzu, *The Art of War*

The journey through hyperspace to the frontier was long, tedious, and tense. The only compensation was, as Jamil said, that everyone had a chance to catch up on their sleep.

Those who could sleep.

Xris was not among that number and, from the ragged-edged looks of her, Tess—for all her talk—wasn't slumbering soundly, either.

Good! thought Xris. Being in a Macbeth-like mood, he hoped she turned into an insomniac.

If she was worried that they were going to attack her in her sleep, she needn't have been. Xris could have told her as much. Not that the team was idle. Each had his assignment and at least one had come up with something, apparently.

"I need to talk to you," Harry said in a low voice, bumping into Xris in a corridor.

Xris nodded. "Where's Tess?"

"Back with the robot."

"What's she doing?" he asked.

"Running an analysis on that machine of Grant's. I asked her and she said that she wants to know how it works before she presents it to her boss."

"Fine. Get the others. Meet in the galley."

Harry's face brightened. "Lunch," he said, and hurried off.

Xris entered the galley, where the others were seated around the table. Raoul had made more sandwiches, but only Harry was eating.

"Well, what is it?" Xris asked.

Harry, mouth full, chewed rapidly, swallowed. "I ran the computer scan for the bomb. I found it," he said, and took another bite.

Xris reached over, snatched the sandwich out of his hand. "You can eat later. Where is it?"

"It's attached to the recovery bay structural girder, about three-quarters back."

"That bomb's the size of Harry's brain," Jamil commented. "If it did go off, how much damage could it do to this spaceplane? The plane's built to withstand laser blasts."

Quong corrected him. "The *shields* are built to withstand laser blasts. That's why they are there, in order to protect the hull. The bomb wouldn't have to do much damage at all. We are in hyperspace. The tiniest crack could rip us apart."

Xris chewed a wad of soggy twist. "Okay, we've found the bomb. Can we disarm it, Doc?"

"Not without risking setting it off. I examined the bomb when it was in Jamil's possession. It is very sophisticated, very delicate. Face it, my friend. She has us by the shorts, as Tycho would say."

Xris spit the twist into the trash compactor. "How's this? We set off the bomb, blow up this plane and everyone in it. Including the robot."

Tess's voice came from behind. "That would be the noble thing to do." She stood in the doorway, was regarding Xris gravely. "But you won't do it."

"I won't, huh?" Xris eyed her. "You think I don't have the guts to do it? Or that maybe these guys wouldn't go along?"

"Do it," said Jamil briefly.

"Sure, go ahead, Xris!" Harry was grim.

Quong nodded his head. "An appropriate sacrifice in the name of humanity. I concur."

Tycho nodded. "My insurance is fully paid. And I have set up a tax-sheltered annuity for the death benefits. My family would make considerable profit."

Raoul's eyes glistened. "I have often wondered what it would be like to die by some violent means. And this . . . the terrible expectation, the mounting fear, and then the blast itself . . ."

The Little One made two fists of his hands, slammed them together in a gesture Xris had come to know meant the telepath was emphatically with them.

Xris turned to Tess. "The vote's in and counted, sister."

Tess stood leaning against the door, her arms crossed over her chest. "Oh, you'd do it. I have no doubt. If Xris gave the order, you'd blow up yourselves, me, the robot." She snapped her fingers. "Like that. But Xris won't give that order."

Xris knew darned well that he wouldn't, but he was interested in hearing her reason. "Why not?"

She looked at him and smiled, not a cocky smile, not a smirk. Just a smile, a warm smile. An affectionate smile. "Because that would be giving up, admitting that you were defeated. And that's something you'll never do, not as long as there's breath in that shiny metal body of yours. Am I right?"

Xris took out another twist. He said nothing.

Tess spread her hands. "Look, guys. Nick Harsch is a businessman. He made a deal. He'll stick to it. The worst that can happen is that he'll dock you a couple of thousand credits for being late. But seeing as how the robot is more than he ever anticipated, he might give *you* a bonus. You'll be on your way home soon enough, with money in your account."

"And a Lane-sucking robot in the claws of the Corasians." Xris rolled the twist between his thumb and forefinger. "A robot that's already killed a thousand people."

"We don't know that for sure," Harry said.

Xris ignored him. "Sorry, sister. Counting money may help you get to sleep at night, but it doesn't do much for me."

Tess regarded him thoughtfully. "Harsch misjudged you. I guess I did, too."

"It's a common mistake—misjudging people. I made it, too, sister," Xris said. "Big-time."

Tess flushed faintly. "What I came in to tell you is that I just looked in on Jeffrey Grant. He's coming out of sedation. I informed him of what was going on. That there's a bomb on the plane and we're flying it to take the robot to Harsch. I'm not a doctor, but it's my opinion that Grant might need to be sedated again. Well, I'm back to work. You *will* let me know if you plan to blow up the plane, won't you?" She walked off.

"Resourceful, energetic, an expert on explosives. You know"—Jamil gazed after Tess in mock admiration—"I believe I might marry that woman. That is, if you don't want her, Xris."

"Personally," Quong said coldly, "I would enjoy shoving her out the air lock."

"Doc," Harry asked, "is there any way we could sabotage the robot? Make it useless to the Corasians?"

"Yes," Quong returned, in a bad mood. "Bring me the bomb. I'll put it in the robot and we'll blow it up. That would be the only way it would be useless to the Corasians. They do not need to know how to use the robot to build Lanes. Not anymore. All they need to know is how to use it to take the Lanes out."

He left to attend to his patient.

Tycho shut off his translator, said something no one understood, and went out after the doctor.

"Does this mean we're *not* going to blow up the plane?" Harry wondered.

"I trust we're not," Raoul said. "The more I think about it, the more I think that such a catastrophic event would absolutely ruin my day. To say nothing of my outfit at the time." He looked at Xris, the usually vacant eyes suddenly snapped into focus. "I could poison her coffee."

"And what would you do about the bomb that's set to explode in six hours? Poison it, too?"

"Ah. I had not thought of that. Oh, well." Raoul smoothed his hair with a delicate hand. "That's why you are the leader, Xris Cyborg, and I am around for visual effect."

Xris left, walked back to the empty cockpit, sat down, stared out into the black nothing of hyperspace.

He should blow up the plane. He knew that. Admit failure. Admit that Tess and Harsch had outsmarted him. Admit that he'd been beaten at his own game.

Corasians would get hold of the robot. They'd use it to take out the hyperspace Lanes. Make the Royal Navy useless. Leave planets isolated, cut off. The Corasians could come in and pick them off, one by one.

He should blow up the plane. He knew he should.

You won't, she had said.

Xris took out a twist, put it in his mouth. This time he lit it, watched the smoke twine up from the glowing end. No one would be able to enter the cockpit until the noxious fumes were sucked into the ventilation system. But then no one was likely to come in here anyway.

She was right, of course. She knew him inside out.

Damn it all to hell and back again.

CHAPTER
39

Tempt them with profits, instruct and retain them.
Thus double agents can be obtained and employed.

Sun-tzu, *The Art of War*

They emerged from hyperspace into empty space.

The frontier—the galaxy's outer rim of stars—looks very much like the more civilized interior: black, with pinprick smatterings of light. But those who live and work on the frontier will tell you that it is different, a difference which they swear they can feel on board ship or spaceplane, planet or inhabited moon. It is the idea of living on the edge—literally. Of being far removed from the majority of living species. It is a loneliness that can drive you mad—or become addictive.

Xris knew the frontier. In the "old days," when he was just starting out in the mercenary line of work, it had been his custom to frequent the moon known as Hell's Outpost, conduct business in the infamous Exile Café. Xris was not one who had been seduced by the romanticized loneliness. He had stayed at Hell's Outpost only long enough to pick up work. He was always glad to return to the interior, to the realm of breathing, snuffling, gurgling humans and aliens. He enjoyed the knots, the twists, the tangles, the challenge of life among the teeming masses.

Right now, though, he had to admit—he kind of liked it lonely. He'd been afraid he'd find himself surrounded. As it was, there were no planes or ships in sight.

Odd. Hell's Outpost wasn't exactly overpopulated, but there were generally planes in the vicinity. The Exile Café attracted a small but loyal clientele.

"So where's your boss, sister?" Xris asked Tess.

"Sister," she repeated, frowning. She glanced back at him. "Do you realize how insulting you make that sound?"

"Yes. Where's your boss? That moon over there is Hell's Outpost. Do we land or what?"

Tess swiveled the copilot's chair away from him, stared out the viewscreen. "We're to meet Harsch at this location. You'll receive your instructions at that time."

"There's no one out there," Harry reported, peering at his instruments and seeing no signs of a plane, or a ship.

"Hey," said Jamil, "we got here on time. If the client can't make it, screw him. Turn this thing around, Harry, and let's go home."

"That would *not* be a good idea," Tess said.

"He's there," Xris guessed. "He's looking us over. Isn't that right, sister?"

Tess didn't reply.

"We're being scanned," Harry reported at almost the same instant. "Pretty damn powerful, too."

"I assume you gave your boss a complete description," Xris said.

"Right down to every last nut and bolt," Tess returned.

"You referring to me or the PRRS?" Xris asked.

Tess flicked him a glance. The strain was showing. She had been staring intently out into space, tapping a fingernail on the console. When she caught Xris's gaze on her, she ceased the tapping abruptly, turning away.

Interesting, Xris thought. What the devil is she afraid of? She's bringing home the bacon.

"Something's out there," said Harry in an ominous tone. "I'm picking it up now. According to my readings . . . hell, I've never seen readings like this! What—Holy shit!"

Darkness engulfed the stars, swallowed them up. A darkness that grew and solidified as they watched. A huge ship, devoid of lights, emerged from behind the moon that was Hell's Outpost. The bullet-shaped ship came into view, visible on their instruments, visible to the eye only as a black hellish mass that blotted out heaven.

A Corasian mothership.

So that's it, Xris said to himself, defeat a hard, cold knot in his stomach. Tess isn't bringing home the bacon. She's bringing the pigs to be slaughtered.

Harry turned. His eye lids were open so wide, his eyeballs looked as if they might roll out of his head. "Xris! Do you know what that is? A Corasian mother—"

"I know. Get us out of here! Fast!"

Harry was already on it. The engines roared, the PRRS bucked and lurched, went nowhere.

"Tractor beam," Harry said. His cheeks were blotchy. "They got us."

"Break loose!" Xris shouted over the whine of the engines.

"No way in hell!" Harry yelled back.

The PRRS was a gnat trying to free itself from the sticky web of an enormous spider.

"Shut down the engines. I don't want to burn out." Xris was on the comm, ordering everyone to the bridge. Stat.

Tess hadn't moved; she hadn't said a word.

Xris grabbed her by the shoulder, spun her around to face him. He leaned over her in the chair, put his hands on the armrests, fencing her in.

"You knew they'd be waiting for us."

She sat cold and still beneath his touch, her jaw muscles clenched tight. She nodded once, stiffly.

Xris stood up, released her.

"They're hailing us," Harry reported. He switched on the comm.

"Greetings, gentlemen," came the voice over the comm.

"That's Sakuta," Xris said, "for the benefit of those of you who haven't had the pleasure of meeting him."

"Not quite correct, Xris. Sakuta is one of my personae. Another is Nick Harsch, to whom you are now speaking. I understand that you are bringing Professor Lasairion's robot to me. Well done, gentlemen. Well done."

"Yeah, well, it was one hell of a job," Xris said, chewing on a twist. He took it out of his mouth to add, "You weren't exactly up front with us. A few little details you neglected to fill us in on. Like how much your flesh-eating friends are planning to pay you for bringing them a real live Lane-laying robot in prime working condition. My guess is that what you're paying us is squat compared to the profit you'll be making."

"Your point being?" Harsch sounded amused.

Xris put the twist back in his mouth. "We want our fair share. That's all. Cut us in for a percentage."

Tess was looking at him in undisguised admiration, a half smile on her face.

"Captain Strauss told me you were the best," Harsch said. "That's why I hired you. I only hire the best. Captain Strauss herself is extremely impressive, don't you agree?"

"Yeah," Xris said through teeth clenched over the twist. "Impressive."

Tess turned away, stared back out the viewscreen at the Corasian ship.

"I was considering making you an offer to join *my* team, but Tess tells me that you can't be trusted. You have a streak of common decency in you."

"It runs right up my back," Xris said wryly. "I take it this means we're not going to get any extra money?"

"No," said Harsch pleasantly. "But I am. The Corasians are paying me an additional sum."

"Let me guess—for the fresh meat?"

"A very crass way of putting it, but yes, if that's how you want to refer to yourselves."

"Tell them not to be surprised if they find this meal a bit hard to digest. Harry, shut that bastard off."

Harry switched off the comm. Tess sat, unmoving.

"What is going on, Xris?" Dr. Quong was on the comm, his voice loud in Xris's ear. "Did you say something about a Corasian mothership—"

"That's what we got, Doc," Xris said.

"A Corasian mothership!" Quong was terse. "We should leave the vicinity immediately!"

"Love to, Doc," Xris returned. "But they've got us in a tractor beam. Tycho, you read me?"

"I copy, Xris. Did I translate correctly? Corasians? Those we call in my language Corpse Eaters?"

"A bit inaccurate," Xris said dryly. "They prefer their meat live, when they can get it. What's the weapons stockpile on this ship?"

Tess was on her feet. "Xris, you can't—"

He ignored her, concentrated on Tycho.

"Standard for a military vessel," he reported. "Four beam rifles, four .22-decawatt lasguns, one stun grenade, and a utility knife."

"Hand 'em out," said Xris. "Jamil, go help Tycho distribute the weapons."

"Xris, this is crazy!" Tess protested. "You can't win! Harsch has men of his own on that ship. And God knows how many Corasians—"

"We're being pulled in," Harry reported. "All systems are shut down. What's the plan, Xris?"

"It's pretty simple," Xris said. "They're going to tractor the PRRS on board the Corasian mothership. Once we land, they'll have to blow the hatch to get to us; we're sure as hell not going to open the door for them. When they come on board, we start shooting."

"Yeah," Harry said, eager. "Then what?"

"That's it, Harry. That's the plan."

"But I don't get it, Xris. How do we escape?"

Tess was quiet, watching him tensely, her hand clutched over the back of the chair.

"You remember that Corasian 'meat locker,' Harry? The time we went in to rescue those people."

"You mean your wife?" Harry said. He thought back, nodded slowly. "I guess I understand now, Xris. We shoot until they kill us."

"That's about the size of it." Xris was back on the comm. "Yes, Raoul, what is it?"

"Jamil has just explained the situation, my friend," Raoul's voice was calm. "I want you to know that I have located certain supplies in the pharmacy which would allow me to prepare cocktails for everyone."

Xris was about to say that this was a lousy time to be thinking of martinis when it occurred to him what type of cocktail the Loti meant.

Feeling no pain, as the saying went. Permanently.

"Thanks, Raoul," Xris said. "Not for me. That's not the way I want to go out. But ask the others."

"Yes, Xris Cyborg. You do not mind if that is the way . . ." Raoul hesitated, then said, "I am such a hopeless shot with a gun. . . ."

"Your choice. Same goes for the rest. Tell them I said so."

"Thank you, Xris Cyborg, and may I say that it has been a pleasure working for you. Far more than for my late former employer, Snaga Ohme. The Little One asks me to express his admiring feelings as well and to tell you that we will meet in the picnic area of the park. I am not certain," Raoul added solemnly, "but I believe this to be a reference to his people's vision of the afterlife."

"It's been a pleasure working with you, Raoul," Xris said, and was surprised to find that he meant it. "Same goes for the Little One. I'm just sorry I got everyone into this mess. Xris out."

A loud clatter sounded from the plane's interior—hasty hands dropped a beam rifle on the deck. His team was going about their business swiftly, efficiently. It was a pleasure working with them all, every one.

Tess stood in front of him. "Xris, this isn't the way! Please! Listen to me—"

He put his hand on her arm, gave it a pat.

"Feel free to detonate that bomb anytime your little heart desires," he said, and walked past her.

Jeffrey Grant was confused. Extremely confused.

He wasn't used to all this upset and turmoil. His emotions had never taken such a flight. Up one minute and down the next, up again—soaring—and then dive-bombing, plummeting toward the ground. At first it had all been exhilarating. But now he was only exhausted and somewhat light-headed from the hypos the man who called himself a doctor had been giving him.

Grant was certain of at least one thing—he wasn't going to take any more sedative! The drug dried out his mouth and made it seem as if everything around him had turned to jelly and he was trying to swim through it.

Having made this decision, Jeffrey Grant sat up in his bed. He was in sick bay, he saw, along with the robot, which was spread out on a metal table. Groggy, Grant slid off of the bed and tottered across the deck to look at his friend.

He thought of the 'bot as his friend, and then immediately felt horribly guilty for doing so. The robot was, undoubtedly, a murderer. A mass murderer.

He gazed down at the 'bot. It lay on its back, its sad eyes staring up sightlessly at the ceiling, its reticulated arms stretched out in front of it or dangling off the edge of the table.

Some of the arms were damaged. No lights flashed. The robot did not speak. It had not been strapped down when the cockpit ejected. The violent upheaval—Grant had not realized just quite how violent the ejection would be—had flung the 'bot through the canopy. He could imagine, with a kind of horror, the thump of its head striking the steelglass viewscreen. It lay on the table, limp and lifeless.

"I should rejoice," Grant murmured. "The robot will not kill again."

And part of him was glad, but part of him was deeply grieved and part of him was angry. The robot should not have been disturbed. It should have been left to rest in peace, not raised, unhallowed and unblessed, from the dead.

Grant was angry at the cold and callous manner in which the doctor on board had poked and prodded at the 'bot, talking to a recording device all the while, speaking of the robot as he might speak of any machine. And the man had the effrontery to laugh when Grant had meekly suggested that he treat the robot with respect.

At which the doctor gave Grant another injection,

which sent him into a realm of jelly, with the robot's sad
eyes staring accusingly at him.

It was Grant who felt like the murderer. Removing
the sheet from his own bed, he placed it gently, respectfully over the robot.

"You," came a voice behind him. "The civilian."

Jeffrey Grant turned, apprehensive and somewhat indignant. He thought, after all he'd been through, that he
deserved something better.

It was the woman, Captain Strauss.

Grant was immediately on his guard. He looked behind her for the doctor.

"I won't take any more injections," Grant stated
unequivocally.

"Good," Tess said vaguely, not really hearing him.
She had entered the room in a great hurry, but had now
come to an abrupt halt, was staring at him, studying him,
measuring him with her eyes. And it seemed she was
not completely happy with what she saw, for her hand
went to her furrowed forehead, rubbing the skin as if
she could smooth away the lines.

She finally said "Mmmm," and was in motion again,
moving swiftly and surely toward what must have been
her goal in the first place, before the sight of Grant
distracted her. She opened a locker and pulled out a
canvas belt with two canisters hanging from it. Grant
recognized them: grenades. Probably some sort of nuclear devices. They looked truly frightful.

"Something's going on, isn't it?" Grant said.

When the captain didn't answer beyond an incoherent
mutter, Grant pressed. "Someone said something about
Corasians. Are you giving the robot to the Corasians?"

"Not giving," Tess said, straightening from her task.
She looked over at him. "Selling's more the word.
Look," she went on, as he was sputtering with shock
and outrage, "I don't have time for all this. Something
very bad is about to happen. And I don't want you to
get hurt. The others"—she glanced back over her shoulder, out the door, where Grant could hear the sound of
voices, speaking in tight, tense monosyllables—"they

came for the money. And me—I'm in it ... well, for my own reasons.

"But you." She gazed at Jeffrey Grant and her expression softened. Her eyes shifted to the robot lying on the cold steel table. "You came after a dream," she said. "I suppose it's more worthy dying for a dream than for money. But you're still just as dead." Her gaze—now it was a searching look—left the robot and flicked over the sick bay. Her eyes fixed on a small steel door, as if her own morbid thoughts had led that direction.

MORGUE was stenciled on the steel door in white letters.

"By God," she said. "That's it. Look, do you know what's going on?"

"I don't know how I could be expected to know, after—"

"Fine. Never mind. I'll tell you. Corasians are about to board this ship. Hundreds of Corasians. Have you ever seen a Corasian, Mr. Grant?"

He had, but only in vid games.

"Let me tell you about them," Tess continued. "They are some form of mostly energy, we don't quite know what. They look like blobs of molten lava, but they're intelligent blobs. They have a great fondness for human flesh. They devour their victims slowly, starting at the feet and working upward, encasing the person in what might be termed gelatinous fire. It is a terrible way to die, Mr. Grant. That's why those men there—Xris, I mean Captain Kergonan—and the rest, are getting ready to fight to the death. They don't have a prayer, a hope of surviving. They don't *want* to survive. A laser blast through the head is much less painful."

"Are ... are you going to shoot me?" Jeffrey Grant asked, thinking that this was what all this had been leading up to. He wondered how he felt about being shot, but his emotions were so drained that he really couldn't decide.

"No," said Tess. "I'm going to give you a chance to save your skin. Through that door are tubes, which are built into the spaceplane's bulkheads. Those tubes are meant to hold corpses, to keep them in storage until autopsies can be performed, or until proper burial can be arranged. If you have the courage, Mr. Grant, you can hide in one of the tubes. I don't *think* the Corasians will find you."

"You don't *think*. You can't be certain. . . ." Jeffrey Grant stared at the steel door marked MORGUE. Images of being buried alive filled his mind.

"I can't be certain of anything, Mr. Grant," Tess said tensely. "It's up to you. I've got to go. You don't have much time, Mr. Grant. I suggest you make up your mind."

She started to leave, the belt with the grenades in her hand.

"What are *you* going to do?" Grant wondered.

"What I have to do," Tess responded, and hurried out the door. She made certain it was shut and sealed behind her.

"Humpf," said Jeffrey Grant. He opened the door marked MORGUE, found himself in an extremely small room. A neat stack of bags—presumably body bags— were piled up in a corner, took up about one-third of the deck space. Directly opposite him, mounted on the bulkhead, were three small hatches, each with a spin-lock.

Grant touched experimentally a button beside one of the hatches. The hatch swung open. He peered inside, then crawled inside, to see what it would be like.

What it was like was cold, with a peculiar smell— disinfectant. Lying prone in the tube (there was no room to sit up—which function, of course, most occupants of the morgue were not expected to perform), Grant discovered that it was going to be difficult, if not impossible, to operate the hatch from the inside. Which made him wonder how he was supposed to get out, once he got in.

A lever labeled EMERGENCY HATCH RELEASE proved to be the answer. Either the designers had thoughtfully provided an exit in case someone was placed here by mistake or, more likely, this was a standard safety requirement, perhaps for those who entered to clean and disinfect.

Jeffrey Grant climbed out again. He opened the door on the second tube, was looking inside and considering his next move, when the ship jounced, rocked, dropped, and then settled into place with a horrendous bang. The jolt threw Grant off balance. He fell on the pile of body bags.

Obviously, the PRRS had landed. No one had, of course, bothered to inform him where, but then, "I'm a civilian." Grant growled to himself.

He made up his mind then and there to go ahead with his plan. He might be a civilian, but he knew that the robot should not, on any account, under any circumstances, be allowed to fall into enemy hands.

Outside, he could hear Captain Kergonan shouting, something about "blow the hatch."

Jeffrey Grant gathered up one of the body bags and, lugging the bag in his arms, he hastened over to the steel table on which lay the dead robot.

"They're going to blow the hatch!" Xris yelled. He could hear the clamping sounds of explosive charges being placed on the outside. "Everyone set?"

He and Harry, armed with beam rifles, stood well back from the hatch, behind a girder. When the hatch blew, they would pour blazing death at whatever tried to get inside. The others were spread out through the PRRS. Jamil was prepared to blow out the viewscreens. Tycho, with his sharpshooter's aim, would pick off anyone attempting to enter the plane from that direction. Bill Quong stood to one side, armed with a pistol and the stun grenade. He would toss it in when the firefight was turning the wrong way.

Raoul wandered into view, carrying a tray of drinks. He was dressed in a vibrant orange suit with wide, flowing pants and long, flowing sleeves, cut low to reveal the Adonian's shoulders.

"I won't be buried in olive drab," Raoul remarked in passing.

Xris could have told him that he wouldn't be buried at all, decided to skip it. The smell of lilac lingered in the air. "Jamil, Tycho, Quong, report in."

Silence.

That was definitely not right.

Xris tried again. "Jamil! Report in! That's an order!"

Nothing.

"Tycho, turn on your translator!"

No apology from the chameleon.

"Quong? Where the devil are you?"

Silence.

What was going on now?

"Harry, stay here. I think my comm's out. I'm going to check on—"

He turned, saw Tess standing right behind him. She held up a grenade for him to see, then tossed it into the small enclosed area in which they were standing.

The grenade rolled to a halt, almost at Xris's feet.

"I'll save you!" Harry cried.

He flung his body full length on the grenade.

"Harry, it's a—"

There was a muffled *whump*, a soft hissing sound. Yellow-gray fog curled up from beneath Harry's broad stomach. Harry grunted. A funny look crossed his face. He lifted his head.

"Sleep-gas grenade," Xris said.

"Yeah, I—" Harry's eyes blinked, his head lolled, thumped down on the deck.

Tess lifted a gas mask, placed it over her nose and mouth, and set off another grenade.

Xris tried to raise his gun, to fire, but the weapon fell from his hand. He keeled over, halted his fall with his hand, tried to push himself back up, fighting the gas, fighting the darkness that was his brain shutting down.

He lost, pitching forward onto the deck.

"I'm sorry, Xris." Tess's voice, muffled by the gas mask.

Yeah, right.

CHAPTER 40

Unless someone has the wisdom of a Sage, he
cannot use spies; unless he is benevolent and
righteous, he cannot employ spies.
. . . It is subtle, subtle!

Sun-tzu, *The Art of War*

Xris woke to a blind darkness, numbing cold, and a
throbbing pain behind his eyes. Memory was blessedly fuzzy for a few minutes, then he saw Tess with the
gas grenades and heard her "I'm sorry." He knew then
what had happened and where he was. Dark, cold, like
a refrigerator. Very much like a refrigerator. He was in
a Corasian "meat locker."

He lay still, trying to think, to force his brain to work
when it would have much preferred to crawl off in a
hole and howl. The pain was nothing more than the
aftereffects of the sleep gas. It would go away. The gut-
twisting knowledge of defeat, the certain knowledge of
the horrible fate which awaited him and the members of
his team would not go away. He asked of the Creator
only one thing before he found himself listed on the
Corasian dinner menu as "Catch of the Day." He
wanted to get his hands on Tess. Preferably the hand
with the vise grip.

It was at that moment that he realized he had another problem.

His hand was missing.

"Shit!" Xris sat up.

"Xris is awake," said a voice in the darkness—Tycho's, by the mechanical sound.

Xris readjusted his cybernetic eye to infrared, was then able to see the warm bodies of his friends, though nothing else.

Corasians have no eyes and therefore have no need for lights on board their spacecraft. The darkness was absolute. Xris was the fortunate one. He could at least see heat sources. His fellow team members, not gifted with his augmented vision, were effectively as blind as if their eyes had been gouged out.

He made a quick count. At least they were all here and, since they were all radiating body heat, they were all still alive. Xris felt better. Not much, but some.

"How are you, my friend?" Quong asked, peering into the darkness in the completely wrong direction.

"Over here, Doc. I'm wonderful, absolutely wonderful. Well rested. Don't know when I've slept better. How about the rest of you?"

"The same," Jamil said lightly. "I'm thinking of going jogging."

"I'm okay," said Harry. He cleared his throat. "Uh, about that grenade, Xris—"

"You saved my life, Harry," Xris said solemnly, suddenly glad of the darkness that was hiding his smile. "Well, you would have, if that grenade had been the exploding kind. But that was still the bravest thing I ever saw anyone do. I mean it, Harry, I owe you one."

"Naw, you don't, Xris." Harry was pleased, probably blushing. "You've saved my skin plenty. Don't give it a second thought."

During the conversation, Quong had crawled over in Xris's direction, found Xris by clutching at him.

"Do you think the place is bugged? Do you think Harsch is listening?" he asked in a low voice, using their subcutaneous commlinks.

"Wouldn't you?" Xris replied dryly. "And he might be able to pick up even that much noise. Keep it down. Way down." He added aloud, "Say, do any of you guys happen to know what happened to my hand? I can't seem to find it anywhere."

"Maybe you left it in your other pants," Raoul said, and burst into a fit of high-pitched laughter.

"What's the matter with him?" Xris asked.

"He's been like that ever since he woke up. I am afraid that the sleeping gas mixed with some other chemical substance in his blood. The Little One won't wake up at all. Well, he will, but he keeps drifting off to sleep again."

"The bastards took off my hand, didn't they? Fortunately it was the cosmetic one. Keep talking, Doc. I have to check something."

Under cover of Quong's long-winded diagnosis of the Little One's condition, Xris pulled up his pants leg. He snapped open the compartment, felt inside, sighed in grim relief. His weapons hand and his tool hand were still there, along with various assorted small rockets and other implements.

Quong finished. "Are they there?"

"Yeah. So, Harry," said Xris loudly, "tell us more about Professor Lasairion."

"Huh? Now?"

Tycho, sitting next to him, nudged him in the ribs.

"What? Oh, yeah, sure. Let's see. I think I can remember most of it. Mom always said I had a photogenic memory. Professor Lasairion was born in Belfast, Ireland, Earth, in the year 2069. He was one of twelve children . . ."

"The Corasians took your hand," Quong said softly. "I was just coming around and I saw two of them in here, working on you. The blobs lit up the place nicely, plus the humans carried nuke lamps. A man, whom I assume was Harsch, was with them, plus four other humans, probably his bodyguards. *And* the charming Captain Strauss."

"Bless her little heart. She must have told them I was a cyborg. I'm probably damned lucky that's the only piece they took off me," Xris said.

Quong shook his head. "It is only a matter of time, my friend. According to their discussions with Harsch, the Corasians consider you an ideal subject. They plan to copy your mechanics, to give their own robotic bodies greater capabilities. The Corasians wanted to start operating then and there. Strauss told them not to. For the time being, at least."

"That was sweet of her." Xris gave a few seconds to the prospect of having his body pulled apart without benefit of anesthetics. A few seconds was more that enough. "What's she want to keep me around for?" He waved his remaining hand. "Other than as her sex toy, of course."

Quong grunted. "Seems there's some questions Harsch wants to ask you about the robot."

"Yeah? Like what?"

"Like where is it?"

Xris stared at the infrared outline of his friend. In the background, Harry was droning, "The professor attended MIT for two years, but was expelled for being in possession of a controlled substance—"

"Oh, that's too much!" Raoul doubled over, helpless with laughter.

Xris said cautiously, "Okay, I give up. Where *is* the robot?"

Quong shrugged. "Search me. The last I saw, it was in sick bay. I was preparing to dissect it— Oh, sorry." He patted Xris on the shoulder, the shoulder that was missing a hand. "I wasn't thinking. Anyhow, the 'bot's not there now, apparently. And someone else is missing, too."

Xris glanced around the room. He counted six faintly glowing bodies, including his own. "Who've we lost?"

"Jeffrey Grant."

"Son of a bitch. I forgot all about him. Where is *he*?"

"He's not here, that much I know. And no one's said a word about him. No one—catch my drift?"

"You mean Strauss?"

"Yes. I don't think she's mentioned him to Harsch. I told the others to keep quiet. According to what I overheard Strauss tell Harsch, the robot was on its own."

"Strange," Xris said, trying to account for this and not having much luck. "Maybe she's keeping Grant on ice, plans to cut a little deal for herself after Sakuta's gone. Although that doesn't make much sense. Wouldn't be

worth the risk, in my opinion. But then, what do I know?
I've been operating in the dark this whole fucking job."

"... married," Harry was saying, "to Greta Jean
Schnickbaum, a Ph.D. in nuclear physics. They had no
children. They used to say that their robots were their
children...."

"Four humans." Xris was adding up the score.
"Armed?"

"To the teeth. Their teeth may be armed, for all I
know. They're walking arsenals. Looks like each one has
an anti-Corasian dampener device."

"What the hell's that?" Xris demanded.

"It fires a blast of oppositely polarized energy, short
circuits them, so to speak. Say you had a battery—"

"Say I didn't. What else?"

"They each have several high-caliber needle-guns, designed to crack open plastisteel."

"Looks like Sakuta doesn't exactly trust his Corasian
hosts." Xris glanced around at his team. "I presumed
they searched us while we were out. I don't suppose
they overlooked anything?"

"They missed nothing," Quong said glumly. "They
even took a small corkscrew which I hake a habit of
carrying in my wallet."

"Those guns would outfit us nicely," Xris said in
thoughtful tones. "Give us a real edge."

"Against the thousand or so Corasians on this ship? I
admire your notion of fair play, my friend."

Xris smiled. "Beats throwing Raoul's high heels at
them."

Quong was not to be deterred. "Not to mention the
fact that we are locked in this cold-storage compartment
with no way out—Jamil couldn't find a door."

"He won't. Not in a meat locker. The Corasians don't
like to have to chase their lunch around. Only one way
in, and that's from outside."

"And," Quong continued, "you are the only one who
can see in this confounded nightmare, with the possible
exception of the Little One, who may have natural
infrared."

"And that's the *good* news." Xris slapped Quong on

the back. "It's what I like about you, Doc. Your optimistic viewpoint."

"I feel it is my duty to identify the difficulties," Quong said stiffly.

"I know, Doc. I know," Xris said. "It's just—"

A clanging sound interrupted him, coming from the wall.

"Company," Xris warned. "At my signal, Doc, jump them. Pass the word."

"Jump whom?" Quong demanded. "With what?"

"I have my weapons hand," Xris said softly.

"Oh, well." Quong grumbled. "That makes all the difference. Why didn't you say so in the first place?"

"And tell Jamil not to let them shut that door!" Xris ordered.

Quong grunted again and stumbled off into the darkness, hands outstretched, feeling his way along. He bumped into Tycho, imparted Xris's orders. Tycho told Harry. The word spread quickly, to judge by Raoul's partially stifled laughter. The team spaced themselves within arm's length of each other, reaching out their hands to keep in touch.

A giggling Raoul shook the Little One, propped him onto his feet.

The Little One's head slumped; the fedora tumbled onto the floor. Raoul prodded him. The Little One's head snapped up. He gazed around sleepily, and then apparently the mental turmoil struck him, for he was suddenly alert and wide awake. He shifted his gaze toward the wall. The banging sounds continued. Apparently they were attempting to open the door and not having much success.

The Corasians are obsessed with obtaining human technology, primarily because they are so bad at it themselves. Almost all of the technology they have ever acquired has been stolen from the human and alien residents of the Milky Way galaxy next door. Often the Corasians borrowed the mechanics, without having any real clear understanding of how they operated, which meant that machinery breakdowns were frequent occurrences.

Unfortunately, it had been Xris's experience that the breakdowns usually happened only to mundane equipment—such as hatch seals. Corasian' weapons, which were attached to the robotic bodies and operated by impulse energy from a computer "brain," worked just fine.

Xris boosted his hearing. Beneath the banging and clanging, he could hear swearing. A human voice, probably Harsch's, though it was too faint to be able to tell. The voice didn't sound happy.

Xris grinned. Harsch was in one hell of a spot. He'd promised to deliver one Lane-laying robot and was now faced with the prospect of explaining to this bunch of flesh-devouring fiery globs of goo that he wasn't going to be able to keep that promise. Harsch must be sweating—literally. No wonder he was keeping those bodyguards close. And they would likely be paying more attention to their Corasian hosts than to a sorry group of unarmed prisoners. The bodyguards wouldn't be expecting an assault from that quarter.

It was a chance. Not much of one. The guards were well armed and it wouldn't take them long to shift their thinking and their aim. And there was always the Corasians. But a chance, even a slim one, was better than no chance at all.

Xris ripped the sleeve from his cybernetic arm, tore off the fleshfoam, laying bare the metal "bones," the instruments, the flashing lights. He popped open the panel on his steel leg. Taking out his weapons hand, he attached the hand to his wrist. Fortunately, he was so accustomed to doing this that he could work in the dark. He felt the hand click into place, made adjustments. A green light blinked on; the hand was operational.

Xris looked around. Everyone was set. He could talk now; the banging would cover his voice.

"I have my weapons hand attached and ready to use. At my signal, jump the guard nearest you. Don't worry about the Corasians; I'll take care of them. When you take out the guards, grab their weapons. Jamil, whatever happens, don't let that door shut. Understand?"

He heard a chorus of affirmatives and one hysterical

hiccup. The banging had ceased for the moment. Harsch came across clearly now, loudly berating someone. A computerized voice offered explanations. The voice was tinny, mechanical, without feeling, and a shiver started at Xris's tailbone, went up his spine.

Soon he might be listening to those voices talking about him, talking over him, as he lay stretched out on a table while they slit him open and tore out . . .

He shook his head angrily. What was he doing, letting his imagination run amuck!

A small body barreled into him, grabbing him by the knees. Startled, Xris looked down.

The Little One had hold of Xris's pants legs, was tugging on them emphatically, nearly pulling them off.

"What the—" Xris was keyed up. "Raoul, what the devil is wrong with him? Get him off me! Hurry! They've almost got the door mechanism fixed! They'll be in here any second! I can't fire with him hanging on to me!"

Raoul, chuckling, sauntered over to retrieve his small friend. "I know that you are fond of Xris Cyborg. We are all of us fond of him. But this is neither the time nor the place in which to express your—"

Raoul stopped talking. He stared at the Little One, who was clinging to Xris's trousers with one hand, gesticulating with other.

"Oh! I see!" Raoul cried in delight. "I see! You were right all along! My friend!" He turned to Xris, who could have sworn that the Adonian's eyes glowed red in the darkness, like a cat's. "The Little One says to tell you that Tess works for Naval Intelligence!"

"I bloody well know that!" Xris shouted, fuming. The banging had started again, was accompanied by an ominous-sounding clank, as if a seal had given way. "Get him off me!"

"Company coming," Jamil reported from his position near the door.

"She's only pretending to work for Naval Intelligence. She's really working for Harsch!" Xris attempted to pry the Little One's clutching hands loose.

Raoul was performing some sort of mad, insane dance,

revolving on his tiptoes, his hands clicking in the air like castanets. "She's working for NI, working for Harsch, working for NI!" He made it a little song. "She's been working for the Naaa-vy!"

"Good God! He's stoned out of his skull!" Xris muttered.

He ripped the Little One's hands loose, shoved the empath away. The Little One stumbled into Raoul. The two collided, tumbled onto the deck.

"And stay there!" Xris ordered. "Keep your fool heads down or they'll get blown off."

The Little One made a frantic attempt to regain his feet, but he tangled with Raoul, who was attempting drunkenly to accomplish the same task. The two weren't having much success.

Xris hurriedly thrust the hand that was no longer a hand but a rocket launcher into the front of his uniform jacket. He stood cradling the limb as if ashamed to reveal the fact that the arm was missing an appendage.

The door—little more than a crack in the wall—was starting to open. A hideous red light welled through. Heat radiated.

Jamil was plainly visible now, flattened against the wall near the door. Sweat beaded on his black skin. He was peering out the opening. He raised a hand; it was bathed in red light. One finger—that was Harsch. Another finger—probably Tess. Four fingers—the bodyguards. Two more fingers—Corasians.

The door swung wide. the Corasians rolled inside. The light and the heat grew brighter and stronger.

The implications of what the Little One had been saying struck Xris.

Working for Naval Intelligence, working for Harsch, working for Naval Intelligence!

A . . . triple agent?

Was that possible?

Yes! Something in Xris shouted hopefully, but he ignored the voice, because he refused to listen to the part of himself that was talking; the emotional, irrational, damnably romantic part of himself who wanted very much to believe that Captain Tess Strauss was on his side.

Xris didn't trust that part of himself and he didn't trust her. He couldn't trust her! His life and, more important, the lives of his people were at stake.

The door opened wide enough to allow the Corasians to enter.

Orange blobs of molten goo encased in plastisteel bodies that trundled about on wheels. The Corasians were more repulsive than frightening—that is, unless you've seen them ooze out of their robot cases, swarm over a living human being, burn the flesh off the bones, then start on the bones. . . .

The Corasians were followed by Harsch, his four bodyguards crowding on his heels. Tess entered next. Xris was supposed to be watching Harsch, watching the bodyguards, waiting for an opening. But his gaze kept going to Tess. Could he read the truth in her face?

Of course not. She was good. Very good. Whichever side she was on. She refused to make eye contact with him, had glanced in his direction only very briefly, and that to make certain she knew where he was and what he was doing. Her gaze took in everyone else at the same time. Her face was set in concrete, hard, without expression. Her eyes were dark as the darkness in the corridor behind her.

Xris cursed the Little One, cursed him for putting doubt in his mind. Xris had been going to kill her; he could have killed her with a clear conscience, without regret. Now he wasn't sure. . . .

Harsch held a lasgun in his hand. He turned the gun on Xris. "Where is the robot?"

Xris shrugged, nursed his maimed arm. "I don't know."

"I don't believe you."

"I don't blame you," Xris said. "I don't much believe myself. But it's the truth. We don't know where the robot is."

"We could help you look," Quong offered politely. "Where did you see it last?"

"Did you try under the bed?" Tycho was helpful.

"You gentlemen are funny." Harsch glanced at each of them, a slight line marring his smooth forehead. One side of his mouth twitched, one hand flexed. He was angry . . . and scared.

"Very funny. Unfortunately, my customers don't have much of a sense of humor. They are growing impatient. Tess . . ." Harsch stepped back. "You know these men. Handle it."

Tess raised her lasgun, aimed it at Quong. Her gaze flicked to Xris. "Tell us where the robot is or your friend the doctor dies. You have five seconds. I'll count. One."

Her hand holding the gun was steady, never wavered. The eyes were empty.

The Little One was wrong.

"Two."

The small rockets mounted on Xris's weapons hand were of his own invention and design, intended to be used specifically against the Corasians. He owned the patent. He'd sold it to the Navy, made a small fortune. It was that fortune which had allowed him to put the team together. With one rocket, he could take out one Corasian, plus Tess and Harsch.

But the moment he lifted his cybernetic hand, aimed, Tess would fire. Quong would be dead. And there would be nothing Xris could do.

"Three."

That left the four bodyguards and one Corasian. Xris would take out that Corasian with his second rocket, and by that time the bodyguards would have recovered and he would be dead.

"Four." Tess was frowning, not pleased.

Quong stood still, stoic. He knew the score. Harry was balancing on the balls of his feet, ready to hurl his bulky body at the nearest bodyguard. Jamil was by the door, the only escape route, for those who survived. Raoul, giggling, had made it to his feet. He staggered, stumbled, veered in Harsch's general direction. The Little One's hands were hidden in the raincoat pockets. Tycho's skin tone had altered to red.

"You won't tell me where the robot is?" Tess kept her gaze fixed on Quong, addressed Xris.

He needed to make her shift her attention to him.

"Now!" he yelled loudly, and jerked his weapons hand out from his coat. He jumped forward.

Tess shifted her aim, fired.

The laser blast burned through the back of Nick Harsch's skull, exited the front.

Xris had never seen anyone look so surprised.

CHAPTER
41

Do not remain on isolated terrain.

Sun-tzu, *The Art of War*

Harsch died standing on his feet, his mouth gaping nearly as wide as the hole in the back of his head. His bodyguards—hearing the sound of the blast—turned to see what was happening, discovered that their jobs had just become superfluous. Harsch started to crumble.

"Now!" Xris yelled—again.

Harry, bellowing like a bull, charged his man, caught him amidships. The guard's beam rifle flew from his hands, hit the deck. Tycho was on hand to grab it. He turned, fired, took out another bodyguard, who was lining up on Quong.

The third guard was swinging his rifle around to take out Xris. He hoped somebody would deal with that, couldn't take time to do anything himself. A Corasian was standing directly behind Tess.

"Strauss!" Xris bellowed over the laser blasts and whines of the beam rifles and screams of the wounded. "Down! Get down!"

Tess dropped face first to the deck, covered her head with her arms. Xris fired one missile, struck the Corasian in the robot head. The head exploded, destroying the computer "brain." That didn't kill the Corasian. Its plastisteel body cracked open; the fiery amoeba form began to crawl out, oozed toward Tess's feet.

Xris dashed forward. "Die, damn you, die!" He swore

helplessly at the Corasian. Laser blasts didn't affect the aliens. They appeared to thrive on the energy. Xris's missile used a negative charge that drained the alien, negated the energy. This time he'd failed, obviously. The lavalike blob was almost on Tess, was creeping up to her booted foot. She kept her head down, couldn't see the danger.

Xris had watched the Corasians kill humans before, had seen them devour the living flesh in flame. He would have to fire again, although that left him only four missiles and they still had a long way to go. He took aim.

The Corasian's red-orange glow began to dim. It continued to move, but more slowly. The blob began to blacken.

Xris reached Tess. He grabbed her roughly by the shoulder, dragged her behind him, put his body between her and the dying Corasian. Tess's head jerked up, startled. She saw the Corasian, sucked in a breath, and scrambled the rest of the way on her hands and knees.

"Xris!" Jamil's voice, urgent, warning.

Xris swiveled. Corasians, being each single units of one gigantic collective brain, had the ability to communicate with each other instantly. The second Corasian had apparently alerted central control. The door was sliding shut. And once it shut, there was no way to open it from the inside.

Jamil stood in the doorway, prepared to use his body to try to keep the door open. Unfortunately, the metal door was heavy, massive. Jamil wouldn't be a doorstop very long. He'd be jelly.

Xris fired a second missile at the remaining Corasian. His aim was low; he hit it square in the massive body. The missile exploded on impact, but only cracked the plastisteel case.

Tess was on her feet at his side. She fired her lasgun. The Corasian's head blew up. The lavalike larva inside the case was still alive, but one of the shots had damaged the case, destroyed the mechanism which allowed the case to open. For the moment, the Corasian was trapped.

And so were Xris and Tess. Laser fire flashed in front of them, lighting up the dark room. The two surviving bodyguards were using the dead Corasian's broken case for cover, trading shots with Quong, crouched behind a girder, and Tycho, lying flat on the deck. The chameleon was so excessively thin that he was a difficult target, as long as he kept his head down. It looked to be a stalemate. Xris didn't have time for stalemates.

Harry had added his weight to the fight with the door—he was wedged in tight—and, for the moment, the door was holding. Jamil had disappeared; presumably he'd gone out the door into the corridor. Outside, the red glow was steadily brightening.

More Corasians.

Xris was suddenly very tired.

Why fight it? he asked himself. It would be a whole lot easier on everyone concerned if we just gave up right now.

Tess tugged on his sleeve. Leaning close, she shouted, "The spaceplane! The PRRS! It's in the docking bay at the end of this corridor!"

He eyed her grimly. "You really work for the Navy?"

"I really do." She smiled. "You want to see my pension plan?"

"I just want to see you live to collect it. The rest of us included. You say that the plane's nearby?"

"Not one hundred meters away."

"You had this all arranged?"

She shook her head. "Not really. I'm making it up as I go along."

"Great!" Xris grunted. "Well, you haven't done bad so far. When this is over, remind me to kiss you."

"It's a deal." Tess peered out through the smoke and laser flashes. "My plan only works if we make it to the door. How do we get rid of these two? It looks like they're figuring on settling down here."

Xris readjusted his weapons hand to fire a laser. "I'm going to try to circle around behind them. You keep them busy."

"No, Xris!" Tess said. "They'll—"

The moment Xris moved, one of the bodyguards looked that direction, shifted his aim, fired.

Xris went down flat, hugging the deck, Tess at his side. The blast took out a chunk of bulkhead behind them.

"—spot you," Tess finished. "The light reflects off the

metal on your arm! To say nothing of those flashing doodads. What about one of those Corasian-killing missiles of yours?''

"I have three left. We're going to need them once we're out of there."

Another blast burst over them. Tess scrunched down. "Times like this, I wish I was flat-chested!" She shook her head. "Look, Xris, if we don't make it out of here alive, we won't need those three missiles!"

Xris conceded she had a point. He aimed, was just about to fire when a smothered giggle and a hand on his shoulder interrupted him.

"Excuse me, friend Xris. Don't shoot." Raoul, crawling on his hands and knees, was pointing at something in the semidarkness. "But would you look at that? Did you ever see anything so silly? He's going to get himself killed!" Tears of mirth rolled down the Loti's cheeks.

Xris looked. The Little One, raincoat flapping around his ankles, had done what Xris was going to do, had circled around behind the two remaining bodyguards. The Little One was visible only intermittently, small body showing up vividly when the laser light flashed, vanishing into the darkness when the light died.

"What the hell—" Tess began. "He's not even armed." She started to get up.

"Wait!" Xris caught hold of her arm, pulled her back down. He yelled, hoped the comm would pick up his command. "Tycho! Quong! Fire high! Aim for the ceiling!"

The Little One took up a position directly behind one of the bodyguards. The small figure reached his hand into a pocket of the raincoat, pulled out what appeared to be a stick. He clapped the stick to his mouth.

The bodyguard, intent on his battle, probably never felt a thing. Or, if he did, he might have thought it was a sliver of flying metal from a ricochet burst.

It wasn't. The bodyguard suddenly ceased firing.

In the next flash of light, Xris could see the man slumped over his gun.

The Little One moved on, creeping up behind the second bodyguard. Quong and Tycho were keeping the guard busy, though he must have been wondering what had happened to their aim, for the laser blasts were now bursting on the overhead, raining down showers of sparks.

The Little One made the same motion—hand to mouth—with the same result. The guard lurched forward, head first, toppled over in a heap.

"What—" Tess was mystified.

"Blowgun. Poisoned darts. Come on!"

Xris jumped to his feet, helped Tess to hers. He took a moment to assess the situation. The only light remaining in the meat locker now was coming from the trapped Corasian, crawling all over the inside of its robotic case. By the red glow, he could see Harry wedged in the door opening, Jamil standing outside, keeping watch on another red glow that was growing in intensity. Tycho and Quong were up and heading for the door. Xris started in that direction, remembered.

He turned, reached down, snagged a handful of Raoul, hoisted the Loti to his feet.

"Can you walk?" Xris demanded.

"No," said Raoul in a lilting voice. "But I can dance."

"Great! Waltz over to the door! Make it fast or you're going to be an appetizer." He shoved Raoul, staggering, in the general direction of the door, waved at the Little One, who was already scurrying back to retrieve his friend.

"Ah!" cried Raoul, and made a dive for something lying on the deck. "My handbag!"

He slung the strap of a dampener rifle over his shoulder.

Having seen Raoul in action on a firing range, Xris's first thought was to take the gun away. His second—that this would entail a fight. Raoul was very possessive of his purse. Xris let it be.

He joined the rest of the team, gathered around Harry and the door.

"Here's the plan," Xris said.

"We have a *plan*?" Quong was impressed.

"The PRRS is down the corridor, to the left." Xris looked to Tess for confirmation. She nodded. "About one hundred meters away. When we get out of here, the rest of you make a run for it." He flourished his weapons hand. "I'll take care of the rear. Okay, Harry, you can move."

"Uh, that's gonna be a problem, Xris," Harry said, his face glistening with sweat and extremely red. "I'm stuck."

"Stuck!" Xris swore.

"Could you hurry, Xris?" Harry continued plaintively. "It's kinda hard for me to breathe."

"They're coming, Xris!" Jamil reported from outside in the corridor. "Corasians! I can count . . . four, five . . . maybe more after that."

"You can bet there'll be more after that," Xris muttered under his breath. "Did you find the controls for the door?"

"Yeah. No luck. I think the door's jammed."

Xris put his cybernetic foot against the metal hydraulic door and shoved.

The door was heavy and it wasn't moving. Harry panted and gasped. A burst of laser fire lit the corridor outside. The range was short, but closing rapidly.

"Hand me one of those dampeners!" Jamil called.

Quong passed his through the opening, above Harry's head. Jamil grabbed it, twisted around, opened fire. He wasn't aiming at the Corasians, he was aiming at the supports of a large piece of metal ductwork on the ceiling.

Xris braced his back against the wall, planted his foot against the door, and, drawing on all his reserves, battery-powered and flesh and blood, he shoved. The door held a moment, then gave way, sliding on its track so suddenly that Xris landed on his back.

Harry, with a groan, staggered out the door. Quong caught him, supported him. Tycho dove through, gun blasting, kept Jamil covered. He blasted away at the ductwork.

The ductwork sagged, dropped at one end. Another few rounds, and it fell, crashing to the deck, blocking the corridor between them and the Corasians. Xris regained his feet.

"Go! Go!" he shouted. "I've got the Little One!" He scooped the empath up under his right arm. "Follow Tess!"

Tess ran for the end of the corridor, yelling and flashing her nuke lamp so that they could see her in the darkness. Harry waved off Quong's assistance and broke into a run. Quong grabbed hold of Raoul, who was doing the tango, and hauled him along. Tycho and Jamil fired one more burst each, then they took off, racing toward the docking bay.

The Corasians were momentarily halted by the fallen duct, but their robotic arms were already grappling with it, shoving it aside. Xris fired one of his special missiles into their ranks. He heard it explode, didn't wait around to see the results. The red glow grew appreciably dimmer, however.

He dashed down the corridor. The Corasians fired after him, but they appeared more intent on removing the ductwork. Xris hung on to the Little One, who was clutching his fedora with both hands, and followed the gleam of Tess's nuke lamp. The rest of the group had disappeared inside the docking bay, were probably already climbing aboard the PRRS.

"By God," Xris said to himself, "we might just actually make it!"

He hurtled through the docking bay door, ran headlong into the rest of the team, who were bunched up together in the opening.

"What's going on?" he demanded. "Why the hell aren't you on board?"

"On board what?" Tycho's translator screeched.

"There's nothing here, Xris," Harry said.

"She lied." Jamil was grim.

"And we are nicely caught in a cul-de-sac," Quong added.

"I want you all to know that I am not the least bit amused. I don't find this at all funny!" Raoul burst into noisy, gulping sobs.

Xris activated the nuke lamp on his arm, flashed it around the docking bay.

Empty. Not a spaceplane in sight.

CHAPTER

42

Make strategic plans for encircled terrain.

Sun-tzu, *The Art of War*

Xris dropped the Little One.

"Tycho. You and Jamil cover the door."

Behind him, he could hear the ductwork barricade scraping across the deck. Xris grabbed the nuke lamp from Tess's unresisting hand, shone the light full on her.

"I swear, Xris! I swear—the PRRS was here! It should still *be* here! I left Jeffrey Grant on board and—" Tess stopped, put her hand over her mouth. Her eyes grew wide. "Oh, dear God! Grant! He stole the plane!"

"Again?" Harry shook his head. "That man's a menace."

"Xris, they're coming!" Jamil shouted.

Xris shut off the glaring white light, tried to think. There had to be another way. . . .

"Harsch's plane," he said. "He had a plane, didn't he? He didn't walk on board."

"Yes!" Tess clutched at him, nearly knocking him off balance. "Yes! Harsch flew here in a Scimitar! I know where—a level above! There's an access from here, the maintenance door!"

Xris switched on the nuke lamp, flashed it around, shone it on a crude lift.

"We can use that!" Tess said. "Come on—"

She started off.

Xris stopped her. "Why the devil should I trust you?"

"No reason," Tess answered softly. "None at all. Except . . ."

She didn't finish, looked back out the door where Jamil and Tycho crouched, firing down the corridor.

Except—Xris filled in the blank—you don't have a whole hell of a lot of choice.

He started to give the command to move out.

Something large and metal clunked on the deck.

"Take cover!" Xris roared. He threw Tess away from him, literally picking her up and tossing her as far as he could before he hit the deck.

The explosion was brilliant, blinding, deafening, numbing. It lifted him up off the deck, slammed him down again hard. Shrapnel flew through the air. A thin, piercing scream tore into his head, hurt worse than the bits of metal slicing through his flesh.

And then everything was dark and silent, except for a terrible bubbling sound and, from somewhere else, a groan.

Xris shook off the concussive force of the blast, heaved himself to his feet. A stabbing beam of light aimed at nothing in particular. The nuke lamp Tess had been holding lay on the deck a few centimeters from Xris's hand. He bent over to pick it up, nearly passed out. He staggered, steadied himself, tried again.

Retrieving the light, he flashed it around, searching for Tess. He found her. She was on her hands and knees, shaking her head muzzily. But she was alive. He continued searching. The bubbling sound had ceased. The groaning continued. And out in the corridor, the red glow pulsed brightly.

Xris stood in the door to the docking bay, aimed at the glow, fired another missile. One left.

The missile hit one of the Corasians standing in the center of the group. Perhaps that Corasian had been carrying more grenades, because the resulting blast was far greater than it should have been. The red glow flickered and died. The corridor was dark.

But there were more Corasians. Once they found out that people were still alive down here, there would be lots more.

"Report in!" Xris gasped. He licked his lips and tasted blood. He could still hear, in his memory, that shrill scream. "Who's hurt?"

"Xris! Bring the light! Over here!"

Xris picked his way through the debris left by the explosion. He found Jamil lying propped up against the bulkhead, one leg stretched out in front of him, a pool of blood beneath. Xris played the light on his friend's face.

"You okay?"

Jamil's face glistened; he nodded, said, "Not me, Xris. Not me." His eyes shifted.

Xris followed with the light. "Bloody hell!" he whispered. "Damn it all to bloody hell."

He crouched down, reached for Tycho's wrist, but he knew he'd feel nothing. Not with a wound like that. He held on to Tycho's thin-fingered hand—about the only part of Tycho that was intact—and yelled savagely, "Doc!"

He heard a crash, a curse, and Bill Quong's cool voice. "Hold the light so that I can see, my friend. I will do you no good stumbling around blind."

Xris held the light, not sorry to move it from the bloody mass that was all that was left of Tycho.

"You hurt bad?" Xris asked Jamil.

"Shrapnel tore through my leg. I won't be running the marathon anytime soon, but I can walk. You?"

Xris looked down. The sleeve covering his good arm was torn and bloody. He couldn't feel anything, for the moment.

"I'm okay. If we have company, keep them occupied."

Grunting, Jamil twisted around to lie flat on his belly, the dampener rifle held in front of him.

"It was a grenade," he said.

"Yeah," Xris responded, holding the light steady. He could see Quong moving about in the darkness, could see Tess pausing beside Raoul. "We were lucky. Whatever that machine is over there contained most of the blast."

"Tycho wasn't lucky," Jamil said. "Strauss led us in here. She led us into a trap."

"I keep hearing voices," Raoul was saying querulously. "Someone's talking inside my head. And this small and unknown personage in a raincoat keeps hugging me." He paused a moment, then demanded loudly, "Where am I? What am I doing here? Why can't I remember my name?"

"Amnesia," Quong said, making his way to Xris. "He was hit in the head. We can only hope it is temporary."

Xris sighed inwardly. Raoul's mind was like a butterfly net at the best of times. Now the net was cut and the butterflies were fluttering about loose. God only knew where they'd land.

Quong took the nuke lamp from Xris's hand, played the beam over Tycho's body, shook his head. "There is nothing I can do, Xris. Our friend never knew what hit him. The blast caught him from behind, as you can see."

No, Xris couldn't. There wasn't enough of Tycho left to tell his front from his back.

"Thanks, Doc. Do what you can for Jamil. And where the devil's Harry?"

"Here, Xris," came Harry's aggrieved voice.

"You hurt?"

"I got hit in the ass. It feels like I'm on fire back there!"

"Just as long as it doesn't interrupt your mental processes."

"No, Xris," Harry returned. "I said I got hit in the ass."

"That's what I meant. Doc, how's Jamil? Can he walk?"

"The calf muscle is torn. He has lost a lot of blood, will be in considerable pain, and he will need assistance. If I had my med kit—"

"If you had your med kit, we'd be on the PRRS and Tycho wouldn't be dead and we wouldn't be trapped like rats on this motherfu—" Xris stopped, sucked in a deep breath. Reaching into his pocket for a twist, he noticed his hand was shaking. He pulled himself together, thrust the twist into his mouth. "Sorry, folks. Jamil, you see anything?"

"Red light. Getting brighter."

"They've figured out we're still alive and kicking.

Most of us, anyway. Harry, you help Jamil. Get him up
and mobile."

"Who are you people?" That was Raoul, irritable.
"Why have you brought me to this awful place? And
why don't any of you know who I am?"

"Quong, calm Raoul down. See if he's got something
in his purse that will tranquilize him—"

"Drugs!" Raoul's voice was shrill. "Are you mad? My
body is a temple."

Xris continued, ignored the outburst. "We've found a
way off this ship. Harsch flew here in a Scimitar. We'll
use it to escape. Tess knows the way. We'll follow her."

They stared at him; all of them, staring at him.

"I know the way," Tess said, her voice strained. "I
think we can make it."

No one spoke. No one moved.

"I'm going with Tess," Xris said. "The rest of you can
come with us or you can stay here. It's that simple."

Harry helped Jamil to his feet.

Jamil draped one arm over Harry's broad shoulders,
pulled himself upright. He tried putting his injured left
leg to the deck, grimaced and grunted.

"This way." Tess held the nuke lamp, led them deeper
into the darkness of the docking bay.

Harry and Jamil both glanced at Xris as they passed
him.

"Tycho had it easy," Jamil muttered out of the corner
of his mouth.

Xris didn't answer.

Quong and the Little One—his fedora had been
crushed, but he appeared otherwise uninjured—were attempting to get Raoul up and moving and not having
much success. "My head aches. My feet hurt. I'm sleepy.
I don't want to go anywhere."

"Tell him he's in a shopping mall," Xris said.

"Shopping?" Raoul perked up. "But what happened
to the lights?"

That brought him to his feet and following after
Quong. The Little One trailed along behind, shaking his
battered hat and wringing his small hands.

Xris stood alone in the darkness next to Tycho. He

knelt beside the body, which was rapidly cooling, fast disappearing from Xris's infrared sight. Xris lifted the limp, dead hand.

He tried to talk, paused, cleared his throat, started over. "I'm sorry, my friend. I'm sorry."

He let the unresponsive hand fall. Standing up, Xris went after the others.

CHAPTER

43

On fatal terrain you must do battle.

Sun-tzu, *The Art of War*

Xris found them gathered around a large metal plate set into the deck. Tess located a control panel on the wall, opened it, tapped the controls. The metal plate shivered and then, with a screech and a whoosh of air, began to rise up out of the deck.

"By the Maker!" Quong breathed. "Pneumatic! A pneumatic lift!"

Corasians, with their wheeled, plastisteel bodies, weren't capable of climbing ladders. The docking bay was probably filled with these lifts, which carried the robots to the catwalks far above the deck.

"There's an access door up above," Tess explained. "It leads to the docking bay on the third level, which is where Harsch landed his spaceplane." She brought the lift to a shuddering halt. "Hop on."

"Ladies lingerie, please," Raoul said politely, stepping daintily onto the lift. He had a brief struggle with the dampener, which was heavy and awkward. He managed to adjust it and was heard to mutter, "I can't think why I chose this style handbag."

Quong lifted the Little One to join his friend. Harry assisted Jamil onto the lift, stood beside him. There was room for one more.

"I'll operate the controls," Tess said. "You get on, Xris."

"I'll wait here with you," he answered.

"Look, Xris, I can understand why you don't trust me—"

"We got company coming." He interrupted her, then switched on the light on his weapons arm, shone it onto the control panel. "I have one missile left. Give the nuke lamp to Quong, I've got light. Start this thing up."

Tess said nothing more, started the lift moving. It took its own sweet time and made a horrendous noise in the process. The people standing on it shook and shuddered from the vibrations.

Xris shifted his gaze to the corridor outside the docking bay. The red glow was again growing bright.

The lift came to a halt, must have been designed to do so automatically when it reached the right level. Xris, peering upward, could see Quong hustling everyone off the lift and onto one of the catwalks. He flashed the light.

"All clear!" came the shout.

"Good," Xris said over the comm. "Keep quiet. If Raoul peeps, slug him."

Tess hit the controls and the lift, with a screech, started back down.

She glanced over her shoulder. "They're getting closer."

"Yeah." Xris said, chewing on the remnants of the twist. "Tycho'll stop them for a time. They like to feed whenever they get the chance. And they don't figure we're going anywhere." He spit the wad on the deck. "One question. Where's the robot?"

Tess's face, in the harsh glare of the nuke lamp, was dead white. Her eyes were moist, glistened. She gave a helpless shrug. "I don't know. I told Grant to hide, showed him a place. . . . He must have hidden the robot, too. I didn't mean for him— I never supposed— the robot was so heavy . . ."

"Bottom line: The Corasians don't have it."

"No. And it would be better if they did. You see, Xris, before I left the plane I—"

"Skip the confession," Xris said. "I'm not a priest."

Tess managed a half smile, shook her head.

The lift was nearly level with them now. As the lift came flush with the floor, it ground to a halt, paused for a moment, then began to rise. Tess and Xris climbed onto it. The lift lurched upward, moving in fits and starts. The platform jounced and creaked.

"This is one of the few times I could wish that the Corasians had made a few more technological advances." Xris looked over the edge of the lift, saw the red glow had come to a halt, was clustered around something in the doorway. The smell of burning flesh was strong, pungent.

Tess gave a little gasp, covered her mouth and nose with her hand.

"Don't look," Xris said, and put his arm around her.

She closed her eyes, sagged against him. "I'm sorry. I should be used to this. I've seen it before."

"So have I," Xris said. "And it doesn't get any easier."

He tried to follow his own advice, tried to look away, but he couldn't. He watched the red globs swarm over Tycho until the rim of the platform blocked them from his view.

The lift reached the catwalk. Quong was there to help them off. "They got Tycho."

"I know. Hand me that dampener."

Taking the rifle from Quong, Xris leaned over the catwalk and fired a blast at the lift's controls. The panel blew off. That lift wouldn't be going anywhere anytime soon.

Xris glanced around. "Where is everyone?"

"Jamil and Harry went to check out the access door. It's at the end of the catwalk to your left. I sent Raoul with them. He's looking for a different handbag, one to match his shoes."

Xris took out another twist. "The Little One?"

"Keeping Raoul from falling off the catwalk."

Xris nodded. Tess went ahead, to join Harry and Jamil at the door. Xris and Quong followed, gathering up Raoul on the way.

"I can't find the handbags," he complained.

"Of course not," Xris said. "You're in men's wear."

Raoul shuddered. "Three-piece polyester suits. How ghastly."

The red glow below them was intensifying. A laser blast burst on the catwalk beneath their feet. Xris and Quong increased their speed, hustling Raoul along at a rapid pace. The Little One trotted along behind.

"Let's open the door, gentlemen," Xris said briskly, coming to a halt at the end of the catwalk. "It's going to be getting warm in here."

Another blast—this time closer. The Corasians were improving their aim.

"Right," Harry said. "We wanted to wait for everyone to arrive, in case there was an escort waiting."

"Can't hear anything," reported Jamil, standing on one leg, propped up against the bulkhead, gun ready. "But that doesn't mean much. This door must be at least fifteen centimeters thick. By the way, these dampener rifles need to be recharged after about fifty rounds. So don't waste your ammo."

Xris held up his weapons hand. "I've got one missile left. Open the door and stand back."

Tess hit the controls. The door rumbled open slowly.

No red glow. Xris cautiously peered out.

Darkness. He looked, saw nothing; listened, heard nothing. All very strange. The Corasians down below must be in contact with their fellow blobs, must have told them their dinner was walking out the back.

Quong remarked, "I have prayed to the Maker. Perhaps this is the response."

Xris motioned for Tess to join him. "Where's the plane from here?"

"The corridor runs in front of us for about twenty meters, then another branches off to the right. The plane's in the docking bay at the end, about another thirty meters." She looked around, uneasy. "This is weird. Where are they?"

"Angels took care of 'em, according to Doc. Watch out for locusts and falling frogs."

"Huh?" Tess stared at him.

Xris turned back to the group. "I'll take point. Tess,

you're with me. Harry, you and Jamil come after. Little One, you're in charge of Raoul."

The Little One nodded. Xris wasn't certain if the empath was reacting to his words of his thoughts, supposed it didn't matter. The Little One reached out a small hand, grabbed hold of Raoul's hand, and clung tightly.

"We're looking for accessories," Raoul said in a low voice.

"Quong, you bring up the rear. Keep your eyes and ears open," Xris counseled, added grimly, "This is all much too easy."

They made their way down the corridor. Xris switched on his light. Tess had retrieved her nuke lamp, flashed it continually along the bulkheads and the deck in front of them. Harry and Jamil came behind, Jamil hobbling, stifling his groans every time the foot of his injured leg touched the deck.

Tugged along by his small friend, Raoul complained that this was a very strange shopping mall and wondered in a loud voice that set everyone's teeth on edge why nobody would turn on the lights. Quong brought up the rear, dampener ready.

They reached the intersection of the corridor, halted, flattened themselves against the walls. Xris peered around the corner.

More darkness, thick, impenetrable, blessed.

He and Tess aimed the beams of the nuke lights down the corridor, and there was the docking bay, its doors wide open.

Xris shook his head. "This stinks."

"You are a man of little faith, my friend," Quong said over his shoulder. The Doc was guarding the rear, facing back the way they'd come. "Take the gift the Maker gives you. Proceed forward with confidence."

Xris proceeded forward, though not with much confidence. His augmented hearing was picking up strange sounds. He tried to place them. Hums, whirs, and occasionally a creak or a squeal.

"You hear anything?" he asked Tess.

She shook her head. "No. Nothing. You?"

"Yeah. If I closed my eyes, I'd swear that we were surroun—"

Xris knew. He saw—or didn't see—the trap into which they were blithely walking.

"Shields! Opaque shields!" he shouted. "Get back!" He raised his arm, aimed the missile—

The laser blast caught him in the left shoulder, spun him around, slammed him to the deck.

Tess dropped the nuke lamp, crouched down beside him. Raising her lasgun, she returned fire. "Doc!" she yelled.

Laser blasts burst in the corridor. Sparks showered down around them.

"Ah," said Raoul, enchanted. "The toy department."

The Little One dragged his friend down to the deck.

Harry and Jamil found cover in doorways, were both firing. Quong ran forward, knelt down beside Xris. "Pick up that lamp," he ordered Tess. "Shine it here, on his shoulder."

"You gotta work on those prayers, Doc!" Xris grunted, as Quong's fingers poked and prodded.

"It was your crack about frogs that did it." Quong peeled off Xris's smoldering uniform. Harry and Jamil were keeping up covering fire. "You were hit in the steel-reinforced part of you, my friend. That is very good news."

"Very bad news," Xris said bitterly, sitting up, with Tess's help. He pointed to his cybernetic arm, at the weapons hand, which hung at his side, dead weight, useless. "What am I supposed to do? Throw the damn missile at them?"

Laser light streaked past them, exploded on the panel above their heads. Tess flung her arms around Xris, shielding him. Quong stood up, heedless of his own safety, poured murderous fire in the general direction of the shot. He continued firing until his gun went dead. He threw it away, crouched back down.

Jamil and Harry were concentrating their fire in the same place. A pop and a clatter and a small flash of light came from the end of the corridor.

"I think we got one," Harry reported.

A laser blast nearly took off his head.

"Or maybe not." Harry ducked back into the doorway.

Xris looked at Tess, who was lying on top of him. "You just can't keep your hands off me, can you?" he asked.

Tess sat up, shoved her hair out of her face, tried to look as if she'd done nothing special.

"It's your fatal charm." She glanced down the corridor. "Speaking of fatal, their aim is rotten today. We should all be dead about now."

"The shields that keep us from seeing them are probably also keeping them from seeing us," Quong maintained. "Disrupting their sensors. You see, my prayers may have been answered, after all."

He was back down beside Xris, inspecting the damage. "Unfortunately, there is nothing I can do about the arm. The connections between the arm and your brain have been fried."

"But the weapons hand itself is okay?" Tess asked.

"It appears to be, yes."

"Can the missile be fired manually?"

"If Doc takes my hand off," said Xris.

"Detach the hand," she said crisply, "and show me how it works."

Quong looked questioningly at Xris, who nodded.

"Go ahead, Doc." He managed a smile. "I'd give my left arm to get rid of these bastards."

"I count two of them, Xris!" Jamil yelled. "One to the left of the door and one to the right. My gun's run out of juice." He threw the useless dampener to the deck.

"Mine, too," Harry reported. "I'm switching to the beam rifle."

Quong took hold of Xris's arm, gave it a twist. The limb came off. Tess took hold of it.

"I can't see!" she complained. "Where's the firing mechanism?"

"You can feel it here, inside the wrist, a small bump."

"I think so." She sounded dubious.

"Don't push on it!" Quong cautioned. "Until you are ready."

Tess nodded. She aimed the arm like a rifle and fired, hit the Corasian on the right. Its opaque shield cracked open. The red glow lit up its companion.

Harry concentrated fire from the beam rifle on their new target. One hit split open the Corasian's side, a second burst blew the hole wide open. The fiery ooze began to crawl out.

Tess shouted at him, "Don't shoot laser energy at the blob! They feed off it! I don't have any more missiles!"

Raoul and the Little One lay on the deck in the middle of the corridor. Raoul kept lifting his head; the Little One kept shoving it back down. Xris, looking back at them, recalled the dampener on Raoul's back.

"Harry!" Xris shouted, and aimed the nuke lamp that direction.

Harry saw the dampener. He made a flying leap, did a belly flop practically on top of Raoul, who shrieked in alarm and hid his face in his hands.

Harry yanked the weapon from Raoul's arm, nearly dislocating the Adonian's shoulder. Flipping over on his back, Harry fired. The weapon's projectile embedded in the center of the glowing mass, exploded. The glow began to fade.

Xris aimed the nuke lamp down the corridor, could find no sign of Corasians.

Raoul's voice broke the stillness. "You beast! Give me back my handbag!"

"What handbag?" Harry was baffled.

"This!" Raoul tried to wrest the dampener from Harry's hand.

Harry stopped him. "Let me keep it awhile. Okay? I'll give it back. I promise. And why don't you let me go first."

Raoul sniffed. "Keep it, then. I never could find anything in it anyway."

Harry walked ahead, dampener at the ready. The rest followed; Quong helped Jamil. Tess and Xris brought up the rear.

"What about your arm?" she said.

It lay on the deck. There was something pathetic about it. Xris was reminded of the robot with the sad eyes. *We give this metal life. Are we the ones who endow it with spirit, as well? Or do we truly understand the definition of "life"?*

"Leave it!" he ordered her, as she bent to pick it up. "The Doc'll make me a new one."

They followed the others. The corridor opened up onto a large hangar deck. And there, inside—a long-range Scimitar.

"Harry, give me the dampener," Xris instructed. "You go get this thing fired up. Tess, you guard the door."

The long-range Scimitar—shaped like the blade for which it was named—was a fighter spaceplane, smaller than the PRRS and much faster.

Harry climbed the ladder leading to the top, opened the hatch. He disappeared inside.

Xris scanned the area for the telltale glow of Corasians. Above him, at the far end of the hanger, he could see faint light.

Xris turned. "Hurry up! They're coming!"

Jamil, hopping on one foot, leaning on Quong, entered the hanger. He looked up at the ladder leading to the Scimitar's hatch and grunted.

"Sorry," said Xris, "but it's the only way."

"Yeah, I know." Jamil paused a moment, drew in a breath, then began to climb.

Quong was right behind him, helping and offering encouragement. "That is correct. Balance the weight on the uninjured leg. I am here behind you. Don't worry about slipping. Don't think of the pain. Tuck it away in a small recess in your mind."

"Doc," Jamil said, pausing, gasping in agony. He pressed against the side of the Scimitar. "Shut up."

"That is very good!" said Quong, approving. "Take your feelings of hostility out on me."

"What's up there?" Raoul asked suspiciously, halting at the bottom of the ladder.

"A café," said Xris. "Meant to look like a spaceplane."

"How quaint," Raoul commented, and climbed the ladder after Quong.

The Little One glanced up, shook his head, heaved a sigh, and ascended the ladder, considerably hampered in this endeavor by the raincoat.

Tess stood at the door, lasgun in hand.

"More coming down the corridor, Xris," she reported.

"Fall back!" he ordered her. "Come on!"

She didn't need a second command. Running to the ladder, she halted beside him, her lasgun in one hand, Xris's arm in the other.

"Up," he said.

Corasians trundled overhead on the catwalks above the Scimitar. Xris could hear the creak of wheels, the whir of the motors in the swiveling heads, lining up the lasguns.

He fired off a round with the dampener, more to force them to keep their distance than because he hoped to hit anything.

"Get a move on!" he called.

Jamil collapsed, almost fell down the ladder. Quong hung on to him, bellowed for help. Harry popped out of the hatch. Between Harry and Quong, they pulled and dropped Jamil inside the Scimitar.

"Live entertainment," Raoul remarked, and dropped down inside the hatch.

Hands reached up to catch hold of the Little One.

"You're next," Xris said to Tess. "I'll cover you."

"Wrong," Tess returned. She plucked the dampener from his hand. "You're a civilian, and wounded at that." She jerked her head. "Get your ass up that ladder, mister."

Turning, she fired the dampener. Her aim was much better than Xris's could have ever been, even if he'd had six good arms. She hit one Corasian; it spun out of control and tumbled off the catwalk.

Xris climbed the ladder awkwardly; it was a difficult task with only one hand, but he made it.

"Tess!" he yelled, afraid for a moment that she was going to try to square things by getting herself killed.

She slung the dampener over her shoulder, scrambled up the ladder. Xris waited.

"Go!" She motioned him.

Laser fire struck the Scimitar. Xris jumped down into the hatch. Tess tumbled after him amid a shower of sparks. He caught her, held her a brief moment, long enough for a smile between them.

Xris started to move forward, heading for the cockpit.

Tess stopped him, gently pushing him down into a seat in the passenger area. "There's nothing you can do. You need attention, and the Doc can't give it to you unless you sit still. Face it, dear. You're useless without your arm and with half your systems shorting out."

"I'm a control freak," he said. "Don't worry. I won't get in the way."

"You're hopeless." Tess gave him a swift kiss on the cheek, then hurried to the cockpit. By the sounds of it, Harry already had the computer convinced that he was today's pilot, and had taken over the controls manually. The engines wound up. Tess sat down in the copilot seat. Xris propped himself up behind her.

Jamil lay unconscious in a hammock. Quong rummaged through the spaceplane's medical supplies.

Raoul glared at him. "Waiter!" he finally called.

Xris, Harry, and Tess stared out the spaceplane's viewscreen into a solid steel wall. The hanger bay doors were shut and the Corasians probably meant for them to stay that way.

"So, any ideas?" Tess asked.

Harry stared at the controls. "It appears friend Harsch had some modifications made to this Scimitar. Watch this!"

Harry depressed a button on the console. Four plasma cannons on each wing blazed. The light was blinding. All of them were forced to shield their eyes.

"Hang on!" Harry shouted. "This is gonna be wild!"

Xris grabbed hold of the ladder.

"Doors gone?"

"Dunno!" Harry returned. "I can't see!"

The spaceplane lurched, bucked, and suddenly shot forward. Xris, his eyes shut against the glaring, painful light, could only hope that this ride wasn't going to be really short.

The light vanished. The plane did not smack into a solid steel wall. Xris opened his eyes, pulled himself back to a standing position.

"My God!" Tess whispered. "That was ... amazing."

The spaceplane, surrounded by millions of tiny pieces of metal, hurtled away from the Corasian ship. The cannons had breached the hull doors, and the pressure of the atmosphere did the rest, blasting the plane and all of the contents of the hangar out into space.

"We ain't out of this yet," Harry muttered.

He swung the plane around and began to program the Jump computer.

And then everything came to a halt.

"What the hell?" Xris clutched the seat for support.

"Tractor beam. Damn it! I thought the blast would throw us clear. I can't break loose!" Harry looked over his shoulder at Xris. "I think they got us this time."

"Then they can have us," Xris said. "I'm too tired. I don't care. ..."

"Maybe not," said Tess softly. "Look."

Shafts of white-yellow light streaked out of nowhere, coming from nothing that any of them could see.

"Lascannon fire," said Harry.

He looked at his instruments, looked up, somewhat sheepishly, at Tess.

"That's the *King James II* out there."

"Yes," said Tess. "I know. Took them a bit longer to arrive than I had anticipated, but—"

The Scimitar suddenly lurched forward. Harry was on the controls immediately, took the spaceplane into a steep dive underneath the lascannon fire.

"Tractor beam shut off," he reported unnecessarily.

The hulk of the *King James II* loomed into view, the enormous vessel surrounded by other large warships, all pouring fire into the Corasian mothership.

Nothing Xris had ever seen looked quite so beautiful.

CHAPTER
44

La vérité existe; on n'invente que le mesonge.
("Truth exists, only lies are invented.")

George Braque, *Le jour et la nuit*

Fighters, short-range Scimitars, and Claymore bombers streaked past, wave after wave, heading for the Corasian mothership. The Corasians hesitated, launched a few of their own fighters, almost immediately pulled them back. The enemy decided to head for home.

The *King James II* battle group, with its six warships, two carriers, and hundreds of fighters, was there to see that the Corasians didn't make it.

"We're free and clear," reported Harry. "Where to?" He was looking wistfully at the fighters, now moving into attack formation.

"Don't even think about it!" Xris said tiredly. "Take us to the *King James*."

Tess looked back at Xris. "All right if I use the comm? I have to report to the Admiralty. I'll tell them about you and your team, Xris. How you got us off that ship. I'll put in for commendations."

At the look on his face, her voice trailed off. She bit her lip, lowered her eyes.

"Commendations." Xris was bitter. "Just have them send that to Tycho's mother, will you?"

Tess said nothing. She turned away, reached for the comm.

Okay, it was a cheap shot. Xris knew he'd hurt her,

knew she didn't deserve it, but he didn't much care. He was feeling rotten inside and out, didn't see why everyone else shouldn't feel the same way.

"Good news, guys," he announced, climbing the ladder, emerging into the small living quarters aboard the Scimitar, "we're all going to get commendations."

"Make mine black, with lace," said Raoul drowsily. He was swaying gently back and forth in one of the hammocks that served as beds aboard the Scimitar. The Little One sat on a bench below, keeping a worried watch on his friend.

"I've given him a sedative," Quong said. "I believe he has suffered a mild concussion. His memory is starting to return, but he is dizzy and disoriented."

"Back to normal, huh?" Xris took out a twist, fumbling at the box with one hand, his good hand. He managed to get the twist out, but dropped the box onto the deck. Swearing, he started to give it a kick.

Quong intercepted him, picked up the box. He handed it back to Xris.

"I will give you a sedative, too, my friend. Are you in pain?" He looked at the mangled hardware, the frazzled wires sticking out of Xris's left shoulder.

"Hell, no!" Xris chomped down on the twist, almost bit it in two. "It doesn't hurt, Doc. It's not real!"

"I wasn't referring to your arm," Quong said quietly. He handed Xris a cup of coffee.

Xris shook his head, accepted the coffee. "That kind of pain, no sedative in the world can touch."

Quong nodded his head, returned to Jamil, who lay stretched out in a hammock, his leg bandaged. He was now awake and alert.

"Boy, I can pick 'em, can't I?" Xris said to Jamil, while sitting down on the bench beside the Little One. "What are we down this job? One Claymore, one PRRS, one Lane-sucking robot, one civilian, my arm, your leg, Raoul's mind, and two friends." Xris leaned back against the bulkhead, closed his eyes. "Two friends."

He raised his coffee cup. "Here's to Darlene Rowan and Tycho." He sipped at the coffee, took too big a mouthful, burned hell out of the inside of his mouth. He suffered in silence.

"I dunno," Jamil said after a moment. "I think it was better Tycho went the way he did. When he found out how much money we've lost on this job, the shock alone would have killed him."

"And we don't know for certain that Darlene is dead," Quong said.

Xris shook his head again, sat holding the cooling coffee. It tasted like mud.

Tess climbed the ladder, came to join them. "How are you feeling?" she asked Jamil.

"Terrific. Nothing like a little shrapnel tearing through your leg. Makes you appreciate life. Grab me some coffee, will you, Doc?"

Quong moved over to the small dispenser, poured coffee, brought a cup for himself and one for Jamil. The Little One huddled into a ball, buffeted by waves of rough emotions. Raoul fell asleep. Down in the cockpit, Harry could be heard, talking to the *King James II*, requesting clearance to land.

Tess stood, hands on her hips. Her gaze swept all of them, halted when it came to Xris. "Look. I'll say it. I'm sorry. I'm damn sorry. About your friends, I mean."

"Don't apologize," Xris said. "You did your job. You did what you set out to do. At least, that's what I'm guessing."

"I'm not apologizing for doing my job," Tess said. "You're right. I *did* do what I set out to do. I stopped Nick Harsch from selling technology to the Corasians. I kept that robot out of his hands and out of the Corasian galaxy. Who knows how many lives we saved?"

"I only know that we lost quite a few on the way," Xris said.

"Stop whining! So the job didn't turn out to be the easy, cushy chance to make a fortune that you expected. The mercenary trade is a risky one. If you can't take it, I suggest you find another line of work!"

She was angry now, too angry to talk. Small red dots burned in her cheeks, her eyes glinted. She headed for the ladder, for the cockpit below.

"Tess," Xris said. "One question."

She halted, not looking around. "What?" Her voice was hard.

"Why didn't you tell us the truth?"

"We would have helped you nail that bastard," Jamil said.

"You only had to ask politely," Quong added.

Slowly, Tess turned back, faced them. She glared around at them, truly exasperated. "Tell you the truth! How the hell could I? How could I trust you?"

"Ah," said Xris, enlightened. "*You* couldn't trust *us*! I get it now. This from a woman with so many angles she would have made an honors class study for geometry."

The corner of Tess's mouth twitched. She tried to stay mad, but she couldn't. She even managed a small chuckle. "All right. I guess I earned that one. I'll tell you everything, okay? Then you can judge for yourselves.

"Navy Intelligence has known about Nick Harsch and his dealings with the Corasians for years, but, like I told you earlier, Xris, we could never catch him. He had a contact in the top levels of the Navy, someone feeding him information. We found out who the person was and took him out—very quietly, no publicity. What we refer to as 'early retirement.' We figured Harsch would try to find someone else. NI chose me for the job. I set myself up. Lost lots of money at the gaming tables, let it be known that I needed credits and needed them bad or my career was down the toilet.

"NI thought for a while Harsch wasn't going to bite, but then we intercepted one of his shipments to Corasia, confiscated the weapons. Harsch lost big. Shortly after that, one of his agents contacted me. After some negotiation, I agreed to work for him.

"I proved my worth, warned him in advance of a couple of raids. Problem was, I never met the man. He handled everything third- or fourth-hand. We needed something big to lure him out."

"Lasairion's sad-eyed robot," said Quong.

"Exactly. It was perfect. The Pandorans were kicking up a fuss about the robot. The Admiralty promptly overreacted, made it all hush-hush, level-one security, for-your-eyes-only, DNA-check-your-spit type of stuff. Of course, as you said, Dr. Quong, these Lane-laying robots were programmed to respond only to Lasairion. So we didn't think there was much danger."

"I can't believe Harsch didn't know that," Xris said.

"He was a deal maker, an entrepreneur. He's like a used vehic dealer, who wouldn't know a gravator from a generator. What he did know was his customers and what they wanted and needed. When he told the Corasians about the robot, they were wild to have it. They promised to set him up in luxury for life."

Tess sighed, ran her hand through her hair. "That's when everything started falling apart."

"Coffee?" Quong asked, and went to get her a cup.

"Thanks. Everything was going according to plan. I became Captain Strauss of the Army and managed to get myself stationed on Pandor, which was easy, because most military personnel are busy trying to get themselves transferred *off* Pandor. No one on base knew I was working for NI, not even the colonel. That's how secret this operation was.

"I examined the robot myself. I swear to God"—Tess gave Xris a wry grin—"that 'bot was broken. I couldn't get it to function. Of course, I didn't dare move it, not then, not while we were trying to smooth things over with the Pandorans. But I scanned it and it checked out as unworkable. What the devil did you do to it?"

"Bumped into it. Jostled it. I don't know."

"A broken connection," Quong said. "A short in the wiring. Something that wouldn't necessarily show up on scans."

"At any rate, I reported to NI that the 'bot was safe. Boy, was I wrong on that one!" Tess sighed, sat nursing the coffee cup in her hands, as if trying to warm them. "We figured Harsch would ask *me* to steal the robot. We had it all planned. I was going to snatch it, put the bomb in it, hand it over to Harsch. I made sure it would go to Harsch himself. That was part of the deal. I refused to deliver it otherwise. He agreed.

"We wanted to catch him alive, of course, to interrogate him, find out just what secrets he'd passed on to the enemy. But if that didn't work out, the bomb would see to it that he never sold anything to the Corasians again. Unfortunately, Harsch had other ideas. He didn't want me to steal the 'bot, he didn't want to risk my being caught. He said he would hire someone to steal the robot for him. He asked me if I knew anyone."

"You recommended us," Xris said, starting now to see the whole picture.

"The Lord Admiral recommended you. I gave your name to Harsch. From that point on, you know what happened. I arranged for Jamil to be transported to the *King James II* without causing suspicion, arranged for you, Xris, to sneak off base. If everything had gone according to plan, you and Jamil would have put the bomb in the robot yourselves, delivered it to Harsch at Hell's Outpost—"

"He sells the 'bot *and* us to the Corasians." Xris shook his head. "Thank the Lord Admiral for the recommendation, but tell him from now on we find our own jobs."

"I don't think Harsch planned to double-cross you. Not at the beginning. He was a sharp businessman and he knew when he had a good thing going. But nothing went according to plan."

"I still don't see why you couldn't have told us all the truth," Jamil said. "You told us part of it."

"Well, I didn't want to blow my cover, for one thing. If this failed, NI would still need me to spy on Harsch. And for another, what was I to think when the whole damned team showed up? Maybe you're going to try to double-cross Harsch. Maybe you're working for him. Maybe you're in this up to your eyeballs. Maybe you'd help me and maybe you'd sell me out. How could I know?"

"You knew," Xris said softly. He stared at the cold coffee.

Tess sat down beside him, put her hand on his knee. "All right. *I* knew. And if it had just been me—my life—on the line, I would have told you. But there were more. Countless more. Everything was falling apart, all around me. First the robot works when it isn't supposed to.

Then Grant shows up with the professor's unit. Then the
robot escapes and takes Grant with it. Then the blasted
robot begins taking out Lanes. Then Harsch hears that
the robot's taking out Lanes—"

"From you."

"Not from me. Apparently he's got more than one
spy in the Navy. Anyway, he passes the news to the
Corasians, raises the price.

"The Corasians are so excited that they send one of
their motherships over here to pick up the 'bot in person. They tell him to bring the 'bot to the ship directly.

"Harsch wasn't pleased about that, but he didn't have
much choice. The Corasians let Harsch know that they
would be very unhappy if he didn't deliver, might start
attacking a few of our outposts.

"And so now what do I do?" Tess appealed to them.
"If the Navy flies in to take out the Corasians, we lose
Harsch. If we lost the robot, we lose Harsch. Harsch
loses the Corasians. The Corasians attack our outposts.
God! I got lost myself trying to solve that one.

"But then, suddenly, everything's all right!" Tess
spread her hands. "We recover the robot. I think, fine,
we can carry out the mission as planned. Everything's
on track. And then you"—she looked at Xris—"want to
chuck the whole thing and run off on some godforsaken
rescue mission!"

Xris sat silent, sucking the flavor out of the wad of
the twist in his mouth.

"All right, so I have a suspicious nature," Tess said.
"In my business, that's what keeps you alive. I wondered: Were you really ready to chuck the job and go
off on a mission you knew was hopeless? Or did *you*
intend to steal the robot, now that you knew how valuable it was? All my doubts came back. I had to do one
thing: Get the robot to Harsch. And I had to do it fast.
Maybe I made a mistake, threatening to blow up the
plane. Maybe I should have just told you the truth, but
even now, looking back on it, I don't see where I could
have reasonably made any other decision."

"She's got a point, Xris," Jamil said. "A lot of what
we did wasn't real bright."

"All's well that ends well," Quong observed with a shrug. "Harsch will never again sell technology to the enemy. And the Corasians will not be able to build space Lanes or take them out. Tycho died for a worthy cause. He deserves a commendation."

"I'm not sure the rest of us do. One thing." Xris lifted his head, looked at Tess. "Why did you gas us when we landed on the Corasian ship?"

"Because you were going to fight to the death. I knew that. I couldn't allow that to happen. I knew then that you were on the level. It was my responsibility to see that you came out of this alive, if I could. I figured that once we were on board, we'd at least stand a chance. As it turned out, I made yet another mistake."

"You lost Jeffrey Grant."

"That was a last-minute thing. I don't know quite why I did it or what I hoped would happen. It's just . . . I felt so sorry for him. He was the innocent bystander. He didn't ask for any of this. I knew Harsch and the Corasians would come on board the PRRS to pick up the robot. I figured that once they found it, they'd leave without bothering to search the rest of the spaceplane."

"What did you plan to do with him then?" Quong asked.

"When I boarded the Corasian mothership, I sent a secret signal to the *King James II*, giving them our location. I knew the Navy was on its way. I figured Grant would stay hidden until I could come back for him. What I didn't count on was the fact that Jeffrey Grant not only hid himself, he hid the robot, too."

"So that's what happened to it," Xris said.

"That's all I can think of. Harsch was furious when he couldn't find it. Furious and scared. He knew what the Corasians would do to him if he came up empty-handed. At least it gave me a chance to keep you alive, Xris. The Corasians wanted to dissect you on the spot. I told Harsch that you had hidden the robot. He ordered the Corasians to keep you alive until he found out where."

"We owe you our lives, Captain," Quong said for-mally, and made a little bow. "I, for one, extend my thanks."

"Me, too," said Jamil. "And if Xris there doesn't offer to take you someplace romantic and treat you to champagne and a chance to watch the moon rise over the ocean, you let me know."

"You don't owe me anything," Tess said, her face flushed. "I botched this job from the beginning. If it hadn't been for you, for all of you ..."

Xris took out another twist. "Let's call it even."

"Xris!" Harry shouted up the ladder. "Message for you. From the Admiralty."

Xris wondered what this was all about, figured it must be Dixter waiting to offer his heartfelt thanks. At the moment, Xris wasn't in the mood. He stood up reluctantly, walked past Harry, headed for the cockpit.

Xris threw himself into the pilot's chair, faced the comm.

"Xris here," he said.

A face appeared, but it wasn't the rugged, aging face of the Lord Admiral. It was ...

"Darlene!" Xris breathed. He was on his feet, leaning out to the screen, actually touching the screen as if he could touch her, make sure she was alive.

"Hi, Xris," Darlene said. "Good to see you."

"It's damn good to see you!" he said fervently. "What happened? Are you all right?"

"I'm fine. So's everyone on board the cruise ship. We didn't make the Jump into hyperspace. We weren't in the Lane when the robot took it out. But the ship was damaged by the explosion and we lost communications."

"Explosion? What explosion?"

"When my window blew out."

"Your ..." Xris stared at her. "What—"

Darlene grinned. "It's a long story. I'll have to tell you later. The captain won't let me talk long. I'm under arrest."

"Arrest!" Xris was completely baffled. He didn't even know where to begin. "Look, just answer me one thing. Are you okay?"

"The captain's turning me over to the Navy. I'm under

twenty-four-hour guard. I'm fine, Xris. Good-bye for now. I'll see you soon. Tell little Harry and the rest of the 'kids' I said hi." She waved at him.

Her image faded away, was replaced by the grinning face of Mendaharin Tusca.

"Don't worry, Xris," Tusk said. "We know what's going on. We'll keep her safe."

"Thank you, Tusk," said Xris. "I mean that. And tell the Lord Admiral thanks, too."

"And our thanks to you, Xris. You and your team. Oh, by the way, we recovered your Claymore. We'll have it fixed up, returned to you. And the Navy will probably be able to find some money to reimburse you for your time."

"Do me a favor, will you, Tusk? You heard about Tycho? Send that money to his family. I'll let you know where, who to contact."

Tusk nodded. "Sure thing. See you on board, Xris."

The screen went dark.

The Scimitar cruised toward the massive *King James II*. Harry turned over control to the computer, went up to give the rest the news.

Xris spent a moment alone, gave his thanks to Whoever might be listening. He took another moment to ask that same quiet Listener to take good care of Tycho.

Then he called up, "Tess, can you come down here a second?"

She came to him, her expression troubled. "What is it, Xris? You sound so solemn."

He took hold of her hand with his good hand, his only hand. "Is Jamil right? Are you into champagne and moonlit beaches?"

Tess smiled. "Actually, I'm more into beer and cheap motel rooms, but—"

He took her into his arms—make that arm—and kissed her.

Up above, Jamil whistled, Harry chortled, the Little One stomped his feet, Quong scolded the others for being crass, and Raoul—waking briefly—asked for someone to bring him his lip gloss.

"One more question," said Xris, when he was free for

talking. "What happened to Jeffrey Grant and the robot?"

"We're not sure," Tess said. "We hope to find him soon. The robot is immensely valuable to us now. For the first time, we have one that works and we have the professor's unit."

"So what's the problem?" Xris asked. "Find Grant and take the robot back. He won't be happy, but then, he's a civilian."

"I wish it were that easy." Tess sighed. "You see, I told you one other little lie. I didn't plant a real bomb in the PRRS. The bomb Harry found when he scanned was a decoy.

"I put the real bomb in the robot."

CHAPTER
45

Heard melodies are sweet, but those unheard
Are sweeter; therefore, ye soft pipes, play on . . .

John Keats, *Ode on a Grecian Urn*

Jeffrey Grant managed to escape the Corasians quite easily. He simply sat down in the pilot's seat, ordered the computer to launch the PRRS, and then flew off. He expected someone to shoot at him.

No one did.

He expected to be caught in a tractor beam.

No beam appeared.

The Corasian collective mind was focused on other, more important details, such as endeavoring to discover the whereabouts of the robot and the acquisition of several prime hunks of meat. The collective mind paid no attention to Jeffrey Grant.

One might say it was the story of his life.

Mildly amazed at the ease of his escape, expecting any second to be surrounded by Corasian fighters, Grant nervously ordered the computer to find the nearest space Lane and jump into it.

The computer located the Lane, but reported that access was prohibited. Another ship or plane was occupying it at the time. Afraid that the Corasians were going to catch him, Grant flew on and eventually located another Lane.

This one was free. The PRRS made the jump.

The ship in the first Lane was the *King James II,* but Jeffrey Grant was never to know that.

While in hyperspace, on his way back to XIO, he spent the time polishing the robot, making it ready.

It occurred to Jeffrey Grant, just prior to landing, that the people at the rental-plane agency might take exception to the fact that he had lost their plane. While still in orbit above the planet, Grant contacted the agency, and attempted to explain.

"I had it parked on Pandor, you see, and left it only for a moment to go look—"

"Trant?" said the young woman. "Jeremiah Trant?"

"Grant," said Jeffrey humbly. "Jeffrey Grant. I was only gone a mo—"

"Ah, Mr. Grant! No need to worry. Your rental plane was returned."

"It was?" Grant realized a bit late he shouldn't sound surprised. "I mean . . . so it was. Should have been. I'm glad. Is . . . is everything all right?"

"Yes, Mr. Grant. The gentleman returned the plane, said that you would no longer be requiring it, and paid the bill in full."

What she did not tell Jeffrey Grant was that the pilot who had returned the plane had arrived under Naval escort, had flashed his Naval Intelligence ID and had asked to be contacted if anyone named Jeffrey Grant turned up inquiring about the rental plane.

Jeffrey Grant was relieved and bothered at the same time. He was relieved over the fact that the plane was back—he had been wondering how he was going to pay for its loss.

He was bothered by its unexpected return.

He had the feeling that someone was following him.

All kinds of wild schemes and evasion plans flooded Grant's mind, caused it—like an old-fashioned gas-powered engine—to stall out. Eventually Grant did what he had been planning to do ever since he escaped the Corasian mothership. He landed the PRRS in a field about fifty kilometers outside on XIO City.

Once down, he packed the robot in its crate. Using

the remote control, Grant activated the robot's crate, guided it to the hatch of the PRRS. Before he left, Jeffrey Grant wrote out a brief note of apology to the Royal Navy, explaining that he hadn't really meant to steal their spaceplane, thanked the Navy for all it had done for him and the galaxy. He left the note on the console.

Grant made a final tour of the plane, picked up a briefcase which one of the Army officers had left behind, then exited the PRRS. Grant made certain the door was locked, then—briefcase in one hand, remote in the other—he led the robot, concealed in its crate, out of a corn field and onto the main highway.

They hitched a ride with a gravtruck into town.

Jeffrey Grant sat at the cluttered desk in his small museum, penning meticulously and neatly the words on the placard.

LANE-LAYING ROBOT. CIRCA 2180. INVENTED, DESIGNED, AND BUILT BY COLIN LASAIRION, PH.D. FOR FURTHER INFORMATION, ASK CURATOR.

Grant had been a bit hesitant about adding that last notation—foreseeing endless questions from tourists—but he believed that it was his duty to do what he could to educate his fellow man. He printed in bold letters across the bottom, DO NOT TOUCH.

He allowed the ink on the placard to dry, then set the placard in its stand.

Jeffrey Grant stepped back. Folding his hands together, he silently, calmly, proudly regarded a dream.

The robot with the sad eyes stood in the place of honor in the quiet little museum, against the far wall, directly across from the front door. The machine, designated as a Collimated Command Receiver Unit, stood at the robot's side. The blue light no longer flashed, the machine no longer hummed. But the soothing light from its screen—light which Jeffrey Grant had always found very attractive—glowed brightly.

Perhaps it was the angle of the light, shining up from underneath the robot, that caused the humanlike eyes of the robot to change expression. They looked—at least to Jeffrey Grant—almost happy. Either that, or the robot, now surrounded by familiar items from the past, felt truly at home here. Jeffrey Grant hoped that it was the latter.

He studied the exhibit a long time. He rearranged one of the robot's telescopic arms at a better, more lifelike angle. He dusted all the rest of the objects in the museum, arranged and neatly stacked his old books.

Then he went on a search throughout the rest of the building, looking for other occupants, thinking that perhaps someone might have moved in while he was gone.

But no one had. It was a holiday on XIO. The building was empty.

Grant returned to the museum, waited for an hour or so to see if tourists would arrive.

None came. The street, as usual, was deserted.

Grant took one last look around, to make certain that all was as it should be.

It was.

He picked up the briefcase, walked out the door, made certain—fussily—that the door was locked. He walked down the street, walked several blocks, until he was in sight of his house.

Something unusual was happening at his house. Police cars, their lights flashing, were parked out in front, along with several expensive-looking vehics that were not marked. His neighbors had gathered in his yard. As he watched, a vid news crew pulled up.

Jeffrey Grant sat down on a bench at a bus stop. He could see, up the street, the building that housed his museum. He could see, down the street, his house.

Jeffrey Grant opened the briefcase. He reached inside, and pressed a small red button.

The explosion blew out the front of the museum, took down the entire building, sent a cloud of dust and debris a hundred meters into the air. The tremendous blast shook the ground.

Men in uniform dashed out of Jeffrey Grant's house at a run. Heads turned. Fingers pointed to the rising column of smoke. The neighbors surged after them. Police sirens began to wail. Police cars sped past Jeffrey Grant.

The unmarked expensive vehics soared into the air. They flew past Jeffrey Grant.

The vid crew, which had, by purest chance, a vidcam aimed in the right direction, was going on the air, live. The crew roared past Jeffrey Grant.

Jeffrey Grant's neighbors, who mostly didn't know him, ran past him, hastening to the scene of the disaster.

Jeffrey Grant sat on the bench at the bus stop and happily explained to a young child, who had come out to watch the police cars, all about Professor Lasairion's wonderful Lane-laying robots.